CHINA BRIDE

HENRY LUK

TOR®

A TOM DOHERTY ASSOCIATES BOOK
New York

This is a work of fiction. All the characters and events portrayed in this book are either products of the author's imagination or are used fictitiously.

CHINA BRIDE

Copyright © 1998 by Henry Luk

A Tor Book
Published by Tom Doherty Associates, LLC
175 Fifth Avenue
New York, NY 10010

www.tor.com

Tor® is a registered trademark of Tom Doherty Associates, LLC.

ISBN: 0-812-54018-2
Library of Congress Catalog Card Number: 98-11925

First edition: May 1998
First mass market edition: November 1999

Printed in the United States of America

0 9 8 7 6 5 4 3 2 1

CHINA BRIDE

ONE

You don't know what kind of men these are.
They might also decide to rape you.

1

BETH WORKED HER HANDS and wrists against the rough, tight rope that lashed her wrists behind her back. She felt tingling in her hands and felt them becoming cold. She struggled. The rope burned her skin as she slipped it back and forth, straining to loosen it, even if only a little bit. She could move it. Gradually she was able to move it more, then still more, as it grudgingly loosened. Maybe . . . *Oh, God help her, maybe!*

She lay on a blanket in the rear of a van that worked its way down a steep hill and through narrow streets clogged with traffic. She heard horns honking and the driver cursing. When he slammed on the brakes, she was thrown forward. When he made a quick turn, she was tossed. Her hips and shoulders were bruised.

She was bound, blindfolded, and gagged, but almost no gag could prevent a person from mumbling understandable words—all you couldn't do was scream—so she could mutter to Michael, "*Ai rien,*" she said. It meant "darling" and was one of the few Chinese expressions she had learned. "Are you okay?"

Michael, too, was blindfolded, gagged, and bound—perhaps more tightly than she was. "I . . . suppose," he mumbled.

At last the van stopped. Two men pulled the doors open, and the smell of dirty seawater rushed in with the fresh air. The men spoke Chinese, and Michael forced words past his gag: "We've got to sit up. We're going aboard a boat."

Beth twisted her body and rose to a sitting position. One of the men grabbed her by the arms and pulled her out of the van. He used a knife to cut off her blindfold, so she could see where she was walking, then he led her down a flight of stone stairs and across a stone wharf. The boat was rising and falling, and she was not sure how she would cross the gap from wharf to deck. That problem was solved for her. A man behind her gave her a hard shove. She grunted in panic, but the shove was so hard that she fell across the dangerous gap and into the arms of another man.

The boat was an open launch, some thirty feet long. The kidnappers pushed the pair toward the stern and shoved them down on a cushioned bench on the left side. She heard the engines roar to life—three of them, she guessed, meaning that this was a fast, powerful boat. The men pulled the mooring lines aboard, and the boat eased away into choppy water.

Beth stared at Michael and saw that he was staring at her. She was reassured to see that he was unmarked and cognitive, for she had thought she heard someone hit him just after she was blindfolded. Light reflected off the water struck his eyes, and she saw love as she had long seen love there—plus now, agony and sadness. She tried to show him love with her eyes.

"I love you, Michael," she muttered through her gag.

The magnificent Hong Kong waterfront was behind them as the launch moved out into a busy harbor. Beth was from Boston and had seen the New York waterfront besides, but no city in the world—at least none that she had seen—was anywhere near as impressive as this. Just behind the docks a hundred or more high-rise buildings rose into the night sky.

She turned her attention back to the rope that bound her hands. Her skin was raw now and stung as she rubbed the cord on one wrist against the cord on the other. She was probably bleeding, but it began to seem possible that she could work one or the other of those lengths of rope over one of her thumbs and slip loose.

She glanced around to see if the kidnappers were watching closely or if they were near enough to hear what she was going to say—assuming any of them could understand English, which none of them had spoken so far.

"Michael," she whispered. "I think I can get loose."

"If you can, do it fast. You don't have much time."

2

SHE AND MICHAEL HAD met on Harvard Yard. As a student at Boston University, Beth had had access to the main Harvard library and had come to borrow three books she needed for her senior paper on American transcendentalism. She had been hurrying to catch a bus. Michael was a graduate student, one year from his MBA, and had been hurrying toward his car, thinking of an expiring parking meter. As they rushed across the Yard they had accidentally collided, she staggered and nearly fell, and the three books she was carrying fell to the ground.

"Oh! *I'm so sorry!* I'm so sorry! Please . . . Please let me help you."

He squatted to gather up her books. She knelt beside him to receive the books as he picked them off the ground.

"It was as much my fault as yours," she said, focusing her attention on the embarrassed young man. He was handsome, roughly her own height, well put-together and well dressed. He was of Chinese or Japanese descent.

"Uh . . . I . . . Miss . . . Am I wrong, or are you Mary Elizabeth Connor? I mean Beth Connor of the Barcelona Olympics."

She smiled faintly, not entirely pleased to be identified. "Yes. I am Beth Connor."

"It is a pleasure to meet you," he said.

"Well, I suppose it is a pleasure to meet you, Mr. . . . ?"

"Chang. My name is Michael Chang."

They stood, and Beth smiled. "I guess you're not Irish."

"No. No, no," said Michael Chang. "I am Chinese, from Hong Kong. I have been in the States for five years—studying."

"Hong Kong. I've met several Chinese people but don't think I've ever met anyone from Hong Kong. From all I hear, it's a very interesting place—a world unto itself—and I hope someday to see it. But isn't Hong Kong being returned by the Brits to China?"

"Not until July first, 1997, two years from now. I'd enjoy telling you more about it. Would it offend you if I ask you to join me for a beer, Miss Connor? Buying you a beer is the least I can do for—"

"It doesn't offend me at all, but—"

"Of course. I understand. It is abrupt of me to invite you for a beer, when we have just met. I am sorry."

Beth was touched. He was so genuinely apologetic that she feared she would really hurt his feelings if she refused to have a beer with him. And he was so deferential and courteous that she could not believe he was just trying to hit on her.

"Well, I'll tell you," she said. "I'll join you for a beer if you will call me Beth, Michael."

He smiled. "Yes. Of course. And thank you."

As they walked out of the Yard and across the street to a student bierstube, she caught herself glancing sideways at him and rather liking what she saw.

"You are an exceptionally beautiful girl, Beth," he remarked ingenuously as they walked. "Am I too direct?"

"Yes," she said, letting him see a smile.

"Even so, I think you are beautiful."

"I might be if I were not so . . . big," she said. "My father calls me 'a strapping big girl.'"

"I'm not sure exactly what that means," he said soberly. "Anyway . . . I am very glad to have met you, even if it had to be in so awkward a way."

Beth was twenty-two years old, a tall blond sometimes called not just strapping but husky. She was a full-figured woman with generous breasts, a visible though not protruding belly, and a well-defined tush. None of her was loose or soft. To the contrary, she was athletic: she had competed as a runner in the Olympics three years ago— having failed to achieve her real ambition, which was to compete as a swimmer—and her body was sinuous and firm. She still swam, though, and she had given up competitive running. That autumn day she was wearing a white Ralph Lauren polo shirt and a black miniskirt that exposed her muscular legs.

In the bierstube they found a booth and sat down opposite each other. The rugged, old wooden table was scarred with cigarette burns and deep scratches that had been darkened with ballpoint pens. Although they had a degree of privacy in the high-backed booth, they were noticed by some of the others at the bar, two or three of whom nodded a greeting.

"You are known all over the world," Michael said.

"I think one of them at least was saying hello to *you*."

"Ah . . . Well, perhaps. I have been at Harvard five years and have made a few friends. But you—everyone knows the name Beth Connor."

"I could wish not so many did, Michael," she said regretfully.

"It was an accident," he asserted firmly. "I am Chinese, and *I* didn't think you did anything wrong."

The guileless sincerity of his statement caught her. "Well . . . many thought I did." She smiled wryly. "After all, most of the Chinese think I did something wrong, and there are a lot more Chinese than there are Americans."

Michael shrugged. "The Chinese support and admire their athletes the same way Americans do, the same way the Brits do. When you and Xiang Li collided and she fell, many Chinese were immensely disappointed. They had expected her to win a gold medal."

"They didn't have to accuse me of knocking her down intentionally," Beth said tartly. "They didn't need to accuse our coaches of putting me—'a gawky, muscle-bound amazon'—on the two-thousand-meter for the very purpose of knocking down Xiang Li."

"Only the New China News Agency XinHua said that. I don't think anyone much believed it, even in China."

"I had a good chance of winning a medal myself, you know," said Beth. "Maybe not the gold. But I was knocked off stride and came in ninth. Then the New China News Agency launched a propaganda campaign against me. I resented it, Michael."

Michael smiled widely. "You had every right to. But, you had your say, didn't you? What was it you said on NBC, that athletes from a 'murderous dictatorship' like China should not be allowed to compete in the Olympics at all? 'The butchers of Beijing,' I believe you called them."

She shook her head. "You know something, Michael? My name and face became more widely known than those of anyone who won a medal at Barcelona. When I came home to Boston—to Southie specifically, where the Irish live—I was more of a heroine than if I had won five golds. I was nineteen years old, and I was the girl who'd called the dirty Commies 'dirty Commies.' It's not a very good kind of heroine to be."

As they talked, Beth was studying Michael Chang. He was wearing a gray tweed cashmere jacket that she recognized as expensive, a white shirt, rep tie, and charcoal-gray slacks, plus Gucci loafers. Except for his almond eyes and brush-cut black hair, he looked like an American preppie from a moneyed family. His complexion was smooth and satiny, not shiny as were the complexions of some Chinese she had seen, and it was by no means yellow. She had heard that some Orientals called Westerners "long-noses." If so, Michael was a long-nose; his nose was not flat but well-defined and sharp.

"So, you've been in the States five years," she said.

"Yes. I was educated at a Jesuit preparatory school in Hong Kong, then came to Harvard."

"Does that mean you are Catholic?" she asked.

He chuckled. "I was baptized. But the Chinese are not a religious people, Beth. We are superstitious but not religious. My parents wanted to send me to this fine Jesuit prep school. On the application form, under the column 'Religion' my father put down, 'Willing to be Catholic,' meaning the whole family would convert to Catholicism if that would land me in that fine school."

Beth smiled. "Sounds like a variation of what we used to call rice Christians. Did your parents have to be baptized for you to get into that school?"

"No. The Jesuit fathers won't accept that kind of fake devotion. I got one of the eighty places by merit, beating out two thousand other applicants in a nine-hour examination." She heard in his voice his pride in this achievement.

"But you eventually volunteered for baptism, didn't you?"

"I admired the Jesuits, their dedication. They were from Ireland and taught me to despise the British colonial administration who believed Her Majesty's servants were one cut above the Chinese, and the Irish for that matter. My faith weakened after I came to America. Now I am a non-churchgoing agnostic."

Beth laughed. "That describes me, too," she said.

"Surely, as an Irish—"

"No."

"Would it offend you if I invite you to dinner one night this week?"

She had been anticipating some such invitation. She was accustomed to receiving them. She attracted young men, not just by her comely face and sensual figure but by her enduring notoriety. Young men who dated her expected it to be noticed that they had gone out with Beth Connor. Almost invariably, they had other expectations as well. She wondered why Michael Chang wanted to take her to dinner, what expectations *he* had. She asked him—

"Why do you want to take me to dinner, Michael?"

As she was to observe many more times, he was all but obsessively literal and actually obsessively sincere. He did not lay on his answer the ironic tone an American would have used for self-protection, to suggest that if she declined his invitation he could pretend he had not meant the invitation to be taken seriously anyway. He said—

"Because I think you are exquisitely beautiful, supremely intelligent, and boundlessly interesting."

She smiled warmly and shook her head. "Michael . . . after hearing you say that, how could *I* possibly say no?"

He grinned playfully. "I was hoping you couldn't."

They went to dinner the next evening.

He took her to the Chinese restaurant high in the Hyatt Regency Hotel. The hostess asked if he had a reservation, at which point the maitre d' rushed up and said, "You don't ask *Mr. Chang* if he has a reservation. Just seat him and his guest." In fact, the maitre d' himself seated them, on a banquette on a curved riser, where they had a view of the Charles River and the city.

Michael suggested to Beth that she might like Scotch for her before-dinner drink. She nodded, and the maitre d' asked, "Glenfiddich as usual, Mr. Chang?" Michael nodded. Beth took careful note of this interplay between Michael and the maitre d', also of the deferential welcome their waiter offered.

Beth was glad she had chosen to dress more elegantly than she usually did. She wore a red-orange-yellow-green beaded floral silk chiffon minidress given to her by a Boston department store for which she had modeled it. It was a dress she could not have afforded to buy, and she had worn it only twice before. One of the roommates with whom she shared an apartment near Boston University had suggested this must be an important date, for her to wear the Oleg Cassini dress.

She had almost *not* worn it. After all, why should she try to impress Michael Chang? She decided, though, that he must be trying to impress *her*, too. He had picked her up at her apartment, dressed in a handsomely tailored dark-blue suit and driving a silver BMW. Her roommates saw him, and while Beth was in the bedroom picking up her wrap, one of them said, "My God! When you said Chinese, I thought, Poor little fellow. Poor little fellow my achin' ass! Go for him, Beth! *Go, go, go!*"

She saw him glancing at her legs as they sat side by side on the banquette facing white linen and heavy silver, and she was glad she had worn a short dress. She thought her breasts were big, and she'd had to defend them against the hands of at least twenty men, but she liked her legs. Dark stockings blurred the image of an athlete's muscles, and her legs were long and sleek.

"So you are Irish," he said, a transparent conversational gambit.

Beth grinned. "It depends on who you ask. When my great-grandfather came to Boston from Ireland in 1911, his name was O'Connor. He dropped two things: the O and his Catholic faith. Some in the family still complain that he left them neither fish nor fowl: micks who couldn't deny their Irish ancestry but outside the embrace and shelter of the mother church. In Southie the Connors are considered an odd family to this day. My father is proprietor of an Irish pub. He keeps a blackthorn shillelagh on a shelf behind the bar."

"What in the world is a shillelagh?"

"It's a wicked cudgel, supposedly for bashing the heads of any man who gets drunk and rowdy in the pub. Actually, it's for show. He's never used it."

"An Irish tradition, I imagine," said Michael solemnly. "I'd like to visit your father's pub."

"I'm not sure you *would* like it, Michael. The Irish of Southie would very likely tease you unmercifully. They would do it in what they think is a good spirit, but I think you would find it difficult to accept. Most of them are very, very provincial."

"My people can be that way. I mean, the Chinese. Also, my family. They are not easy people to understand. Many of us still like to think of ourselves as people of the Middle Kingdom, the center of the universe."

One of the things she was beginning to like about Michael was that his sense of humor was gentle and restrained. He did not trade banter. He did not tell jokes; in fact, she doubted he knew any. He was more mature than most young men she knew.

But he was also literal, which was why she suspected he could be hurt by the rough humor the pub regulars would direct at him. She determined to protect him from that, even if he never saw her father's pub, where one or two evenings a week she perched on the bar for half an hour or so and sang Irish songs while her father played an accompaniment on his concertina.

After they'd had two drinks, he said, "I suggest you would like the pressed duck. They do it well here." She listened to him order their dinner and a bottle of vintage Bordeaux suggested by the sommelier.

They had toasted each other with their first sips of Scotch, but now he raised a glass of their second drink and saluted her. "I am really grateful that you came tonight, Beth," he said gravely.

It was the sort of thing an American man would never have said. She had never met an American man who would lower his defenses that way. For that was what Michael was doing: abandoning his every defense—with his dignity if she put him aside—and exposing his feelings with honesty that was almost outside her experience. When, tentatively, he laid his hand on hers, she turned her palm up and closed her fingers around his.

He smiled gratefully and innocently.

Beth squeezed his hand. She leaned toward him and kissed him quickly and lightly on the neck.

3

ON THE WEEKEND HE took her to a play on the MIT campus. When, the next week, he asked her for their fourth date—he suggested he would cook dinner for them in his apartment—it left her with a significant decision to make. If she went to his apartment, their relationship would enter a different stage. It was an appealing idea: to be alone with him, perhaps to share with him something more than the calm, dry kisses they had exchanged so far.

On the other hand—

She had read of the Chinese that they were reasoning, purposeful people who identified goals and pursued them. Michael was so *American*, yet still Chinese. She believed he respected her, but it was also obvious that he was making a rational approach to something meaningful. If she accepted his invitation to visit his apartment, it would signal her willingness to share something more meaningful. If she didn't, she would have in some sense rejected this kind, thoughtful, warm-spirited man—a man like none other she had ever allowed to kiss her. She said yes.

The building was new, and the apartment was spacious and comfortable. He had a large living/dining room, a kitchen separated from the living room by a counter, two bedrooms, a bathroom, and a powder room. He had rented the apartment furnished but had supplemented the rented furnishings with a couch covered in soft tan leather, a glass-topped table covered with magazines and books, and ranks of Barnes & Noble bookshelves. He had bought posters and prints for his walls. She noticed in particular a poster based on a Matisse paper cutting, advertising a Paris exhibit of Matisse work.

Nothing about the place suggested it was the home of a Chinese. He subscribed to many magazines: *Time*, *Newsweek*, *The New Yorker*, *Vanity Fair*, *George*, *Playboy*, and *Penthouse*. His books were American biographies and histories, and American novels. His tastes seemed to be for everything American.

"You can tell something about a person by looking at how they keep their living quarters," she said.

"Is the person you see reflected here a person you would allow to kiss you?" he asked earnestly and ingenuously. "I mean, kiss you not like brother and sister but like— How do I say it?"

"You don't have to explain," she whispered. "I know what you mean. You're the kind of person, Michael. You *are* the kind of person."

She stepped closer to him, opened her arms to receive him, and moved into his embrace. They kissed gently at first, then fervently, finally so hard that she tasted blood on her lips.

"Michael . . ." she whispered.

"You are *perfect*," he said soberly. "Simply perfect."

At this point in any other relationship she'd had, the man began to come on heavy. Michael did not. They sat on his couch, and he kissed her on the neck and ears, on the cheeks, and again on the lips, but he did not offer to touch her legs or breasts.

She had come to the apartment wondering what he would serve. He grilled steaks rare, which he served with buttery mashed potatoes and a Caesar salad. He opened a bottle of red wine. She went into his kitchen while he was cooking and found it was stocked with American foods: steaks and potatoes, frozen peas and corn, frozen pizzas, chicken breasts and thighs with Shake 'n Bake, ice cream, Coca-Cola, and beer. He had no rice, no noodles, no chopsticks.

After dinner he essayed tentative caressing of her breasts. She put her hands on his and pressed his hands down, to make him caress her more firmly. He pulled back her skirt and stroked her legs. She let him. And that was as far as he went. He seemed to marvel that she would let him touch her that intimately. When he kissed her, his kiss was more prolonged and more passionate and involved their tongues. . . .

4

WHEN HER ROOMMATES BEGAN to make jealous little jokes about Michael, especially about how very wealthy he must be, Beth found herself becoming defensive about him. She saw in Michael a modest, quiet, self-controlled, intelligent man.

He made concessions. He didn't understand American football and didn't enjoy the games, but he took her to one game and he sat with her in his living room watching NFL games on television, often asking her to explain what was going on. She found she was comfortable with him. She did not have to fear aggression. He listened respectfully to her opinions and deferentially offered his own, sometimes leading her to change her idea. They discovered mutual interests in films, in art, in food.

After a time he suggested he would prepare a Chinese dinner for her. When she arrived at his apartment that evening she found him busy in the kitchen.

"It must be a sort of *American*-Chinese dinner," he said. "At a real Chinese dinner, many things are served: at least one course of meat, fowl, and fish, with vegetables and soup. All the diners share from all the courses. For us I am making just one course. Pour us two drinks, please."

Beth poured Scotch. She did not ask what he was cooking, just watched while he heated a wok and poured in oil, added a dark paste from a can, then chopped garlic, and then ground pork.

"This is called *Ch'ao-lung-hsia*," he explained. "Lobster Cantonese."

He stir-fried the pork, added soy sauce, salt, sugar, and a chopped scallion. He put in the cut-up meat of a lobster and stir-fried that. Finally he added what looked like chicken stock, a white mixture that probably was corn starch and water, and two beaten eggs.

"Cook for a few minutes," he said, putting a lid on the wok.

Michael lifted his glass and saluted Beth. He kissed her, tenderly at first, then more urgently. Because he knew she would allow it—would in fact welcome it—he lifted her skirt and pushed his hand down inside her panties to caress her rear. It was cold, and he rubbed it as if he could warm it.

With the lobster Cantonese he served rice and a mixture of snow peas, mushrooms, and bamboo shoots that he had stir-fried earlier and now reheated in his microwave.

They ate with chopsticks.

"When and how did you learn to use chopsticks?" he asked her.

"I've eaten in Chinese restaurants more than a few times."

"When you can lift a single peanut from a bowl of peanuts with your chopsticks, then you will be wholly adept with them."

After dinner they experimented with that. Michael did not

teach her. He let her struggle. After a few awkward mistakes, losing peanuts on the floor, she mastered the technique.

That night she let him discover her beauty mark: a small dark mole on her right breast, halfway between her armpit and nipple.

"It's a witch mark," she told him, "the place where Satan suckles. Oh yes, he suckles me and takes me on midnight rides through all the world." She laughed. The conscious or unconscious wickedness in her laugh almost suggested that she spoke the truth. "Three hundred years ago, women were burned alive for having a mark like that."

Michael stared thoughtfully at the little mark and for a very long moment was unsure how to react. Finally he smiled and said, "I see. You have three nipples. May I kiss like Satan?"

"If you are willing to take the risk," she said in a throaty whisper.

"Risk?"

"A man who is seduced by a witch never escapes her."

"I do not want to escape you, Beth," he said with that literal sincerity she found so appealing. "You see— *I love you*."

"Oh, Michael! *I love you, too!*"

Before they went in the bedroom they agreed he would not take her back to her own apartment, that she would stay with him all night.

5

AND NOW— THE MAN she loved was in agony. He sat bent forward, his arms pinned behind him, his gag distorting his mouth.

She worked desperately on her bonds, feeling her skin tearing away under the rough rope as she worked it toward her hands, suffering pain that was all but unendurable, but gaining in confidence that she *was* going to break loose.

They were going to marry, which was why she had flown with

him to Hong Kong—to meet his family and confront them with their decision. But to be kidnapped on the very morning of their arrival, before they even had a chance to see his family and tell them of their decision! She never thought his Chinese family was going to like it any better than her Irish family did. But they were going to get married, come hell or high water.

She knew she loved him. She knew he loved her. During the rest of that fall and all the following winter and spring, she lived with him as though they were husband and wife. She continued to pay rent on the apartment she shared with her roommates, but she moved all her things to Michael's apartment. They did all the domestic things a married couple might do: loved and quarreled, shared excitement and boredom, explored each other's likes and dislikes. He bathed her—they never took a shower apart. He loved to see her nude. When she was, he kissed her all over, kissed her feet, kissed her backside, and even nuzzled in her pubic hair, kissing her there though not pressing his tongue into her.

One late-spring evening while they were in bed, Beth had on sudden impulse pushed her face into his crotch and had given him head—the first time in her life she had even considered doing such a thing. It was very quick, took but a minute. When she finished she had sat up and stared into his flushed face, waiting for him to say something. Both of them were startled.

"Oh, Beth . . ." he had whispered hoarsely.

"If you had even a little doubt that I love you, I guess that settles it."

"We must marry now, Beth. Not next year. We must fly to Hong Kong. I will introduce you to my family. As soon as you graduate next week, we will fly to Hong Kong and we will marry."

If they survived this ordeal.

"Escape if you can, Beth," he mumbled. "They may throw you overboard, once we are a little farther out.".

"And let me drown?"

"They might."

She struggled against her bonds, with new determination born of desperation. At last, with a final painful effort, feeling blood ooze—she was sure—she shoved one piece of the abrasive cord over the knuckle of her right thumb. The rope loosened. She looked around to be sure none of the kidnappers could see, then slipped the rope off entirely. She kept her hands behind her back, as though she were still tied.

"Michael," she whispered. "I'm loose!"

"Really?"

"Yes. I'll untie you, and we'll slip overboard. We can swim back or to another boat that can pick us up."

"Beth, I can hardly swim. I will certainly drown."

"I'll stay with you, then," she sighed.

"No! I'm valuable to them, and they won't hurt me until they get what they want—or decide they can't get it. I can't promise what they'll do to you. It could be . . . very bad. You don't know what kind of men these are. They might also decide to rape you."

Beth snatched in breath.

"If you can, slip over the side into the water," Michael whispered. "The water's dirty and choppy, and there's a strong current running, but it's not cold. You— You *must* do this."

She rubbed her wrists hard, trying to restore circulation in her hands.

She stared at the water he was telling her to jump into. Even at this hour—long after midnight and not long until dawn—the harbor was crowded with water traffic: every kind of boat from huge container ships to tiny motorized sampans, coughing rusty lighters to swift jet foils and catamarans, all of them sharing and somehow avoiding collision in the heaving water.

The kidnappers were paying Beth and Michael little attention. They supposed their prisoners remained helpless. Beth stared at the shadowy figures. To her they were faceless, very much of a kind: thin, coarse men with impassive visages. Except one. One—who seemed to be the leader—had an exceptionally ugly face, because a part of his lower lip had been cut away, leaving a jagged red-and-white scar.

"They may shoot at you," Michael whispered hoarsely. "I know you are a strong swimmer, even underwater. Beth— I am suggesting a terrible risk. Do you think . . . ?"

"Yes," she said simply and resolutely. "I will go get help."

"Go for shore, where we just left. With any kind of luck, somebody will pick you up. Watch out that you're not run over. Go as quickly as you can, before the distance is too great. If you slip over quietly, this boat may move on some distance before they notice you've gone."

Beth stared at the dark, choppy water, gathering determination.

"I love you, *ai rien*, and I'm deeply sorry I got you into this."

Beth swallowed and nodded. "I love you, too, Michael. *Zai jian. Zai jian.*" The Chinese words meant—not good-bye exactly, but "until we meet again."

The kidnappers weren't watching. She loosened her skirt so she could tear it off just before she went in the water, so it would not impede her swimming. She stared at the kidnappers. She stared at the water. Then she snatched off the skirt, kicked off her shoes, and threw them over the side. With a last glance at Michael, she rolled over the gunwale and dropped to the water.

6

AS MICHAEL WATCHED, BETH went over the side quietly and disappeared. She simply disappeared. He did not see her stroking or swimming; he did not see her head bobbing among the waves; it was as if she had sunk and drowned immediately. Well—if he didn't see her, the kidnappers wouldn't see her. He kept silent. If she hadn't drowned, the more time that passed before they discovered she was gone, the better.

Of course, they did discover, within a minute. One of them screamed. The engines stopped, then reversed.

Their leader, the man with the scarred mouth, was a brute

known by his coarse nickname Dai Gul Dai, which meant Big Prick, and he dropped to his knees in the middle of the boat and tore away the plastic sheeting that wrapped a rifle. The others grabbed long, powerful electric torches and began to scan the water.

"Son of a pig-shit whore!" Dai Gul Dai yelled at Michael in Chinese. "Where is she?"

Michael nodded at the water and mumbled.

Dai Gul Dai shoved the rifle into the hands of another man. He was an expert with the knife he now whipped out and used to cut away Michael's gag, which he was able to do in one deft movement, cutting the gag without cutting Michael—as this morning he had deftly slit a man's eyelids without injuring his eyes.

"*Where?*" he demanded, pressing the knife against Michael's throat.

"In the water. She jumped overboard."

"With her hands tied?"

Michael hesitated briefly. If they thought she had jumped with her hands tied, they would assume she had drowned. He nodded. "Yes."

"*Why?*"

"She was terrified. She thought you were going to rape her, maybe kill her."

Dai Gul Dai shook his head and sneered. "She was a fool. We were going to enjoy her for a while, then drop her on one of the little islands. Too bad, Mikego Chang"—Michael winced whenever Dai Gul Dai mispronounced his name—"what a waste, to have brought a fat whore—we call her Dai Baw Dai, She of the Big Tits—all the way from America, only to have to see her commit suicide."

He gave a signal, and the engines began to drive the boat forward again. Michael stared at the water behind the boat and wondered if Beth were still alive. He had not prayed often since leaving the Jesuit high school, but now he started to mutter, "Our Father, who art in Heaven . . ." He fervently wanted God to hear him now in a plea for the life of the girl he had learned to love extravagantly.

TWO

"The horses will run, and the club girls will dance."

1

MICHAEL HAD BEEN RIGHT — the water was not cold. In the moment before plunging into it she had elected a tactic, which was that she would dive deep, swim under the boat, under its chopping propellers, and come to the surface on the right side of the boat, the side opposite where she had entered the water. They would be looking for her—if they looked—on the left side, and she would have a minute or so to make distance before they discovered her.

She could not have guessed how filthy the water was. Since it was dark anyway, she did not open her eyes, but she felt every kind of debris around her, brushing against her as she swam. Her hand got caught in a sheet of limp plastic, and she had to fight it off. She bumped against what felt like a huge dead fish.

She could hear the menacing propellers whipping the water. Then, ominously, they stopped. That undoubtedly meant they had noticed her going over and had stopped to recover her—or kill her. She swam strongly, knowing she had only seconds before she had to surface. She was in good shape, but she knew she had to go up for air very shortly.

She broke the surface as quietly as she could. She had made only ten yards from the boat, but she was on its right side, and she could see everyone peering to the left, shining powerful flashlights on the water. The boat's propellers were reversed, and it was easing slowly backward, moving closer to her. Beth drew two deep breaths, then submerged again and swam underwater until she had to come up for air. Now she was amidships of the boat, but she was thirty yards away. She could hear the men yelling. Their words were incomprehensible to her, but the voices were angry. She swam on the surface now, still away from the boat, not yet turning toward shore.

The roar of its engines almost spoke enraged impatience as the boat gained speed again and moved on out across the harbor.

Her prison though it had been, with a crew intending to murder her, that boat now speeding away had been the floor under her feet, and now there was none; she was afloat on her own in oil-fouled, garbage-filled, heaving water. The distance to shore was not impossible, she had swum that far before, but she had never been in water like this.

What was more, she might easily be run over. Heading toward her right now was a squat tugboat not much different from a New York Harbor tug, pulling a heavily laden barge by a cable. She swam out of its course, aware that stroking hard to get out of its way depleted some measure of her endurance. It passed, but she found herself bobbing in its wake, struggling to avoid being overwhelmed by its big bow waves. After that experience, she spluttered and gasped and swam again, more slowly, toward the lights of the Hong Kong waterfront.

A small steel boat she could not identify moved past, slowly and not making much wake. She waved and yelled, hoping the crew would see her and fish her out of the water, but it slid quietly past. She had to realize that she was all but invisible.

Grimly, she began to stroke toward the waterfront again. After a few minutes her arms and shoulders ached, and she stopped and treaded water. Then she realized she couldn't do that—the current would carry her away.

She began to despair of ever reaching shore. She tried to settle into a steady, not-too-demanding stroke, making slow progress. But now she was faced with a new menace. Bearing down on her was a huge, sleek, fast boat: a jet-foil catamaran accelerating. There would be no getting out of *its* way. She waited until it was almost upon her, then drove herself down, hoping to go deep enough to avoid its murderous onslaught. She dove as deeply as she could, maybe twenty feet, and she not only heard it but felt a powerful shock as it passed above her. When she could stay down no longer she stroked to the surface and found herself spinning in the vortexes of its wake. Her mouth filled with water as she surfaced, and she spat the vile stuff and retched.

Conscious that her strength was dwindling, she assessed her situation. She could not reach shore. Her only hope lay in being seen and picked up. She looked around for a boat she could swim close to.

Good luck! Here came a black-hulled boat with a white super-structure, showing blue lights. Surely it was a police boat. She swam toward its course and began to wave and yell.

The police boat glided majestically past. No one on board had been staring down at the water, no one had seen the desperate figure of a young woman flailing and waving. They weren't expecting anything like that; they weren't looking for it, and they didn't see it.

Beth sobbed, but she knew she could not waste her strength on weeping. She had very little chance now, and what chance she had depended on being fished out of the water.

She saw a rusty, dilapidated old boat coming. Its cranky engine clattered loudly. As it came closer she could see that part of its rail was broken away. Ropes dangled over the sides. Again she yelled and waved desperately.

She saw the man at the helm, spinning the wheel, turning the little craft toward her. Its engine stopped, it drifted close, and a man reached toward her with a pole. She seized it gratefully, and the man pulled her toward the boat. Two men reached down and grabbed her wrists. They pulled her out of the water and onto the deck of the little boat, where she collapsed, exhausted, and for a whole minute lay facedown on the wet deck.

The engine sputtered and began to turn the propeller again.

Beth rolled over and looked at her rescuers. She knew they couldn't speak English, but she tried to thank them—

"Oh, thank you, thank you! I was drowning. Thank you!"

They stared at her, curious and utterly uncomprehending.

She tried to put into her tone of voice the meaning she could not express with words. *"Thank you!* I'm so grateful to you." She tried to convey her meaning with gestures, but what was the gesture for gratitude? She wished Michael had taught her a few more Chinese phrases. But he had assured her that Hong Kong was a thoroughly Westernized megacity, that English was spoken everywhere. Well, it was not spoken or understood on this small boat.

The men turned away from her and went back to whatever they had been doing before.

She pointed back toward the Hong Kong shoreline, in the hope they might understand that was where she wanted to go, on the remote chance they might turn around and take her there. Solemnly they watched her point and listened to her plead. They exchanged glances. But they did not turn the boat around.

All these men were small, thin as skeletons, and none of them had a full mouth of teeth. They were dressed in ragged khaki shorts and stained white vest undershirts. All were barefoot. They were busy at some sort of work and gave it, not her, their attention.

The deck of their boat was cluttered. She could not guess what most of the clutter was, but she did recognize that part of it was nets. This was a fishing boat. They were cleaning their nets, pulling litter out of them. One of them was repairing holes.

One of the men brought something to her. It was a whole raw shrimp. He gestured, pointing at the shrimp and at the water, and she understood this was a shrimp boat and these men were fishermen. They were leaving Hong Kong, maybe having sold their catch there, and maybe they were on their way home, probably to the New Territories that, according to Michael, was a large tract of semirural land north of Kowloon (still part of Hong Kong) and south of China, where fishermen and farmers lived.

She pointed again at the Hong Kong waterfront and at herself. "Please! I must go back. *Oh, God!*" She wept. *"Please!"*

The fishermen had been a bit compassionate for a young woman who had somehow found herself in this water and had been strong enough to survive, until now. But they withdrew their sympathy when they saw her becoming hysterical. Four of them stared at her without feeling, then turned their backs on her.

Beth lay on the deck and whimpered. Exhausted, wet, and cold, she shivered. One of the fishermen—she would never know which one—tossed a piece of sailcloth over her. She clutched it to her and raised herself to a sitting position against a gunwale. She ceased trembling, ceased crying. She just sat disconsolate and stared at the deck.

So . . . she was off the boat where kidnappers had decided to murder her, and she was out of the water, all of which she should be very grateful for. She was aboard a boat with men who seemed to mean her no harm—had in fact stopped to rescue her—and that she could not guess where they were taking her was maybe no great worry. Sooner or later they would encounter someone who understood English, and then she could explain who she was and ask them to contact the United States consulate.

2

THEY TRAVELED FOR WHAT seemed a very long time, across open water far from lights and far from land. They were always in substantial traffic—boats and ships were always around them. She wondered how the captain found his way in this dark water, how he distinguished the lights of the place where he was going from the thousand other dim lights on the shore. But it was obvious he did know where he was going. The boat was not wandering but making a straight line to some destination well known to the captain and crew.

As they crossed broad open water, daylight came. She could see a misty coast ahead, and in time she was able to see that they were heading toward one particular cluster of buildings. As they came nearer it became apparent that this was a village, probably the home village of this boat.

The place was picturesque beyond imagination. She wondered why Michael never told her such a pretty place existed in Hong Kong. Houses—hovels, they would have been called somewhere else—stood high on stilts. The tide was out now, but the marks on stilts and pillars showed how high it reached when it was in. Each house had a sort of porch, facing the saltwater inlet that split the village in two, and behind that the house itself was enclosed in wood and corrugated steel. The villagers were up and about, though it was barely after dawn. Some were in boats, tugging the cords of their outboard engines to start them. Others were already poling sampans along the narrow inlet. Dogs prowled on the wet tidal flats, sniffing at what they hoped was edible.

As the fishing boat approached a stone jetty, the captain sounded a horn. A few people rushed from houses and ran down to the jetty. They yelled what was obviously a cheerful welcome. They began to laugh, and children danced up and down with excitement. In the dim red light of a foggy dawn, the people looked like marionettes dancing on a stage. The captain yelled something that caused even greater excitement. Beth guessed he had said they had had a successful voyage and sold a good catch of shrimp.

With ropes in place securing the little vessel to the jetty, the captain at last shut down the clanking engine. The crew began to leap to the jetty. Two of them helped Beth from the boat.

Instantly she was surrounded by curious people. The crewmen began to speak in staccato Chinese, probably explaining how she had come to be aboard the boat.

"Does anyone understand English? Please, does anyone understand anything I'm saying?"

One of the women began to speak to her, gesticulating sharply. The woman wore a loose gray cotton shirt and loose ankle-length pants. She was barefoot. On her head she wore a hat of golden woven straw, a tapered cylinder above a brim; it looked like a lampshade.

Beth realized she had to be a strange sight to these people. Apart from being conspicuously Caucasian, she was wearing nothing but a polo shirt, panties, and her bra—plus her little gold wristwatch, which she had not taken off. Harbor oil smeared her skin and blackened her clothes.

"Does anyone speak English?" Beth asked again, not really daring to hope anyone did.

People backed away from her, as if she were somehow a threat.

The gesticulating woman, who assumed the lead in trying to communicate with this strangely dressed young woman, spoke more slowly, gesturing elaborately, apparently hoping that by speaking at a deliberate pace, accompanying her words with clarifying hand signals, she would be understood. It was like the old cliché the English used: that anyone could understand English if it were spoken slowly and distinctly. But the case was hopeless, and the woman turned her back on Beth and walked away.

"I must return to Hong Kong Island. Is this the New Territories?" Beth said, pointing out to sea. "Hong Kong Island. I must go there."

The words "Hong Kong" seemed to frighten these villagers. They stared hard at her, tipped their heads as if to understand her better, and kept their distance.

A man taller than the rest, dressed in a white shirt and black trousers, approached. Beth spoke to him. "Do you understand English? I must go back to Hong Kong."

The man regarded her with intense curiosity, mixed, she thought, with a little sympathy, but he turned to the Chinese woman in the lampshade hat and spoke peremptorily. The woman frowned, as if to protest, then curtly gestured to Beth to come with her. She led her along a narrow stone-paved walkway toward one of the houses on stilts.

On the way they passed stalls that were already selling live, dried, and smoked fish. The smell of all these fish oppressed Beth's nostrils. She enjoyed fish, but this village was immersed in them.

The woman's house was furnished with a table and four chairs, a television set, which was on—the program being some Chinese period drama—and a small iron stove. A tiny gas flame burned under an aluminum teapot. One corner of the room was given over to a little shrine, in which incense burned before an icon of a goddess and a silk cloth on which some Chinese characters were painted.

For the next hour Beth sat in the woman's house, uncomfortably conscious that the woman did not want her there but was obeying an order. She was probably a little frightened by having this foreign stranger in her house and she was unsure of what consequences would follow. Even so, she was not hostile. She gave Beth hot water to drink—not tea, hot water—and heated some gruel for her to eat. She also gave her rancid chicken fat to rub on the rope burns on her wrists. Beth was unwilling to rub this smelly mess on her wrists but recognized that the woman was probably right and so reluctantly rubbed the fat onto her ravaged skin.

The man Beth took for some kind of village headman returned and sat down facing Beth across the table. He tried to talk to her and became visibly annoyed when this odd young foreign woman persisted in her inability to understand simple Chinese. All Beth could understand was that he was trying to ask her questions. But all she could answer was, "Hong Kong. I must go to Hong Kong."

After a while he gave up, and they sat in silence. They seemed to be waiting for something, and Beth wondered what that might be.

3

THE SIGHT OF THE sampans in the inlet reminded her of something Michael had told her of his family. One evening she had spoken apologetically about being the daughter of a pubkeeper, the granddaughter of a trolley-car conductor.

"Ha," he had muttered. "My great-grandfather was named

Chang Zi Hin. The name means Self-Prosper. He owned sixty or seventy sampans. They were little floating brothels. A man came aboard, slipped inside the little tent in the center of the boat, and pleasured himself with the girl there—very likely a fragile child of fourteen or fifteen. While the man was with the girl, the boatman rowed a short distance out into the harbor and then returned, pretending he had no idea why the man inside had given him so much money or what he was doing under the cover of the tent. The commerce made my great-grandfather wealthy. He had no pangs of conscience about it. He ran a business. If he hadn't engaged in that business, someone else would have."

Beth had shrugged. "Many Boston fortunes were founded in the slave trade."

"When the British sent out a colonial governor full of Christian fervor and determined to stamp out prostitution, my great-grandfather Chang Zi Hin had to go out of business. The city swarmed with prostitutes, but the ones on sampans were conspicuous. So—he sold his best girls to onshore whoremasters and used his fleet of sampans to smuggle arms. Don't be ashamed to be the daughter of a pubkeeper."

" 'Chang Zi Hin.' What is your Chinese name, Michael?"

"I am Chang Po Ka. It means Protect-the-Chang-Family."

He had proved very reluctant to talk about his family's business and fortune. She had pressed him—

"What business is your family in, Michael? Maybe that's prying, but if I'm going to marry you, I have to know."

"It is not customary in Chinese families to reveal—"

She had interrupted. "*Michael.* I remember vividly how in *The Godfather* another Michael, Michael Corleone, told Kay he would allow her to ask just *one* question about his business, after which she must never ask anything again. Well—I can't live that way. If I'm going to be your wife, I'm going to be your partner in every aspect of your life."

"If I speak to you in confidence, you won't tell anyone, not even members of my family, what you know?"

"Husbands and wives have secrets," she had said. "But not from each other."

He had nodded, smiling faintly. "Very well. I will tell you a great many things. You will know more than my mother has ever known, more than my sister knows or ever will know."

"I think you know about all there is to know about me, Michael. I want to know as much about you."

He had admitted that his family was prosperous. "Prosperous" was not the word. They were wealthy. The descendants of the brothel-keeper and arms-smuggler were heavily involved in real-estate development. Michael had insisted he had no real idea of his family's net worth, but it was one of the wealthier families in a community where great wealth was risked and earned every year.

In contrast to *her* family.

The Connors found it difficult to accept him. They had invited him to dinner, and on the way there Beth told him her mother had asked if she should have chopsticks for him. Her parents and her younger sister, Kathleen, watched him eat lamb and parsley potatoes with knife and fork, gradually relaxing as he used those utensils dexterously.

Her father, Curran Connor, was a burly, sandy-haired Irishman. "We have always been told," he said to Michael, "that your people take more than one wife. I suppose that custom has changed, hmm?"

"That custom has changed, Mr. Connor. I have promised Beth without qualification, not just that she will be my only wife, but that she will be the only woman in my life."

"A hard promise to keep," Beth had said with a mischievous smile.

"Where will you live?" her mother asked. Beth had probably inherited her size and athletic ability from her mother, for Margaret— invariably called Peggy—Connor was taller than her husband and at least as robust. Like her daughters, she was a striking blond.

"We'll have a home in Hong Kong and one in the States, too," said Michael. "I'll have responsibilities to the family business, but they won't be so heavy that Beth and I can't spend a month or more in Boston every year. I'm really thinking about keeping my apartment in Cambridge on a long-term lease."

"What happens to your family when the Chinese Communists take over Hong Kong?" Kathleen asked.

"We don't expect things to be very different. The word from Beijing is, 'The horses will run, and the club girls will dance.' It's not in Beijing's interest to interfere in Hong Kong capitalism. Hong Kong Chinese are investing significant amounts of money in China—and the mainland Chinese have invested a lot in Hong Kong. Anyway, my family has funds on deposit in other places, so we could leave if we had to."

"What's this ongoing battle between the last governor of Hong Kong, Chris Patten, and the Beijing government that we read so much about in the *Boston Globe*? I got the idea that China was going to swallow Hong Kong and spit out her bones."

"Not at all," Michael replied with confidence. "Journalists like to focus on the doom and gloom and not talk about the positive things. Britain and China signed a deal in 1984 returning Hong Kong to China in 1997. China promised to keep Hong Kong's legal, social, and economic systems unchanged for the next fifty years. Beijing drafted a set of basic laws, and Deng Xiaoping invented the notion of 'one country, two systems' to preserve Hong Kong's unique advantages. Except for defense and foreign affairs, Hong Kong will govern itself with a new chief executive to be selected later next year. Most of the Western influences in Hong Kong will remain; only a few cosmetic changes will take place. The Jockey Club and the Hong Kong police have already dropped the 'Royal' from their names."

"Then why the public row with the British governor?" Curran Connor pressed on.

"Several years ago, Governor Chris Patten, without consulting Beijing, introduced popular legislative elections in Hong Kong, something the British had not seen fit to do for a hundred and fifty years. Now only a few years prior to returning Hong Kong to China, the colonial government suddenly introduced mass democracy overnight, by brute force according to some. Beijing suspected Britain had a hidden agenda of providing a small group of China-bashers a visible and public forum to criticize and embarrass China. That's what the argument was largely about."

"Isn't it true many Chinese people left Hong Kong out of fear?" Mrs. Connor asked, with evident concern.

"Yes and no, Mrs. Connor. From 1990 to 1994, fifty to sixty thousand of our middle- and upper-middle-class people emigrated every year. Beginning in 1994, many of these emigrés started to return to Hong Kong to take part in the economic boom. Net emigration is down substantially. In our family, we all have multiple passports and can leave on very short notice."

"Do you think they would let you leave?" Curran Connor asked. "We understand they won't let anybody leave China."

"To the contrary, Mr. Connor. They let *anybody* leave—except a few political dissidents they want to silence. Even members of the Politburo send their children to the States to be educated, but quietly, under assumed names."

"All we have to do is keep a low profile, and we'll be perfectly alright," said Beth. "I've talked to other people about it. Professors. They confirm what Michael is saying."

"Your family must be quite wealthy," her mother remarked ingenuously.

"Prosperous," said Michael dryly.

He and Beth had laughed over that in the car on their way back to Cambridge. Both of them had noticed her father staring at Michael's Rolex watch, while trying to pretend he was not staring at it. They could guess that only a wealthy man, not just a prosperous one, could afford a watch like that.

Then there was the gift he brought them: a case of Old Bushmills Irish Whisky. That hadn't come cheap.

The Chang family was wealthy. That was why the kidnappers had seized Michael. For them, *she* had been an accident.

4

HER CLOTHES DRIED, PARTLY. She thought of Michael, wondering where the kidnappers had taken him and what they were doing to him. The woman busied herself about her house, cleaning a fish with a sharp knife and putting it in oil to fry.

Finally, she heard the sound of an engine. Two uniformed policemen appeared in the door and entered the house. Beth breathed a sigh of relief. At last she would be rescued. They spoke—rather sharply, she thought—to the man she took for the local leader.

One of the policemen gestured to Beth to stand up. He unhooked from his belt a pair of handcuffs and curtly gestured that she should extend her hands. When she didn't move fast enough, he grabbed her hands and locked the handcuffs on her wrists.

"Why?" she cried. "Why? I am an American. I—"

There was no point trying to talk to the policemen. They didn't understand any more English than did the fishermen.

Suddenly a horrifying thought occurred to her. She looked at the insignia on the policemen's caps. These badges were red, with stars. My God! Had these fishermen crossed into mainland China? Was she ashore in the People's Republic?

She didn't have time to think about it. The woman who had fed her pretended not to see what was happening. The man nodded as if he approved. The policemen led her out to a utility vehicle, something like a Jeep Cherokee but boxier, and put her in the back seat. And they set off along a road—to God knew where.

5

FOR A WHILE THEY drove along a narrow, rutted road, but shortly they entered a six-lane superhighway, and the driver accelerated to the speed that highway allowed. The highway signs were in English as well as Chinese, but Beth did not recognize any of the names. She did recognize the symbols on the signs, and she wondered idly why the fork-and-knife symbol, meaning food was to be had at the upcoming exit, was not a pair of chopsticks. She stared disconsolately at the countryside through which they passed. She saw tall buildings and factories, clusters of squalid houses, growing crops, much red earth, and an occasional water buffalo. It was all depressing to her. This was China, and they were speeding deeper into it, away from Hong Kong.

Part of her attention was fixed on her handcuffs. It was not that they hurt, which they didn't, but the adamantine steel manacles that chained her wrists close together definitively fixed her status. She was a *prisoner*. She was a prisoner in Red China and—what was even worse—no one knew she was here. She had no idea why they were holding her prisoner, but she feared they might decide to hold her indefinitely, for whatever incomprehensible reason they might have, and because no one knew where she was, no one could help her. Staring at the handcuffs, she realized they were bright and new, as though they had never been locked on anyone before.

After what seemed like a two-hour drive, the vehicle entered a big city. She had gathered from the highway signs that its name was Guangzhou, though that name meant nothing to her. It was a huge place, lying under the thickest smog she had ever seen. Traffic was heavy and chaotic—trucks, buses, cars, motorcycles, motorbikes, bicycles, all moving fast in what looked like vehicular anarchy, governed, if by anything, by a cacophony of truculent horn-honking.

The city was crowded, busy, and noisy; everything seemed to move faster than natural, like a scene in an old silent movie. Nothing she saw was "Chinese"—that is, nothing had the aspect of a Chinese city as she had seen them in movies, or even on television news programs. Except for the Chinese characters on all the signs, and except that all the people were obviously Chinese, Guangzhou could have been a city anywhere in the world. Like any other modern city, it was under construction. New high-rise buildings were going up. Scores of high-rise buildings already stood, some of them more than fifty or sixty stories, some apparently office buildings, others apartment buildings, still others luxury hotels.

Many of the streets were broad boulevards. But after a time the driver guided the vehicle into a tangle of narrower streets. Desperately anxious to have some idea where she might be, Beth stared at the street signs, which were in both languages. Beijing Lu, one said. She knew she was not in Beijing; they hadn't driven *that* far.

Finally the driver turned into a street that was torn up for construction, where he used his horn to clear the way through a crowd of bicycles and pedestrians, including scores of schoolchildren in uniforms.

They reached a walled compound, where a policeman stood guard at the gate. The driver turned in. He stopped in front of a doorway to a square, gray stuccoed building.

The two policemen led their prisoner inside. The building was a police station. An officer of conspicuously higher rank took charge. He ordered one of the men to unlock her handcuffs. Then he led her down a flight of stairs and along a short corridor flanked with barred doors. As they entered the corridor she saw a room that had to be a bathroom. She pointed to it and asked to be allowed to use it. Her need was urgent. With a hand on her shoulder he hustled her along. He opened the door to a cell. As she stepped inside, the man turned a big key, and she was locked in.

The cell was maybe eight feet long and six wide. The walls were of concrete block painted institutional beige. The steel bars were painted a cheerful light blue. There was no bed, only a wooden shelf without either a pad or a blanket. A wooden bucket with a wooden lid served as toilet, and—for some reason she could not imagine—an old-fashioned brass spittoon sat beside the bucket.

The place was grimly functional. Its purpose was to confine one human being in a cage, and that was what she was: confined.

She nodded toward the bucket and gestured that he should go away and leave her her privacy. The man leaned against the opposite wall, folded his arms, and grinned.

She shook her head. "No! Not while you're staring, goddamn it!"

The guard grinned more broadly, showing gold teeth.

Which was worse—to do it in the bucket while he watched, or to let it go in her panties and have it run down her legs? She had to do one or the other. She had no more alternatives.

Beth squatted over the bucket. With a skirt she could have covered herself, mostly, but she had no skirt. She slipped down her panties and let her stream run into the bucket. The man stared, laughed, and said something in Chinese she could no more understand than anything that had been said to her since she was pulled from the water of Victoria Harbour.

The man left now. Beth stood and pulled up her panties. Instinctively she seized the bars in her hands and pressed her face between them as far as possible, to see whatever she could. All she could see was part of the cement-floored corridor, now deserted.

The jail was not silent. She could hear someone hacking and spitting in another cell. What was more, the sound of construction work outside was oppressive and unceasing: the noise of jackhammers, mostly. Also, she could hear the constant blaring of automobile horns.

"Does anyone in here speak English?" she called out through the bars, not really expecting that any other prisoner did.

No one responded.

Beth sat down on the shelf and began to cry. She couldn't help herself; she wept until it exhausted her. She went to the bars again and peered out. The corridor was still deserted. She sat down on the shelf.

Where was Michael? What had they done to him by now? How and when could she get out of here and get back to Hong Kong where maybe she could do something for him? All of this . . .

it was all *insane!* She couldn't believe it. But it was totally, oppressively real. She sobbed again. She was absolutely helpless. She could do nothing for Michael or for herself. She sat slumped and softly wept.

THREE

I would sign a confession that
I murdered my grandmother if
that would get me back to Hong Kong.

1

BETH STILL HAD HER watch and knew what time it was. She managed to go to sleep for a little while before noon. Maybe the word was that she crashed. Many hours had passed since she last slept— in the hotel room in Hong Kong, with Michael lying beside her. Even in her stupor she struggled with the thought that she might be held in prison for a long, long time. All that drove her into fitful sleep.

She had to use the bucket again. She didn't want to but knew she had no choice. She squatted over it and urinated, then replaced the lid, pressing it down as tight as she could. What she would do when she had to relieve her bowels, she couldn't imagine. She grabbed the bars again and tried to look up and down the corridor. For the short distance she could see, the corridor was still bare and desolate.

She sat down again, awake and oppressively aware—aware especially of how very slowly time was passing. Someone in another cell hacked constantly and spat noisily, which was probably why the cells had spittoons. Somewhere along the corridor a woman was quietly, hopelessly weeping. Beth wondered how long that poor soul had been in here, and what fears burdened her.

A little after noon a woman came and without a word handed a bowl and a glass through a horizontal slot in the barred door. It was the midday meal: rice, in which some vegetables were mixed, and a glass of tea. She sat and ate, with her fingers. The rice was tasteless, but she ate it and drank the weak, unsugared tea. Starving herself would serve no purpose.

When the woman had delivered rice to the other cells, she returned and stood outside to watch Beth eat. She watched, open-mouth curious, also scornful, until Beth handed her the empty bowl and glass.

Shortly after she finished eating, a uniformed woman unlocked the door and beckoned her to come out of the cell. The woman led her up the stairs into the police station and into a small square room furnished with a wooden table and two wooden straight chairs.

A man came in. He was of middle age and wore a uniform: an open-collared shirt and a cap, which he put down on the table. He carried a pad and pencil and a file folder.

"You speak English?" he asked as soon as he was seated opposite her.

"Yes." She decided that it would be better to respond to questions and see where the conversation led, rather than to gush out the demand that she be returned to Hong Kong.

"You confess you have enter China illegal?"

"I didn't intend to. I fell overboard from a ferryboat and nearly drowned. I *would* have drowned except that a shrimp boat picked me up. The fishermen took me to their home port, which I suppose is in China, not Hong Kong. I didn't mean to enter your country illegally. For that matter, I didn't intend to enter at all."

She had decided to say nothing about the kidnapping. She could not be certain the kidnappers were not from mainland China; she had read about crime and corruption in China. Anyway, to say that she had fallen overboard was far simpler and did not raise an issue that did not need to be raised.

The man nodded. He was humorless and apparently struggling

to speak and understand English. He was, as she judged, a functionary doing a routine duty. He shoved his pad and pencil toward her. "Please to write out confess you enter China illegal."

"Illegally, yes. But involuntarily," she said.

"Write so. Write name, where you from, and how and why you enter China illegal."

Beth took up the pencil and wrote on the pad:

> My name is Mary Elizabeth Connor. I am an American citizen from Boston, Massachusetts, USA. I came to Hong Kong yesterday to marry a Hong Kong citizen. Last night, after midnight, I accidentally fell overboard from a ferry boat. I would have drowned, except that a shrimp fishing boat picked me up from the water. The fishermen brought me to their home port, which is in the People's Republic of China. I had no intention of entering China illegally or otherwise. I request that I be returned to Hong Kong as soon as possible.

She signed the note and shoved the pad across the table to the officer. He read it, frowning, probably because some of the words she had used were not within his English vocabulary.

"We must keep you here," he said, "until facts you say proved. Maybe not long. Anything need? Book for read?"

"One thing," she said. "I would be most grateful for some toilet paper."

"Toilet—? Oh, yes. Very good. Go to cell for now. Maybe not long you stay."

He opened the door and summoned the woman who had led Beth to this room. He spoke to her, smiling a little, and she returned his smile. The woman took Beth in custody and led her away. Instead of going immediately back to the basement prison, she led her to the bathroom at the end of the cell corridor. It was primitive, but it did have a toilet and toilet paper. While the woman watched, Beth used the toilet and cleaned herself. Then she submissively followed the woman to her cell again, to be locked in. The bucket had been emptied, and a stack of tissue paper lay on the wooden shelf, also a book for her to read while she was confined—a ragged, faded paperback of Erskine Caldwell's *Tobacco Road*.

2

BETH TRIED TO REMEMBER some of the writings she had read, about how it was to be a prisoner. *Darkness at Noon* occurred to her. Some writers had even insisted it was an uplifting experience, that they had come out of it stronger people. All she wanted was to come out of it as soon as possible, one way or another. She found nothing uplifting about it.

Maybe not long, the man had said. How long was not long? How much time would they need to confirm the facts?

If Michael was still in the hands of the kidnappers, it was essential that she report the kidnapping to the police, since Michael had said his family wouldn't. If he had been freed, he would suppose she had drowned. Every hour she spent in here . . . Oh, *Jesus!*

Driven by impulse, not by any rational notion that she would see anything, Beth pressed her face still again to the blue-painted bars. Once again, all she saw was the empty, hard-walled corridor. She resolved not to hang on the bars like a monkey; it was irrational.

She returned to the shelf, sat down, and picked up the tattered copy of *Tobacco Road*. She remembered it was a somewhat scandalous novel about the lives of a poverty-benighted family in the South. She had never read it. She might as well; there was nothing else to do in here.

She spent the afternoon apathetically reading, finishing half the book. Despite her resolution, she spent some time gripping the bars and staring at the corridor. Twice she heard the sound of a man urinating noisily into his bucket.

She could not get comfortable on the hard boards of the shelf. Already she was developing new little bruises on her hips.

At five o'clock a woman brought her a bowl of noodles with vegetables and bits of meat in it, a bowl of oily soup, and another glass of tea. She ate and drank. This seemed to mean that she *would* have to spend the night here. When the woman came back for the bowls and glass, Beth tried to ask her what was going on, without confidence that the woman would understand her, which she didn't. The woman only shook her head, and Beth found it impossible to read either sympathy or scorn in her expression.

About seven o'clock the monotony of confinement was broken for a moment when a struggling, cursing man was hustled along the corridor by two policemen. They shoved him into a cell, and he spent some minutes screaming and rattling the door. In a minute the two policemen returned. Beth heard—did not see, but heard and could imagine—the beating they gave him. The thuds of the truncheons were sickening. The man groaned and gagged. She imagined he vomited. The policemen left, and she heard the prisoner weeping and moaning. When he fell silent, she wondered if he were alive.

After that the jail was quiet except for the hacking and spitting in one cell and the soft weeping in another—plus the incessant muffled racket of the street work outside.

Worse was to come. About eight, when Beth was sitting, trying to interest herself in *Tobacco Road*, the lights went out.

She panicked. For a moment she had to suppress an impulse to scream. Though confinement was almost unbearably oppressive, she had not before felt the horror of claustrophobia. In the dark she was afraid. She stumbled to the door and shook it. She stood there breathing heavily, moaning softly. Thank God the corridor was not *totally* dark—faint gray light from somewhere outside leaked in, enough that she could distinguish the corridor floor from the wall. That faint light allowed her to recover a bit of equilibrium and subdue her panic.

The darkness in the cell, though, was so complete she could not read her watch. Desolate, with nothing else to do, she lay down on the boards and stared at the faint gray light on the corridor wall opposite. Staring at that dim gray light and hearing the noise from the other cells and from the street gave her a sense of time and place that preserved her sanity, which she might have lost in total darkness and total silence.

3

SHE TRIED TO FIX her mind on pleasant memories.

At Christmas they had set up a Christmas tree in his apartment and had invited a few people—her roommates and five of his friends from Harvard Business School, two of them Chinese. From a restaurant Michael ordered *yu-cha-hün-tün*, wontons stuffed with pork, shrimp, water chestnuts, and scallions, also *tsao-ni-hün-tün*, wontons stuffed with dates, walnuts, and grated orange rind. He served the *yu-cha-hün-tün* hot with wines and cocktails, the *tsao-ni-hün-tün* cold with tea and coffee. That evening Beth wore a *cheongsam*, Michael's gift: a beautiful emerald-green, ankle-length silk dress that clung liquidly to her figure. It was decorated with embroidery, with gold and silver threads. High slits in the skirt showed her thighs when she walked. During the party, he gave her a pair of earrings: pieces of the darkest green jadeite set in circles of tiny diamonds.

She saw, to her absolute amazement, that the two Chinese friends—both of them from Hong Kong—treated Michael with deference that amounted almost to obsequiousness, so much that she was uneasy with it.

On Christmas Day, Beth's parents came to the apartment and sat down to a turkey dinner, very American-style. She had insisted she would cook, but Michael had said he would not see her cooking and ordered everything catered. The dinner was delivered shortly before the Connors arrived. The caterers even laid it out on the table.

Her parents were not entirely able to conceal their dismay at seeing their Irish daughter wearing her Chinese dress, no matter how exquisite and expensive it was.

"Is this how you will dress in Hong Kong?" her mother had asked.

Michael had answered. "On formal occasions, when everyone wants to pay her honor."

"Dressed like a goddess," her father said. "And couldn't a Southie family live three or four months on the cost?"

Their Christmas together, just six months ago, had been a warm and memorable experience. She was proud of the calm poise Michael had evinced with their guests and her parents. He had shown them his affection for her, enough to make it evident and certain, not so much as to let it seem callow. Everyone saw how comfortable they were with each other. Everyone saw how proud she was of Michael and how proud he was of her. She would never forget that week, no matter what happened.

4

SHE SLEPT A LITTLE, fitfully, turning on the hard shelf and unable to find the least comfort. All kinds of dread tortured her. She clung to the man's bland assurance that she might not have to remain imprisoned long, but she could take no confidence in it. How long was "long"?

She couldn't see the bucket and had to feel for it. She wondered if they would again take her out to the real toilet in the morning.

The night passed. The lights came on again, and she could look at her watch and see that it was seven o'clock. She received morning noodles and tea. So began her second day in jail.

She had just finished *Tobacco Road* when a uniformed woman unlocked the door and gestured that she should follow her. It was ten o'clock. The woman led her this time up two flights of stairs and into a room where the officer who had taken her written statement was waiting.

"You will go now to see the deputy governor," he said. "It is improper that you should go so dressed. So . . ."

The uniformed woman who had taken her to the toilet entered the room. She led her through a series of corridors and to a bathroom. There she pointed to a shower stall and gestured that Beth take a shower. Beth used the toilet first, then took a shower. That was welcome enough. The water was hot, and there was soap. She was able to wash the harbor oil off her skin and out of her hair. There was no curtain, and the woman watched her with critical interest as she bathed. When Beth was finished, the woman handed her a towel. Then she handed her a white cotton blouse, a black knee-length skirt, and a pair of rubber-and-canvas shoes. Beth dressed, and the woman handcuffed her again.

She was put in the rear seat of a car, and the woman and another policeman drove her again through the teeming streets of Guangzhou, to a modern, handsome building that sat behind a wrought-iron fence, a paved forecourt, and an expanse of green lawn. One sign was in English. This was the headquarters of the provincial government of Guangdong Province.

Inside, the woman led her to a comfortably furnished office, took off the handcuffs, and pointed to a leather-covered armchair. Beth glanced around the office and saw a collection of photographs of a man shaking hands with several older men—one of whom she recognized as Deng Xiaoping.

A man entered the office. He was the man in the photos. "Good morning, Miss Connor," he said in accented English. "Welcome to Guangzhou, the city you used to call Canton. My name is Shek Tin. I am deputy governor of the province of Guangdong."

He was a man of what she supposed was average height in China, below-average height for Americans, and she guessed his age as roughly fifty. His jowly face was unremarkable except for two small moles on his left cheek. His dark hair was combed down over the right side of his forehead, up and back on his left. This was his office. His jacket hung over a chair, and he wore a white shirt, apparently freshly laundered but wrinkled even so, with two pens in the pocket, also a red-and-gold-patterned tie. She guessed he was a man who had once worn a Mao jacket and hated it and now didn't even own one. He had the air of a self-confident man of affairs, maybe a little weary, maybe a little cynical, with a half smile on his wide mouth. She guessed he was a practical man who would do his job, and she could hope his job would mean sending her back to Hong Kong.

"I am pleased to meet you," she said. She didn't know what else to say.

"Yes. Please be seated. Now. Your confession is incomplete. You say you came to Hong Kong to marry. To marry whom, Miss Connor?"

"Michael Chang, the son of Chang Wing Hing."

"Ah. And as he was taking you across Victoria Harbour on the harbor ferry you fell overboard."

"Yes."

Shek Tin shook his head. "This does not ring true, Miss Connor. The story is incorrect in several ways. For one point, the harbor ferries do not run after midnight. But tell me—you are the Beth Connor of the 1992 Olympics, are you not?"

"Yes. That was an accident."

"So. Perhaps. You say, I understand, that you entered the People's Republic of China illegally."

"Illegally," she said, "but wholly involuntarily."

"Yes. The fishermen—"

"I would be dead but for them," she said simply.

"Yes."

"Mr. Shek, can I go back to Hong Kong?"

"Technically you should explain your illegal entry in testimony before a People's court. I should prefer you do not have to do that.

It is who you are, actually, that makes a small problem. Would you be willing to sign a confession that you intentionally knocked down Xiang Li?"

"Mr. Shek, I would sign a confession that I murdered my grand-mother if that would get me back to Hong Kong."

Shek smiled. "I understand your little joke, Miss Connor. Un-fortunately, my government takes the Barcelona incident very seri-ously. My government believes you were sent to the Olympics with the specific assignment of putting our best woman runner out of the race."

"I promise you that was not so."

"In addition to that, you said very bad things about our country and government."

"Yes. I did. I am sorry. But your news agency called me ugly things—which made me angry."

Beth's mind was running fast, keeping ahead of the conversa-tion. This seemed to be turning into some sort of negotiation. Maybe she could negotiate her way out by making some sort of con-cession. It could all be straightened out later. No one outside China would believe anything she said in these circumstances. The whole point was to get back to Hong Kong and find Michael. There were not many concessions she wouldn't make to achieve that.

"Please read this statement," Shek said. He handed her a paper. It read:

> I acknowledge that in the 1992 Olympics at Barcelona I in-tentionally knocked down the Chinese runner Xiang Li. The American Olympic coaches specifically placed me on the team to do that, for the purpose of denying a gold medal to the run-ner from the People's Republic of China.

"Will you sign?" Shek asked.

"May I have a pen?" Beth asked.

He handed her a pen.

She edited the statement—

I acknowledge that in the 1992 Olympics at Barcelona I ~~intentionally~~ *carelessly* knocked down the Chinese runner Xiang Li. ~~The American Olympic coaches specifically placed me on the team to do that, for the purpose of denying a gold medal to the runner from the People's Republic of China.~~ *Except for this unfortunate incident, the Chinese runner would almost certainly have won a gold medal. I apologize to the people and government of China for the intemperate statements I subsequently made about the Chinese government.*

Shek smiled over her amendments. "Miss Connor," he said, "you are a clever young woman. I believe I can accept your statement if you will agree to one change."

Beth nodded.

"After the word 'intemperate' I add the words 'and untrue.' Agreed?"

"Agreed," said Beth.

Shek picked up a telephone. A secretary came in. He handed the amended statement to her, to be retyped.

"You must understand, Miss Connor, that the Olympic incident is a great deal more important here in Guangzhou than it is even in Beijing. Xiang Li is a local girl. She is quite popular here."

"She has done well in other games," said Beth. "She may win her gold this year."

"We hope so."

5

AFTER BETH HAD SIGNED the statement, Shek escorted her to a chauffeured car. She wondered where they were going but decided it best not to ask.

Sitting in the back of the comfortable car, no longer handcuffed, she began to wonder if the worst were not over.

Shek Tin was nothing like what she had expected in a Chinese bureaucrat. To use an American expression, he didn't talk the talk or walk the walk.

As she was driven through the streets of Guangzhou, she saw not a single Mao suit or cap. The badly dressed were badly dressed by anyone's standards. The well-dressed wore Western styles. Some women wore filmy-thin ankle-length skirts, many others wore minis. The climate was too hot for business suits, and few men wore them; they were dressed in polo shirts and slacks. Young women clung to young men driving motorcycles. Many young women drove their own motorbikes, their skirts flying.

She saw no portraits of Chairman Mao, nor of Deng Xiaoping for that matter. A few billboards seemed to be political, but only a few; the signs everywhere advertised consumer goods—television sets, VCRs, personal computers, cars . . .

The car pulled into something like a plaza. There, in English, the sign said "Friendship Store."

"We dress you correctly," said Shek with a playful smile. "After all, I can't send Miss Beth Connor to Hong Kong looking like something we fished out of the water."

The store was like the very best of American department stores, only better—with marble and parquet floors, muted music, subdued lighting. The merchandise on display was like what an American would find in Saks. The only thing markedly different was that all the clerks wore photo-identification badges.

Shek led Beth up escalators to a floor where women's clothing was displayed: the latest styles in rich fabrics, on stiff, slender plaster mannequins. He identified himself to a clerk, who immediately became elaborately obsequious.

The clerk took Beth into a dressing room, not a tiny dressing room as in an American store but a room bigger than the cell she had occupied only this morning, deeply carpeted and furnished with an armchair and a love seat upholstered in pink silk.

"The Governor say, bottom to top," trilled the clerk with a tiny, embarrassed giggle. "You let . . . sizing?"

Beth did not know what the girl meant, but she nodded. The clerk produced a tape measure from a pocket in her skirt and proceeded to measure Beth's bust, waist, and hips. She disappeared then, out of the dressing room. After a minute or two she returned, carrying a black lace brassiere and a pair of sheer black bikini panties.

"You try?"

Somewhat reluctantly, Beth took off the blouse and skirt she had been given at the police station, then her bra and panties. She pulled on the black panties first. One size fits all, just about, and they stretched snugly around her hips. The bra was not so good a fit, but it was good enough. It lifted her breasts and thrust them forward, which was what it was for.

The clerk opened the door and Shek came in. "It would not have been proper for me to be in the room when you were . . . naked," he said. "But now . . ."

Beth didn't think now was much better, but she thought it impolitic to object.

The clerk left again and returned with a black lace garter belt and a pair of dark sheer stockings.

"This is as you dress at home, correct?" Shek asked.

"Something like this." Beth agreed, though in fact she had never dressed quite like this in her life. Another clerk knocked, opened the door, and came in with several boxes of shoes. A pair of black Prada heels fit. Then the original clerk brought in a spectacularly elegant, garnet-red rayon-and-Lycra catsuit with a black lace camisole top and a twisted belt of black lace across the hips. Beth slipped into it. The suit was form-fitting but not tight. A two-button jacket of the same color and fabric would cover her bare shoulders and arms. Beth looked at the label and recognized the designer's name: Versace.

Togged in these pricey, stylish clothes, Beth could not help but admire herself in the mirror. A hairdresser came, frowned over the state of her hair, but combed and sprayed it, saying something that sounded apologetic to Shek. Finally Beth sat and submitted to the ministrations of a cosmetician, who darkened her eyebrows and lashes and applied a light lip coloring with a brush.

"Ah, so," murmured Shek. "We have a photograph made of you."

And it was done. A photographer posed her in front of a huge spray of yellow roses in the main room of the clothing department.

They did not return to the car. Shek simply led her across the street via a pedestrian walkway to the Garden Hotel—the sign was in English as well as Chinese. There they went to a private dining room, where several men waited—apparently officers of the provincial or municipal government. Again photographs were taken.

Then— "Someone you know, Miss Connor."

The someone she knew was the Chinese runner from the Barcelona Olympiad: Xiang Li. The runner was a husky, athletic girl, robust like Beth, not tiny like the clerks in the Friendship Store. As strobe lights flashed, she embraced Beth, and the two of them faced cameras and video cameras, smiling, for more photographs. Then they sat down side by side at a table.

Xiang Li spoke English. "Was unhappy, that accident," she said softly, out of earshot of the cameramen and others.

"You will win your gold medal this year," Beth said, equally quietly.

"I hope . . ." Xiang Li said in her ear.

"You are world champion," said Beth. "You will win your medal. There was no conspiracy to upset you in 1992, and there will be none this year."

"Thank you," said Xiang Li sincerely. "You not run this year?"

"No," said Beth. "From the time I was a child I was exploited by people who wanted to make something from my athletic ability. I was even exploited by my parents. Running and swimming were my two sports. I wanted to be a swimmer. More glamorous. And I worked hard at it. But the truth was, I was a better runner. In any case, the decision was never mine to make."

"I know," said Xiang Li. "They make you do what you can do."

"Not just in China, though," said Beth. "If I'd wanted to play the piano, I wouldn't have been given the chance. I was a big girl, and

I could run and swim. They chose running for me. I was an *asset* to coaches and trainers. They made their reputations and their living off young bodies like mine. And of course—I had the young body. So, what the hell? I figured I might as well get what I could out of it."

"Yes. Yes," said Xiang Li in a whisper that was almost a hiss.

Beth remembered how she had explained all this to Michael, in almost the same words. She went on. "When . . . what happened . . . happened . . . at Barcelona, I saw how false and hollow the whole thing was. It's nothing but a huge scam, staged for immense profits, and I decided I wanted no more of it." She reached for the Chinese girl's hand under the table. "One bad part of it for me was knowing I could make a choice and get out of it—but probably *you* and many, many others couldn't. Li . . . go out there this summer and *win it!* I won't be there, but I'll be watching on television, and I want you to know I'll be cheering for you. Get your gold. Don't let my cynicism discourage you."

Impulsively, Xiang Li hugged her and kissed her cheek. Strobes flashed. The video cameras ground out tape. Beth understood that Shek had found a way to use her, to generate propaganda that would be seen all around the world. She didn't much care. Xiang Li understood what she had said, just as Michael had and a million athletes the world over could. And maybe nobody else. However much they were using her—and they *were* using her, for damned sure—this was her way back to Hong Kong. To get back there, and to Michael one way or another, counted more than any propaganda ploy. She could kill the propaganda later, for sure. And she would, when the chance came—when she and Michael were together again.

An hour after the luncheon, Shek led her back to the car. "Now the airport," he said. "You will fly to Hong Kong, where you will be met by a representative of your government. We arranged that with the United States Consul General here in Guangzhou."

Shek's driver threaded the car through the formidable Guangzhou traffic. They passed a low building marked with an immense clock. "The railroad station," said Shek.

Then, as they drove under an overpass, Beth spotted men sleeping on the pavement, cars and motorbikes barely missing their feet.

Shek saw her staring. "Migrant laborers," he explained. "They come here from all over China, looking for work in this busy, prosperous city. Of course, many would like to go to Hong Kong. We will not allow that, not even after July 1997 when Hong Kong returns to the motherland. When Comrade Deng Xiaoping visited your country, President Carter was critical of our policy of not letting people like that leave China and go wherever they wish. It was a matter of human rights, he said. So, Deng Xiaoping said to him, 'Maybe you are right, Mr. President. Maybe we should let them emigrate. How many would the United States like to take? Two million? Five million? Ten?' " Shek smiled broadly, obviously genuinely amused. "How many?"

There was a sudden commotion in the middle of the road. A crowd gathered quickly. Traffic ground to a halt.

Shek spoke curtly to his driver in Chinese. The driver got out of the car and squeezed into the crowd.

A Chinese man of about thirty, his hair cropped short, with blood streaming down his forehead, burst out of the crowd and dashed in front of their car. Close on the wounded man's heels were two Chinese uniformed policemen wielding batons.

The bloodied man fell against the side window of the car, hitting his head against the window. The policemen caught up with him and clubbed him on the head, spilling more blood. The policemen dragged the man away, putting handcuffs on his wrists.

Shek tried his best to appear normal. Beth said nothing, but her sympathy was clearly with the beaten man. Whatever he had done, he should not have been beaten that severely. But she wasn't going to jeopardize the chances of her imminent release by any ill-chosen words.

The driver came back, slipped into the driver's seat and reported to Shek in Chinese as he was driving the car through the dispersing crowd.

"The man you just saw, with blood on his face, killed another man in a fight. The dead man's friends would tear him to pieces, so police must beat him to calm the people. I hope you understand human rights, which your country value so much, is a luxury we cannot always afford with so many people in so little space."

"I hope the man who was beaten agrees with your philosophy," Beth said with obvious sarcasm that seemed to escape Shek's notice.

At the airport he took her aboard the Southern China Airlines plane, leading her along the aisle to her seat. Passengers gaped. Some of them had seen the car pull up to the airplane, and they saw the cabin attendants treating the man and woman with elaborate deference.

"So," said Shek. "It has been a pleasure to meet you, Miss Connor. I regret the early discomfort in your visit. We remedied it as soon as we realized who you are."

"Thank you, Mr. Shek," Beth murmured. She knew he had found a way to use her, but she was grateful anyway.

Shek grinned. "Not bad fellows, after all, hmm—the representatives of that 'murderous dictatorship' and 'bloody-handed regime'?"

He bent down to kiss her hand, and she rose and kissed him lightly on the cheek. "Not a bad fellow, Mr. Shek," she said. "You are not a bad fellow at all."

He grinned and blushed. "Yes," he said. "Probably I will never see you again, but I wish it were not so."

"So do I," she said. And she meant it.

Shek Tin left the plane. As Beth sat in her seat staring out at the Guangzhou airport, she returned to reality. Still she had no idea where Michael was, or if he was alive, and if he was alive he had no idea where she was, or if *she* was alive.

FOUR

She is not dead. Maybe we will have to remedy that.

1

DURING THE DAY, MICHAEL heard chickens. Mornings, cocks crowed, then all day he could hear hens busy about the yard, clucking, scratching, occasionally squawking when they were mounted. He could smell salt water, too, though it was not close by. He heard engines straining, pulling cars and trucks up a grade, though this, too, was at a distance.

From all of this he guessed he was in a mountainside house, undoubtedly a thoroughly isolated mountainside house—and very likely across the border in China. He judged that from the amount of time he had spent on the boat after Beth slipped over the side. While he had remained bound, the boat had growled and bucked its way across a lot of water, including open water that heaved.

The rooms in which he was held were spacious and comfortable: a sitting room furnished with a not-too-old leather-covered couch and a plush-covered easy chair, plus a coffee table and a television set; a bedroom furnished with a double bed with two night tables and a dresser; a bathroom equipped with a Western-style toilet, a basin, and a tub and shower.

The windows were blocked with steel mesh, then steel bars, then heavy shutters he could not reach but guessed were nailed tightly shut. The only exit door, the one from the sitting room into a hall outside, was of heavy wood reinforced with iron straps. The suite had been built years ago, he supposed, to hold prisoners the triad wanted to keep secure but probably not harm. It was a triad prison. Of that he had no doubt.

Most of the time he had company. One or two of the kidnappers sat and watched television all day and all evening, sometimes but not usually engaging him in conversation. He had no privacy from them. The door had been taken out of the doorframe between the sitting room and bedroom.

Apart from the simple fact of being locked in and his gnawing worry about Beth, his confinement was not unbearable. They fed him well, and they kept him supplied with beer, wine, and spirits. He had to be confident that his imprisonment was temporary.

He was, as he had assured Beth, an asset. He was worth something to these men. Very likely, if they could not negotiate terms satisfactory to them, they would release him—just as they would release him if they *could* negotiate something. They would be, above all, practical men; and killing him would be of no practical value to them.

Beth . . .

He could only *hope* she was alive. Once she disappeared over the side of the boat he had seen no further sign of her. Neither had the kidnappers, for that matter. He had been torn between hope of seeing her swimming and dread that he would see her, and *they* would see her. Fortunately they had not seen her. On the other hand, that could well mean she had drowned.

He despaired, but he kept hope alive. Beth was smart and strong, and if anyone could survive, she could.

He could not decide whether time was for him or against him. This was his third day in captivity: a terribly protracted amount of time for a simple kidnapping for ransom. Of course, he knew now it was not a simple kidnapping for ransom. He was in the hands of a triad, and the triad either wanted an immense amount of money or something besides money—in either case, something his father was unable or unwilling to concede.

Michael realized that he was living in an unusual period. The handover, the return of Hong Kong from Britain to China, was only a year away. The traditional triads, vastly enriched in Hong Kong, were in an awkward situation. The British had treated them harshly, strictly as members of an outlaw organization. Mere membership subjected one to imprisonment. But at least with the Brits the triads knew where they stood and they had learned to cope, if not thrive, with the British colonial system.

But with the Chinese Communists taking power in Hong Kong next July, the triads faced uncertainty. The patriach Deng Xiaoping did say that some triads could be "patriots" (it was historical fact that triads began as secret societies aimed at overthrowing the Manchurians who had invaded and ruled China since the sixteenth century). Representatives of the Beijing government had met with triad leaders, much to the chagrin of the British establishment, to discuss ways to ensure a peaceful handover. The triads knew that the Communist rulers in Beijing ultimately would stamp them out, not so much for their illegal acts as for their organizational abilities. For the autocratic Chinese government ultimately would not tolerate any other locus of power, any shadowy governing structure, especially one so well financed with wealth rivaling Fortune 500 companies and small nations, and one as secretive and well organized as the CIA and Chinese secret police. It was ironic, Michael mused, that the triads would most need the rule of law and the recognition of human rights after the handover because they were more likely than ordinary citizens to suffer at the hands of the rulers from Beijing.

Some triads in the mid-level hierarchy had opted to move out of Hong Kong. But like other emigrants, they wanted to make a quick financial killing and leave with plenty of cash. Michael wondered if he was in the hands of one of these emigrant triads, desperadoes who were asking such a huge amount of money that his father balked. After all, he was a second son and ultimately expendable.

His guard was watching, for God's sake, *The Flintstones* on Hong Kong television and was much amused by it.

Another man came in who was not amused. Dai Gul Dai, Big Prick—the knife wielder and leader of the kidnappers. Without a word of apology to the man who was watching *The Flintstones*, he switched to a Chinese channel that was broadcasting the news, then dropped heavily on the couch beside Michael. He was a big, coarse man with a nervous tic—his lip and jaw twitched just beneath his knife scar, as if some nerve had been damaged.

The news program covered a number of stories—the Japanese claim to a group of tiny islands just north of Taiwan, which were also claimed by China and Taiwan; the approaching ninety-fourth birthday of Deng Xiaoping; labor on flood-control projects being performed by soldiers of the People's Liberation Army; and final preparation by Chinese athletes for competing in the Atlanta Olympics. That story segued into a story from Guangzhou, where the American runner Beth Connor was shown meeting with the Chinese runner Xiang Li. Miss Connor, the story explained, had nearly drowned after falling overboard from a boat in Hong Kong Harbour but was rescued by Chinese fishermen and taken to their village in the Pearl River estuary. And so on. The final picture showed the American runner being put aboard an airplane for a flight to Hong Kong.

"Thank God!" Michael muttered.

"So, Mikego Chang," said Big Prick. "It appears that your fat whore of the big tits somehow survived her dive into the harbor. You lied to me! You said her arms remained bound."

"I knew she was trying to break loose."

"So. It seems she did. She is not dead. Maybe we will have to remedy that."

Big Prick heaved himself up from the couch and stormed out of the room, leaving Michael almost weak with joy at having seen Beth alive on television. Of course Michael trembled at hearing Big Prick say, "Maybe we will have to remedy that."

Before Michael could think much about the threat, Big Prick came back. "You have a visitor, Mikego Chang," he said in a surly voice.

Michael looked up and shrugged. "What visitor?"

"You know him," said Big Prick. He sharply ordered the guard to switch off the television set and leave the room. "Your family solicitor, Qiao Qichen."

Qiao was a man of minatory presence. Even the formidable Dai Gul Dai blenched under his withering glance and retreated from the room. He was not a big man, just balding and late-middle-aged—but supremely self-confident. He wore a dark-blue suit with faint pinstripes, a white shirt, and a dark-blue polka-dotted bow tie. He looked something like a Chinese Winston Churchill.

Michael stood up, smiling. "Hello, Tom," he said. Tom was the nickname the two younger Chang brothers had bestowed on Qiao Qichen after he sat with them and watched a tape of *The Godfather*. Tom Hagen was the Corleone family's *consigliere*, counselor, and Qiao held an analogous position with the Chang family. He was not just their solicitor; he was their trusted adviser and confidant. "You've come to pay the ransom, I suppose. I can get out of here now, hmm?"

"I am afraid not, Michael. Things are quite complicated," Qiao said somberly.

The petite Chinese girl who served the food here came in with a bottle of Black Label, glasses, water, and ice. She was a pretty little thing, dressed in a white T-shirt and a black vinyl miniskirt. The T-shirt was printed with a picture of Calvin and Hobbes.

"Then you have things to explain," Michael said, disappointed and angry. "At least I know that Beth is alive and well. I just saw her on television. Of course, you don't know that I am engaged to be married to Beth Connor."

"We do know," said Qiao. "The whole family knows. She told Shek Tin, the deputy governor of Guangdong Province, that she was engaged to be married to you. Naturally, he contacted the family. I spoke with him. I knew nothing of any such engagement, but I checked with John, who was able to confirm that you were bringing an American girl to Hong Kong."

"Yes. John was to have met us at the airport. But, how did she get to Guangzhou? And why did she talk to a deputy governor?"

Qiao shrugged. "I don't know, Michael."

"Does my father understand that I plan to marry her? Does Frederick understand that? For that matter, do *you?*"

"Plan . . ." Qiao murmured gravely. "Your plans will have to be changed."

"Why? I have no intention of changing them."

"There is much that you don't know."

"I suppose you've come here to tell me what I don't know. If you did not come to pay the ransom and arrange my release, then just how *do* you come to be here?"

Qiao picked up his glass and took a swallow of Scotch. "Listen to me, Michael. Listen to it all. Don't make any judgment before you hear all that I have to tell you."

"This is going to be quite a story," Michael said skeptically. He, too, took a swallow of Scotch.

Qiao lifted his chin high, drew breath, and seemed reluctant to begin. He sighed. "In the first place, Michael, you must understand you have been kidnapped by a Taiwanese triad called Chung Yui Hui. It is one of the most powerful and most vicious of all triads."

"Taiwanese . . ." Michael muttered scornfully.

"Need I remind you," Qiao asked, "that members of a Taiwanese triad went to California and murdered an American citizen a few years ago, because that American had published articles critical of the Taiwanese dictatorship? Even Chairman Mao never dared do a thing like that. They are utterly ruthless."

"So—"

"You have been away too long. Maybe you don't know that more and more the Taiwanese government and economy is controlled by black gangs. They have gone far beyond gambling, prostitution, loan-sharking, extortion, and the like. They muscle their way into major enterprises, including big building projects. What is more, they solve small problems by killing the source of the small problem."

"Am I a small problem?" Michael asked bitterly, tossing back a swallow of his whisky.

"You are not a small problem. There is something more you do not know. Your elder brother Frederick is dying. You are the heir now. You will be the head of the family. The Chung Yui Hui triad holds prisoner the next head of the Chang family."

"Frederick . . . is . . . dying? Dying how? Of what?"

"Of AIDS," said Qiao softly.

Michael's jaw dropped. His cheeks reddened. "AIDS—Frederick? How?"

"Do I have to tell you how? You know his lifelong penchant for—"

"—squalid cathouses. Cheap whores," Michael grumbled. "A man married to Anne." He shook his head. "What did he want? My God, did he infect her?"

"No. She has been carefully examined. What is more, your father won't allow him in her bedroom."

"When? When will he die?" Michael asked.

"Soon. The doctors have sent him home to die. Anne refuses to believe it. She is frantic. She's hired a qi gong master. You know, a faith healer, so to speak: a charismatic fraud. It's like having Rasputin in the house. Whatever he tells her to do, she does—all the qi gong hocus-pocus: squatting, doing breathing exercises, and meditating. He has made her half believe that AIDS is not a real disease but a state of mind that can be overcome by exerting a benign influence, mind to mind."

Michael had long carried a mental image of his dramatically beautiful sister-in-law as the Dragon Lady of the comic strip "Terry and the Pirates." She was tall and statuesque. She usually wore her glossy black hair in bangs and her silk dresses sleek and tight. She was a thoroughly Westernized woman, who had been educated at McGill University in Canada and had returned exuberant with what American women called "lib." Though Frederick's wife had to be of a good, traditional Chinese family—her name was Liu Soong Qin—she had sometimes scandalized the Chang family with her miniskirts, her makeup and hairstyles, and her western expressions. It was difficult to imagine her distraught and already mourning her husband, the father of her two children. It was more difficult to imagine her mindlessly adhering to a cult. Michael found it all but impossible to imagine she could have been ensnared in *qi gong*.

Michael shook his head. "Tell me what else I don't know," he said dully.

"Something more that you *do* know, first. You know what an immense project Western Reclamation is. Fifty or more tall buildings on the landfill. Apartments, offices, shops: a mini-town with all the goods and services of a small city. It is estimated that the project will be worth more than ten billion U.S. dollars, eighty billion Hong Kong dollars. Under the exclusive auspices of Wing Lung Properties."

"The largest project the family has ever undertaken," said Michael.

"The largest project the family has ever undertaken to date—and all but certain to generate an enormous profit. But a problem has arisen. For many years, the family did much important business with the Nationalists in Taiwan. The Kuomintang had money, after all, much of it from the Americans, who simplemindedly—"

"Yes, yes. Our family has had a longtime alliance with Taiwan—that is, with Taiwanese *money*. Much of the money that went into our last bank tower was Taiwanese. And I do know that from time to time a Taiwanese triad was involved."

Qiao reached for his glass and drank some whisky. "Since 1984 we have known that on July first, 1997, Hong Kong will be Chinese, no longer a British crown colony. The mainland Chinese are very practical. They are willing to accept investment capital, no matter where it comes from—almost. But there is a limit. They want no joint enterprises with the Nationalist Chinese in Taiwan."

"I know," said Michael.

"Beginning next year," Qiao continued, "our businesses will be subject to new law and policy. Knowing that, your father has gradually shifted allegiance from Taiwan to China. We have no choice, don't you see? And the People's Liberation Army is a major investor in Western Reclamation."

"But—"

"Do you remember the name Fu Wei Jien? He was also called Four Finger because his little fingers on each hand were cut off in a fight early in his career?" Qiao interrupted. "Whether you do or not, Four Finger was a close business friend of your father for many years. He accepted, regretfully and resentfully, the idea of your father shifting to the mainland Chinese as his source for new partners and investors. Even so, he had a special interest in the Western Reclamation project and demands a piece of it, which we cannot let him have because—"

"Because the PLA says no," Michael guessed.

Qiao nodded. "The People's Liberation Army says no. With them it's a matter of ideology and face. They will not be associated with a Taiwanese entrepreneur, especially not with Four Finger, who was a close political ally of the heirs of Chiang Kai-shek.

"The triad, Qiao. What has all this to do with the triad?"

"The Chung Yui Hui triad is Four Finger's partner in all his enterprises. It forced itself on him, as he tells it. And they are forcing your father to agree to let them in on Western Reclamation by holding you captive. Four Finger says he is sorry about your kidnapping but has no influence over that aspect of his business."

"Which leaves me in the goddamned middle," Michael said bitterly. "What are they going to do, start cutting pieces off me and sending them to my father?"

"There is always a way, Michael," said Qiao Qichen. "Always there is a way, if one uses brains and patience."

"You're telling me to be *patient*?"

"Listen," Qiao said curtly. "Do not underestimate your father. Or me. We are working on an arrangement that will allow Four Finger and his Taiwanese triad to invest in Western Reclamation and share in its profits—while keeping its participation a secret from the People's Liberation Army."

Michael managed a wry smile. "The Bahamian connection," he said.

"Precisely. The Taiwanese money will be funneled in through the Bahamian corporation. The PLA will be told the Bahamian corporation is a tax shelter—"

"Which it is," said Michael.

"Ah. But we will say it is a tax shelter for some Germans who want to invest in Western Reclamation. This is how we will do it. But making such arrangements takes time. You were kidnapped Sunday. This is only Tuesday."

"The family must take care of Beth," Michael said urgently. "We *must*. The first thing is to let her know that I am alive. Then we must protect her against Dai Gul Dai. He threatened her a little while ago. It may well be that he wants to kill her. She would recognize him if she saw him again. She'd call in the police."

"*She must not do that,*" said Qiao. "Police interference could cost you—"

"Then take her inside the mansion and guard her."

"First we will have to find her," said Qiao.

Michael sighed. "Where am I, Qiao?"

"In China."

"Where in China?"

"I don't know. I was brought here in the back of a van and could not see out."

"Alright. Tell my father I will do my best to be patient."

"Your father asked me to emphasize the importance of your being so. John asked me to give you his love and sympathy. He has volunteered to search out Miss Connor."

"No! Not John. I don't trust him. I *can't* trust him."

Qiao nodded gravely. He tossed back the last of his Scotch. "So," he said quietly. "You are a shrewd fellow." He shrugged and smiled ironically. "So. What should I expect of the son of Chang Wing Hing, the grandson of Chang Joi Hing?"

"John was supposed to meet our plane on Sunday. He didn't. And Beth and I were attacked by kidnappers on Peak Road."

"Surely you don't think John *knew* the kidnappers would be lying in wait?"

"I don't want to think that. I don't want to think that ill of my younger brother. But I have to face facts. If Frederick is ill and dying, then only *I* stand between John and the inheritance."

"That is true," said Qiao somberly. "I knew you would be aware of it. Your father cannot bring himself to think of it."

"In America," said Michael, "an inheritance is often *shared* among the sons and daughters."

"Yes. And fortunes are fractionated. Our way is better. Only one can be the heir and head of the family. Control is in his hands alone. He will be kind to his brothers and sisters—so far as he sees fit—but the fortune will remain one: intact, inviolable."

"I never expected much kindness from Frederick," said Michael. "I will treat my siblings more generously than he would have. He thinks of John and me as inferior pups, because we are of our father's second marriage—to the giddy girl who had been his concubine. He imagines that John and I are illegitimate. But we're not. John and I were conceived only after Frederick's mother died and my father married our mother. We are just as legitimate as he is."

"He holds you in higher regard than you think," said Qiao. "Higher than you hold John, apparently."

"What am I to think? Why wasn't he at the airport? Why wasn't he in our car when the kidnappers got us?"

Qiao stood. "I promise you I will do what I can to find your girl and surround her with protection. But you must understand—your father and I trust you *do* understand—that marriage between you and Miss Connor is impossible. You *cannot* marry her."

"I am *going* to marry her."

Qiao shook his head. "You can *have* her, but you can't marry her.

We will set her up in a comfortable home, where you can see her as often as you wish. Your wife—a Chinese girl of respectable family—will know about her, of course, but—"

"Will know I have a concubine."

"I was going to say 'mistress.' We'll give her money. We—"

"Tom—I *love* Beth Connor!"

"Nobody doubts it. But you can't marry her."

"I *will* marry her."

"This is not the time or place to talk about it. Once you are free and come home and talk with your father, everything will be settled. Even Miss Connor, American though she is, will see the wisdom of our way and will be happy with the arrangement we will make."

2

AFTER QIAO QICHEN LEFT, Dai Gul Dai looked in and grinned. One of the other triad guards came in and switched on the television again—Charlton Heston as El Cid. Michael remembered how he and Beth had sat together in his apartment only a few months ago and watched this endlessly rerun movie. He had never been a big fan of Charlton Heston, and he was in no mood to see him doing derring-do. But he doubted he had any influence as to whether or not the television remained on.

The girl arrived with food, this time a Western meal of rare roast beef with potatoes, also a bottle of red wine. The guard glanced at the meal with a sneer that suggested only *kwai-loh* ate such nauseating victuals. Or maybe his sneer was out of envy. Michael didn't care. He ate.

Heston moved across the screen, alternately pontificating and clattering. The movie had subtitles in Chinese characters, which the guard obviously was reading.

So . . . Frederick. Frederick dying? That commanding man, that vital man, dying? In a small sense it was as if Qiao had brought news of the fatal illness of God. Michael had been aware of his father's mortality. He was, after all, an aging man. But Frederick—

Michael wanted to speak with Frederick before he died. More than that, he wanted to see Beth, to reassure her and once more to declare his love. He was sitting here wasting his time while others schemed and plotted and decided things about his life without consulting him.

Worse than that, the brutal Dai Gul Dai had threatened Beth's life.

Michael remembered the slight hesitation in Beth's demeanor when he first told her they were going to Hong Kong to break the news of their pending marriage to his father.

"Michael, I'm afraid. What if . . ."

"Beth, do not be afraid. We'll be together for the rest of our lives. No matter what. No matter what it might cost me—" At which point Beth prevented him from saying anything more with a long, passionate kiss.

Enough! He sat here and ate beef and drank wine, while everything about his life was being decided by others. Maybe all of them had derogated a factor they did not appreciate: *him*.

Half the wine remained in the bottle. He shoved the cork into the neck. He stood and with a quick, efficient movement, brought the bottle down hard on the skull of the television-besotted guard.

The man slumped forward, blood gushing from his head and wetting his shirt and the chair.

Michael slipped out of the room, checked the hallway, and found a way out of the house. He stood outside, in bright moonlight.

3

LOOKING AROUND, HE DISCOVERED that the house was part of a small villa, isolated as he had suspected on a high mountainside with a view of water that could have been anything from the mouth of the Pearl River to Mirs Bay. A narrow, rutted road wound down the mountainside.

Michael decided not to trot along that road but to work his way directly down the steep slope below the villa. He began, slipping in loose soil, colliding with rocks, tearing the thin soles of his Italian shoes.

It was impossible to be quiet. When he was fifty meters or so away from the villa, he stopped, crouched, and listened. Everything above was silent. Beth had slipped over into the water and swam to safety. Maybe he could move on down a kilometer or so before they noticed he was missing. By then he—

He heard shrieking. They had found the guard he had slugged with the bottle. Suddenly the soil and rocks and scrub vegetation were awash with light. Men ran out of the villa. A huge dog came bounding down. Michael grabbed a big rock, and when the dog lunged at him, fangs bared, he struck it on the muzzle with all his strength.

The dog yelped and fell away, rolling and rubbing its muzzle on the ground. Michael ran, stumbling through the bushes, scratching himself on opposing limbs, bruising his feet on rocks, terrified by the noisy onrush of pursuers coming from above. His Gucci loafers were wholly unsuited to running down a rocky mountainside, and shortly the heel tore off his right shoe. Then the sole came loose. He could not run without a shoe, for sure; he had to keep the shoe on even if it slowed him down.

Yelling men kept crashing down from above. The beams of their electric torches passed over him. So far they missed him, but a beam would hit him sooner or later. There was no place to hide. His breath came hard, burning in his lungs. The dog had come back to life, too. He could hear it. He remembered its fangs. He stumbled on down the slope, moving as fast as he could.

Then a beam of light stopped on him. Men yelled. And then they caught up with him: three of them with drawn knives.

4

THEY TOOK HIM INTO an outbuilding with a concrete floor, stripped him naked, and forced him down into a galvanized steel laundry tub that was bolted to a wall. Two pairs of handcuffs fastened his hands to two of the legs of the tub. His ankles were locked together with leg irons, and a rope ran through their chain and was tied to another leg of the tub. He could not move.

This greatly amused Dai Gul Dai, who stood by, staring at him. "You have the cock of a goat, Mikego Chang," he said in Chinese. "And hanging balls. So hanging! You're not ruptured? I hope you are comfortable."

Michael knew what they were going to do. He had heard of it. They were going to inflict great pain, without leaving a mark on him.

Two men came in dragging big bags of heavy waxed paper. They were filled with ice: small clear cubes frozen from distilled water, bought from some warehouse that supplied ice to restaurants. Dai Gul Dai whipped out the blade of his ugly knife and slit the bags. Laughing, the men poured the ice into the tub, covering Michael to the bottom of his ribs.

He shuddered. His body shook from the chill. But he knew this discomfort was nothing compared to the pain that would follow.

Dai Gul Dai pushed the ice down, compacting it so the tub could hold more, and he curtly ordered more poured in.

"Well. Your woman was a skillful artist of escape. I think even *she* would find it impossible to slip the steel that holds you now. And so. We will leave you to a pleasant night. Before morning you will melt your ice. Before morning you will piss in your water, which will warm it. Tomorrow you will be a more subdued *guest*, don't you agree?"

Michael hung his head. The ache had begun, and it would worsen and worsen until he would suffer agony.

Dai Gul Dai ordered the others to leave. He himself stayed,

standing with his hands on his hips, smirking. "Tell me, Mikego," he said. "Why are you so anxious to leave us? Have we not treated you well?"

"You threatened to kill my bride. Am I expected to love you?"

Dai Gul Dai sneered. "If all works out as we wish it, nothing of that kind may be necessary."

"Your time is coming to an end," said Michael. "Hong Kong now, Taiwan next, falling under the control of the People's Republic of China. What will happen to you? What will happen to the triads?"

"Emperors came and went," said Dai Gul Dai. "The republic, Sun Yat-sen . . . the Japanese came and went. Chiang Kai-shek and Mao Tse-tung are dead. The triads remain. And we will remain. You know why? Because we represent the best of the Chinese culture. Worship of money and power for one and efficiency and secrecy for another. We shall live forever."

Dai Gul Dai went out, turned off the lights, and left Michael alone.

He shifted a little but could not lift himself two inches off the floor of the tub, and could not begin to escape the ice.

The ache was of course in his testicles and scrotum, less in his penis but very real there, too. Even his navel rebelled against being immersed in ice and caused a special nausea. His parts throbbed. They would throb and ache all night, until all this ice melted and the water warmed from his circulation.

The pain hardened. It was like concrete inside his scrotum, which seemed to have swollen, though he knew it had in fact contracted. No, not like concrete. Like a pair of hands that squeezed his testicles. It was like being kicked in the balls, except that a kick was one impact, one shock, and this shock endured and tortured him.

He tipped his head back. Oddly, his face was wet with sweat. He felt it running into his eyes. He tasted it on his lips.

Michael groaned.

This night was going to be an unrelieved horror. But he knew he would survive. That was why they had chosen to torture him *this* way: because they knew it would not kill him.

That he would survive what lay ahead was not so certain.

But he *had* to survive. Beth had survived. And what more had she done? In these few days she had somehow escaped drowning, then reached China, then won the grudging respect of a government official. She was a marvel! His family must realize that. His father must understand that he had not fallen in love with an ordinary woman, one who might have been content to live as the pampered mistress of a wealthy man. His father, who had lived his life according to old traditions, would find this marriage very difficult to accept—but he would have go accept it.

He was going to have to accept more than that very shortly. Many traditions and archaic ways of thinking would be swept away when Hong Kong reverted to China.

Paroxysms of the pain caused convulsions. And the ice had not even begun to melt.

5

HE WAS NOT SURE he was conscious when the girl came in. Maybe the body had a way of having mercy on itself. More time had passed than he had been aware of. He knew because the ice was slush now; the cubes jostled around in a little water.

The pain was worse. Ice-cold water penetrated where ice itself did not, and he felt a new ache in his anus.

The girl. The cute little girl who brought his food was there. She stood beside the laundry tub, looking at him thoughtfully. His eyes had adjusted to the dim remnant of the night's moonlight, and he could see her clearly, even the expression on her face: curious, yet a little lofty, as if she scorned a man in such adversity and wondered how he had managed to get himself into it.

"Help me," he pleaded weakly, speaking Chinese.

The girl shrugged.

"Look on my wrist, my left wrist," he muttered. "See the watch?" He was talking about the gold Rolex, worth no small money in the States where he'd bought it and worth a fortune in China.

She lifted his hand and examined the watch. "*Ayeeyah!*" she exclaimed.

"It's yours if you help me," he said.

"It's mine if I choose to take it," she said with a little shrug.

"And what if I tell Dai Gul Dai you took it? Help me, and you can have it, and I won't tell."

The girl pulled the watch off his wrist and put it on hers.

She set to work then, shoving a big wooden tub across the floor, bringing it close to the laundry tub. Then with a bucket she began to dip the ice from around him.

She used the bucket and her hands, and in ten minutes he sat shivering with only a little ice around his buttocks, around his drooping scrotum.

That latter ice she pushed away.

She put her hands on his penis and scrotum, clutching them gently, trying to impart the warmth of her hands to his aching organs. Michael gasped.

"*Xie xie,*" he murmured. Thank you.

The girl tried massaging him, but that hurt, and he grunted. She cupped her hands over her mouth and breathed on them, to give them more warmth, then clasped his scrotum again, almost too tightly. It warmed him a little but not enough to relieve the pain. He moaned.

"*Xie xie . . .*" he whispered.

For some fifteen minutes she held his penis, and alternately as much of his scrotum as she could. The pain gradually subsided.

Finally she massaged him gently, which restored his circulation. When he sensed his penis stiffening in her hands, he blushed.

She conscientiously ran her fingertips all over his lower body, feeling for cold. She decided, apparently, she had warmed him enough to earn the Rolex.

She left him and busied herself getting rid of the ice. She dumped it somewhere outside, where it would melt quickly in the subtropical heat. She drew water from a tap, carried it near, and poured buckets of water into the laundry tub until he sat up to his ribs in cold water but not ice. The girl moved the wooden tub and the bucket back to their places, stared at him for a long, silent moment, then slipped out.

Alone and too miserable to sleep, Michael wondered if they wouldn't kill him now. Dai Gul Dai may have left him to suffer all night only to satisfy his sadism, then to kill him in the morning after he had suffered. Dai Gul Dai was without a shred of humanity; he was a cold and vicious killer. The Taiwanese triad was a band of killers.

He wondered if he could trust Qiao Qichen. Could his father *actually* have consented to his kidnapping? Couldn't he even trust *him?* Then there was John. . . .

6

DAI GUL DAI WALKED down the worn stone steps toward the quay, being careful not to lose his footing on the slime a higher tide had left on the steps. He glanced around. Victoria Harbour was busy as always. Star Ferries crossed the water, carrying thousands between Hong Kong and Kowloon. The jet foils rushed out of slips, taking gamblers to Macau. If the *kwai-pau*—it was the female equivalent of *kwai-loh*, meaning foreign devil, the epithet the Cantonese had affixed to the hated Westerners two hundred years ago—had slipped overboard ten minutes later, she would have been outside this harbor traffic and would almost surely have drowned before she was picked from the water.

He regretted now what he had regretted that night: that she

had escaped before he'd had a chance to lie on the deck with her. He'd had in mind he would make her *hum gul*, that is, blow his flute. After that—maybe after the others had enjoyed *dew*—that is, had fucked her—he would have put her overboard in open waters and let her drown.

He had not meant to capture her Sunday morning on Peak Road, but she had made such a fuss that he'd had her bound and shoved into the back of the car, rather than hear more from her. If he'd had any idea she was a famous young woman whose disappearance would be noticed, he would have handled her differently.

Too late now.

Women. . . . All right. The one he was looking for was on the quay, smoking a cigarette and waiting. Ah. To *dew* with this one would have been supreme, much better than anything the *kwai-pau* could offer. She had long, shapely legs and wore her skirts short. Tonight, though the air was warm and damp, she wore a raincoat, also a wide-brimmed hat. She paced the quay with conspicuous impatience, as if she supposed he might not come. She should have known better than that. He was Dai Gul Dai, wasn't he?

"A pleasant night," he said.

"What is a pleasant night?" she asked. Her face was shadowed by the hat, but it was, he knew, a strong face: beautiful, yet cruel. "You are late."

"I had to come a long distance."

She raised her chin, and her face emerged from shadow. He had never seen a woman as desirable. Beside her, the American was nothing. "I have been away from the house too long. Let us understand each other quickly."

"Quickly," he repeated.

"I offered you a great deal of money to—"

"I cannot do it so long as my leader has any use for him."

"And when he doesn't?" she asked.

"Easy . . . then."

"Your leader has no use at all for the *woman*."

"You want her—?" He was surprised.

"Don't you? She is a witness against you. And being a *kwai-pau*, she will betray you to the police. You told me she saw you. Who sees your face doesn't forget it, Dai Gul Dai."

"She who sees what gives me that nickname doesn't forget, either," he said.

"Let us confine our talk to business. For her, let's say, five hundred thousand. After all, silencing her is as much in your interest as it is in mine."

"Five hundred—"

"Here it is. In advance."

She shoved toward him a fat manila envelope. He glanced inside. A thick wad of notes was in there: yellow thousand-dollar Hong Kong bills. "It is well," he said.

"Immediately," she said.

"Immediately. Well . . . as soon as I can find her."

"And don't forget, there will be many times that amount when you accomplish the other task I have set for you."

7

THE SUN WAS SHINING outside when Dai Gul Dai returned to the laundry room. He carried a towel. He grinned at Michael and pulled up a wooden bench and sat down.

"So," he said. "I trust you have spent a pleasant night."

Michael nodded.

"Yes. Most pleasant. But, Mikego, really, you should not give away an expensive watch. If you wanted to do some good with it, you should have given it to me."

He unrolled the towel. Unrolling it exposed a severed hand, cut off above the wrist. The Rolex was on the wrist. Dai Gul Dai pulled it off and slipped it on his own wrist.

Michael vomited.

FIVE

*I can offer you one million American dollars
if you will go back to Boston immediately.*

1

BETH ROSE AT EIGHT and took a shower. A crisp young man from the United States consulate had met her at Kai Tak Airport and brought her to this modest hotel. He had promised he would return at nine-thirty this morning.

At the airport she had barely given him a chance to introduce himself before she asked him for word of Michael.

"What sort of word are you looking for?" he had asked.

"That he's been released by kidnappers. Or—or maybe something bad. Is there any word? What do the newspapers say?"

"There's no public word that anyone has *been* kidnapped," he had said. "Why do you ask?"

"Michael Chang is my fiancé."

"I see," he had said quietly, with evident skepticism.

Besides a very modest hotel room, the United States government had provided her dinner: two Big Macs with fries and a Coke the young man picked up on the way.

The room was small and spartan, but it had a television set that received just four channels, two in Chinese. Last evening, while she was eating, a movie had been broadcast on one of the English-language channels—Charlton Heston in *El Cid*. It had brought tears to her eyes. She and Michael had watched it in their apartment in Cambridge only a few weeks ago.

After her shower this morning she watched the Chinese news. For her it was a curious experience. Although the talk was impossible for her to understand, she gathered from the maps and pictures that the lead story had to do with some islands north of Taiwan and conflicting claims to them by Japan and China and Taiwan. Then— My God, there *she* was! The scene was the luncheon in Guangzhou. She saw herself smiling and talking with Xiang Li, then talking with Shek Tin, and finally boarding the plane for Hong Kong. Shek had made a propaganda show of her, just as she had expected.

The young man from the consulate was named William Hodding, and he returned exactly on time, nine-thirty, bringing her breakfast: an Egg McMuffin and coffee. He handed her a temporary passport and an envelope containing five hundred U.S. dollars, for which he asked her to sign a receipt. It was money from a contingency fund the consulate kept to help stranded Americans, and she would be expected to repay the loan as soon as she could.

"I saw you on television last night," he said briskly. "Also this morning. I had been told you were a celebrity, but I didn't quite make the connection. Do you have any complaint of your treatment in China?"

Beth shrugged. "It was pretty rough at first. I spent a day and a night in a jail cell. Once they figured out who I was, they became quite civilized. They treat their citizens, particularly murder suspects, much harsher than we treat ours. But hell, it's their country."

"We wish you had not made the statement you made," said Hodding.

"Mr. Hodding, I would have confessed I was carrying an atomic weapon in my bra if it would have helped me get back to Hong Kong."

"I see. Well, there is a flight to the States leaving at one-thirty. You can be on it. It will arrive in New York, and with the cash I've given you on loan, you can easily catch the shuttle to Boston."

"I don't want to go back to Boston," she said. "I came here to marry Michael Chang. I have to find out what's happened to him."

"Are you referring to the son of Chang Wing Hing?"

"Yes. My fiancé."

Hodding shook his head incredulously. "You came to Hong Kong to marry the son of one of the wealthiest men in Southeast Asia?"

"I don't know he's *that* wealthy."

"He is, Miss Connor. Believe me. He is. The Chang family lives in a compound, something like the Kennedy compound on Cape Cod, maybe more like the Corleone compound shown in *The God-father*. Chang Wing Hing is a billionaire. The Chang family owns Wing Lung Properties—one of the biggest land-development companies in Hong Kong."

"Well, that's probably why Michael has been kidnapped. And if there's no word of it, that's why I have to go to the police."

"Miss Connor, the *family* will go to the police if they want to."

"Mr. Hodding, *I* am going to the police. Will you take me, or do I have to find a police station by myself?"

Hodding sucked in a deep, impatient, disapproving breath. "Very well. Much good may it do you, Miss Connor. But the police you will see."

Even at this late date in the history of the British crown colony, it was an Englishman who received Beth and heard her story—in the presence of a young Chinese detective sitting respectfully to one side, with a steno pad balanced on his knee. The Englishman did not see fit to introduce him.

Chief Superintendent Lionel Bannister had a flushed red face and a bristly military mustache, and he listened to her with unconcealed skepticism.

"Well," he said, "we should think, should we not, that the kidnapping of a member of so prominent a family as the Changs would have generated a report? In point of fact, Miss Connor, we've heard nothing of such an incident."

"It happened on Peak Road," she said. "One of the Chang bodyguards pulled a gun and was immediately struck by a thrown knife. The man came to him and recovered his knife, then used it to slit the bodyguard's eyelids. Is there no hospital report of a man with a knife wound and slit eyelids?"

"No, none," said Chief Superintendent Bannister dismissively. "That, too, one should expect to be reported, shouldn't one?"

"*I'm* reporting it. I'm reporting it now," Beth asserted impatiently. "Michael told me his family would not report it."

"At what time did this happen?" asked the Chinese detective.

"Sunday morning. The flight arrived at six forty-five or about that, and we were met by two Chang bodyguards. We were stopped on the Peak Road by a Bentley and a van that blocked the road."

"You are reporting something of which we have no other evidence," said Bannister in a cool Oxonian accent. "I am sorry, Miss Connor, but there is really nothing to do, don't you see? For you to suggest so serious a crime as kidnapping, involving so prominent a family as the Changs, when we have no other report of it, simply muddies waters. Your own notoriety is no advantage. I suggest you return home. If anything develops, we will inform Mr. Hodding, who will inform you."

"Well, *thank you very much*, Chief Superintendent," Beth said with emphatic scorn. "I had better cooperation from Chinese police authorities in Guangzhou. Maybe you'll be going home next year when the Chinese take over here, and maybe things will be done more effectively. Unfortunately the kidnapping of Michael Chang—which *did* happen whether you like it or not—can't be ignored until next year." She turned a hard glare on Hodding. "I find myself at the mercy of bureaucratic assholes."

"Good *morning*, Miss Connor," Bannister said dismissively.

The Chinese policeman who had been there to take notes—and in fact had taken none—approached her in the hall outside.

"Miss Connor, I am Senior Inspector Huang Han Gai. English-speaking people usually call me Mark Huang. The Chief Superintendent summoned me to listen to what you have to say. I react rather differently to your report. I am willing—it will have to be only quasi-officially—to look further into what you are telling."

"Miss Connor will be going back to the States this afternoon," said Hodding rigidly.

Beth glared at Hodding. "I am *not* going back to the States until I find out what's happened to Michael," she said, putting as much hard emphasis on her words as Hodding had placed on his.

"It might be a shame to leave before you at least talk to Mr. Chang," said Senior Inspector Huang.

"She will miss her flight if she does anything but go to the airport," said Hodding.

"Nevertheless, I am willing to take her to see the Changs."

"She becomes your responsibility if you do this," said Hodding.

"Not precisely," said Huang. "But that's a point we won't argue."

"Well, then . . . As you wish, Miss Connor."

Hodding turned and strode away, leaving Beth with the Chinese detective.

Senior Inspector Mark Huang was stouter than most Chinese men she had seen, some of whom, especially the shrimp fishermen, were skeletally thin. She had discovered that she had difficulty estimating the age of Chinese, especially the men, and if she guessed Huang was thirty, likely he was thirty-five or forty. In any case, he had broad shoulders and something of a paunch. His face was wide and flat and open, and when he first spoke to her he showed her a ready smile. He was an appealing man, in contrast to the dour Hodding and the arrogant Bannister.

He was wearing a double-breasted blue blazer, a white shirt and blue tie, gray slacks, and polished black loafers. He didn't look like a policeman, in her judgment.

2

SENIOR INSPECTOR HUANG DROVE a blue Toyota—air-conditioned, thank God. He drove her up a winding highway, climbing a mountain.

"I recognize this road," she told him. "The signs—Peak Road. I remember reading that name on signs. This is where we were kidnapped."

As they ascended the peak, suddenly she exclaimed— "Right here! This is where we were kidnapped. The road was blocked by a van, and— Right here! It happened right here!"

"This would have been Sunday?" Huang asked.

"Yes. Sunday morning."

"I see. There would have been little traffic on Peak Road on a Sunday morning."

"And a man was seriously injured!" Beth insisted. "As I tried to tell that patronizing idiot Bannister, a man threw a knife. It went right into the bodyguard's stomach. Then he pulled it out and used it to slit the man's eyelids."

"Details like that are what interest me in your story," said Huang. "I will explain later. The Chang mansion is just a little farther up. Can you describe the man who threw the knife?"

"He was ugly! He sneered. I got the impression, then and later, that he was the leader of the kidnappers. They wanted Michael, not me, but I insisted I would not be separated from him. I screamed, and they threw me in the back of the van, tied my hands behind my back, and blindfolded me."

"Because of the way the kidnapper used a knife I'm quite sure this was a triad job."

"Triads? I've heard of them from Michael. Are they as powerful and wealthy as the Mafia in the United States?"

"Far more powerful and much richer. You must remember, Miss Connor, that triads started out as secret patriotic societies trying to overthrow the Mongolians and the Manchurians who invaded our country centuries ago. To finance wars and revolutions you need money, plenty of money. Many patriotic Chinese, especially overseas Chinese who struck it rich, gave lots of money to the triads to evict the brutal foreign occupiers."

"How did the British, people like that ass Bannister, look at the triads in Hong Kong?" Beth asked.

"In Hong Kong, the British regard everything we Chinese do with suspicion. The Chinese rarely take their disputes to the British courts, if they can help it. Many businessmen would rather let the triads resolve their disputes for them. Your fiancé's forefathers were part of the triads. Everybody who was anybody was at one time either actually or loosely affiliated with the triads. Without the triads' benign tolerance you can hardly get rich in this place. And getting rich is what it's all about. The successful triad members try to bury their past. They engage in legitimate businesses, whitewash their crimes, buy peace from their former triad members with money, and go on to collect M.B.E.s, O.B.E.s, and even knighthoods from Her Majesty."

"What a life," Beth sighed.

"So . . . we approach."

Hodding had said the Changs lived in a compound, and he had been right. The mansion and associated houses were on a branching driveway, all close together, all clinging to the steep mountainside and looking as if their foothold were precarious. Although the mansion stood behind an eight-foot stone wall, she could see it was a grand Edwardian stone edifice. The other houses, all of white stucco, were open to the driveway. She saw three such houses. Probably there were more, farther up and out of sight.

Huang headed his Toyota up to an ornate, solid-steel gate, emblazoned with a European-style coat of arms.

The Senior Inspector got out of the car and pressed a button on the stone column beside the gate. A small window in the gate opened, revealing the face of a turbaned Indian with a fierce beard and swarthy face. Huang identified himself to the Indian, and stated the purpose of his visit. The window closed.

While they waited, Beth noticed that closed-circuit television cameras scanned the driveway. Powerful lights would illuminate the whole area at night. Men watching the Toyota from doorways were obviously guards.

After several minutes the window in the gate opened, and the Indian spoke to Huang, then opened the gate.

Huang's Toyota became the seventh car parked on a circular, crushed-stone driveway that ran all the way around a small, carefully kept green lawn on which reposed two large stone Oriental lions. One of the cars on the driveway was a Mercedes stretch limousine, another a Rolls-Royce Silver Cloud.

"Look at the license plate on the Rolls," Huang said quietly to Beth.

The number was one black digit on a yellow plate—

8

"That license plate is worth more than the car," Huang told Beth. "First, because it's a single digit. Far more importantly, because it's eight. To the Cantonese, eight is a lucky number. In Cantonese, 'eight' rhymes with 'prosperity.' Mr. Chang could sell that plate for two million U.S. dollars. Literally."

Besides the mansion, there was another house inside the wall. Huang explained it was the guest house and contained several suites. Beth caught a glimpse of a swimming pool and guessed the guest house served the pool as a sort of cabana—though it was big enough to contain six cabanas. The land below the walled enclosure swept down at a steep angle into a wooded valley below. Fifty yards down a chain-link fence seemed to mark the limit of the property. Beth spotted four large dogs patrolling the fence. Still farther down, the slope was heavily wooded, and she could not see the bottom of the valley. Another steep, wooded slope rose opposite, and she saw half a dozen hovels clinging to that slope three-quarters of a mile away.

The mansion dominated the enclosure and dominated Beth's attention. It was Michael's family home, where he had grown up. Until now she had guessed that the Chang family lived comfortably, but she had not guessed that they lived in splendor—isolated splendor. The rambling stone house stood four stories tall, with distinct wings reaching at angles. Some of the windows were stained glass. The coat of arms she had seen on the gate was also carved into the stone above the great oaken doors of the main entry.

A man in a loose white shirt came to the car, spoke with Huang, and led them along a stone walkway and down stone stairs, where he showed them into a stone-pillared veranda with a stone balustrade and a mosaic floor. Though the day was hot and the veranda was not air-conditioned, it was shady, and a breeze blew through it. The tables and chairs—including several tiny children's chairs— were all of wicker. Potted palms and shrubs stood at intervals along the balustrade, separated by pieces of Asian and European sculpture. A small stone fountain gurgled in the middle of the veranda, its bowl the home of a dozen or so large goldfish.

Ironically perhaps, the principal view from this luxuriously appointed and comfortable veranda was of the opposite slope and the hovels. They were partially hidden by the potted palms and shrubs and by the sculpture, but they could be seen. To the left, the veranda overlooked a wing of the house. To the right it overlooked the lawn with lions.

Beth wondered if as a young boy Michael had not spent a great deal of time in this pleasant place, if indeed he had not once sat in one of the child-sized wicker armchairs.

Beth and Huang sat down and again waited. A maid appeared with a tray, offering cups of tea and a plate with slices of two kinds of melon. A man came in and sat down without offering to shake hands. He was a calm, shiny-faced Chinese, maybe fifty years old, wearing a gray linen jacket over an open-collared white shirt.

"I am Qiao Qichen," he said to Beth. "I am Mr. Chang's solicitor. You are the American we've been seeing on television, Miss Connor, and you say you have some business with the family. Please state it."

Qiao Qichen regarded her with skepticism that verged on hostility.

"I am engaged to be married to Michael Chang," she said. "He brought me to Hong Kong to meet his family. But—" Her voice broke, and she had to pause to recover it and wipe tears from her eyes. "We were kidnapped on Peak Road. We were held all day in a . . . a hot-sheet hotel, then were taken to a boat in the harbor.

Michael believed the kidnappers were going to kill me and urged me to escape by throwing myself into the harbor. I—"

Qiao Qichen frowned hard and interrupted her. "I am afraid you are mistaken, Miss Connor. Mr. Michael Chang has not been kidnapped."

"Then where is he?" Beth demanded in a choking whisper.

The solicitor shrugged. "In Cambridge, Massachusetts."

"He is not! He was kidnapped! I swear it! Ask his brother John. He was supposed to have met us at the airport."

Qiao Qichen nodded. "Very well. Let's see what John has to say." He snapped his fingers. The man who had led Beth and Huang to the veranda appeared. Qiao Qichen spoke to him, and the man hurried off.

While they waited, Beth sipped tea, and Huang ate a bite of watermelon.

Then a young man came out.

"This young woman says that Michael brought her to Hong Kong on Sunday morning. She says you were to meet Michael at the airport."

The young man fixed an appraising stare on Beth—erotically appraising. He was a slight young man, smaller than Michael, and his golden complexion shone as Michael's did not. He wore silver-rimmed round eyeglasses. He was calm, shrugged his shoulders, and said, "Michael is in America, so far as I know. Why would he bring *her* here?"

"We don't know. She offers a reason, but I don't think we can accept it. Thank you, John." Qiao Qichen smiled at Senior Inspector Huang. "Either this young woman is hysterical or she has some motive for suggesting what she does. Which do you take to be the case, Senior Inspector?"

"I intend to find out," said Huang.

"Without embarrassing anyone, Sir," said the solicitor, a new hardness in his voice. "Without embarrassing this family, I am prepared to offer her a small amount of money, for her silence, for her agree-

ment not to meddle in family affairs. Let us say the price of a first-class ticket home, plus perhaps ten thousand Hong Kong dollars for her incidental expenses."

"No," said Beth firmly. "I didn't come here to extort money from Michael's family."

"Let us not use a word such as 'extortion.' Would you consider twenty thousand? If not, what *would* you accept? You see, Miss Connor, we know who you are—we saw you on television last night and read about you in the morning papers, and it is important to the family that your name not be associated with the name Chang, at least not in any way that implies a scandalous connection. Think about it. Twenty thousand Hong Kong dollars is two thousand six hundred American dollars. I can perhaps offer more."

"I am not here to ask for money," Beth said, a note of desperation in her voice. "I came to Hong Kong because I love Michael and he loves me. I am not going home until I find out what's happened to him."

Qiao nodded. "Let the question remain open," he said. "You may decide that accepting a bit of money from the family, and a little help, would be most wise. Another offer, final for now. The family is most anxious that it not be touched with scandal. For your cooperation and silence, Miss Connor, *for your silence*, I can offer you the following—"

He realized he did not entirely have her attention. She had noticed a man standing at a window on the second floor of the wing to the right of the veranda, and she wondered if that were not Michael's father. He stood behind a red velvet drape he had pulled partly open, and she saw he was staring at her. Apparently he noticed that she had seen him, and he let the drape fall shut.

"Miss Connor—"

She returned her attention to the solicitor.

"It is essential, Miss Connor, absolutely essential, that the Chang family's privacy be left inviolate—for reasons greater than simply a family's natural wish not to have its personal affairs come to public attention. For that reason, and until we can discover exactly what *is* the relationship between you and Michael, the family is prepared to offer you a suite of rooms in this house, as well as a generous allowance of money."

"I didn't come here for money," Beth repeated. "Michael has proposed marriage, and I have accepted."

Qiao Qichen glanced at Huang, as if to appeal for help in making this young woman understand. "Marriage between you and Michael is quite impossible," he said gravely. "You must accept that." He paused, staring at her with an expression in which she could imagine she saw a hint of sympathy. "Very well. It is *difficult* to accept. I concede that you are genuinely in love with Michael. But—" He paused. "All right. Let's put the matter on a different plane. I can offer you one million American dollars if you will go back to Boston immediately and not communicate with Michael except through his family."

Beth's eyes flooded with tears. "I don't *want* a million dollars. I want—"

"*Two* million dollars. And that's absolutely our last offer."

"*No!*"

Qiao Qichen frowned at Huang. "Is this . . ." He paused and pondered for a brief moment. "Is this what American romantic love means? Or is she holding out for a higher bid?"

Huang shook his head. "I don't think so."

The solicitor grimaced. "She has seen too many American motion pictures," he muttered.

Beth wiped her eyes and looked away from both men. She looked toward the window where the man she took to be Michael's father had appeared. Now the curtains were parted again, and a woman was staring at her. The woman was older than she was but was not old enough to be Michael's mother. She was beautiful. That was all she was, just beautiful, in a way that justified itself, no matter *who* she was or *what* she was. She was Chinese: tall, slender, with long black hair, wearing dark-red lipstick, dressed in a deep-cleavage black dress. This woman—whoever in the name of god she might be—glowered darkly. For whatever reason—and Beth could not imagine a reason—the woman stared at her as if she wished her to drop dead. If she were not Michael's mother, which she certainly couldn't be, was she his *wife*? A lover? *Who?*

Like the man before her, the woman saw that Beth was looking at her and let the drape fall shut.

Qiao Qichen spoke to Huang. "So that discussion may not be closed, I am prepared to give her ten thousand Hong Kong dollars right now."

"I think the discussion *is* closed, Sir," Beth said coldly. "I have seen too many American movies. Maybe you haven't seen enough. I came here to marry Michael. Until *he* tells me it's impossible, it's not impossible. And I don't believe he will ever tell me that."

3

IN THE CAR AS they drove back down Peak Road, Senior Inspector Huang used his cellular telephone—the ubiquitous communicator that nearly everyone in Hong Kong carried—to check with Immigration.

"Damn," he said when he put the telephone down. "Mr. Qiao was lying. Michael Chang entered Hong Kong on Sunday, just as you said."

"Are you surprised? The more Mr. Qiao talked, the more apparent it became that he had lied at first, that Michael is in fact here, and that he probably knows where."

"When you told me the bodyguard was wounded by a thrown knife, that said triad to me. The men of the triads favor knives for weapons, and often they throw them. Also, when you said the man slit the eyelids of the bodyguard, that too said triad. I have in my files a great number of crimes committed by triads. I can't help but take a special interest in them."

"He'd had a knife used on *him* some time ago," said Beth. "Not his eyelids. On his mouth. Somebody cut him."

Huang frowned. "His *mouth?*"

"Ugly scar. Like somebody once tried to carve his lower lip off."

"I see," said Huang thoughtfully. For a moment, he took his attention from Peak Road and studied her face. Then he picked up his cell phone and punched in a number. "Emily? Huang. Can you meet me for a late lunch? Usual place? Please do." He put down the phone and spoke to Beth. "Emily Parker may just have a useful insight. It's a long shot, but we'll see."

"Anyway—?"

"This may explain also why the Changs say Michael was *not* kidnapped. They are probably engaged in protracted negotiations with the triad. But—Miss Connor, really? What about the money? Why don't you reconsider Qiao Qichen's offer? I am sure he will enrich it. You can take home a fortune if you play your cards right."

"I don't even want to *talk* about money," she said wearily, sadly.

"Well—what, then, do you intend to do?"

"I'm going to stay here until I find Michael. I *love* him, and he loves me. I won't betray him. I am not leaving Hong Kong until I find out what happened to him. Even if it's—" Her voice caught, and she swallowed. "Even if it's the worst possible news."

"You will have to live somehow. Hong Kong is an expensive place. Be realistic. Maybe you had better let the Changs give you some money."

"No. They'll think I'm an opportunist. I plan to marry Michael, and I won't have the Changs thinking I came here to take money from them. Anyway, my five hundred dollars American—what is it, four thousand Hong Kong?—ought to last me a week. After that, I'll have to think about getting my hands on some other money."

"Money is the best you are going to get from the Chang family, Miss Connor. Michael Chang's family will *never* accept you as a daughter-in-law. No matter how much Michael wants to marry you, they will force him to marry a Chinese girl of whom they approve. They might be willing to help him set you up in luxurious circumstances as a mistress—a concubine, we used to call it—and smile benignly while he spends most of his nights with you, but his children will be borne by a Chinese girl. You have to face it."

"I will face it when Michael tells me so."

"Then why not live in the Chang mansion until he does tell you so? Or tells you otherwise?"

Beth sighed heavily. "Senior Inspector Huang, *please!* If I moved into a suite in that mansion, I would be a *prisoner* there—as surely as I was a prisoner in that cell in Guangzhou. Why else do you think they offered me a suite? Out of generosity? No. To *control* me. To be sure I don't have any chance to embarrass the Chang family. The way things are, how can I be sure I wouldn't just permanently disappear?"

"Well . . . then I think you should phone *your* family."

"Only as a last resort. They gave their consent and blessing to this trip—to our marriage—only reluctantly, after great soul-searching. They've learned to accept Michael, even to admire him. For me to go home and say . . . The disappointment would . . . Mr. Huang, I went home from the Olympics without a medal. Even if I wanted to, I couldn't go home from Hong Kong without a husband, so long as . . . so long as Michael is alive."

"Your five hundred American dollars will not last you long in this city," said Huang. "If you refuse to take money from the Changs, you are going to have to find a way to fund your stay here, not to mention your flight home. I still think you should contact your family in Boston. At least they can wire you a few dollars."

"Short of death by starvation," she said, "I will not ask my family for money, and I will not take money from the Changs."

Though sympathetic, Huang was not incapable of impatience. "Your pride is something to contend with."

"Why can't I take a job somewhere and earn a little money?"

"In the first place, you don't have a Hong Kong work permit. In the second place, you don't speak Chinese, and the lowliest clerical or secretarial job requires that. You couldn't work behind the counter in a store—half your customers wouldn't be able to talk with you."

"In stores like the Friendship Store in Guangzhou?" she asked.

Huang shook his head. "For every job like that there are fifty applicants. You have to be realistic."

"I know how to be a waitress. I've carried beer to tables in my father's pub. Maybe my pride is not so great as you think."

"Even for that your want of fluency in Chinese would be a handicap. I say again, you have to be realistic. You've been offered a lot of—"

"I won't take money from the Changs. I won't become a prisoner in their compound. This is only Wednesday, Mr. Huang. Surely my five hundred American dollars will support me for the rest of the week, and by the end of the week surely I will know something about Michael."

4

SENIOR INSPECTOR HUANG TOOK Beth to lunch in a dim sum shop in Kowloon. It was a busy little restaurant, serving quick lunches to men and women from the offices in nearby buildings, also longer lunches to people who wanted to linger and talk. It was, Beth reflected, something of a Chinese McDonald's. The table had no cloth but was supplied with a stack of paper napkins. Chopsticks came in envelopes, and the pair had to be split apart. Each place was set with a small plate the size of an American salad plate, to which food from the serving plates was to be moved with chopsticks.

Huang ordered food, and they began to eat before Emily— whoever that might be—arrived. Beth recognized wontons and took two to her plate, one filled with vegetables, the other with meat and vegetables.

Beth sipped from a beverage he had suggested she try: a glass of chilled, sweetened soy milk. It was something she had never tasted before—had never in fact even heard of—but it was tasty and refreshing. "I'm glad Emily is not here yet," said Huang. "I'm going to tell you something about her. She works as a hostess in a very luxurious, very expensive nightclub in Kowloon. She knows her way around. She might be able to help you find a room."

"She's a friend of yours, I gather," said Beth.

He did not respond to that. "Emily," he said briskly, "is from London. She was engaged to be married to a young man named Blake. Blake left her in London and came out to Hong Kong to establish himself in a job he'd gotten with Domino's Pizza. Oh, yes, we do have Domino's Pizza shops in Hong Kong. He was to send for her, to bring her out as soon as he was settled. Well . . . need I tell you what happened? He did not send for her. Emily came out on her own, to learn that Blake had married a Chinese girl who was about to have his baby. Emily didn't have the money to go home, so she became a club girl. That's not exactly a prostitute, Miss Connor, but it's something close. She's a hostess at the Pearl Club. She entertains men, encourages them to spend money on champagne and food. I say 'entertains.' She does not always end the evening in bed with the man she entertained. In point of fact, more often than not she doesn't. She is in a sense like a geisha. But from time to time she—the term we use is 'go out.' She goes out with a man. When she does, she earns significant money."

Beth nodded gravely. Huang was about to introduce her to a hooker.

"The reason I invited her to join us is that she might, just might—on a very long chance—know something about the man with the scarred mouth."

Emily Parker arrived. She was a slight young woman, three or four inches shorter than Beth. Her short, unruly hair was sandy-red, almost orange. Her blue eyes settled on Beth with a straightforward, appraising focus. Her mouth was wide, with a fleshy lower lip. Her shoulders were narrow.

Huang quickly sketched out for her why Beth was here. "The

leader of the kidnappers had a very ugly scar on his lower lip," he told her. "Does that say anything to you?"

"Big Prick," said Emily. "Dai Gul Dai."

"What I was afraid of," said Huang. "Has he been in the club the past few nights?"

"No. Odd. He's usually in every night or so. He works for Mr. Wu, you know. He's a member of Chung Yui Hui."

"I'd know him if I saw him," said Beth grimly. "I'll never forget that face. Why can't I go to the club and—"

"You can't just hang around in there," said Huang. "A young woman who goes there, *works* there."

"Couldn't you take me?"

Huang smiled and shook his head. "I can go in and out on official business," he said. "If I were to sit down at a table, I'd have to spend money. Miss Connor, your five hundred American dollars wouldn't cover the cost of one evening at the Pearl Club. Anyway, suppose you saw Dai Gul Dai—and he saw you. His knife would fly."

"I suppose there's one way she could be in the club a few nights," said Emily. "She could work there."

"I couldn't," Beth whispered, lowering her eyes and shaking her head.

"No. I suppose you couldn't. I didn't think I could, either. It's not as bad as you think. Anyway, I don't suggest you try it. But you don't have to work as a hostess. We have waitresses, too. Waitresses don't go out. Ever."

"Too much risk," said Huang firmly.

"*Not* much risk," said Beth. "He won't be expecting me there, working as a waitress, and if he sees me he won't recognize me. All I need is one glimpse of him. I'll know him, and then we'll know who kidnapped Michael. *It's the key to the whole thing.* I've got to work there. If you won't help me— *Oh, please!*"

"Will you give me your absolute promise that you won't do anything but call me? If you see him and identify him, you must be sure he hasn't seen you and then leave the club immediately. If you try to do something you think is brave— Miss Connor?" Huang asked.

"Alright. I promise you, absolutely, I won't try to do anything brave. All I want is a chance to find out where Michael is . . . if he's anywhere. Senior Inspector—*this may be the only chance I have*. Do you know what it means to love someone and . . . ?"

"Qiao Qichen tried to say he didn't know. I doubt that's true. I imagine he does know what it means. Alright— I'll do everything I can for you, Miss Connor, except let you throw away your life."

"Call me Beth," she whispered almost tearfully. "I like to think I have friends."

Huang put his right hand on hers. "I was educated in a Jesuit school, as your Michael was. They baptized me Mark. You can call me that . . . Beth."

She turned his hand over and squeezed it. "Mark . . . and . . . Emily. *Help me!*"

SIX

Nobody needs to know I was a whore
for two years in Hong Kong.

1

WHEN BETH WENT TO the bathroom, Emily told Huang she figured Beth was the same sort of victim *she* had been—a victim of a
man who had tricked her into coming to Hong Kong and then
found some reason to abandon her. "What you want to bet he had
the kidnapping staged, just to get rid of the poor girl?"

Huang left them on the street outside the dim sum shop, saying
he would go and make the arrangements for Beth to work in the
Pearl Club for a few nights. He would come by Emily's room to confirm it. Maybe Beth could find a room in the same hostel, or the
same building at least.

To Beth's surprise, Emily Parker immediately and generously be-
friended her. "If you are only going to be here a week or so," she said,
"you might as well come bunk with me. I don't live fancy, but my
place is clean, with room enough for the two of us. You can chip in
something on the rent. We'll have to stop on the way and buy you
some different clothes. You can't wander around day and night in a
designer catsuit. Also, the waitresses wear leotards and pantyhose,
so you'll have to get some of them."

They entered Emily's hostel no earlier than four that afternoon.
It was on the fifteenth floor of a building that called to Beth's mind
the word "warren." There were several hostels in the building, sharing space with tailor shops and other small businesses. The building

stank of burned cooking oil. People congregated in the hallways, apparently to escape the confines of their shops and living quarters. Besides Chinese, the building was occupied by dirty-looking Pakistanis who cast suggestive leers on the two young women as they made their way up in a slow elevator and through the hallways.

This hostel was a group of ten rooms rented out by a late-middle-aged Chinese woman who sat in a big and well-worn maroon plush chair in the middle of her group of rooms and watched television. Sticks of incense burned in a little shrine mounted on the wall behind her chair. As they passed by the woman, Emily handed her a bill. She rented her room by the day and paid cash.

The room Beth was to share with Emily was not much bigger than the cell in Guangzhou. It had no window, was lighted by two bare bulbs in a ceiling fixture, and was furnished with two single beds, one green vinyl-covered chair, a small fiberboard dresser, and a television set on a shelf high on the wall. Beth was surprised to see that the room also had a telephone. It sat on the floor. Emily's clothes hung on hooks. Some lay on the bed that would now be Beth's. A few paperback novels also lay on the bed.

The bathroom behind the bedroom was smaller still. It had a toilet and basin and a shower head sticking out of one wall. The tiled floor sloped toward a drain in a corner, meaning that the entire bathroom was also the shower stall. It had no door and no curtain.

Beth tried not to show Emily her reaction to these cramped quarters. The room was, as Emily had promised, clean. The door was equipped with a secure lock. It would be all right for a few days. Surely, a few days was all she'd have to live here.

"Beth . . . I know," said Emily. "I know what you're thinking. I live cheap. I'm not in this room much, only when I sleep. And I'm saving a bundle of money. Every quid I don't spend in Hong Kong I'll have when I go home. *In London* is where I'll live fancy."

They rearranged the room a little—there was not much rearranging to do. Beth had bought jeans and a T-shirt. She took off the catsuit and folded it into a drawer that Emily cleared for her, then pulled on the jeans and shirt. She had also bought the black leotard and dark sheer pantyhose Emily had said she would need. She shoved them in their bag under her bed.

Mark Huang came by. All was set. Beth could work as a waitress at the Pearl Club for a few days.

Emily urged Beth to take a nap before they left for the club. They would not be home much before dawn, she said.

When Beth woke, a little before seven, Emily was taking a shower. Because the whole bathroom was the shower, Beth would have to wait until she was finished before going in to use the toilet.

It seemed that no one she had met this week looked like what she had supposed they should: Huang not like a detective, Shek not like the deputy governor of a Chinese province, Emily Parker not like a young woman who earned her living the way Huang said she did.

She was too delicate for it, as Beth judged. Nothing about Emily was coarse. She did not look world-weary or used. It was difficult for Beth to believe that the slender young body she saw under the shower was sold to men. Her belly was flat. Her breasts were youthful: two firm hemispheres that stood, did not hang, on her visible rib cage. Something in the forthright, almost ingenuous way she looked at Beth seemed to contradict what Huang had told of her.

"I can read your mind," she said as she raised her head and rinsed the soap suds off her face. "You wonder how I can do it."

"You don't have to talk about it."

Emily shrugged. She soaped her breasts and sharp little pink nipples. "I had to figure what the hell. Who was I, anyway? I needed the money bad. And you know, Beth, once you do it—you do it *just once*—you've defined yourself. It's like, you were a virgin once, but you're never gonna be again. Okay? You sell yourself once, you're a whore. You are, and you can't deny it—not to yourself anyway. You decide that's what you are, it makes it easier. I've been out here fourteen months, and I got money in the Hong Kong Bank. I'll go home before they turn the place over to the Beijing Chinese next July. I'll take with me enough money to buy into something good back home: a share of a nice little pub maybe. That'd be nice. And nobody needs to know I was a whore for two years in Hong Kong. Nobody's the wiser."

Beth nodded. "You're a brave girl."

"Nobody ever gave me nothing. Whatever I get, I earn it."

Beth nodded. "I guess I can't say the same, exactly."

Emily grinned. "Strip off and c'mon in here. You need a bath, too, before we go out. Uh . . . hey! I'm not gonna hit on you. A bath, I say. Just a bath."

Emily rubbed soap over Beth's wet skin and turned her to rinse as she had promised: affectionately but in no sense whatever erotically. It was simply another manifestation of Emily's artless, almost childlike nature.

2

THEY ATE CHEAPLY, IN another dim sum shop, and walked on to the club. A pair of Western girls dressed in blue jeans and T-shirts attracted no attention on the streets. There were plenty of others, most of them tourists.

The Pearl Club was located in Tsim Sha Tsui East, a high-class version of New York's Times Square that had until recently been all ocean. Now a string of five-star hotels, office towers, and plush nightclubs stood on the landfill.

Despite what she had been told, by both Mark and Emily, Beth was in no way prepared for the Pearl Club. The place was lavish. She had no experience at all with nightclubs, and this one was beyond her wildest imagination.

On the street, valet parkers took patrons' cars. Bearded Indians in long, red, gold-embroidered coats and white turbans welcomed men and probably occasionally enticed into the club a man who had not meant to go there. Inside, patrons passed across a thick red carpet to a bank of elevators.

Leaving the elevator, they faced a broad, red-carpeted stairway that customers and working girls alike climbed one more floor to reach the club. Gilt and marble dominated the decor. At the top of the stairs, Beth followed Emily along a columned hallway, on a flower-patterned carpet, between black columns decorated with golden leaves and flowers.

Inside the club at last, Beth entered a contrived fantasy world, conspicuously designed to extract the most money from men at the fastest possible rate. At one end of the club was a stage, at the other a bar. In the large room in the middle, men and girls sat on couches or in armchairs, facing tables. The club was dimly lighted by scores of chandeliers that shed a golden glow.

The Pearl Club was open and already busy. A dozen hostesses sat with men at the tables. Others sat at the bar, waiting. Hostesses wore revealing clothes of one kind and another: skimpy-cut, thin, or both. A few—the Chinese hostesses in particular—wore sheer bras that exposed their breasts as much as if they were topless. The men at the tables, most of them Chinese or Japanese, only two or three of them Western, leaned toward their hostesses, engaged in what looked like profound conversation, not light, erotic banter.

No man sat alone. Every woman in the club worked there, Emily explained.

Emily led Beth toward the bar and to a tall, slender blond wearing a tight, black ankle-length gown.

"Ilse. This is Beth."

Ilse appraised Beth skeptically. She was what, oddly, a club like this called the Mama-San. She was the madam, in a broad sense. More precisely said, she was the manager of the girls: hostesses and waitresses. Emily had explained that the Mama-San interviewed each man who came in, asked him what kind of girl he wanted, then assigned a girl to him. From time to time, she checked with each man and asked if he was satisfied with the girl he had or if he wanted to see another one. She was the supervisor of the hostesses and ruled them with an iron hand.

"Temporary, I suppose," said Ilse dryly.

"Well . . . probably."

Ilse smiled wanly. "It may be more temporary than you expect." She spoke perfect English with a slight accent that Beth suspected was German. "You are a waitress, not a hostess. The men are supposed to leave you alone. If a man tries to play touchy-feely with you, tell me about it, and I'll take care of it; don't try to solve the problem yourself. See the girl over there? That's the way you do it. You squat beside the table and take the order. You squat to put the order on the table. If a hostess is having trouble, she'll try to tell you, quietly. You bring that word to me, fast. Okay?"

"Okay."

"Don't worry about what a man orders. You don't even have to know what we serve. The hostess takes care of all that. All you have to do is go to the bar and kitchen, pick up what's been ordered, and carry it to the table. The quicker the better. I'll assign you five tables. You keep a close eye on all of them. A hostess will signal you if her table wants anything.

"Now, sooner or later a man will decide he likes the waitress better than the hostess and will ask you to sit down with him. Just say it's against the rules, so you can't. Then you come and tell me."

Each girl had a small locker. Beth received a key and opened her locker, number fourteen. She put her jeans and T-shirt inside and a small plastic purse she had bought, in which she was carrying her money and her travel document from the consulate. Dressed in a tight-stretched black leotard, dark sheer pantyhose, and high-heeled black patent-leather shoes, she was ready to face her job.

Emily changed into a black satin microskirt that rode low across her belly. It would ride up when she sat down and would show her white panties. Her loose, blue-green nylon blouse closed in front with a single tie that left it open between her small breasts and wide open over her navel and hips.

Ilse led Beth to her station, showing her where to stand so she would have a clear view of each of her tables and could respond immediately to a signal from a hostess. The waitress stations were squares of translucent plastic, and pink light shown from below.

Though the waitresses displayed nothing but their legs, they were lighted to be seen.

Shortly Emily came to one of Beth's tables and sat down beside a Japanese man. She spoke briefly with him, then nodded to Beth, who hurried over and squatted beside the table.

"Mr. Tanaka," said Emily, "would like a bottle of champagne, also some melon slices."

Beth stood and went to the bar. The bartender handed her first an ice bucket, which she carried to the table. Then he gave her the champagne, opened, and she took that to the table, squatted, and put the bottle in the ice. She returned to the bar for a small tray with two glasses, and delivered those. The kitchen was a little slower with the melon slices, but they arrived on the bar after two or three minutes, and Beth went to the table and squatted to put the plate and some napkins before Mr. Tanaka, who was already nuzzling Emily's neck and stroking her legs.

A floor show began, gaudy and loud. The eight chorus girls were all Westerners of one kind or another, none Chinese. They wore tiny flesh-colored sequined G-strings and transparent bras spangled with glittering sequins. They smiled woodenly, danced woodenly, and changed costumes often—that is to say, they changed plumed hats, fluffy boas, and feathery fans.

No one onstage essayed comedy. The languages understood in the club were too various. An American black wearing a white top hat and white tails sang. He had a good voice and was apparently the star of the show.

Beth's hostesses kept her moving. She carried more ice buckets and champagne to her tables, also bottles of whisky and brandy. One table ordered a tray of hors d'oeuvres for four: two couples.

Beth was a little disturbed that her leotard slipped up and exposed more of her hips and bottom than she had meant to show, but it was no great embarrassment. Other young women in the club were so much more exposed that she doubted any of the men noticed her nether cheeks. In any case, she had no time to brood on how much she was showing; she was kept too busy for that.

When she had worked an hour and a half, Ilse told her to take a break and put another waitress on her station. She guided Beth to a cluster of stools in a corner behind the bar, where hostesses and waitresses not immediately on duty congregated and relaxed.

Besides herself, only four girls sat there—two Chinese waitresses and two hostesses: one a delicate-looking Australian with glossy light-brown hair and freckles, the other a moody-looking woman probably ten years older than the rest, who turned out to be French and spoke heavily accented English.

Of these four the Frenchwoman was the only one who was all but bare-breasted, wearing a sheer bra that revealed small breasts and dark, pinched little nipples. She sucked hungrily on a cigarette, drew the smoke down deep, and said little. Beth sympathized with her. She was perhaps the handsomest woman in the club, but her youth and freshness were fading, and she obviously knew it. If she had not saved her money, she was in imminent trouble.

The Australian girl, whose name was Barbara, was bright and voluble. She wore a yellow bikini bathing suit under a white silk jacket, showing extravagant breasts. She said she was nineteen and had worked here and in another Kowloon club for about a year and a half. She also said she would never go back to Australia. "You can't *imagine* what a *boring* place it is. In another year, I'm going 'ome, which when an Australian says it means I'm going to England. To London, which is where it's at. I'll have just about fifty thousand quid. I'm going before the Handover. Beijing says, 'The 'orses will run, and the club girls will dance.' The 'orses may trust 'em, but we club girls don't trust them types. They're *political*."

Emily came by. "Figured this would happen. Mr. Tanaka is too timid or too cheap to ask me to go out. I call him empty tank, if you catch my meanin'. So . . . back on the line. Damn it."

As Emily went out to sit and wait for another customer, the Australian girl smirked and said, "Not 'er best opportunity for the night, anyway. She's got a *real* one, I mean a real . . . wot is it you Americans call it? A sugar daddy? She's got a connection that's *unbelievable!* There's not a girl works here but doesn't envy her. I wish

I knew wot she's got! I mean, she's a *nice* girl, but she's no ravin' beauty, now, is she? Tits? My two would make *six* of 'ers."

Ilse recalled Beth to her station, and for the next hour and a half she carried bottles and trays to her five tables. She made no effort to calculate what the hostesses took as commissions on the drink and food they cajoled the men into buying. They earned it. She watched the men fondle the young women, and from time to time she saw a man and woman leave a table and go to Ilse to pay the price for releasing the hostess for the rest of the night.

A Chinese man and a man she guessed was Korean reached down and ran their hands over her legs as she squatted to serve their tables. She said nothing to Ilse, she just took care the next time she went to their tables to serve from another side, where they couldn't reach her.

The American black man came out in a standard black dinner jacket, leaned against a piano, and sang to the accompaniment of a Chinese woman pianist. He had a pleasant voice, and so far as Beth could tell none of the requests that came from the tables confounded him or the pianist. The requests seemed to concentrate on songs by Andrew Lloyd Webber, and the man knew them all. He winked at her and murmured, "Miss Connor," as she passed in front of him. So far as she could tell, he was the only one in the club, Emily and Ilse excepted, who knew who she was.

But when she took her next break, Ilse summoned her and led her to an office off the main room of the club. Ilse knocked. A voice invited her to open the door.

The man sitting at a massive desk in an ornate office rose and came around the desk. He extended both hands to Beth, and Beth extended hers and let him take her hands in his to greet her. Ilse slipped backward and left the room, leaving Beth alone with this man.

"You would not know my name, but I am Wu Kim Ming," the man said. "I am honored but also astounded that Beth Connor should be working in my club. You may relax in my assurance that I will not make publicity about it. I am sure you have a reason—I mean, a reason beyond the modest compensation you will be paid here. Pleased be seated."

Beth sat down in the leather-upholstered armchair he pointed to. She saw him react to the liquid swish of her nylon-clad legs as she crossed them.

"I am curious to know, Miss Connor, if you would be willing to spend the night with me in my suite at the Mandarin Oriental Hotel."

Emily had warned her of such an invitation and had coached her on how to respond to it. "I don't see how I could possibly do that with a man I have just met. I am not—"

"Not a prostitute."

"No, Sir. I am not."

Wu Kim Ming smiled. "So . . ." he said softly. "At any price. So be it. In fact, I am glad to know it. I would have been disappointed in you, Miss Connor, if you had accepted my proposition. I would have acted on your acceptance, but I would have been—in the more real sense—disappointed."

She could not remember ever having met a man so completely self-controlled. She guessed him to be in his early fifties—again allowing for her inability to judge the ages of Chinese people. She made that judgment by the gray at his temples, though he showed not a single wrinkle, even at the corners of his eyes. He was handsomely dressed, in a dark gray suit with faint white pinstripes. He spoke English without an accent.

"Do you want to tell me why you are working here?"

She drew breath. "It is a place where I can make a few dollars for a few days, without obtaining a Hong Kong work permit," she said.

"As in America without a green card," he said.

"Something like that."

"I wish I could advertise to the world that Miss Beth Connor is working at the Pearl Club. You would quit if I did that, wouldn't you?"

"Sir, I—"

"Not to worry. I won't. If you decide to stay longer, we will get you a work permit and make you the star of our show—whether you can sing or dance or not."

"I am grateful."

"Regard me as a friend, Miss Connor. I am more than pleased to have you here. Let's explore in our minds the many possibilities your working here may afford. Afford both of us, that is to say."

3

WHEN BETH LEFT THE office, Wu stepped out and summoned Ilse in. He sat down behind his desk but did not invite her to sit.

"Are you sure of your information?" he asked.

"All I know is what Inspector Huang told me," said Ilse.

Wu rubbed his hands together before his chin and frowned. "Engaged to be married to Michael Chang. Potentially the daughter-in-law of billionaire Chang Wing Hing."

"I can't imagine Mr. Chang would allow that marriage."

Wu shrugged. "Alright, then—potentially the *concubine* of Michael Chang. In a sense, that might be better than daughter-in-law. In any event," he said crisply, "watch out for her. Don't let anything bad happen to her here. I want to her feel she's— How shall we say? I want her to feel she has friends in you and me. A day may come when our having cultivated that feeling in Miss Beth Connor may be quite valuable."

Ilse nodded. "I've kept an eye on her all evening. I've got a feeling that girl can take care of herself."

"Let's hope she doesn't have to." He sighed. "What's Emily doing?"

"Nothing much. She's been with a Japanese gentleman three times, and he spends money on champagne and food but never asks her to go out. Incidentally, Beth Connor is living in her hostel room with Emily."

"Oh, ho! That's interesting. Well, send Emily back here. I'll take her. She's a biddable girl, I'll say that for her."

4

IN THE BATHROOM ADJOINING Wu's office, Emily changed into a *cheong-sam* of glistening pink silk decorated with gold, silver, and blue brocade in a flower pattern. The dress shaped itself to her body, clinging sinuously to her every curve and angle, and she had to wriggle into it. It fit so close that she could not wear either panties or a bra under it—they would have shown. The skirt was slit on the sides, almost to her hips. A high collar rose under her jaw, but it was open, and the bodice was split low, showing wide but shallow cleavage between the hemispheres of her breasts. Mr. Wu—and that was what she invariably called him; she could not imagine calling him by any familiar name—had bought it for her a couple of months ago, to wear when she went with him to the Mandarin Oriental Hotel. The first night he took her there she had been wearing her microskirt, and he had taken her up on a freight elevator.

At the hotel they walked through the lobby and to the private elevator that would carry them to Wu's suite, and Emily was conscious as she always was of the stares they attracted—on him out of awe and deference, on her out of curiosity about a slight English girl with orangish hair dressed in an elegant *cheong-sam*. Those who guessed at her identity probably guessed she was the daughter of a Brit nabob of some kind. None guessed correctly that she was a club girl being honored by Wu Kim Ming.

His suite was the most luxurious she could imagine. While he went to a bedroom to change, Emily stood at a window and looked out over Victoria Harbour. Wu returned. He was wearing a black silk robe and carrying a small glass flask. He approached her, and she stood and put her hands in his.

"Let us kneel," he said solemnly. "Try to do as I do. Breathe deeply and try to clear your mind of inharmonious thoughts." He dropped his robe and knelt naked on the floor. Emily knelt beside him. She knew he didn't want her naked. Wu closed his eyes and began to draw deep breaths. "Clear your mind," he whispered. "Let nothing intrude."

For a minute, she kept her eyes closed and listened to him. He drew long breaths and let them out audibly. She tried to do the same. It was *qi gong*. She glanced repeatedly at his jade stem, which was the term he liked to use for his male organ, and saw it grow visibly as he breathed and meditated. She had seen this happen each time she had been with him and could not decide if *qi gong* caused the increase or it was caused by simple lickerishness.

He continued the deep breathing for several minutes. She tried following him but as always could not sense that it made any difference to her. Finally he took her hand, rose, and helped her to rise with him. He raised the flask he had brought from the bedroom and drank quickly. She knew what he was drinking: powdered rhinoceros horn in white wine. She understood that the Chinese believe rhinoceros horn is a powerful aphrodisiac.

She bent down and began to lift the hem of the *cheong-sam*. "No, Precious Lady Yin," said Wu. "The dress enhances your beauty. I would rather make love with you when you have it on."

Emily nodded. Only once had she been naked when they coupled.

"We are going to make love in another of the Nine Glorious Postures," said Wu. "Come. I sit here."

He sat down on a small couch made of bamboo with a thin, silk-covered pad for a seat. He leaned back on this couch and extended his legs before him, his heels together.

"Now . . . raise your dress and bring yourself astride me. Lower yourself onto me."

For Emily it was awkward and challenging. But she did it. She raised her skirt around her hips, then had to spread her legs wide to straddle him. She bent her knees and lowered herself until his jade stem was at her jade gate. He guided his stem with his hands, so that as she lowered herself it entered her. Nodding encouragement and making gentle signals with his hands, he encouraged her to settle down on him until their hips were firmly pressed together. Immediately she understood why this was one of the Nine Glorious Postures. This penetrated her more deeply than she had ever been penetrated before, even in others of the Nine Glorious Postures.

"This is called 'The Bouncing Infant,' " said Wu. "You are in control. You lift and lower your hips—with perhaps a slightly twisting motion—until we achieve the supreme. And we must *both* achieve it. It is a failure if I do and you don't. I know you think a girl like you should not let her feelings run loose. Let them run, Lady Yin! Let your body do for you what it is capable of doing. Never eschew what the moment may give. You cannot know whether or not another such moment will ever again happen to you."

Emily began to move, tentatively at first, then more determinedly—because she knew how much it could profit her—she raised and lowered her hips. She closed her fists over the top of the back of the couch, so she could use her arms to help move her hips. She leaned forward over him until her breasts were almost touching his face. He pulled her *cheong-sam* open and kissed her nipples.

"Traditionally, in this glorious posture I am supposed to contemplate the beauty of mountains," he whispered. "I prefer to contemplate the beauty of your lovely *hung.*" It was the polite Cantonese word for breasts. He licked her nipples. "Precious Lady Yin," he murmured.

Emily took the cue and whispered, "Strong Lord Yang."

She became more vigorous, lifting her hips, thrusting them down, feeling his engorged stem sliding back and forth in her most sensitive places. She stopped trying to withhold anything. In one more minute her body tensed with rhythmic spasms. His body stiffened, and his hot fluids shot into her. She could feel them.

She felt him doing what a man does: minifying. But he did not want to disjoin. He clasped her and held her in place. She realized abruptly that the chafing of her inner parts had made her surfaces more sensitive, so that she could feel the slightest movement, even the faint pulsing of his shaft; she had to imagine he was feeling something similar. His diminished jade stem still subtly stimulated her jade gate.

"Tell me, Precious Lady Yin, what sort of woman is your new friend Beth Connor?"

Emily was surprised that he should ask such a question at such a time. "She is an American innocent," she said. "She is a very lovely girl."

"So innocent and lovely she would not be interested in *fang si*"—which meant chamber matters and was an old and traditional Chinese way of speaking of sex—"with me?"

Emily started. Was Mr. Wu interested in Beth? "I . . . She is very much in love with her fiancé."

"Michael Chang."

"Yes. I am surprised you know."

"Oh, you understand how the world moves, Emily. Word circulates. I just wondered if this American girl would be interested in *fang si*."

"Don't I satisfy you, Mr. Wu?" Emily asked.

He took her breasts in his hands and squeezed gently. "You do, Precious Lady Yin. I am not thinking of substituting your new friend for you. Except for my honored wife, you can be my only woman. Even if Miss Connor and I should . . . well . . . that would only be temporary. You and I will still *shang chuang*." His Cantonese phrase meant they would "climb the bed"—and was a little vulgar.

"But Beth . . . interests you."

Wu sucked her left nipple into his mouth and worked his tongue over it for a quarter of a minute. "Think, Precious Lady Yin. Think! The wife—more likely the mistress—of Michael Chang. And you her best friend in Hong Kong! Then think of yourself, my sole concubine, living here in my suite, with a generous allowance of money to lay away in the bank every month, against your eventual return to London. *Think!*"

"What do I have to do to earn these privileges?" Emily asked.

"Nothing! Just be her friend. She needs friends. Senior Inspector Huang Han Gai is her friend, too, but he has his special loyalties and can be trusted only in a limited way. Just be her friend—and keep me advised of what she says and does."

Emily lifted her hips, meaning to retreat off him. Wu circled her with his arms and pressed her down again, once more penetrating her deeply and arousing in her feelings she had meant to avoid.

"I don't have to betray her in any way?" she asked softly.

"To the contrary. Her prosperity and success are our prosperity and success."

5

BETH LEFT THE PEARL Club a little after three in the morning. Even at that hour the streets were busy, and she walked through bustling crowds. Again, as she had been in the fishing village, she was uncomfortably conscious that probably she alone, among all these people, spoke English. She had made a big point of learning the way between the hostel and the club, knowing that Emily might not be with her when she returned.

The building was neither dark nor silent, nor was it as well lighted or as busy as it had been earlier. It was still full of the heavy stench of burned cooking oil and of tobacco smoke. She showed her key to the entrance guard and walked to the elevators. For the first time, she thought of the building as dirty and oppressive.

The elevators were slow. She had noticed that before. She had to stand in the dimly lighted hall and wait, listening to the sound of the elevators moving in their shafts but with no idea where they were. The ones coming down forced air out through the cracks between the doors, so she judged two were descending.

A man walked up to her. Beth had seen racism in the States, had recognized it as ugly, and was determined not to be racist. Even so, she was repelled by the sight of the Pakistani, or whatever he was, who approached. He was a slight, thin dark man, with a black mustache and oily black hair.

He touched her.

He put his hand on her arm. "Brit, no?" he said in a thick accent.

She stepped away from him. "American," she said.

He smiled and reached out to touch her arm again. "Handsome," he said. "Beautiful. You, me, *dew*, yes?"

She had learned very few Chinese words, but Michael had explained to her what one word the kidnappers had used meant. *Dew* meant "fuck." It was the most vulgar term the man possibly could have used.

"We no *dew!*" she yelled at him. "*Get away from me!*"

He grabbed her left breast and squeezed. She felt a shock of pain and screamed.

The man laughed. "*Baw!*" he said. "*Baw*. Big. Good."

She struck. Beth was strong. Her fist crushed his nose, and his blood flew.

The man's dark face changed to a mask of fury. "*You . . . hurt . . . me!*" he yelled. "Now! We *dew!* We *dew!*" He pulled a knife.

Beth stepped back in terror. Stepping back she collided with another man, who had come up behind her. He brushed past her and attacked the Pakistani with the knife. He slugged the would-be rapist hard, first with a fist to the belly, then one to the face. The would-be rapist dropped his knife and slumped against the wall, where the new man continued to slug him time after time. In the cell in Guangzhou Beth had heard bones breaking when the guards worked over the riotous prisoner, and she heard them again now: ribs and the bones of the man's face. He dropped to the floor, and her rescuer began to kick him in the face, in the belly, in the crotch.

She had never seen this man before, the one who had come to her rescue. He was Chinese. He was not much bigger than the darker man who had assaulted her, but he was stronger, and he was ruthless. She wondered if he did not mean to kill the man.

An elevator came. The door opened. The Chinese man pointed to the door and gestured that she should enter and go up.

When the elevator door closed, he was still kicking.

SEVEN

*No one walks out on a corps commander
of the People's Liberation Army.*

1

IN THE ROOM, BETH trembled as she locked both locks. She opened her purse and pulled out the card Senior Inspector Huang Han Gai had given her. It had his home telephone number as well as his office number. She punched in the home number. After a few rings a woman answered.

"I'd like to speak to Senior Inspector Huang, please."

The woman said something in Chinese.

"Inspector Huang. Inspector Huang. *Please!*"

Silence followed, until finally, after what seemed like a whole minute, Huang came on the line. "Who's calling?" he asked. His tone was sleepy and annoyed.

"Beth Connor. I've been assaulted! A man tried to rape me. Here in the building. I—"

"Which building?"

"The hostel. I'm in Emily's room. A man tried to rape me. Another man beat him. I mean, the other man beat him . . . maybe to death."

"Is Emily there?"

"No. She went out."

"Alright. Don't let anyone in but Emily. If the police come and want to talk to you, tell them through the door that Senior Inspector Huang is coming. I'll be there in . . . say half an hour."

Emily arrived before Huang. She held the tearful Beth in her arms and stroked her hair. After a while Emily said, "I need a bath, I do. Come on, we'll take a shower together, the way we did before. Believe me, there is nothing like warm water to make a person feel better."

It was as before. The two young women washed each other. Emily's touch on Beth's naked body was affectionate and comforting, not in the least amorous or sensual—as was Beth's touch on Emily. Beth did feel better when they had dried each other, and she was grateful.

Huang arrived.

"You have a way of telling the most distressing truths," he said to Beth. "The floor outside the elevators is covered with blood. The security man swears he heard and saw nothing. He said no attempted rape or beating could possibly have occurred. He says the blood is probably chicken blood. Frankly, I'm going to leave it at that. I took a sample on a handkerchief, but I'm not going to have it analyzed for the moment. I see no point in getting you involved in another investigation."

Beth was dressed in her jeans and T-shirt. Emily had pulled on a T-shirt and panties and sat on her bed, combing her wet hair.

"I probably know who tried to rape her," said Emily. "It's a shame, you know, how many dirty Pakis we've let into Hong Kong. I bet the Chinese stop that next year."

"Having said that, who do you have in mind?" Huang asked.

"A Paki," Emily sneered. "There's a bunch of them in the building. Maybe twenty. They leer. They leer and leer. At white girls. One of them in particular. Filthy bahstard! She being a new girl . . . What you bet I don't see that one anymore?"

"If you've got him identified, I bet you don't see him," said Beth. "The man beat him almost to death and was still beating him when the elevator doors closed."

"I'd like to know why," said Huang. "A Chinese man, you said. Why would he attack and beat—?"

"Took a look at him, is why," said Emily. "Every time I see one of those bahstards I wish I could break his face."

"Emily . . . I'd like to know why. People don't beat other people half to death without a reason. What's more, if he killed him he took the body away. Let me use your phone."

While Huang made a call, Emily pulled on her jeans and pronounced herself hungry. Beth agreed she was ready to go out to breakfast.

Huang put down the phone. "No report," he said. "No hospital's reported receiving a man seriously beaten. So where's the—can we call him victim?"

"*Here's* the victim," said Emily, nodding at Beth. "Meant to be, anyway. I *hope* the bahstard's dead."

Huang accompanied the two young women out to breakfast. They went to the coffee shop in the Sheraton Hotel, where Beth ordered bacon and eggs. Emily ordered eggs, too, but with kippers. Huang settled for a croissant and marmalade.

"Something else happened that I'd like to tell you about," said Beth. "Ilse took me in to meet Mr. Wu."

"Wu Kim Ming?" the detective asked.

"Yes. He was very polite, very kind. He did ask me to go to his hotel for the night, but when I said I wouldn't, he accepted that and went on being polite and kind."

"I've been to his suite in the Mandarin Oriental," said Emily. "If you go there, you'll learn a few things."

"And pick up more than a few dollars," said Huang wryly.

"Is he the owner of the Pearl Club?" Beth asked.

Huang and Emily exchanged glances.

"Beth . . ." Huang said quietly. "I told you a little about triads. Wu Kim Ming is the chief of the Hong Kong chapter of the Chung Yui Hui triad. The name means Association of Righteous Harmony, and it is one of the most powerful triads in Asia. Owner of the club? It's a front for him when he's in Hong Kong. His chief base is Taiwan. If you understood Chinese and heard him speak it, you would never take him for a native of Hong Kong. He speaks Mandarin. We here in Hong Kong speak Cantonese."

"Wu Kim Ming speaks a better language than that," said Emily with a little smile. "He's initiated me into five of the Nine Glorious Postures. I'm no virgin, of course, but— Wu's a . . . whatta you call? An *expert!*"

"A virtuoso," said Huang dryly.

"You are calling him a major criminal," said Beth to Huang.

"It's difficult to know what words to apply to a man like Wu," said Senior Inspector Huang. "He's not a criminal in the sense that Al Capone was. He's far too smart and subtle for that. Not in the sense that Richard Nixon was a major criminal. Nixon tried to subvert your democracy, but I would think murder was beyond him. It is not beyond Wu Kim Ming. Remember what I said about the ambivalence of the triads toward next year's handover. Like other Hong Kong citizens, the triads don't mind Hong Kong divorcing Britain, but many fear the forced marriage between a prosperous Hong Kong and a still-backward China. It's like an arranged marriage in the old days. The blind marriage could turn out to be great, or disastrous, for the bride, that is."

"*Something else,*" Beth whispered hoarsely, seizing Huang's hand. "Emily said this man—what's his name? Dai . . ."

"Dai Gul Dai," said Huang.

"Big Prick," said Emily.

"You said he worked for Mr. Wu! Does that mean it is possible that Mr. Wu has something to do with the kidnapping?"

Huang turned down the corners of his mouth. He had a special capacity for looking lugubrious, likely the product of his Chinese ancestry combined with his English education. "Dai Gul Dai is apparently a member of Chung Yui Hui, though we cannot know for certain who is and who is not a member, but he is what you might call a freelance hoodlum, sometimes involved in crimes that cannot be attributed to the triad."

"Mr. Wu seems like such a gentleman—and a *gentle man;* I am sure you know the difference."

Emily's kippers all but turned Beth's stomach. She had observed the breakfast before, in Barcelona where some of the British athletes ate the smoked and oily fish with their eggs, the way Americans ate bacon. She had reached a point where she avoided sitting at tables with them.

"The man who beat the Pakistani," said Huang. "Would you know him if you saw him again?"

Beth shook her head.

"Does it occur to you at all—to either of you—that it's an odd coincidence for a stranger to appear out of nowhere and attack a man who was assaulting you? We may be very glad he did, but isn't it curious? Not only that, he took care to remove the dead or injured Pakistani from the premises. And I think he was dead, too, since he didn't show up in hospital. You are assaulted by a stranger, a Pakistani you do not know; another stranger happens out of nowhere and kills the man, then disposes of him, dead or alive, so there's no police report of the whole incident. Just how, *damn it*, did that man happen to be there?"

"The Paki was there because he wanted a piece of ass," said Emily. "He wanted any he could get. Filthy bahstard."

"Maybe so. But what motivated the other man?" Huang insisted. "The Chinese are very practical people. They don't come to the help of strangers without a reason—or in any case, they don't go so far as to kill a man without a reason. I keep asking, *What was his reason?*"

"An' I keep telling you, Huang—Beth and I *don't know.*"

"Well . . . maybe the Chang family has put a bodyguard on you, Beth," said Huang.

"Would one of Mr. Chang's bodyguards *kill* a man? Would the family sanction that?" Beth asked.

"It's not inconceivable," said Huang. "The Changs would not actually order a man killed, but if the man ordered to protect you judged it necessary to kill a man to achieve the purpose—"

"Purpose," Beth interrupted. "What purpose? To protect me, do you really think? Or to keep an eye on me? They've got a lot of bodyguards. How can we be sure one of them isn't sitting at one of the tables not far from us, watching us talk, trying to listen? All this kind of thing is new to me. I don't know if I'm—"

"Advantaged or disadvantaged," Huang finished her sentence. "I will suggest to you, Beth, that you are immensely advantaged."

"You got a guardian angel, luv," said Emily.

"Maybe I need one," Beth said sadly.

2

AS BETH AND EMILY walked to the Pearl Club that evening, they kept glancing around, to see if they could identify a man following them. If in fact they were followed, they did not spot the man— which meant, Emily suggested, that he was probably an experienced tail who knew how to keep himself inconspicuous. Beth thought it would be easy for nearly any Chinese to remain inconspicuous in the midst of these teeming crowds.

Inside the club it might not be so easy. If the man did not sit down at a table and allow a hostess to join him, his incognito would fail. But they saw no one. They changed and went to work: Beth in her leotard and pantyhose, Emily in her microskirt and, tonight, a loose black halter.

After about an hour Ilse came to Beth and told her to take over one of the pricey private rooms situated along one side of the main clubroom. Actually the compartments were private only in that their walls subdued the raucous sounds from the stage and made it easier for men and women to talk; the top halves of the doors were glass, so the Mama-San or anyone else could look in any time. The room was furnished with two handsome leather-upholstered short couches—love seats—facing each other across a low marble-topped table. Light came from a small crystal chandelier in which bulbs burned at low wattage, casting a dim golden glow. Two distinctly Chinese watercolors hung on the wall: wading birds in a misty river scene with distant mountains in the background. A thin stick of incense burned in a vase on a round corner table.

"I'll give your regular tables to someone else. You wait on that room only. Stand just outside and be ready anytime one of the hostesses signals you," Ilse said.

"Okay," Beth said dubiously.

"One of the men recognized you and asked me to assign you to his room. I guess he'll tell all his friends tomorrow that he was served here by none other than Beth Connor. Don't worry about it. It's the same as working your tables. Same rules. No hanky-panky. I'll be keeping an eye on you. Also, I'm assigning Emily to the room, so you'll have a friend there."

Beth nodded. Before she went to the private room she paused to tug her leotard down on her hips so as not to show too much of her derriere. She walked toward the private room, where Emily was already seated beside a young Chinese man and a Chinese hostess was sitting beside a much older Chinese man.

Beth stopped. Through the glass in the door she could see the young man with Emily. He was John, Michael's brother!

For a moment she thought about going back to Ilse and saying she could not handle this. What was going on? Why was John here? Which of these men had asked for her as waitress? And why? But she stood her ground.

Conscious that she had been wearing a Versace catsuit when she met John and was now going to face him in a black leotard and dark sheer pantyhose that exposed not just her legs but a good part of her butt—was going to face him as a waitress at his beck and call—Beth opened the door and entered the private room.

"Miss Connor . . ."

"Mr. Chang."

"I apologize to you, and I owe you an explanation that I can't give now. The gentleman sitting opposite is Bo Yu Tang, who used to be a corps commander in the People's Liberation Army until he was cashiered, for reasons I can't go into now. He speaks almost no

English and becomes impatient when people converse and he can't understand."

John turned to the former general and spoke to him in Chinese. Beth understood just two words—"Beth" and "Connor."

Bo Yu Tang was as Chinese a man as she had ever seen—in *her* frame of reference, by her definition. He looked like a character out of *The Good Earth* or some other movie supposed to be set in decades-ago China, though he wore no queue and none of the clothes worn by those characters. His face was flat, dominated by his cheekbones and wide, thin mouth. She could only guess—and likely her guesses were wild—that he was a man whose origins were in a peasant village, where his family had labored on the soil for millennia, and had risen to prominence in a milieu where he *could* rise: the PLA. She had guessed of Shek Tin that he had once worn a Mao suit and detested it. She guessed of Bo Yu Tang that he had worn his as evidence of revolutionary fervor and had been proud of it.

He should not have been proud of the suit he was wearing now. It was gray, rumpled, and ill-fitting.

He might not like English, but he was going to hear some yet. "Where is Michael?" she demanded coldly of John.

"Michael is alive and well. He knows you're alive."

"Where *is* he?" Beth asked urgently.

"I can't tell you right now."

"This is no coincidence, John," she said, her eyes hard and glittering. "How did you know I am working here?"

"We can't talk about it now. Bo Yu Tang has a short fuse."

"Better take our order, luv," said Emily. "We'll have champagne, of course. But what Bo really likes, he's already told John, and John told me, is cognac."

Beth squatted to put her pad on the edge of the table and write the order.

"With some first-class cheese," said Emily. "And meats and fruits. And *shrumps*. Yes. I'm sure the general will want shrumps. With sauces."

Beth scribbled. "Fruit?" she asked.

"Later," said Emily. "With the tea."

Suddenly the chubby hand of Bo Yu Tang touched her hand and closed on it. He smiled and essayed a little English. "Not ever American girl."

Whether he meant he had never before met an American girl or had never before had sex with one, she could guess but didn't want to.

"We are very different from Chinese," she said. "Americans are very different."

He looked to John, and John translated.

"Say much things." .

"He means," John explained, "that he has heard all kinds of rumors about American women."

"Like what, John?" Beth asked coldly. "That we're easy lays? Tell him he'll be disappointed in that." She pulled her hand away and stood.

"Be careful, Miss Connor," said John. "He is potentially a very dangerous man."

The Chinese hostess that Ilse had sent to sit with Bo Yu Tang caressed his cheek and guided his hand to her breasts. He spoke sharply to her.

"He doesn't want her," John said to Beth. "He wants you to sit with him."

"I don't sit with men," Beth said with cold, angry emphasis. "I am a waitress, not a hostess." .

"You may be a lot of things you didn't expect if he insists on it. I warned you. He is a powerful and dangerous man, accustomed to having his way."

"Well, he's not going to have his way with me," said Beth as she left the room to carry the order to the bar.

While she was at the bar, Wu Kim Ming passed her on his way to the private room. She saw him step inside. Bo Yu Tang rose to shake his hand. They spoke cordially for a minute or two, then Wu left the room and came back. As he passed Beth this time, he smiled and nodded at her.

The champagne was ready first, and she carried the ice bucket and bottle into the room and put them down. Bo said something apparently addressed to her before she went back for the tray of glasses, and she pretended she had not noticed. When she entered the room again, he looked up at her and left no question but that he was speaking to her.

John translated.

"He saw you on television. That's why he's here tonight—because I told him we might be able to get you for his club companion. He is a blunt man, who wastes no words. He wants to know if you will go out with him tonight."

Beth suppressed a shudder. "Tell him I'm a waitress, not a hostess, and it's against the rules for me to go out with a customer."

Bo Yu Tang spoke again, and again John translated. "He says the rules of the club will be waived if he asks."

She made the reply she had been rehearsing in her mind in anticipation he would say something like that. "Then tell him he's interested in Beth Connor, not a whore, and tell him Beth Connor doesn't make a decision like that when she's just met a man. I would have to know him a good deal better before I could consider such an invitation."

"Well said," John commented dryly. Then he translated.

Bo spoke to John, and John translated to Beth. "I am sorry, but he asks— The Chinese words are maybe more polite. He wants to know if the hair on your *yü-men*, which means your jade gate, is the same color as the hair on your head."

Beth drew in an audible breath. "Tell him that's not the kind of question a gentleman asks a woman who is not a whore. Remind him I am not a whore and assume he doesn't want a whore."

John translated. Bo Yu Tang seemed to take the answer in good spirit—causing Beth to wonder if John had really told him what she had said. Then Bo grinned and spoke again. "He wants to know how much money you would accept for having sex with him tonight."

"Tell him to go to hell," said Beth curtly. She stood and left the room.

The brandy was ready on the bar. She carried a tray with bottle and snifters to the private room. She squatted by the table to serve the cognac.

"I didn't translate what you said," John told her. "I just told him you wouldn't do it for any price."

"That is correct," said Beth. "Not with him, not with any man—for any price."

Bo Yu Tang pointed at Beth's breasts and laughed as he said, "*Dai baw dai.*"

"He says you have beautiful breasts."

Emily shook her head. "He said you have big tits."

Bo went on laughing. "*Dai law dai!*"

"He's being insulting," said Emily. "Since you won't go out with him—"

"What'd he say?"

"He said you have a big butt."

Beth stood and opened the door. Bo spoke angrily; she could hear a threat in his voice, though she could not understand his words.

"Miss Connor!" John blurted, aghast. "He forbids you to leave! He says no . . . no—"

" 'Stinking cunt' is what he said," Emily explained. "Excuse me, but I've heard a lot of this kind of talk."

"He says no one walks out on *him,*" John finished his translation. "The situation has become hazardous, Miss Connor."

Emily poured cognac into Bo's snifter. "Here, luv," she said soothingly. "Have a little drink."

Bo Yu Tang glared at Beth. Then he spoke to John. His voice was firm but the fury had gone out of it.

"He says he will forgive your impudence if you will drink a glass of brandy with him."

"I—"

Beth meant to say that she could not, that it was against the rules of the club; but the anger in the private room had come to Ilse's attention—the Chinese hostess had been frantically signaling—and Ilse now stood in the doorway, blocking Beth's exit. She was capable of being a formidable figure.

"Bo wants Beth to drink with him," said Emily. "He's been very insulting—and vulgar, what's more. He wants her to go out with him. He wants her tonight."

"He's in a very bad mood," John said to Ilse, "and I don't suppose I need tell you that having Bo Yu Tang angry at this club is not promising for your future."

Ilse stared at Beth for a moment. "Have a drink with him," she said calmly. "Let's smooth over the situation."

Bo spoke, and John translated. "He wants Beth to sit down with him. Emily can go."

"No," said Beth. "He'll paw me."

Ilse spoke to Bo Yu Tang in halting Chinese. Then she explained to Beth. "I told him you are a special waitress—the Olympic athlete and all that—and simply are not available to go out."

Bo spoke to Ilse.

"Alright. But he wants you to drink with him, to tell him about America."

"I won't sit on the couch. I couldn't keep his hands off."

"Sit on the floor," said Ilse. "Let's try to make peace. I know what he is and how he talks. But—"

"I'll do it," said Beth, "for the sake of being able to get in a few questions for the little shit." She nodded at John.

"You know who *he* is?"

"An insufferable little liar is who he is."

Ilse flushed angrily. "Too damn much is at stake here for you to play saint. For god's sake, try to make peace!" She turned and left the room, closing the door behind her.

Beth sat down on the floor. Bo Yu Tang smiled benignly and poured a snifter full of brandy. He pushed it toward Beth, then placed beside it a yellow one-thousand-dollar note.

"What's this?"

"When you finish drinking that much cognac, the money is

yours," said Emily. "They play that game in these clubs. Getting a girl drunk makes her more—how do you say?"

"Compliant," said Beth. "Alright. We'll see."

For ten minutes Bo asked questions about America and heard John's translations of her answers. He asked the meaning of the names Boston Red Sox and Chicago White Sox—did they have political significance? He wanted to know how much a man earned by working in, say, an automobile factory. He asked if American men could purchase wives as Chinese men still could in some parts of rural China, albeit illegally—and if so, what prices did attractive girls fetch? Most of his questions, though, were sex-oriented. He wanted to know if many American women had breasts as big as Beth's, though now he used—as John explained—the polite term *hung* rather than the vulgar term *baw* that he had used before. He wanted to know if, as he had heard, all American women shaved their pubic hair and colored their pudenda with cosmetics. He asked for a serious affirmation that American women really did not, as a long-standing tradition, practice oral sex as a method of birth control.

Beth answered his questions. She drank the brandy in her snifter, then picked up the thousand-dollar note, and stuffed it in her cleavage.

Bo Yu Tang filled her snifter again and laid a second thousand-dollar note on the table.

Beth took one swallow from the second snifter and shook her head and pushed it away. There was a very fine line between euphoria and helplessness, and she felt herself approaching that line.

Bo Yu Tang spoke harshly to John. His mood had shifted again.

"The general says the game is over. He says you *will* come with him to his hotel *now*."

Beth looked into the man's angry face. "Go to hell," she said brusquely as she scrambled up from the floor and reached for the doorknob.

Bo Yu Tang lurched to his feet and lunged at her. He grabbed her leotard and ripped the top away, exposing her breasts.

That was a mistake. Beth Connor was an Olympic athlete, still in near-perfect physical condition. Last night she had broken the nose of the Pakistani who assaulted her, and now she broke the nose of the former Chinese general with a powerful left jab, and followed that with a looping right cross that caught him squarely on the jaw and knocked him sprawling over the table.

3

AN HOUR LATER BETH sat with Wu Kim Ming in the dining room of the Mandarin Oriental Hotel. She was dressed in her Versace catsuit. On the way from the club, Wu had ordered his driver to stop at her hostel, and two bodyguards had accompanied her as she went to the room she shared with Emily and changed her clothes.

"You must understand who Bo Yu Tang is. He was a career officer in the People's Liberation Army and rose to corps commander. A year or so ago he was forced to retire. He'd too often dipped his fingers in money that wasn't his. He's still influential just the same. He has powerful friends, some of them in the triads. It wouldn't be safe for you to go back to your room tonight. Bo doesn't want to kill you, but he wants to see your bottom bared and beaten bloody with a bamboo cane. I offer you once more the hospitality of my suite. I will place you in a room of your own and promise not to venture near it during the night—great though the temptation might be to do otherwise."

Beth stared into Wu Kim Ming's face. "I believe you are a man who keeps his word," she said simply.

"Tomorrow," he said, "we must find you another place to live. Bo will have men looking for you. I think you should not go to the club anymore."

"I must," she said simply.

"Because you hope to find a clue as to what has happened to your fiancé."

Beth sighed and nodded. "Mr. Wu, Qiao Qichen offered me two million dollars, American, if I would go home and forget Michael. I refused. He couldn't believe that love could be that powerful a motive and said I'd seen too many American movies. But . . . I can't go home without doing all I can—which may not be much—to help Michael. I simply can't."

"You are a very brave young woman—a foolish one, perhaps, but very brave."

"I have a terrible sense that I have entered a world I don't know and don't know how to handle."

Wu Kim Ming tapped the tablecloth with one finger. "Michael Chang's father is a rich and powerful man. Why can't *he* help his son?"

"I don't know. Apparently he can't. Michael has been held since Sunday."

"Why is he held?"

Beth spoke tearfully. "I know nothing about it, Mr. Wu—except that everybody lies to me and nobody seems ready to do anything."

"It is unfortunate that you made an enemy of Bo Yu Tang."

"Should I have submitted to his brutal demands?"

Wu patted her hand. "No, no. But you caused him not just pain but a terrible loss of face."

Beth dropped her chin to her chest and shook her head. "I seem only to have made things worse."

"You need help. I—"

She interrupted him. "I am told *you* are a powerful and influential man, Mr. Wu. Would you help me?"

"I hope you would understand that I have helped you already."

"I *do*. I do."

"Alright. I will make your problem mine, Miss Connor. I will see what I can do to help you."

EIGHT

*Here in Hong King . . . love is not unimportant
but does not solve all problems.*

1

CHANG WING HING STROLLED out onto the veranda where the
young American woman and the Senior Inspector had talked with
Qiao Qichen and Po Ji—John. He reached into a pocket of his
jacket and withdrew a crust of bread, which he crumbled into the
water of the fountain, for the goldfish. He put his hand in the water,
and three of the fish came to his hand. They allowed themselves to
be stroked like pet dogs or cats.

The weather was exceptionally warm; and, though the house
was air-conditioned, Chang preferred the open air of the terrace,
where the wind off the ocean blew through, faintly scented by the
odors of the sea. The terrace was one of his favorite places.

His youngest son, John, bowed to him. "Honored Father," he
said.

They spoke Chinese. "Good morning, Po Ji," the father said to
his youngest son. The name meant Protect Self. Michael was Po Ka,
Protect the Family. Frederick, the eldest brother, was Po Kuok, Protect the Nation.

Each of the sons had been educated at a Jesuit day school in
Kowloon, and each had been baptized with a Christian name that
they used when they spoke English.

The elder Chang had never been baptized, had not been so educated, and was not a Christian by the remotest stretch of imagi-

nation. He had long endured the arrogance of British Christians and had never cared to associate himself with their offensive mythology. He honored his ancestors and honored the gods, but he worshiped nothing, prayed to nothing, and expected nothing of "gods."

He was supremely pragmatic. He knew what was good. It was things you could touch and hold, not ephemera, not wisps of the imagination, unseen and never seen.

He would have preferred the British to stay on. He had learned to live with the insufferably stuffy, arrogant Brits and had prospered. But he had also accepted the reality of the Handover once the 1984 Sino-British Agreement was signed by then–Prime Minister Thatcher in Beijing. Initially Chang considered moving his entire family and business to Vancouver, as some of his wealthy friends did. Then he made trips to that wonderful city on the Canadian Pacific Coast, nicknamed "little Hong Kong" because of the influx of a quarter million new immigrants from the territory. Chang noticed a fair amount of resentment from the indigenous Caucasian Canadians against nouvelle riche Chinese like himself. The locals especially disliked the no-nonsense pragmatic attitudes of the Hong Kong immigrants who knocked on doors of houses or mansions they liked, asked for a price, and paid in cash without even bothering to bargain.

Chang saw a further downside of moving to Canada. Even though his wealthy friends lived in mansions and ate and shopped in sections of Vancouver that had turned into a mini–Hong Kong full of Cantonese restaurants and shops, his friends looked older, almost depressed, as if leaving the fast-moving Pearl of the Orient had drained them of their very essence, leaving them but empty shells. His friends were simply wealthy old men in retirement, living in anonymity, rather than in grand style like the captains of industry and finance they used to be. Chang had decided to stay put in Hong Kong and bet his and his family's future and fortune on co-existing with Beijing.

"Honored Father," muttered his eldest son, Frederick, who sat slumped weakly in a chair, drawn, looking older than his father, resigned to the inevitability of his approaching death.

"Po Kuok," said the father solemnly. "Today's pain . . . ?"

"It is endurable, Honored Father."

Chang's thought was that it was not endurable to *him*, but he said nothing of the kind, only nodded.

Michael's father was one of those Chinese men whose age Beth, among many others, could not have guessed. He was in fact sixty-two, but his hair was black, without a trace of gray, and his face was taut and unmarked by wrinkles. He had an air of courtliness, the bearing of a man who had met challenges and overcome them, the mien of an aristocrat who expected and received deference—all of this in a restrained way that invited acceptance and offered no offense.

Though the day was hot, he wore a white dress shirt and a dark-blue dotted necktie, a blue blazer, and gray trousers—in contrast to his sons who wore Izod knit shirts and khaki slacks.

Chang was the father of three sons—that is, three *legitimate* sons—and one legitimate daughter. His daughter, Chang Mei Ling, educated by Maryknoll nuns and known also by the English name Cheryl, was there on the terrace. Her husband, Tsao P'ing, was a chartered accountant, and they were the parents of two sons and two daughters. Mei Ling was Westernized, as the family believed. She was wearing tennis whites, showing her legs as only she and Anne ever did in the house, and had in fact played tennis earlier. She was tall and was widely regarded as a beauty.

Liu Soong Qin—Anne—sat beside her frail husband and held his hand. Her glossy black bangs reached almost to her eyebrows, and her dark-red lipstick made her mouth a sharp slash across her face.

Qiao Qichen was there, too.

Po Ji—John—spoke. "After the unfortunate incident at the Pearl Club last night, Beth Connor was taken from the club by Wu Kim Ming. She did not return, either to the club or to her quarters, before dawn. He dined her like a princess at the Mandarin Oriental Hotel, after which they left the dining room, and I think we must imagine he took her to his suite. The girl is no fool. In a very short time she has formed a powerful alliance."

"And foolishly made a powerful enemy," said Qiao.

"This girl," said John, "must be brought under control."

"I gather from all I've heard," said Chang, "that she may be a fool but is a strong and determined personality. And . . . there does seem to be a potent relationship between her and my middle son—in the American romantic idiom."

"He has been allowed to spend too much time in America," Anne said censoriously.

Chang cast a hard glance on his daughter-in-law, to remind her that she was privileged to be here but was not expected to express her opinions on matters of family business. "However the case may be," he said sternly, dogmatizing now as head of the family, "she must not be allowed to continue working in a Kowloon nightclub. As my youngest son describes it, she is on display in immodest costume and carries food and drink to tables as a servant. However little we may wish it, this young woman has formed an attachment to Michael and likely will be associated with our family in the future. It is unacceptable that she should be a nightclub girl."

"How will we establish influence over her?" asked Qiao. "I have spoken with her, as you know. She is self-willed, in the extreme."

"Contact Senior Inspector Huang," said Chang. "Tell him she must come here if she expects to help Po Ka."

2

BETH WAS AWAKENED BY a gentle knock on her bedroom door. Wu had been true to his word: it was morning, the sun was shining through the windows, and he had not come to visit her during the night.

"Who is it?" she asked.

A small, female voice—"Mister Huang is here to see you, miss."

Huang? How . . . ? "Tell him I'll be out in a minute."

She dressed as quickly as she could, taking no time to brush her hair or apply any makeup. She came from the bedroom into the big living room of the suite and found Mark Huang sitting there with Mr. Wu. They were engaged in a solemn conversation.

Both men stood.

"Beth . . ." said Huang quietly. "It's Emily."

"*Emily!* My God, what—"

"She is alive. And she is going to survive. But she was severely beaten last night. She is in hospital, sedated. She'll be alright, in time. She's in shock. She's badly hurt, but she's not injured."

Beth felt herself go rigid, felt the skin of her face burning. "What do you mean?" she whispered.

"She was whipped," said Wu. "With a bamboo cane probably."

"The flesh of her buttocks was cut deeply, and she bled heavily," said Huang. "The pain . . . I can't imagine it."

"It was meant for me," Beth said somberly, settling weakly onto a couch.

"Yes. I'm sure it was," said Huang. "She was seized just outside the door of her hostel room. Almost certainly the thugs who did it were in the hire of General Bo. He would not have had a personal part in it, and his thugs must have mistaken Emily for you."

Beth covered her face with both hands and wept.

"She's asked to see you. She wants me to bring you to the hospital."

Beth nodded and rose from the couch.

"You are under my personal protection, Miss Connor," said Wu gravely. "I will extend that word to everyone. At least two of my men will be within sight of you at all times—for a few days at least. And you may tell Emily that she will be paid until she can return to the club. What is more, the expenses for her care will be paid."

The first chance Beth had to speak privately with Huang came after they were in his blue Toyota. Two dark-visaged men had accompanied her and Huang down in the hotel elevator, through the garage, and to the car. They followed now, in a black Honda.

"Paid . . ." she said bitterly, derisively.

"It would occur to a Chinese, Beth," he said. "We are a highly practical people. Wu is sympathetic, of course, but his sympathy extends to the practical: doing something to be sure Emily is taken care of financially while she recovers."

"She is *going* to recover. You promise me?"

He nodded emphatically. "She was beaten in the cellar of the building. They made no effort to gag her, and her screams woke half the building. Uniformed police were there within five minutes."

"Five minutes . . . ?"

"In five minutes the bullies whipped her and escaped. When the police arrived she was on her hands and knees on the cellar floor, shrieking and moaning. Five or ten minutes after that she was in Queen Elizabeth Hospital, being attended to by doctors and nurses. She was tortured, Beth. There is no other word for it. She is still in severe pain. But she will survive."

"Take me to her, Mark," said Beth.

3

EMILY LAY ON HER stomach, her head resting on her arm and a pillow. A frame of some sort supported the sheet so that even that light fabric would not touch her injured fundament. When Beth came to her bedside, Emily was weeping softly.

Beth touched her hand.

Emily looked up. Her eyes and cheeks were wet with tears. "It doesn't hurt so much now," she said in a low voice, just above a whisper. "They've got me sedated. When it wears off—" She shook her head.

"It was meant for me," Beth said quietly.

"Yes. I know it was. But don't think it's your fault. It's not, not in any way."

"Mr. Wu said to tell you that your pay will continue until you can go back to work, and your medical bills will be paid."

"I won't be going back, luv. I'll be going home now. Everybody who ever talked sense to me told me what I was doing was dangerous."

"You could probably have gone on for the one more year you wanted, with nothing like this—except for me. I'm so damned sorry, Emily!" Beth sobbed. "You won't have all the money you wanted."

"Maybe . . . maybe Mr. Wu—"

"Yes. He's provided bodyguards for me. Maybe he'll help you, maybe change your circumstances."

"I'm going to have a funny-looking arse," Emily said sardonically. "Some men will like that. Perverts. Beth . . . they bent me over a barrel. One man held my arms, another man my legs. The third man pulled my knickers down and went to work on my bum with a birch. Wasn't it Singapore where the American lad got three strokes? Well, I got twenty. Maybe more. I'll have scars back there for the rest of my life. It'll be weeks before I can sit on it."

4

AT TWO THAT AFTERNOON Beth arrived by taxi at the gate of the Chang mansion—the taxi closely followed by the black Honda. With grim pleasure in the irony of it, she had used Bo's thousand-dollar note—plus part of the five hundred American dollars from the consulate—to buy a loose cream-white linen jacket and a pair of matching stirrup leggings. She had used up nearly all the money she had, but she was determined to appear before the Changs as something besides a supplicant and something other than a waitress.

She came alone. She and Mark Huang had agreed it would be

better if he did not accompany her this time. They had agreed also that if he did not hear from her by six o'clock he could take it that she did not remain in the compound willingly.

The turbaned guard opened the gate immediately, and John hurried out to meet her.

"Last night I didn't have the opportunity to expand on my apology," he said as they walked toward the house. "You see . . . I *couldn't* talk to you truthfully in the presence of Senior Inspector Huang. Not that day, anyway. Miss Connor, Michael's safety depended, and still may depend, on the police not knowing—"

"I am beginning to understand these things," she interrupted.

"We know that Michael loves you. We know you love him. You must understand, Miss Connor, that here in Hong Kong, among us, love is not unimportant but does not solve all problems."

They did not this time go to the veranda but entered the grand house through the main entrance. Inside, they were in a great two-story entry hall. All was stone: the floor, the walls, and the curving stairways that ascended on each side. In spite of the multicolored light afforded by sunshine coming through the prismatic leaded-glass windows to both sides of the doors, the hall was cold and gloomy—or would have been except for the presence of a magnificent jade castle that stood on a heavy mahogany table, lighted by subtly concealed lamps that cast a gentle glow on it. The castle was five feet tall, elaborately carved and ornamented, of dark-green, not milk-green, jade. Michael had given Beth a little education in jade, and she realized this was the finest, the most expensive, and made the castle an object worth tens of millions of American dollars.

John led her to the right and up one of the curving stairways. Incongruously, two big niches on the stairway displayed Renaissance suits of armor. In the second-floor hall, seventeenth-century pistols shared display-case space with a medieval chastity belt. Crossed halberds hung on the wall.

They entered a sitting room on the second floor. Here, too, style clashed with style, as if someone had obsessively sought for eclecticism. The floors were parquet, the walls were of plaster molded in flowery patterns, the woodwork was elaborately carved, a Persian carpet lay on the floor, gilt-framed mirrors hung on all sides, and the furniture was a mixture of Louis XIV, Louis XV, and Empire styles. Here, in this English Edwardian house, was a French sitting room, a salon, as it were.

The Changs formally received her now: Chang Wing Hing, the head of the family; Chang Po Kuok, Frederick, the ailing eldest son; and the *consigliere*, Qiao Qichen, whom Michael had nicknamed Tom.

Chang Wing Hing extended both his hands and received hers in a gentle, warm clasp. "I am most pleased to meet you, Miss Connor," he said. "I believe my middle son has committed his affections to you—which I can well understand now that I see you. I hope you understand I could not accept this until . . . it was confirmed."

"Michael has confirmed it?" she asked.

Chang drew a breath, then nodded. "Yes. He is alive and well. I hope I may anticipate your cooperation in doing whatever we must to gain his release."

"It's the only reason I'm here, sir. I would even—" She stopped and stared for a moment at Qiao. "—go back to the States without seeing him if that would save Michael's life."

Chang nodded gravely. "Then we are in concert," he said. "Please, Miss Connor, sit down and allow us to serve you some refreshment. Tea? American—well, that is, Scots—whisky?"

Beth smiled. "Being Boston Irish," she said, "I'll drink a tot of whisky with you, if you'll join me."

Chang nodded at John, who went to a cabinet that concealed a bar.

She decided she was favorably impressed with Michael's father. He opposed their marriage and *would* oppose it, but she believed she could understand why, and she believed she could win him over, given time and Michael's assistance.

The eldest brother, Frederick, was a surprise. Michael had described him as big and strong—formidable, in fact. The man who sat before her was a wraith. If . . . Abruptly she experienced a striking insight. If the eldest brother, the heir apparent, were what he looked as though he might be—a dying man—then *Michael* would become the heir apparent! And that would change many things.

"Miss Connor," said Qiao, "we hear that your new friend Emily Parker was attacked last night and severely injured."

"I am beginning to think Hong King is not a very safe place," she said. "I arrived here on Sunday and was kidnapped. Early yesterday morning, a man attempted to rape me. Early this morning Emily was attacked and viciously beaten. The beating was meant for me. Senior Inspector Huang believes it was arranged by your friend"— she nodded at John—"Bo Yu Tang."

"I warned you," said John as he poured drinks. "I told you the man is dangerous. He has a gross but sensitive ego, and everyone is laughing at him: the big one-time general who got his nose broken by a *kwai-pau*, a foreign woman."

"I don't give a damn about his nose," said Beth. "Emily is badly hurt. I visited her at the hospital this morning. She will carry scars for the rest of her life: on the part of her body where she was whipped and . . . psychologically."

"We grieve to hear of it," said Chang solemnly. "But, you say *you* were attacked? Someone attempted to rape you?"

"Yes. A Pakistani."

"But you escaped?"

She sighed audibly. "A man came out of the shadows and attacked the man who wanted to rape me. He kicked him repeatedly. I think he killed him."

"You cannot continue to live in Miss Parker's room in the hostel," said Qiao. "Bo Yu Tang will discover that his thugs beat the wrong young woman, and he will send them to find you. Wednesday you declined an offer of an apartment here, for reasons that I suppose were good enough for you. But now . . . you need protection."

"It would appear that I have it," she said crisply. She accepted a glass from John. "It is no coincidence that a man beat my would-be rapist. I suspect it was no coincidence that I was not at the hostel this morning."

"You refer to Wu Kim Ming," said Qiao. "Are you aware of who he is?"

"I've been told."

Chang Wing Hing sipped whisky. "Miss Connor," he said in a voice that was soft yet firm, "it seems your name and the name of the Chang family are about to be inextricably intermixed. Po Ka—Michael—when you see him, will explain to you why marriage is out of the question. I know you will not accept that from me, but I believe you will accept it from him. You impress me as a fine young woman. I endorse my son's judgment. I *want* you to be associated with us. But marriage . . . well . . . with us it does not make so much difference. If it is my son's wish, the family will honor and support you—and love you—even if you are not his official wife."

"With due respect, Mr. Chang, I have every intention of marrying Michael and becoming your daughter-in-law."

"What's in a name? We Chinese are practical. We just want effective possession, what you call day . . . fact . . ." Chang Wing Hing looked in Qiao's direction.

"De facto," Qiao answered.

"We want de facto control and let others have the empty title if they wish. Take Hong Kong for example. It has been a British colony for over a century. Next July it will once again be part of China. In point of fact China already runs this place in everything but name. American government makes big hue and cry about democracy, as if the British had given us democracy that Beijing would take away. So how does the Chinese government handle this awkward situation? They invented 'one country, two systems' for Hong Kong. Yes, Hong Kong will be reunited with China. But she will have her own laws. Take a lesson from this. Michael shall have in the future, shall we say, 'one family, two households.' You can have Michael every night except for the few occasions when he must sire Chinese grandchildren for us and when he must appear with his Chinese wife on formal occasions. The rest of the time he's all yours."

"Even if I were to agree to such a torturous scheme, I have every confidence Michael would object," Beth said with pride.

"Let us put that question aside for now. May we?"

Beth hesitated for a moment, held back the words she wanted to speak, and nodded.

"Very well," said Chang. "So. Marriage or not, you seem about to become a Chang: I mean a member of our extended family. It is inappropriate, then, for you to work as a waitress in a Kowloon club. Ours is an old and honored name, Miss Connor. We cannot have it associated with . . . that."

"Besides which, it is dangerous," said Qiao. "Michael was kidnapped for a reason. Those who kidnapped him may have decided it is now worth their while to kidnap *you*. And Bo Yu Tang is determined to have his revenge on you."

"Is he a threat to Michael?" Beth asked.

Chang Wing Hing closed his eyes and shook his head. "No," he said quietly.

"When is anyone going to tell me why Michael was kidnapped and why he has been held so long?"

"Miss Connor . . ." said Chang patiently and still in a quiet voice, "it is a matter of *business*. Michael will explain. In time. For now, you must trust us. Believe me, Miss Connor, we know what we are doing."

"And I don't," she said, resigned.

"We want you to accept a suite in this house," said Chang. "You will have every comfort. You will have a car and driver at your disposal. We will bestow on you an allowance of money, so you may buy such things as were lost when your luggage was lost. We—"

"You are kind and generous, Mr. Chang," she said, "but if I accept your hospitality I will become . . . how shall I say? I will become your *client*. I—"

"You fear you will lose your independence. And you want to retain your independence because you do not entirely trust us."

Beth smiled and shook her head. "Oh, let's try to put it some other way, Sir."

"Alright. Instead, I offer you an apartment of your own, in a central location. You will have money, so you can buy what you need, eat in restaurants, and ride in taxis and go wherever you wish. You will have a cellular phone. And your friend—when she is released from hospital, she can come and live with you. The apartment has two bedrooms. I do not deceive you, Miss Connor. I will know where you are, what you are doing, and whom you are seeing, generally. Unless you make a huge mistake, we will not interfere."

Beth realized she was running out of options. She nodded. "Very well. Thank you, Mr. Chang."

"Before you leave," he said, "I want to introduce you to someone you should know. My wife, the mother of my two younger sons. Po Ji, will you go and bring her?"

John left, was gone only a minute or so, and returned with a woman who obviously had been waiting in a nearby room.

Chang rose, took her hand, and presented her to Beth. "Her name is So Liming. She speaks no English."

The diminutive, sweetly pretty woman impressed Beth as too small and too young to be Michael's mother. Her dark almond eyes gazed up at Beth's face with honest curiosity. It was plain that she was surprised—perhaps not dismayed but certainly surprised—that her son could be smitten by this tall, muscular, blond American girl. She smiled and spoke to Chang.

"She says she is pleased to meet you."

The woman's smile had been formal when she said she was pleased to meet Beth. Now it danced and became genuine and faintly mischievous. She spoke again, and Chang translated—

"She says that if you are going to live here and be a consort to our son, you must learn to speak Chinese."

"I will," Beth said simply.

So Liming extended both hands, and Beth clasped them in hers. She smiled, but she was intently studying her son's young woman.

5

THE PART OF HONG Kong Island called Mid Levels, which was above the waterfront area known as Central and below The Peak, demonstrated the mountainous character of Hong Kong. The streets were as steep as the streets of San Francisco, many of them joined by long flights of stone-paved steps. At one point an outdoor public escalator carried people up and down the toilsome slope.

The apartment that Michael's father provided for Beth, located on the twenty-third floor of a forty-four-story building on Arbuthnot Road, was spacious, handsomely furnished, and comfortable. Beth had all she had been promised: a generous allowance of money in cash and a cellular phone. As soon as she was alone, she called Senior Inspector Huang. He came at six o'clock.

"Very interesting," he said. He leaned close to her and whispered in her ear. "But understand, dear Beth, you are not much more independent here than you would have been in the mansion on The Peak. The Changs own this building. Everyone who works here works for them. If they decide to lock you in and cut off your telephone service, they can do it. And you can be sure that every call you make on that cellular phone is monitored. The place may be bugged. They may be listening to what we say. We will go out to dinner. We can talk over a restaurant table."

6

CHANG WING HING'S ROLLS-ROYCE with the number 8 license plate stopped in front his building on Arbuthnot Road. But he had not come to visit Beth. The apartment he was visiting was on the top floor. The top three floors of the building on Arbuthnot Road could be reached only by a special private elevator not accessible to the others who lived in the building. That elevator could be entered only from the parking garage next door, and only by those who had special keys.

The penthouse was occupied by two women: a pretty teenage girl named Xiu Ling, which meant Little Bell, and her thirty-three-year-old mother. This day—the day when Beth moved into the apartment on the twenty-third floor—was Xiu Ling's birthday. Today she was sixteen years old.

On this day a man could, with her consent, deflower her without risk of being charged with a crime. For nearly four years now she had lived here with her mother, in the understanding that she belonged to the man who owned the apartment and that when she was sixteen she would begin to *zuo ai*—make love—with him. Xiu Ling had been looking forward to this. She would happily have been deflowered when she was twelve, by such a man as the one who was her benefactor.

In the meantime he had satisfied himself with stripping her, kissing and caressing her, then relieving himself with her handsome and compliant mother. Listening to her mother talk about what man and woman do in *fang si*, she had learned how to please the benefactor.

She *would* please him. She was determined to please him. At long last she was old enough. Tonight she would fulfill her destiny and experience the first of ten thousand happy nights.

Her father was a sixty-year-old tailor who lived and worked in a third-floor shop on Cochrane Road. The crowds riding up and down the Central–Mid Levels Escalator passed so close to the windows that they could and often did stare into the workshop and flat. Xiu Ling's mother was not her father's wife, and he had not welcomed the child—another mouth to feed. The girl had grown up knowing she was resented by her father, by her father's wife, and by her father's older children. She did not understand how such things worked, but she understood that her father and her benefactor had been brought together by a woman who brokered such arrangements and that her benefactor had paid her father a great deal of money to buy her.

Nothing finer could possibly have happened to her. She moved from a squalid, crowded flat where strangers stared in, to this beautiful apartment. Eating as her benefactor made it possible for her to do, she had filled out and was—as she knew from glances on the street—a sensual beauty. He had seen to it also that she learned to read and write, which her mother could hardly do and her father could not do at all. He had brought books for her to read, so she knew something of the world.

This afternoon she and her mother had exchanged bedrooms. Xiu Ling had moved into the larger bedroom with the great bed, and her mother had moved into the smaller room with the narrower bed where the girl had slept until now. It was understood between them that from today her mother was Xiu Ling's housekeeper. Her mother had been kind to her, so she would treat her mother kindly.

The benefactor would come at seven—probably bringing gifts. Xiu Ling began at six to bathe and perfume herself, to brush her hair, to apply makeup, to dress in a red-and-blue silk minidress.

He was prompt as always. Though he had a key, he always courteously rang the bell. Xiu Ling nodded. Her mother—dressed in a short black skirt and white blouse—opened the door and bowed deeply to their benefactor.

He returned her bow with a shallow nod and handed her the packages containing his presents, which included a red packet containing a check for ten thousand U.S. dollars to the mother for her years of loyal service in and out of bed. Then he walked across the floor to the girl and embraced and kissed her. Chang Wing Hing had waited patiently for Xiu Ling to grow up, and tonight his patience would be rewarded.

7

CHANG PO KUOK—FREDERICK—slept. He slept more and more lately. His wife Anne stood by his bedside and stroked his forehead.

She wiped tears from her eyes with one long, slender index finger and wiped the tears onto his lips.

It was his own doing. Damn you, Frederick! We were to have been royalty. Except for your neuropathological cruising of the stews of every city you ever visited, we would have inherited it all. Everything would have been ours. And you threw it all away, for nothing better than mindless indulgence of the nerve ends in the tip of your cock! We are brought down by something that cannot be seen even under the lenses of a microscope! You were to have been king of the Chang family, and I was to have been queen—and now the best that remains for me is to be dowager queen at the sufferance of one of your younger brothers.

It is not fair, Frederick! What did you say to me once?—that my time in Canada and the States had left me fixated on the Western concept of *fair?* Well, it does mean something. This is not *fair!*

"Let us save him, Princess."

She turned. She bowed deeply. "Yes, Master," she said.

He was Lung, the *qi gong* master, nicknamed Dragon. Though she remained coolly skeptical, with her own eyes she had seen him turn Cointreau into simple orange juice without a trace of alcohol. He had discovered a tumor on a friend's neck and had excised it by touching it with the tips of his fingers.

Dragon was her own age—in his mid-thirties. He was a wide and solid man who cultivated, unsuccessfully, an appearance of asceticism. His pitted face was too broad and coarse, his hair too unruly, his body too beefy to project an air of fervency or piety. He glistened with sweat, and his ornate white shirt, worn with the tail out, was damp and limp. He sat down beside the bed and crossed his legs, then went into his exercise of deep breathing.

Anne, too, sat down, closed her eyes, and began to draw deep breaths.

Soon Dragon began to tremble. And to sweat—now it streamed from him, redolent. He rocked from the waist and moaned. Finally he spoke—

"The honored father has favored the *kwai-pau*. This augurs ill."

"There was nothing I could do about it," Anne said quietly. "Anyway, he does not favor her. He favors Michael."

"At least we now know where she is, where she may be found."

Anne sighed. "In a secure building where the honored father houses his favorite concubine and several servants."

"Building security will not hinder the man you employed. Besides, she has to go out sometime."

"On the street?"

"In a restaurant. Anywhere. But, if you are right, which I am sure you are, she enjoys favor only through the honored father's affection for his middle son. Now, if Michael—"

"My man dares not move against Michael Chang so long as his leader has use for him. My man would not dare defy the leader of Chung Yui Hui," Anne said.

"Then—?"

"The *kwai-pau*," said Anne grimly. "*You* must carry the message. You must speak with my man. I will tell you how to find him. You must tell him where she is."

"I am your servant, Princess," Dragon said humbly.

Anne's eyes hardened. "Use your powers in my service, Master—or learn the fate of an ineffective servant."

8

CHANG WING HING LED Xiu Ling out of the bridal chamber, back to the living room, after about two hours. She was radiantly beautiful, glowing with youth and happiness. He could have asked nothing more of her than what she had given.

It was unfortunate, actually—and the only unfortunate thing about their evening—that she was as old as sixteen. She would gladly have done all she had done tonight, three or four years ago.

But there were new laws, and puritanical new ideas prevailed in the world. The benefit to a man of relations with very young females was denied, on the outrageous notion that they were harmful to the girls. The contrary was demonstrably true. To enjoy *shang chuang* with a girl-child gave a man long life and good health. And the girls did not fare badly, either. His father had taken one of his concubines when she was twelve; he, Chang Joi Hing, had lived to be ninety-one. The girl was still alive, a woman in her sixties now, supported by the family and living in a comfortable flat overlooking Repulse Bay.

Chang wondered how things would change after next year's Handover, whether Beijing would impose its puritanical and hypocritical moral codes on the loose and fast lifestyles of people living in Hong Kong. Mao Tse-tung's doctor wrote in a biography that Mao had hundreds of pretty party cadets serve his voracious sexual appetites, and he passed on venereal diseases to these unsuspecting party faithfuls. It's the old Chinese saying, Chang mused: "The emperor can burn down a city, but a peasant cannot light a candle." Mao could be as promiscuous as he wanted, but everyone else must toe the line.

Chang knew how careful he had to be whenever he traveled to China for business. His host invariably insisted on supplying him with beautiful young women for the evening. Chang could not refuse and make his host lose face, yet he heard of stories where overseas Chinese were lured into traps and had policemen barge into a hotel room in the middle of the night when a poor sleepy fellow still had a young naked girl in his bed. Chang always took the precaution of staying in a hotel suite with a connecting door to the next room, where a trusted aide would be registered. In an emergency he could exchange places with his aide through the connecting door and his aide would face the police and accept the consequences.

He himself had in fact taken his own favorite, So Liming, the mother of Michael and John, to bed when she was thirteen. When the mother of Frederick died, he had astonished everyone by marrying that little girl. When she was seventeen she bore him his second son, and when she was nineteen she bore him his third. He had no doubt that his continuing rigor at middle age came from her. For him, sleeping with young women was as much good medicine as it was good sex.

NINE

. . . Weighted down. He'll be eaten.
No trace of him will ever show up.

1

SINCE HE HAD GIVEN up his watch, Michael knew the time of day only by the sun and by the meals brought to him. His place of imprisonment remained the same, but the conditions were very different. They had never returned his clothes after they unchained him and let him climb out of the tub. For three days now he had been naked. What was more, they had left the leg irons on his ankles, so he hobbled around in shackles. Apart from that, nothing had changed. He occupied the same rooms, was fed the same kind of meals, and had to endure the constant television-viewing of his guards.

One more thing was different. The man he had hit on the head with the wine bottle was Dai Gul Dai's younger brother, called Big Mouth. Now a personal enemy, Big Mouth glowered at Michael, muttered, and threatened. At least once every hour, he growled, *"Dew neh loh moh,"* which meant "Fuck your old woman"—"Fuck your mother." It was the most grossly vulgar expression the brutish, semiliterate man could think of.

"My brother," Dai Gul Dai told Michael, "has asked for the privilege of disposing of you when we are finished with you. I am not sure I can honor him that way. Unfortunately, we will probably have to return you with your hide and parts intact."

Michael looked up from the couch where he sat enduring another day—this was Friday—of boredom and apprehension. "As the supreme leader of Chung Yui Hui requires," he said coldly.

"Chung Yui Hui? How come you to use that name? What do you know of Chung Yui Hui?"

"I know that if you disobey any element of your orders they will cut off that overgrown appendage that gives you your name."

"You should be careful how you talk, Mikego Chang. It is true that I perform some services for Chung Yui Hui, but I am not its servant."

"Any man who performs services for a Taiwanese black gang is its servant."

"You think you know a great deal. Let me tell you something you do not know. Do you know where your fat whore—the one of the enormous tits—is?"

Michael shook his head. He could not trust his voice.

"In hospital," said Dai Gul Dai with an evil smile. "It seems she so much offended a very important man that he had her caned. I hear that her *dai law dai*"—her big behind—"is an ugly sight to see, all black and red."

Michael shook his head. "I don't believe it," he muttered. His voice trembled. "I—"

"She offended an important general of the PLA, a corps commander. She struck him with her fist and broke his nose. Later that night—early this morning, actually—she was punished as naughty English schoolboys are punished for their offenses, by twenty strokes of a cane across her bare *law*."

"I don't believe it." Michael moaned.

"Why not? You know very well that your *kwai-pau* is no tender flower. She is a big girl, an athlete. They say she struck the general twice and not only broke his nose but knocked him over a table. One strong enough to swim away from our boat as she did is strong enough to knock down a late-middle-aged general."

"Dai Gul Dai, if you are lying to me, somehow, some way I will kill you."

Dai Gul Dai grinned. "I don't think I'll worry myself much over that threat," he laughed.

2

DRAGON HAD NOT BECOME a respected *qi gong* master through Anne's sponsorship. He had been that long before she ever met him, long before she entreated him to save the life of Frederick Chang. He had been honored and deferred to long before—since, as a teenage boy, he had avoided punishment for stealing fruit from his master's cabinet by demonstrating that he could take the limes and oranges from behind its latched doors without opening them, by an exercise of will. He had never revealed the secret—that he had hidden limes and oranges in his sleeves and rolled them out when everyone was staring at the cabinet doors—and made good use of his repute as a worker of little miracles, to small profit at first, later to immense profit.

He was a peasant, born in a village in Hainan Province to a family so poor that he had gone about naked until he was nine years old. He had watched in tears as his father sold two of his sisters for money to buy rice. He was literate only by the chance that the village schoolmaster had seen the half-starved yet pretty little boy playing naked in the dust and had taken him from his parents and had taught him to read and write. Besides being the only teacher in the village, the man had been its *qi gong* master as well—and a notorious, aggressive pederast. In exchange for enduring the most racking—but later exquisite—pain in his anus, the boy had become the first-ever literate member of his family. He had learned a few things besides: something of the wisdom of the sages, something of his country's geography and history, the rudiments of arithmetic—and a body of knowledge far more important to him.

The pederast was a charismatic and a smoothly clever flimflam artist. He had to be to survive. By tricks of magic and miracle cures he won for himself the grudging awe that was his protection. From the first, sometimes barely able to sit because of the pain in his anus, Dragon had watched his master's dodges. The old man had taught Dragon nothing of this sort but did not discourage the boy from learning on his own. He never acknowledged that his apprentice, as he might have been called, was cleverer than he was; he admired him and did nothing to hold him back. And he did not try to hold him back when at age sixteen Dragon left the village to try his own hand at whatever scams he could invent.

In the West, Dragon would have been a magician, a sleight-of-hand artist, a key bender, maybe even a faith healer. In China he was a *qi gong* master.

He made his way in time to Guangzhou and then across the border to Hong Kong.

Anne, on the other hand, was a beautiful but strong-willed and difficult woman who knew how to use money and power. She had a Western education and scorned everything that could not be proved by sight, hearing, taste, smell, or touch. But she was ruled by powerful emotions that overwhelmed her intellectualism. She was genuinely in love with her husband—more accurately, perhaps, genuinely in love with the wealth and power he represented. She was unable to accept the fact of his approaching death.

Her intellect told her that Dragon was a fraud. Her passions overruled her mind and told her to seek a miracle.

She had friends who knew of Dragon, one who knew him personally. She sought him out where he lived, in a flat in Mong Kok. Immediately she fell under the influence of his charismatic personality.

Theirs was a strange relationship. Although she called him Master and believed he had supernatural powers, she made it clear to him that he was her servant. There was never any question about that. She paid him; ergo he was her servant.

Following his instructions, he met the man with the scarred face on the Star Ferry. He recognized him readily enough.

"My honored mistress has information for you," he said to Dai Gul Dai.

"Why doesn't she meet me herself?"

"I don't ask questions," said Dragon.

"What is the information?"

"The *kwai-pau* has been taken under the protection of Michael's father, Chang Wing Hing. She is living in a flat on Arbuthnot Road."

Dai Gul Dai grinned. "Tell your mistress her information is faulty. The *kwai-pau* is in Queen Elizabeth Hospital, recovering from a caning she received early this morning."

"No," said Dragon. "She came to the mansion. Today. I saw her. She is living where I told you. My mistress warns you that Chang Wing Hing has probably set bodyguards over her."

"Then who is in hospital?"

"I don't know. The one who came to the house, the one who is living in the flat on Arbuthnot Road is Michael's *kwai-pau*. My mistress says you will know what to do."

Dai Gul Dai shook his head. "I had assigned a man to do it tonight, at Queen Elizabeth Hospital. Tell your mistress I am grateful for the information."

3

BETH STOOD BY THE bed, stroking Emily's hair and cheek, murmuring words she hoped Emily understood. Mark Huang hovered a little distance away, watching and frowning.

Perhaps the sedative was the origin of Emily's speech; in any case she had lapsed into an East London argot she had probably heard and spoken years ago. "Hit's all swoled up," she said. "The doctor said so. All swoled up, twice the soize of itself. The 'urt's very different. It *ikes* now. That's wot it does; it ikes. Oh, Bef! Oh, god!"

Beth bent closer and spoke in her ear. "The doctor told us this would be your worst night. This is the worst. After tonight you'll begin to feel better. Gradually."

"Tell 'em to give me another shot. Oi got to slipe. Oi cahn't stand no more. Oi got . . . to slipe."

Beth was sorry this visit had awakened her. "We'll tell them, Emily," she whispered. "And we'll be back in the morning."

Emily was asleep before they left the room.

An hour later she was still fitfully asleep. When she drifted awake for an occasional moment and felt the dreadful ache in her fundament, she whimpered and soon slipped away again. She was not even aware of the fact that she had urinated and lay on a wet sheet. The nurses hadn't discovered it yet, either.

A man in the khaki uniform of the Hong Kong police stopped at the nurses' station. He chatted with the two night nurses on duty for a moment, commiserating with two fellow unfortunates who had to work at such hours. He told them that Senior Inspector Huang had sent him to check in on Emily Parker, so he could report to the Senior Inspector. The nurses shrugged. Pitiful case, they said.

They gave him the room number, and he ambled casually along the hall and entered the room.

How fortunate that she was heavily sedated! She would not make a sound. From a scabbard inside his shirt he drew a stiletto. Out of curiosity he pulled back the sheet that lay over the frame and looked at her torn and swollen flesh. Even he winced. But—he had his work to do. He clutched the stiletto and raised it to strike.

Aaeeya! Blood filled his throat and the tubes below, choking off any cry he might have tried to make. In the brief moment he had before blackness replaced light, he knew his throat had been cut from front to back, all the way to his spine, and that he was dying very fast.

As the man settled to the floor, the man who had cut his throat pulled the wire out of the wound. It was twelve inches of strong steel wire wrapped on wooden handles at both ends. He had deftly dropped it over his victim's head and jerked hard. The wire had cut through flesh and muscle and cartilage.

Another man stepped out of the shadows and stanched the blood with two heavy towels. Not a drop of it fell to the floor.

Nor did a drop fall as they lifted the corpse and shoved it out the window. It fell four stories and landed with a dull thud. Moments later, outside, having assured themselves that no one had seen anything, they stuffed the body in the boot of a car and drove away from the hospital.

They were long gone before the floor nurses bestirred themselves to wonder what had happened to the policeman who'd gone down the hall to check on Miss Parker.

4

FOUR FINGER, THE TAIWANESE businessman who wanted to invest in Western Reclamation, sat stiffly in a chair in Wu Kim Ming's suite in the Mandarin Oriental Hotel. He was a man of some sixty years, gray and bald. He wore round gold-rimmed eyeglasses. In the heat of a Hong Kong summer he was not wearing a suit but a pair of khaki slacks and a loose avocado-green shirt. A pencil and a ballpoint pen were clipped in his shirt pocket. He did not bother to hide his missing little fingers.

The buzzer sounded, and the white-jacketed houseboy opened the door to admit Bo Yu Tang. Bo, too, was casually dressed in a loose white shirt and black slacks. A fat bandage covered his broken nose. He was grave and reserved as he shook hands with Wu Kim Ming and Four Finger.

Wu spoke to the houseboy, who opened a door to an adjoining room and beckoned. Three girls from the Pearl Club came out and stood just inside the door, expecting to be chosen by the three men.

"Take first choice," said Wu to Bo.

One of the girls was Barbara, the nineteen-year-old Australian who had chatted with Beth two nights ago, the one with glossy light-brown hair and freckles. The other two were Chinese.

Bo tipped his head to one side and studied the Australian girl. *"Chui siu?"* he asked.

"He asks if you will play his flute," Wu said to her in English.

"You said you'd pay extra for that, Sir."

"You will be well paid for whatever you do. What is more, I promised that no . . . harm would come to you."

"Alright," Barbara said hesitantly.

By gestures Bo indicated that he wanted her to take off her clothes. She glanced at Wu, who nodded. For her entrance to the Mandarin Oriental, she was modestly dressed in a white linen sheath. As she pulled it over her head, Bo grabbed it, tore it off her, and threw it on the floor. He turned her around, unhooked her bra, and tossed it. She dropped her panties, stepped out of them, and stood naked—embarrassed and apprehensive. Bo sat down on the largest couch and pulled her down beside him. He put his left arm around her. He reached up with his other hand and accepted from the houseboy a glass of aged Rémy Martin.

Four Finger sat down once more in the chair where he had been when Bo arrived. The two Chinese girls moved to stand before him. Both were diminutive and pretty. They wore near-identical silk microdresses, one red, one blue. Four Finger nodded at the one in blue, and she sat down on his lap.

The third girl, wearing red, sat down beside Wu on the little bamboo settee where he had introduced Emily to one more of the Nine Glorious Postures on Wednesday night.

"We three," said Wu, "are in a position to increase our fortunes immensely. All we need do is agree."

Bo Yu Tang spoke. "For me to sit down in the same room with Four Finger of the Kuomintang, loud enemy of the Revolution, is a major concession."

" 'Kuomintang,' " said Wu. " 'Revolution.' I am talking about *money*."

"But I must think about principle," said the general. "I am an officer of—"

"*Retired* officer."

Bo frowned.

" 'Letting a hundred flowers blossom and a hundred schools of thought contend is the policy for promoting the progress of the arts and the sciences and a flourishing culture in our land,' " said Wu. He was quoting Mao Tse-tung, which Bo would well understand. "Also, 'An army without culture is a dull-witted army, and a dull-witted army cannot defeat the enemy.' Is it not so, my friend?"

"Practicably said. In a practical way, what do you mean?" asked Bo.

"We wish to achieve the same thing. Western Reclamation. You have invested in it hugely. My friend Four Finger wants to invest in it modestly. Tens of billions of American dollars, hundreds of billions of yuan, are at stake. The Chang family is willing to filter my friend's investment through a Bahamian corporation, so it will not appear that you and your friends have associated yourselves with a Taiwanese consortium. But—" Wu paused and smiled. "Whenever did ideology count for more than money?"

"The masses—" Bo started to say.

" 'Weapons are an important factor in war,' " Wu quoted Mao again, " 'but not the decisive factor; it is people, not things, that are decisive. The contest of strength is not only a contest of military and economic power, but also a contest of human power and morale. Military and economic power is necessarily wielded by people.' People? Who? What people? *We*, my friend, are people. Notice that the Chairman did not say *the* people. He said *people*."

Bo took a swallow of brandy. He dipped a finger in the brandy and rubbed it on Barbara's nipple. "Be specific, Wu Kim Ming. You asked me here to—"

"To enjoy a special evening and in the course of it come to know that the man you have despised is a man like you, like me. That is what counts—that and living well, with money."

"*More specific*, Wu Kim Ming."

"I would like for you to agree that the money coming through the Bahamian connection will not be questioned. Thus you will allow my friend Four Finger to have his small share in Western Reclamation. It will be advantageous for all of us."

Bo Yu Tang glanced around: from the naked Barbara, who had understood nothing of this conversation, to Wu, to the Chinese girls, to Four Finger. "It has come to my attention," he said, "that punishment was administered early this morning to a young woman in your employ who did not deserve it. The one who did—" He shrugged. "—has disappeared. She is the new concubine of the Changs. I am sure the Chang family, in exchange for my consent to the arrangement you suggest, will see to it that she is surrendered into my custody for the punishment she escaped early this morning. Once her *dai law* has been appropriately beaten—and this time I intend to witness the flogging, as you may wish to do—then we stand in agreement on all points."

Wu Kim Ming drew a breath, then nodded. "It will be as you say, my friend."

5

THOUGH THEY WATCHED HIM every moment as he showered and dressed, Michael found to his surprise that he was being moved as Dai Gul Dai had said, to somewhere, God knew where. When he was dressed and ready to go, they handcuffed him and put the shackles back on his legs. They led him out of the mountainside house to a handsome black Toyota with darkened windows so that people inside could see out but people outside could not see in. They put him in the backseat between two guards, one of which was the implacably hostile Big Mouth, Dai Gul Dai's brother, who still wore a thick bandage around his head from the wound he had taken when Michael slugged him with a bottle of wine.

Dai Gul Dai sat in the front seat. Except for Big Mouth, who glowered without cease, the triad men were relaxed, even jaunty, as they moved their prisoner.

Michael discovered now where he had been. The powerful speedboat Beth had jumped from had carried him well north and west of Hong Kong and up into Zhu Jiang Ku, that is, the mouth of the Pearl River. If on the night when he tried to escape he had succeeded, he would have reached a new motorway running through the lakes and hills ten or fifteen miles north and west of Shenzhen. If he had reached the motorway he might well have been picked up by a truck driver who might have been sympathetic and might have carried him back to Hong Kong.

Such was fate, he reflected.

The road from the mountainside house to the motorway was crooked and narrow. The driver dared not gain any real speed. Looking ahead, Michael spotted a police car coming toward them. The two cars passed each other, but immediately the police car turned and chased after the Toyota. Its lights flashed. Dai Gul Dai ordered the driver to pull over.

Two policemen came to the Toyota and looked in. They spotted the handcuffed and shackled Michael. They stared with cold curiosity. "How is this explained?" one of them asked.

"I have been kidnapped!" Michael yelled. "They are holding me for ransom."

"A lie!" shrieked Dai Gul Dai. "He is a profiteer, an enemy of the people. We are holding him until he can be brought before a People's court."

"Allow him to show you the credentials that give him the authority to hold anyone for a People's court," said Michael.

"And your own credentials," the officer said. "Where are they?"

Michael shrugged and pointed at his restraints. "They have everything," he said.

The officer spoke coldly to Dai Gul Dai. "Show me his papers."

Dai Gul Dai turned up the palms of his hands. "We plucked him from the water and put on the chains to be sure he could not escape—which he tried to do."

The officer studied Michael for a moment. "Who are you?" he asked.

"My name is Chang Po Ka. I am the son of Chang Wing Hing of Hong Kong."

The officer spoke to Dai Gul Dai. "And you?"

"I am Tung Si, a poor peasant."

The officer shook his head scornfully. "Your peasant cart is impressive," he sneered.

Dai Gul Dai smiled. "Honored friend," he said. "This unfortunate confrontation can be ended easily. I am prepared to offer you ten thousand yuan—"

"For what?"

"To achieve a lapse of memory about this incident."

"He is a servant of the Chung Yui Hui triad," said Michael. "Ten thousand yuan! He could offer you a hundred thousand. But . . . my father can pay a great deal more—let us say half a million yuan."

"His father offers you a bullet in the back of the head," Dai Gul Dai said angrily.

"And the 'poor peasant' offers you one in the face," said Michael. "Do you suppose a triad will forgive and forget paying you?"

"Half a million yuan," muttered the officer. "Or maybe a million. To be paid when? And how?"

"I offer ten thousand, payable *now*, in cash!" yelled Dai Gul Dai.

"Twenty thousand," said the officer.

Dai Gul Dai nodded. "Twenty thousand let it be. Cash."

Michael knew he was defeated. It was how things were done in certain parts of China. For twenty thousand yuan these policemen would walk away, leaving a shackled man at the mercy of those who paid instantly and in cash. Money . . . money in hand. To some, duty and ideology were weak compared to money.

The policemen sold Michael to Dai Gul Dai, who handed them their yuan in bills. The two policemen grinned as they took the money. They turned and started back to their vehicle.

Dai Gul Dai grabbed an Uzi from under the front seat of the

Toyota. He fired two short bursts, and the two policemen fell. He gathered his money out of the dead hand of one and kicked the other in the face to be sure he was dead.

"You see?" he said to Michael. "You see how it is? Maybe you learn something from this, as a man does."

"The police will be all over here," said Michael. "A missing radio car . . . found with two dead officers."

"All over here, correct," said Dai Gul Dai. "But we will be many kilometers away."

The black Toyota moved on down the mountain road, leaving two dead policemen lying in their blood.

6

AN HOUR LATER THE nineteen-year-old Australian girl sat with the two Chinese girls on the side of the room distant from the big couch. Barbara sat on the little wicker settee and ate from a tray brought to her by the houseboy. She swallowed generous drafts of Foster's lager from a pint mug. She had put on her panties and bra again, but not her dress, and she was flushed and tearful. The two Chinese girls were sympathetic. The one in the red dress caressed Barbara constantly.

Bo Yu Tang had left. Wu Kim Ming and Four Finger sat quietly talking.

"The time has come," said Wu, "to release Michael Chang."

"When what has been promised has been achieved," said Four Finger.

"We have Chang Wing Hing's word. What need for anything more? You know him well, have known him for many years. He is a man of honor, a man of his word."

"Then what of *your* word, given to Bo, to deliver up the *kwai-pau* for her beating?"

Wu smiled and shrugged. "Bo's pride is injured. But he, too, is a practical man. He will not risk his investment in Western Reclamation over what is really a petty side issue. His pride will surrender to his greed."

"And if it doesn't?"

"Then, my friend, we will be between a rock and a hard place, as the Americans say."

7

BETH SAT WITH MARK Huang at a table in a small Austrian restaurant only a block or so from her apartment. Called Mozart Stub'n, it represented for her a relief from dim sum and all the rest of Chinese cuisine. She agreed with the pundit who had said that Chinese was one of the world's three great cuisines—the other two being French and Italian—but she was happy to sit down over a green salad followed by a plate of beef and beets and fried potatoes. Mark had introduced her to Mozart Stub'n in the thought that she would enjoy a European meal, and she made note of its location. If she were going to live in Hong Kong, she would come here often.

"Mark, this dinner is on me. I mean, I will pay for it." She smiled. "I mean, the Changs will pay for it. I am afraid you have taxed your expense account already—or perhaps even your own resources."

Huang shook his head, but he smiled. "I—"

"You are relieved," said Beth. "Don't kid me. Anyway, why not? It's the Chang family, after all, who's really paying. They're so damned anxious to show their generosity, let them show it."

"I accept," said Huang gravely.

"Mark, what's going to happen to you next July? Are you going to stay here? Do you have a passport that lets you go someplace else if things don't work out well?" Beth asked with obvious concern.

"I was born in Hong Kong. I have a passport issued by the British called B.N.O., which stands for British National Overseas. That means I am a subject of the United Kingdom but living overseas. With this B.N.O. I can go visit London without a visa, but I cannot work or live in England permanently."

"What a shame! They gave you a passport but won't let you live in their country?" Beth was incredulous.

"If my rank were higher in the police force, say Chief Inspector or higher, or if I were involved in more sensitive areas, they might have given me right of abode in England. But as it is, I am like millions of Hong Kong–born Chinese, trapped here with nowhere to go. We may have one of the highest standards of living in the world, far higher than the U.K., but we are as insecure as residents in Tel Aviv or Beirut. We are simply not important enough to the world to matter."

"You're important to me. You've been awfully good to me," she said. "I don't know what I'd have done without you—gone back to the States on that plane Hodding wanted to put me on, I imagine, in spite of my vehement protests that I wouldn't."

"I knew you'd have to," he said. "I also knew it would be a great personal tragedy for you."

"I am more than grateful to you, Mark," she said, touching his hand. "For something else, too. You've been a *gentleman*. Another man might have taken advantage of my situation. Mr. Wu did. That is, he tried to."

Huang squeezed her hand, then pulled his hand away. "Don't give me too much credit, Beth," he said. "You are an extremely attractive young woman, and I am an unmarried man, but in all frankness my admiration for you does not extend to the erotic."

Beth grinned. "I'm glad to hear it," she laughed. "On the other hand, I—"

"Let me explain," he interrupted. "I have not been— I have not been, shall we say, 'monogamous' in my relations with women. But I have never had a relationship with any woman but a Chinese." He turned up the palms of his hands. "I suppose in America they might use the term 'racist,' but I simply have no desire for an intimate relationship with a Western woman. I admire you. I admire blonds, but I have no interest in touching one." He lowered his eyes and stared at his plate for a long moment. "Am I offending you?"

Beth shook her head. "The man who tried to rape me was a Pakistani—probably because he was away from home, away from the wife he had back home."

"And got himself killed."

"Who did that, Mark?" Beth asked solemnly. "Who saved me and then beat that man to death?"

"I don't know, Beth. I honestly don't know. My first guess is that Wu put a guard on you. But let's not overlook the possibility that the Chang family may have arranged it. Once it became apparent to the Changs that you were genuinely affiliated with Chang Po Ka—Michael—you may have been taken under their protection."

His cellular telephone rang. He spoke on it for a minute or so, in Chinese, then put it down. "The hospital," he said. "A man in the uniform of the Hong Kong police came to look in on Emily. He went to her room and did not return to the nurses' station, which overlooks the only way out. Emily is alright, but the hospital has put a security guard on her room."

"My god! Are you saying someone came to kill her?"

"And didn't succeed. So who is watching over *her?*"

Beth's eyes were wide, and she gasped and gasped. "Mark— we've got to get her out there! You've told me my building is secure, guarded closely by the Changs. She doesn't need the hospital. We can get nurses to take care of her in my apartment. A doctor can call—"

"How—?"

"Use your cell phone. Call the Chang mansion. Let me talk to Mr. Chang or to Qiao Qichen. Let's see how far the Chang commitment goes."

8

FOUR FINGER SAW NO reason to waste the services of the young woman assigned to him and took her to a bedroom once more before he left the suite. While he was there, Wu sat with Barbara. He gave her ten thousand Hong Kong dollars and thanked her for tolerating the brutish attentions of Bo Yu Tang.

Barbara's face remained red. She whispered, could not speak normally. "I guess you Chinese believe money solves all problems, heals all wounds," she said. "Well—"

"Let us not denigrate each other's cultural heritage, Barbara," he said. "Are you suggesting the money is not sufficient?"

"No."

"If I had offered you that amount in advance, advising you what the man would demand, would you have said no?"

Barbara shook her head.

He caressed her cheek. "Then it was—and is—a business proposition. I have learned that I can depend on you if I am in need of special patience, special endurance. Which I sometimes am. Indeed, now that I think of it . . . the young woman who was attending to me personally will be unable to do so for some time. Would you like to move into this suite and allow me to teach you the Nine Glorious Postures?"

"Emily . . . ?"

"Emily has suffered a misfortune. I expect her to return to my service. In the meantime—"

Barbara wiped away tears. "You will treat me kindly, won't you, Sir?"

When Four Finger came out, Wu sent the two Chinese girls with him in a car guarded by two others. Barbara remained with him, swallowing more and more Foster's and gradually subsiding into euphoria. She was asleep on a couch when the door guard advised Wu that a man had come to see him.

The man was the one who had cut the throat of the assassin who had entered the hospital to kill Emily.

"I thought you'd want to see this," he said, speaking Chinese, and he handed Wu a Polaroid picture.

The photo was of the corpse of the man in the Hong Kong police uniform.

Wu frowned over the picture. "This explains a great deal, doesn't it? Yes. A great deal."

"I knew you'd want to see."

"Where is the body now?"

"Forty, fifty miles out. Weighted down. He'll be eaten. No trace of him will ever show up."

"You promise me that?"

"I promise you, sir."

"Well, then. You are to be rewarded. Would you prefer money, or status?"

"As you judge proper, Honored Leader."

TEN

*I have good reasons to regret the Handover,
but the end of British arrogance is not one of them.*

1

WELL AFTER MIDNIGHT EMILY, heavily sedated, was removed from Queen Elizabeth Hospital and started off by ambulance to the apartment building on Arbuthnot Road. Qiao Qichen coordinated the operation, giving all the orders. John was with him.

Qiao Qichen had suggested to Beth on the telephone that Emily would be safer in the mansion on The Peak, where the family had all the resources necessary to care for her. Beth insisted that Emily be brought to her apartment, saying that what Emily most needed, probably, was love, which she could have from a friend and could not have from strangers, no matter how well-intentioned.

Huang sat in the apartment with Beth, waiting for the group from the hospital to arrive.

"The status of the men sent to do this confirms the bona fides of the Chang family. The *consigliere* himself! And the younger brother! They take Emily's safety seriously."

"It's a very odd situation," said Beth. "I mean—"

"The family across the hall moved out on an hour's notice. I told you this building is a Chang enclave. They are moving only within the building, to another apartment. Don't feel sorry for them. They probably pay no rent."

This was a concession that Beth had felt compelled to make:

that Emily and her full-time nurses would be installed in the second apartment on that floor, not in Beth's apartment.

"It's the same damned thing," she said. "I don't know if I'm being protected or imprisoned."

Huang stood and walked to the window, which overlooked the pointed tower of the Bank of China. He glanced for a moment at the television screen—they had turned down the sound—and at a traditional Chinese opera company dancing and singing. "You can't imagine," he said, "what a threat you represent to the Chang family. By this time next year they will be on the very brink of a change that may bring down in ruin every value they cherish. Then on top of that, their son and heir may wish to marry a *kwai-pau*. Do you know what that means, Beth?"

"A foreign devil, female type."

"And why?" Huang asked. "Because the foreigners—Westerners—scorned a proud people and reduced them to subordinate status. Today still, that arrogant man Chief Superintendent Bannister treats me like an office boy. You know Hong Kong was ceded to the British more than a hundred fifty years ago because China lost the Opium War. Imagine China wanting to ship tons of heroin to your country and your government banning it, China then invading the United States, burning down the White House in Washington D.C., and demanding, among other things, the concession of Manhattan Island in New York as a Chinese trading post. How would you feel about the Chinese even though they turned Manhattan into the world's financial capital? I have good reasons to regret the Handover, but the end of British arrogance is not one of them."

"I am Irish, you know," she said.

"Yes. Well . . . the Brits used to say, 'The Niggers begin at Calais.' But, many Chinese make no distinction between Brits and Germans, or French or . . . Well, I'm sorry. Americans. For Michael Chang to marry one of you is simply impossible."

"It's a new world, Mark," she said solemnly. "It's coming to Hong Kong on July first of next year. Rudely. A new world. What counts to Chang Wing Hing and Qiao Qichen may be utterly meaningless next year. I hope not. But the possibility has to be faced."

He nodded, and as he returned to sit down the doorbell rang. Huang went to the door.

"Good evening," said the woman standing in the elevator hall. "I am the wife of Frederick Chang. I am Michael's sister-in-law. Please call me Anne. The honored father asked me to come and to offer such assistance as I can to the injured young woman."

Beth recognized her. She was the woman who had stared down from the window, who had dropped the curtain when she saw that Beth noticed her.

God, she was *majestic!* She had a presence that anyone could envy. Presence? It was something more, something more formidable. The bangs with which she wore her glossy black hair defined her forehead. The hair hanging around and below her ears defined her face. Her features were perfect: cold black eyes, a modest but chiseled nose, thin lips dramatized by dark-red lipstick. She wore a skintight black silk dress. The skirt was as short as some of those worn in the club. Sleek black stockings clung to her shapely legs.

"I will be in the other apartment," she said.

"Come in, come in," said Beth.

Anne entered the room and glanced around as if appraising. "I am to supervise the care of Miss Parker," she said.

"We know about your husband's misfortune," said Huang. "My deepest regrets, Lady."

"Fate," said Anne curtly.

"Please sit down," said Beth. "We know much of each other, don't we?"

Anne nodded. "I know that my young brother-in-law is a man of exquisite taste." She sat down on the couch beside Beth. "I am not so different from you, Beth. May I call you that? I graduated from McGill. You know the university? In Canada?"

"The finest medical school in North America," said Beth.

"I didn't study medicine," said Anne. "Some say I studied nothing but Americanism. I am thought of by many as far too much Americanized."

"I hope we will be friends," said Beth. She grinned. "I hope you will help me become—may I invent a term?—'Chinese-ized.'"

Anne laughed softly. "I am sure we are going to be close friends," she said. "For the time being I will live in the apartment with the unfortunate Emily Parker. The honored father has given me in trust to see that her every need is met."

"She is the victim of something that's not her fault," said Beth gravely.

"It has been explained to me," said Anne.

"Well, then. Would you care for a drink?"

"I am dying for a Scotch," said Anne.

2

EMILY LAY ON HER stomach on a bed in the apartment assigned to her. A nurse stood over her and gently applied an unction to her savaged flesh. Emily groaned. Beth and Huang stood and watched, appalled. Anne watched and winced.

What they saw sickened all three of them. Emily's beaten buttocks were red and green and blue and yellow and swollen to twice their natural size. Welts oozed black blood.

"Give me a shot. . . ." Emily whispered hoarsely. "If it *kills* me, Oi don't care! Oi want to be unconscious . . . or dead."

The nurse glanced at her watch.

Anne's face was a contorted mask. "Whoever did this," she muttered, "will have it done *to* him."

"Yes," said Huang. "All we have to do is identify the man who did it."

"Sometimes," said Anne, "it is necessary to kill. It is never necessary to do *this*."

"I don't buy killing much," said Beth. "I'll buy it now. Bo Yu Tang . . . Give the word to the honored father. Bo Yu Tang—"

"Must die," said Anne simply.

3

IN THE MORNING ANNE left the apartment, asking Beth to watch over Emily while she was gone—for an hour, perhaps. She walked down to Hollywood Road, along that street for a short distance, then turned down a long flight of stone stairs. Two-thirds of the way down she entered a leather-goods shop and passed through it to a room behind. Dai Gul Dai sat there, sipping tea.

Anne sat down. Dai Gul Dai poured tea for her.

"Is Chang Wing Hing really stupid enough to send *you* to guard over the *kwai-pau*?"

"My honored father-in-law is not stupid. But he doesn't suspect *me*. I am, after all, the mother of his grandchildren."

Dai Gul Dai smiled. His smile, not often seen, was grotesque, menacing.

"We enjoy good fortune in this," she said. "Beth Connor is delivered into our hands."

"That much good fortune!"

"That much. Good fortune has come in a string of events. First, someone stupidly beat the one called Emily when they meant to beat Beth. Then someone equally stupid went to the hospital and tried to kill the one called Emily." She paused and shook her head. "Why, I cannot imagine. Having beaten her severely, why would someone *then* want to kill her? If they wanted her dead, why didn't they kill her instead of beating her? Do you suppose it was not the same men?"

Dai Gul Dai scowled. "The man who tried to kill the one in the hospital was one of my men. We had no idea she was not Michael Chang's fat whore."

"Then you are not the one who beat Emily."

"No. The men who did that did it for Bo."

Anne sighed. "Very well. We still know our objective, and now we can gain it." She pushed a key across the table. "That is the key to the apartment where I am staying with Emily. Whenever I am away, Beth will be there. Even though there is a nurse, she insists that one of us must be with Emily at all times."

Dai Gul Dai sneered. "Someone who cares if she lives or dies."

"Alright. This key opens the apartment. The code you must punch in to enter the building lobby is eight-eight-three-three. I will make an excuse for going out this evening, for an hour or so. About eight o'clock. You watch the building. When you see me leave, Beth will be alone with Emily. The nurse will be gone by then. I suggest you kill them both."

"Have you ever killed anyone?" Dai Gul Dai asked scornfully.

"No. I don't have to. I can hire someone like you to do it."

4

DAI GUL DAI SAT at the table and drank tea for ten minutes after Anne left. She didn't want him seen anywhere in her vicinity. Well . . . for that matter he didn't want her seen anywhere in his.

When finally he did leave the leather-goods shop, he stepped out into bright, hot sunlight and smothering heat. He began to climb the steps toward Hollywood Road when suddenly he was aware that the men on each side of him was not there by chance.

"Dai Gul Dai," the one on his right muttered. "The master wishes to see you."

Dai Gul Dai nodded. "I want to see the master."

They drove him through the tunnel to Kowloon and to the Pearl Club, which was of course closed and all but deserted at this hour. Wu Kim Ming kept him waiting half an hour before he admitted him to his office.

"Honored Master . . ."

"What business have you with Mrs. Frederick Chang?"

Dai Gul Dai cut short a gasp of surprise, of alarm. "She—she wishes me to kill Mikego Chang's *kwai-pau.*"

"Do you intend to do that?"

"With your permission, Honored Master."

"With my permission," Wu sneered. "You didn't ask my permission before you tried to kill her last night."

Dai Gul Dai shook his head. "I did not—"

Wu tossed a Polaroid picture across his desk. "*Your man,*" he said. "He is quite dead, as you can see. He fell out the window at Queen Elizabeth Hospital."

"The big-tit whore was never in that hospital."

"But you thought she was. You made the same error that General Bo's thugs made. Why does Anne want her dead?"

"I don't know, Honored Master."

"Why do *you* want her dead?"

"For the five hundred thousand that Anne will pay for her death."

"*Without* my permission! You didn't ask my permission. And you don't have it. I do not want Beth Connor killed."

Dai Gul Dai bowed and stared at the floor.

Wu stared at him for a full minute before he said, "Do you wish to remain affiliated with Chung Yui Hui?"

"Of course," Dai Gul Dai said humbly. "It is my honor, my life."

"A man like you has no honor," said Wu calmly. "But you do have your life, and I assume you would like to keep it."

"Honored Master . . ."

"Tell me about Michael Chang. Is he well?"

"He is alive and well, Honored Master. Anne would pay well for his death, but—"

"I want him moved to our safe house in Sha Tau Kok. Do you understand? He is to be moved there tomorrow."

Dai Gul Dai nodded. He withheld from Wu the fact Michael had already been moved to Shenzhen without Wu's knowledge or permission. Sha Tau Kok was a border town between China and Hong Kong, and Dai Gul Dai guessed this meant that the triad was about to turn the Chang son over to his family—for what trade-off, he could hardly imagine.

"I expect this thing to be done smoothly. Your man is at the bottom of the South China Sea—where you could be if—"

"Honored Master," murmured Dai Gul Dai deferentially. "Allow me to give you something that may prove of value to you." He pulled from his pocket the key to Emily's apartment. "Tonight at eight the one called Beth Connor will be in that flat with Emily. The code that opens the door into the building is eight-eight-three-three." He allowed himself to raise his eyes and let them meet Wu's, and he smiled faintly. He handed over the key. "For whatever purpose you may find for it."

5

Bo Yu Tang stared skeptically at the gap between the stone quay and the pitching yacht. A young man sprang across the water and landed nimbly on the deck. He turned and smiled at the portly Bo, then ordered a crewman to lay a gangplank across the gap. Even the gangplank with ropes on each side to steady a man on his feet did not make the crossing easy, in Bo's judgment. He stumbled awkwardly as he stepped from the plank to the deck and allowed two men to seize and steady him.

Wu Kim Ming stepped forward to shake his hand and welcome him aboard. Other men gathered around. Some shook his hand. Some saluted him. Among them was Chang Po Ji—John—the youngest of the Chang brothers, the one who had witnessed his humiliation in the Pearl Club.

As Bo Yu Tang stood on the deck, glancing around, ropes were thrown aboard and the yacht eased away from the wharf and moved into the surging waters of the harbor. Bo had never before been aboard a yacht like this one. It was steel-hulled and fifty feet long. Throbbing diesel engines moved it authoritatively through the water. He looked up and saw a radar antenna placidly turning circles above the bridge. The boat moved through the harbor traffic and away from the waterfront.

Wu led the way to a door that opened into an elegant saloon. It was furnished like a luxurious hotel suite, except that all the furniture and fixtures were fastened down against the rolling of the boat. Bo had little experience of salt water and felt queasy even before he left the deck and entered the elegant saloon below. The presence of Wu Kim Ming aboard the boat challenged him to match Wu's sangfroid. Bo forced himself to look pleased and happy but wondered, all the same, how long he would have to endure the rolling of the boat.

Bo Yu Tang was, as Beth had judged when she met him, a peasant from an inland province, and he was surprised at the luxury afforded by the main cabin of the yacht. He sat down in a deep easy chair. The others took their places in chairs and on couches. Everyone sat facing a handsome teak table that occupied the center of the saloon.

"Brandy?" Wu asked Bo.

"Well . . . perhaps when— Where are we going?"

"Not far. And into a sheltered little bay where the boat will not roll and we will have privacy for the evening's entertainment."

"You said you could not promise the entertainment."

"I said I could not promise it *this evening*. But I promised you that you should have it—when I can arrange it."

"Arranged by you. Done by you."

"There are good reasons not to be too severe about it. Believe me, there are reasons. You and I are men of affairs, and you will have your satisfaction. And we will leave some room for flexibility."

"You think—"

"I think you will have your satisfaction this evening. In any case, your evening will be worthwhile. I have brought a companion for you." He snapped his fingers, and one of the men left the cabin and returned in a moment with a pretty little Chinese girl.

"Where is the Australian?"

"Not available," said Wu.

"Very well. You are a gracious host. But let us hope we witness the entertainment this evening."

6

ANNE LEFT THE APARTMENT about eight, saying she needed to make a run up to the mansion to pick up some clothes. Beth came across from her apartment and sat down beside Emily.

"Oi'm honest-to-god beginning to feel loik I moight survoive," Emily said weakly. "No more shots, though? The nurse—"

"I have pills you can take," said Beth.

Emily sighed. "Got to talk like a . . . human being again. Jesus, Beth. In a real sense I'm glad it was me. I'm tougher'n you. I am, you know. I've had to take stuff that you never had to."

"How about some soup, Emily? You've got to eat, sooner or later. In the kitchen there's a package of mix. I can make chicken noodle soup. Jewish penicillin."

Emily glanced around over her shoulder and tried to look at her bare bottom. "Does it look any better?" she asked.

Beth lied. "A little. The swelling has gone down a little."

While she was in the kitchen heating the soup, Beth heard the sound of a key in the lock. Anne had said—

It wasn't Anne. Two men.

"Ladies," said one of them. "Be very quiet. We don't want to have to gag you. We have not come to kill you. By this time tomorrow you will be right here, as you are now. In the meantime . . . a short trip. Miss Connor, you must come with us. If you cause us difficulty, the penalty will fall on Miss Parker."

"Who? Why?"

"You will learn who and why at the appropriate time. We have not come to kill you. You will be back here before the night is over."

Beth looked at Emily. "I don't seem to have any choice," she said.

When the door was closed and Beth was gone, Emily forced herself to roll off the bed and stagger to the telephone. She dialed 999, the Hong Kong emergency number.

"Emergency? Please! Senior Inspector Huang Han Gai. He alone, please! Contact him! Tell him Miss Emily Parker is calling. He will understand. He needs no further message."

7

EVEN THOUGH THEY NEVER took the blindfold off, Beth knew she was being taken aboard a big yacht. From the moment when they hustled her into their car she had been blindfolded and handcuffed with her hands behind her back. Even so, she'd had a reasonably accurate idea about where she was going. They had put her aboard a fast boat. It had to be one much like the one she had jumped from. This time there had been no chance of escaping. Wriggling out of ropes was one thing; escaping from handcuffs was quite another. Now she was led up steel steps from the pitching boat to the deck of a gently rolling yacht or ship.

She wondered if she were going to encounter the horrible Dai Gul Dai again. Or Bo Yu Tang!

They led her through a door, probably into the main cabin. She heard shuffling and breathing—meaning that she was in a room with at least six or seven men, probably more. One man stood to each side of her, firmly clutching her arms. She heard a voice. She trembled. She hoped she didn't recognize it but feared she did: the voice of Bo Yu Tang.

Other hands now grabbed roughly at her clothes. She was wearing her jeans and a white T-shirt. They pulled the shirt up under her armpits, unhooked her bra, and exposed her breasts. Then they pulled her jeans and panties down to her knees. Even through her blindfold she could see bright, sharp flashes. She heard the sound of a Polaroid camera ejecting film. They were taking pictures of her!

She felt hands on her breasts, rubbing them, lifting them and dropping them.

She heard a harsh laugh. *"Dai baw dai!"* Big tits! It was the voice of Bo, using the same vulgar words he had used in the Pearl Club.

Then she felt other hands. Other men stepped up and fingered her breasts, some gently, some not so gently. Some laughed. Some commented in words she could not understand. Some of the words drew laughs.

She gasped and sobbed—not so much for this invasive abuse as out of dread for what she was certain was coming.

They shoved her against a table. When her thighs were pressed firmly against it, they pushed on her shoulders and forced her to lie facedown across the width, not the length, of the table. They unhooked one of her handcuffs and brought her hands around in front and above her head, where they locked the open cuff on her wrist again. Her arms were pulled forward, and she supposed they had tied a rope between the cuffs and something on the deck. At the same time they were tying ropes around her ankles and stretching those, probably to the legs of the table. In a minute she was spread across the table, with her legs wide apart and her bare buttocks exposed. Again she saw the bright flash and heard the Polaroid camera.

As they had done with her breasts, they took turns running their hands over her bottom. They made jokes and laughed.

Abruptly they stepped back and fell silent. She could hear their breathing. Then she heard a loud *whoosh* on the air, followed instantly by the thud of a solid cane on her fundament. Beth screamed. She had never known such an excruciating shock of pain. *Whoosh!* The cane came down again. Fluid shot out of her mouth as she shrieked in agony. *Whoosh!* Beth howled and writhed.

Then she heard something strange: a sharp snap, a finger being snapped. Peremptorily. The cane did not fall on her again.

In a moment she felt a wet cloth touching her backside. She smelled alcohol, mixed with something else—an odor she could not identify. She moaned and sobbed. Could it possibly be they had given her three strokes and wouldn't give her any more?

She heard the voice of Bo, Though she didn't realize it, he was speaking to her. A man translated—

"Bo Yu Tang says he is satisfied. He could demand more, but he will accept this. The rest of us thank you for the fascinating display of big American tits and a big American ass. Some of us will probably see you again. You will never know when someone you meet is someone who saw you tonight. You won't know us, but we will remember you. Maybe you will not in future make exaggerated claims to dignity. In our eyes, you have none. And no pride."

8

SENSING THAT THE CAR was climbing a long hill, Beth allowed herself to hope they were taking her back to the apartment as they had promised. She sat forward on her legs, trying not to press her buttocks down on the seat of the car. She was cuffed behind her back again, and she still wore the blindfold. As the car made a sharp turn and started downhill, one man unlocked her handcuffs. The car stopped. They put her out on the street.

The car sped away with screeching tires. As she lifted her blindfold, she saw a police car hurtle past, blue strobes blinking and horn blaring *hee-haw-hee-haw!* Looking around, her eyes free of the blindfold for the first time in two or three hours, she saw an ambulance. Two paramedics were approaching her.

"Miss Connor?"

She nodded.

"Have you been injured?"

"Yes . . . flogged."

"Can you climb up into our vehicle?"

Beth nodded, and accepted the young man's arm and let him help her inside. She noticed that the other one was using a cell phone.

The young paramedic who helped Beth get inside the ambulance took a long hard look at her.

"Flogged on the backside, miss?"

"Yes."

He pointed to a low table in the middle of the vehicle, covered with a pad that was in turn covered with paper dispensed from a roll. "Will you lie down there, miss? May we lower your clothes and look at your injuries?"

"I'll do it," she said. She pulled down her jeans and panties and lay facedown on the table.

The paramedic frowned over her bruised buttocks. "Not terribly bad. I've seen schoolboys who got worse."

"They put something on it," she muttered. "Alcohol and something."

"Odd . . . People who flog people aren't usually so thoughtful. You got—what?—three strokes. Yes. You've got three angry welts. The skin is not broken. No blood. You don't need an antibiotic, actually. I'll clean this thoroughly and give you a mild sedative in the form of a tablet you can swallow when you get back up to your flat. Senior Inspector Huang is up there and is on his way down."

"People are staring," she whispered. Three men and two women had stopped on the sidewalk and were looking through the windows of the ambulance.

The paramedic pulled a roll of paper from a dispenser and covered her.

Huang arrived and climbed into the ambulance.

9

AFTER THEY ASSURED EMILY that Beth was all right—without giving her details—they left her to slip back into sedated sleep. Anne would stay with her, and Beth and Huang crossed the hall to Beth's apartment.

"I have a hundred fifty questions," said Huang. "The first is, how are you feeling? Do you want to take a pill?"

"I feel angry, I feel violated, I feel afraid," said Beth, "but I'm not in horrible pain. Mark, I was *used* tonight. Someone put on a show with me. My backside hurts. You better believe it hurts! But I'm not injured. *They made a show of me!*"

"Beth—"

"I understand it now. I took three strokes, and God save me from ever feeling that kind of pain again. . . ." She stopped and sighed loudly. "But they didn't break the skin. I have welts. I will have no scars. I took nothing like what Emily took. Mark . . . what they made me do was scream and shriek, wail and whimper—and, *Jesus the pain was real!*—but what I suffered most, as I can say now, was *terror*, crushing terror that . . . that they'd do to me what they did to Emily. That's what they wanted. They wanted to hear me howl!"

"To what purpose, Beth?" Huang asked gravely.

"*They did more!* They exposed me. There were— God, I don't know, maybe twenty men there. They played with my tits. The American expression is, they 'felt me up.' They ran their hands over my naked ass. Then they stood back and watched me take the three strokes and heard me yell. Okay. Bo Yu Tang was there. But there were a lot of other men, and one of them said to me when it was over that I'd never know, when I'm in company, whether or not there's a man present who didn't play with my parts and listen to me scream. I'll have no dignity, he said. No pride."

"Beth . . . ?"

"*The goddamned Changs*, Mark! To make it impossible for

Michael to marry me. How could he marry a girl who's been ogled naked and felt over by . . . by God knows who? How'd they get into this place? They had a key."

"I think you are jumping to conclusions."

"Well, one more thing, then. Why was I kept blindfolded the whole time? *So I wouldn't recognize someone I'd have recognized if I could have seen him!* Qiao Qichen was there. What do you wanna bet? Maybe even Michael's father himself. And some of the most prominent men in Hong Kong played with my tits. So Michael—"

Beth stopped and began to cry. She lowered her chin to her chest and wept. "He could never endure the humiliation of marriage to a woman who had been—"

"Maybe you underestimate your young man," said Huang.

ELEVEN

Being a female is a poor damned thing in this town.

1

THOUGH HE WAS FED and not subjected to physical abuse, Michael was naked and shackled on Sunday morning. He lay on his bed, drenched in sweat and oppressed by pessimism. He heard the straining of truck engines and the clashing of gears in transmissions. He even smelled the exhaust fumes from the tailpipes.

He had a better idea of where he was. The constant heavy truck traffic suggested Shenzhen. Twenty years ago Shenzhen had been a fishing village of twenty-five thousand people. Now it was a metropolis of three and a half million. He had visited there several times. Each time he arrived the city had grown beyond recognition. Huge office and apartment towers went up everywhere, every month producing new ones. People migrated there from Guangdong and other provinces, by the hundreds of thousands a year, seeking construction and industrial work. Other hundreds of thousands were overseas Chinese returning to their home country and wanting to live in the burgeoning, modern neocapitalist city. Every day trucks backed up at the border crossings, on both sides, the lines stretching back for miles. Every route was clogged with truck traffic, carrying goods of every description between Hong Kong and Shenzhen.

The reason was the so-called New Economic Zone, created by

Deng Xiaoping. It was China's experiment with capitalism, and it had been immensely successful. Scores of billions of dollars in investment capital flowed annually into Shenzhen, from Hong Kong and from the overseas Chinese wherever they were. Shenzhen was as burgeoning a city as any in the world, including Hong Kong itself. The Chang family was investing heavily in Shenzhen and would invest more heavily as the focus of enterprise moved to China.

None of this meant anything to Michael as he lay naked and sweating on his bed, with his legs chained together—at the mercy of Dai Gul Dai and the Chung Yui Hui triad. "Association of Righteous Harmony." He sighed. Association of murder and extortion. Qiao Qichen had been right about what they wanted: a share of Western Reclamation. Tens of billions of dollars.

Well . . . goddamn it, if that was what they wanted, why didn't his father give it to them? Was a share of Western Reclamation more important than his son's life?

And Beth—Dai Gul Dai said she had been viciously beaten. He doubted it. But still it could have happened. The worst thing about being kept naked and chained in this house was that he could do nothing for Beth. He loved her. He was more conscious now of his love than ever. And of hers. It was something his father and brothers could not understand. It was American! He had anticipated trouble when he decided to bring Beth to meet his family—trouble with his strong-willed father over his plan to marry a non-Chinese. But never in his life did he anticipate trouble with kidnappers, triad killers!

But the saddest thing for Michael was the physical separation from the love of his life. If he were to die, he wanted to be in her arms, feeling her warmth and her pulse.

"Good morning, Mikego." The loathsome Dai Gul Dai stood beside his bed, smirking. "I have news for you. Today we are moving you to another house." He grinned and shrugged. "Maybe farther from where you would like to be. Maybe closer. In any case, you are to have a heavy breakfast such as the *kwai-loh* eat. Oh . . . Eggs. Pork. Then you are to have a thorough bath, release from your chains, and clothes. We are moving you to another house."

2

WHEN THE DOORBELL RANG, Anne started but went to the door. It was only a little past nine in the morning, and she was expecting no one. She opened the door, leaving the chain to stop it short of opening more than a few inches.

So! By the gods! Wu Kim Ming. She had never met him, but she recognized him as chief of the triad and the chief to whom Dai Gul Dai owed absolute loyalty. She released the chain and let him in.

"Mrs. Chang," he said quietly, his eyes laying on her a glance so intently appraising that its touch was palpable on her body. "My sympathy to you, Lady."

"My thanks, Mr. Wu."

She was dressed in a gleaming black silk dress that clung to her and dramatized a figure that did not need dramatizing. It was embellished with finely worked embroidery representing a small dragon set forth mostly in gold thread but with highlights of green and red. The shirt was short. Her legs, in sheer dark stockings, were exquisite, as he did not fail to observe appreciatively.

Wu wore a dark-blue linen suit, a monogrammed silk shirt, and a blue tie with tiny red dots, each one worked up with thread and not just woven into the fabric.

"I should not have arrived unannounced, but the number of the telephone here is difficult to obtain."

Anne smiled. "I am sure *all* telephone numbers are accessible to you, sir."

Wu smiled. "As they are to the honored Chang family. I am surprised to see you here. I came to extend my sympathy to poor Miss

Parker, who works for me and who I understand has been severely beaten."

"She is here. My honored father-in-law asked me to watch over her. She is a close friend of Miss Connor, who has some kind of relationship to my brother-in-law, Michael Chang."

"Yes. I have met Miss Connor. Is Miss Parker . . . ?"

"Allow me to announce you, Mr. Wu—and to cover her a bit."

When Wu entered the bedroom where Emily lay, he closed the door, leaving Anne outside. He walked to the bed and lifted the sheet to uncover Emily's injuries.

"Precious Lady Yin . . ." he murmured.

"Proud Lord Yang," she whispered.

"The man who did this is a dead man," he said.

"Bo Yu Tang did it. It was a mistake. He meant to do it to Beth."

"The lives of oafs like Bo mean nothing to anyone. Precious Lady . . . I promised that you will be my only woman. And you will."

"I think I should go home," said Emily.

"I will make you a home here."

Emily nodded. "Cover it up, please."

"The pain?"

"Is bearable now."

He touched her cheek. "Precious Lady Yin . . ." he said.

Returning to the living room of the apartment, Wu closed the bedroom door firmly.

"Well, Liu Soong Qin," he said smoothly. "I believe you have a goal of your own. I have evidence that you do. You seem to have recruited one of my servants into your service. You will understand that I cannot tolerate his pursuing a goal that violates my own, even if it is a service to you."

"Your goal is an alliance with the Changs," she said. "You will not achieve it with Michael's father. You certainly will not achieve it with Michael." She stopped and smiled. "And John? Well . . . who knows what ephemera John pursues?"

"What he pursues is obvious enough," said Wu.

Anne gestured to the couch, suggesting that Wu sit down. "Where shall you put your trust, Wu Kim Ming? John is a *child* and will never be anything but. Michael is a man who will remain forever resentful of his kidnapping. Frederick, my husband, is dying. And . . . Ah! With all three dead, the inheritance passes to my young son, who will be under *my control*. What great things we may do, Wu Kim Ming!"

"I had not imagined you were so . . . ambitious," said Wu.

"But I am the key to it," she sneered. "If Michael remains alive, he will take charge of the Chang family fortune and leave us out in the cold. If he does not survive, we control the Chang family through my son!"

"Your father-in-law is not so old a man."

She smiled. "Who knows what misfortunes may befall him?"

"You have thought all this through very carefully," said Wu. "How fortunate that I happened to call here this morning. You could not have arrived at all these ideas during the few minutes I spent with Emily Parker. You have been planning for a long time."

"If I had not met you this morning," she said, "I would have come to you very soon. An alliance between us— An alliance between you and the Changs!"

Wu drew in his lower lip and for a moment frowned and pondered. "An alliance . . ." he said thoughtfully.

3

THE DOORBELL RANG. HAVING lost all confidence in the security supposedly being given her by the Chang family—and with incomplete confidence in the security Huang now assured her she was afforded by the Hong Kong police—Beth peered anxiously through the peephole in the glass before she opened the door. She recognized the man waiting patiently just outside. He was Wu Kim Ming.

She opened the door.

"Good morning, Miss Connor," he said. "I would have telephoned, but it has proved less than easy to get your cell phone number."

"Come in, Mr. Wu," she said. "I have just brewed a pot of tea. I hope you will not find my tea undrinkable. It is Chinese tea that I found in the kitchen cabinet. Why don't you take a seat at the table?"

"I am sure it will be delicious," said Wu. He glanced around the apartment. "Handsome quarters. Provided, I imagine, by the honored Chang Wing Hing for his son's future consort."

"Future *wife*."

"Let us fervently hope so. In any case, I have come to see Emily as well as you, and stopped by her flat for a moment. Her injuries are healing. She will be able to rise and walk soon—tomorrow, I should guess."

Beth poured tea in two cups. She sat down gingerly, putting most of her weight on her legs near her knees, as little as possible on her bruised bottom.

"Miss Connor! Have *you* been . . . hurt?"

Beth nodded. "A little," she said.

"How? By whom? Where?"

"By Bo Yu Tang, chiefly. He is the only one I can identify. I was blindfolded the whole time—that is, from the time I was kidnapped from the apartment across the hall, a little after eight, until I was put out on the street in front of the building, a little before eleven."

"What did they do to you?"

"Caned me. It was like what they did to Emily, only not nearly as hard and only three strokes. I have welts, and they are painful to sit on, but I was not injured the way Emily was injured. As a matter of fact, I think the intention was to shame me more than hurt me. A lot of men were there to witness it all. I was stripped. A lot of them touched me. Then they watched while I was flogged. Witnesses. Many of them. God knows who. . . ."

"Bo's thugs," said Wu.

"I don't think so. I think they were a variety of men. The man who translated for the general told me I would probably see some of them again; though I wouldn't know them, they would know me. The idea of the whole ordeal was to break my pride. I have to wonder who wanted that to happen."

"Bo Yu Tang," said Wu grimly. "You damaged his pride, so he wanted to break yours. I join you in saying, god knows who the witnesses were. I would guess some of them were prominent businessmen. I could not guess who the others may have been."

Beth stared into her teacup. "Have I been so shamed that it will be impossible for Michael to marry me?"

Wu shook his head. "I wonder if Michael's father knows what happened."

4

ALTHOUGH HE GREW WEAKER by the day, Chang Po Kuok—Frederick—was still invited to sit in on business meetings. If by some miracle he might recover, he must not be allowed to become a stranger to the family's affairs. He slumped in an elaborately carved but deeply upholstered chair, looking as though he had to struggle not to topple over.

Chang Po Ji—John—was not always called to meetings, but he was at this one, sitting erect on a nonupholstered but ornamental chair. Qiao Qichen sat on a matching chair.

The patriach, Chang Wing Hing, sat in a high-backed, throne-like, silk-upholstered chair behind a huge ebony desk deeply carved with images of dragons, its leather top bordered with flower designs in ivory and mother-of-pearl. The desk had been acquired by his great-grandfather who had accepted it in payment for skilled and pretty little prostitutes at the time when he closed his hundred sampan brothels. The keeper of an onshore bordello had declared himself short of cash and offered his priceless antique desk in payment for fourteen girls. This much of the provenance of the desk was probably historical fact. The rest was myth. If the myth was to be believed, the desk had been carved for a eunuch serving in the Forbidden City, who had sold it to a merchant of the Canton Co-Hong, who had been compelled to surrender it to a brothel-keeper in payment of gambling debts.

Another element of its romance was that it had no drawers. Instead it had a spacious compartment built in and well hidden. The master could sit behind it with his legs under it as under any other desk, and another person could lie in the compartment and hear everything said across the desk. One version of the myth had it that the eunuch sometimes kept another eunuch in the compartment, hearing and memorizing all that was said, particularly what was said when the principal eunuch excused himself from the room for a minute or two. Another version had it that the brothel-keeper allowed husbands to hide in it while he encouraged other men to talk about their wives.

In any case, the desk was always adorned with delicate vases containing fresh flowers. Chang Wing Hing sat behind it only when he wanted to impress visitors or to cower subordinates. That he sat there now was ominous.

He never sat behind the desk except in a suit with white shirt and necktie. The others, if they had known they were to be summoned to this office, would have come in suits, too. As it was, they wore slacks and golf shirts.

"My telephone rang this morning," said the elder Mr. Chang. "Why do I receive news by telephone? From other people, not from the family? I was told by my caller that the American woman of whom Michael Chang is enamored was last night kidnapped, taken to a yacht, and there exposed naked and caned like an English schoolboy—in the presence of prominent men. Can this be true?"

"I cannot believe it is true," said Qiao Qichen.

"No. It is not true," said John. "I do not believe it is true, Honored Father."

"*I believe it is true!*" shouted Chang. "The man who told me is a friend. He said the spectacle was . . . obscene."

"He must be mistaken," muttered the youngest son.

"This woman," said the father with anger, "is now associated by name with our family. Wife?" He shuddered with revulsion. "Concubine? Would *I* take to concubine a woman who has been exposed and beaten? I gave this woman protection—"

"Which seems to have proven ineffective," Frederick suggested deferentially.

"*Yes!* Where were the guards? Am *I* safe? I placed this woman in a building where my dear little one lives, where I visit her. And a few floors below, the American woman is taken and— Where was Liu Soong Qin when this outrage happened? The English girl called the *police*, and now we have Senior Inspector Huang involved!"

"We need more facts, Honored Father," said John. "Otherwise we jump to conclusions."

"In this as in much else," said his father, "it is not facts but what are *said* to be facts that count. That is the way of the world. The word seems to be spreading in Hong Kong that Chang Po Ka's American woman has been exposed naked to a score of men, many of whom fondled her and then watched her beaten and heard her howl! *This* is identified with *us!*"

"Who is responsible?" Frederick asked weakly. "Who did it?"

"Bo Yu Tang," said Frederick's father. "But he couldn't have done it, he couldn't have arranged for her to be taken, without someone's cooperation. We have been betrayed. . . . I sense it! Someone is a traitor to our family. Who? I will find out." He nodded. "I will find out."

Fifteen minutes after the Changs and Qiao left the office, a panel on the front of the desk slid open, and Dragon, the *qi gong* master, rolled out. The space inside was not cramped; even so he was glad to be out of its total darkness.

5

MICHAEL KNEW WHERE THEY were taking him. Just a few miles west of Shenzhen, on an inlet off Mirs Bay, lay the town of Sha Tau Kok. It was a border town in a very dramatic way, in that the boundary line ran through the very middle of Sha Tau Kok, indeed down the middle of a narrow street. Though the border beyond the town was heavily fenced and patrolled, the town itself was something of a no-man's-land where the Chinese police and the Hong Kong police kept a discreet distance from each other and tried to avoid stepping on each other's toes. At this point, with the Handover only a year away, neither side could see any point in an international incident.

In Sha Tau Kok, townspeople crossed and recrossed the border as if there were no such thing as a border.

The Hong Kong police, obsessively anxious to exclude what Hong Kong called I.I.s—illegal immigrants—relied on its Field Patrol Detachment to turn back the I.I.s at the border. Rather than insist on building a fence through the center of the town of Sha Tau Kwok, the Field Patrol Detachment, heavily armed and equipped with detection devices of every sort, relied on stopping the illegals as they left Sha Tau Kok and tried to make their way deeper inside Hong Kong.

Michael was heartened by the sight of the town. If his kidnappers were going to hand him back to his family, here was the perfect place to do it.

The black Toyota entered the town slowly and proceeded immediately to a dilapidated, rambling building that housed poultry and fish shops on the ground floor and, as he would see, a seedy flat on the floor above. When he entered the shabby living room of the flat, he saw that the living-room windows overlooked the boundary line. Below these windows local people were placidly wandering back and forth between China and Hong Kong, going about their daily business of buying and selling.

If the Chung Yui Hui triad meant to exchange him for whatever it had extorted from his father, this had to be the exchange point.

6

DRAGON ARRIVED EARLY IN the evening. Anne had to authorize the lobby security guard to let him in, and even then the guard would not let him go to the elevators until he had searched through the soft leather briefcase Dragon was carrying. She opened the sliding glass door in the living room and led him out onto the balcony, where over the railing they had a dizzying view to the street far below.

"We speak out here because I suspect the rooms inside are equipped with hidden microphones," she told him. "I am quite certain that calls I make on the cell phone are monitored."

"I have suspected as much," said Dragon, "and have made no attempt to contact you."

"I want you to go to the leather shop and leave word that you need to talk to Dai Gul Dai. When you see him, give him this word: that I have formed an alliance with Wu Kim Ming. That makes it more important than ever that he kill Chang Po Ka. I have a sense that he will soon be ordered to return my young brother-in-law to his father. He should not kill him until that order is given, but it must be done as soon after that as possible."

"*Ayeeyah!* My Lady is the shrewdest of the shrewd."

She nodded. "And now I am nursemaid to a Cockney tart. I'll be glad when she can get up and fetch her own tea."

"Perhaps I can do something about that," said Dragon.

"Perhaps you can," said Anne quizzically.

She went to Emily's bedroom and told her there was a man here who might be able to relieve her pain. "A master of the mystic art of *qi gong*. Have you heard of it?"

Emily nodded.

"Would you like for him to try to relieve your pain?"

"Suppose it can't do me any 'arm," Emily whispered.

Returning to the living room, Anne found that Dragon had taken a saffron silk robe from his briefcase. He fastened the last frog, then settled a squarish yellow silk hat on his head. When he lowered his hands to his sides, his sleeves fell below his fingertips. He settled his hands across his stomach, and his hands were out of sight.

In the bedroom he stood and looked thoughtfully at Emily for a long moment, then said solemnly, "This young woman has been the victim of a grave injustice."

Anne sneered. She had told Dragon about Emily, but his pronouncement suggested that he had somehow deduced it.

"Please to uncover her wounds."

Anne frowned and jerked up her chin. She was not certain if Dragon genuinely thought it would be helpful to see Emily's bruised and swollen bottom or if he just wanted to see her nakedness. "Emily?" she asked.

"Alright," Emily breathed.

Dragon's eyes widened when he saw. Maybe he was genuinely sympathetic, Anne decided.

"Now . . . Emily," Dragon said softly. "Watch what I do, and you do similarly. I mean, breathe deeply and rhythmically, as I do, and close your eyes."

He began to draw deep breaths, to hold them for a moment, then to let them out audibly. Emily did it, too. Anne followed.

"Think peaceful thoughts," Dragon whispered. "Only peaceful thoughts."

He began to tremble, also to sweat. Suddenly he shuddered and ceased pulling the deep breaths. He reached out and touched Emily's swollen flesh with one gentle hand.

"Get up, Emily," he said calmly. "Get up now. You can stand. You can walk."

Emily obeyed him. Very carefully, she rose on her knees and began to back off the bed. Dragon and Anne took her by both arms and helped her. She touched the floor with her feet and put her weight down on them. Dragon backed slowly away from her, and she followed him.

"Hi!" he exclaimed. "Aahh!"

Anne snatched the sheet from the bed and draped it over the naked Emily. She stared open-mouthed at Emily, as though she had witnessed a miracle.

"Do you wish me to return, Lady?" Dragon asked Anne.

"Tomorrow," said Anne.

7

BETH WAS SURPRISED TO discover how expensive it was to dine in a sushi house in Hong Kong. She had supposed sushi was a moderately priced meal, as it was in the States. Well . . . little matter. She and Mark Huang were dining at the expense of the Chang family, and she was firmer now in her suspicion that her ordeal of last night had been connived by the family.

Huang watched thoughtfully as she drank her second Beefeater martini. He was sipping sake. Only once or twice before had he seen anyone drink the notoriously powerful American cocktail, and he wondered how it would affect her.

He had called and suggested she might like to have dinner out. She had agreed that would be pleasant. She could have made an unexciting meal out of what was in the refrigerator and cabinets in the apartment, but she did not like dining alone. She had decided, what was more, that a certain tension and awkwardness existed between her and Anne, so that spending much time with Emily when Anne was there was not appealing. Emily slept much of the time, in any case.

"I checked with the harbor police to see what large yachts were in Hong Kong waters last night," said Huang. "As I warned you, it was futile. You could have been aboard at least twenty-five yachts, and some of those have already gone on to Macau and other places."

"I had the impression of a steel hull."

"That reduces the number to fifteen or so. Large companies, including American companies, keep big yachts here. The owners offer hospitality—to businessmen, politicians . . . They ask no questions about what their guests choose to do aboard their boats."

"I thought a rumor might be about, from crewmen maybe. I yelled loud enough."

"Their employment depends on being circumspect. A screaming girl on board a yacht would attract little attention."

"Nothing will happen, will it?" she asked. "Being a female is a poor damned thing in this town."

"A *foreign* female," he amended.

"Mr. Wu came to see me."

"To offer sympathy?"

She shook her head. "He didn't know—*or did he?*"

"I couldn't be certain," said Huang. "Has it occurred to you that Wu Kim Ming may have been one of the men who witnessed your degradation? And approved of it?"

Beth flushed. "*No!* Well . . . then maybe Chang Wing Hing."

"No," said Huang. "It is not his way. Qiao Qichen . . . ? Not impossible."

"*God almighty!* Who can I trust?"

Mark Huang smiled faintly. "Me," he said simply.

Beth put her hand on his. "I know, Mark. I know."

8

THEY HAD WALKED TO the sushi house and now set out to walk up the steep streets to return to the apartment. They had not covered a third of the distance when Beth's cellular phone beeped.

She unfolded it to answer. "Hello?" she said a little timidly, wondering who had her number and who could be calling her in the middle of the evening.

"This is Qiao Qichen," said the voice on the line. "Arrangements have been made to release Michael. I should like to send a car for you, so you may be present when he is turned over to me."

"Where and when will that happen, Mr. Qiao?"

"At three A.M., in a border village called Sha Tau Kok. I don't want to explain too much on this cellular telephone, but I would like to have a car pick you up about one-thirty. Will you be ready?"

"Of course. But—one thing, Mr. Qiao. I would like to have Senior Inspector Mark Huang with me."

Qiao was silent for a moment. "It has been agreed that no police would be present. But . . . if he will be alone and if he will remain in the background—yes. He may be present."

"I will contact him," she said.

TWELVE

He is acting on his own motives. And he will die!

1

QIAO QICHEN PUT THE telephone into the cradle of the instrument on the leather top of the ebony desk.

Chang Wing Hing, who had been listening on another instrument, put it down, too. "She does not trust us," he said quietly.

"Considering all that has happened to her, it would be surprising if she trusts anybody, would it not?" asked Qiao with a degree of sympathy in his voice.

"Do you, in fact, trust this promise to return Chang Po Ka?"

"Yes. Everything has been arranged. Four Finger is satisfied. General Bo is satisfied. And we could have no better guarantee than the one we have: the word of Wu Kim Ming."

"Wu promises that my son will be handed over at three o'clock?"

"At Sha Tau Kok."

"Perhaps, after all, I should be present, too," said Chang Wing Hing gravely.

Qiao shook his head. "*I* will be there. Wu will be there. The American girl will be there."

"It was a mistake to send her."

"No. Chang Po Ka could complicate the matter. It could be that *his* trust in us has been diminished. He may have his own conditions. But when he sees her—"

"One of us . . . one of the family. My eldest son is *unable* to go.

He is asleep now. Or is he in a coma? And my youngest son? Where is he?"

"Somewhere . . ." said Qiao. "Chang Po Ji has done useful service in placating General Bo. He probably has him in a club somewhere—or in a bordello."

Chang Wing Hing frowned as he glanced at his watch. "Many hours," he said gravely. He shook his head and sighed. Then he formed a resolution. "I will go to my little one and wait there. She will make the hours pass faster."

Once again Dragon bided his time for a quarter of an hour after the room fell silent before he ventured to slide back the panel and roll out of the compartment. Anne had shown Dragon the compartment in which she herself had sometimes hidden. He used the secret compartment in her service usually but sometimes in his alone. He had bought stocks on the basis of what he heard and made a small fortune.

2

EMILY WAS IN THE living room when Dragon arrived at the apartment. She knelt on the couch, propped up by cushions, and watched an American movie on television. Dragon had not brought his robes, but he squatted on the floor and led Emily through breathing exercises and meditation, until she pronounced herself almost comfortable. She stared at him with worshiping eyes as he wiped the heavy sweat from his face.

"The *gong* master and I will go out on the balcony to talk," said Anne, "so you can go on watching your movie."

Neither Anne nor Dragon could be comfortable on the balcony. The distance to the street below hardened their stomachs. Even so—

"They are handing over Michael Chang at three tomorrow morning. At Sha Tau Kok."

"You must go to the leather shop. They will know how to contact Dai Gul Dai. Have them tell him I *must* see him. Tonight. Without fail. He must come into town. Have them tell him I will be at our meeting place on the quay at midnight. Have them tell him it is worth ten million dollars to be there."

3

ANNE WAS OF COURSE known at the mansion on The Peak. She told the cab driver to wait, and the gate guard admitted her immediately to the compound.

"Do not waken anyone," she said. "I will be here only a few minutes. I have only come to pick up some clean clothes."

She let herself into the mansion with her own key and walked upstairs through the darkened house to her private suite. On the way she stopped into her husband's bedroom. He was asleep, breathing so lightly that she needed a minute to determine if he was breathing at all.

She shook her head over the wraithlike figure. "You damned fool," she whispered. "You were too stupid to control yourself and so brought what you are suffering on yourself; yet, you were too smart, too cynical and sophisticated to let Dragon help you. If only you were as naive as Emily Parker. . . ." She sighed. "If only I were. I suppose miracles *are* for the gullible."

She entered her suite. Her children were asleep. So was their nurse. It took all her strength to move the bed she had once shared with her husband to one side and expose the door of the wall safe. On her knees she twisted the dial. She tugged the door open.

Jewelry. And money. She had been accumulating it for a long time. As the wife of the eldest son, she had long had access to money, and she had improved her fortune by investing after she hid in the great desk and listened to conversations. She had never trusted her husband or his family to treat her properly if something came unstuck. What she had in this safe was a pittance compared to the Chang family. To anyone else it was a fortune.

She counted off two million Hong Kong dollars. She took out the envelope containing the cashier's check she had bought three days ago at the Hong Kong Bank's head office in Central, then closed the safe and wrestled the bed back into place.

How to carry it?

Ah . . . simple enough. Lying on the floor of her open closet was the red nylon Adidas bag in which she carried her tennis clothes when she went to the courts. She tossed the dirty clothes aside and stuffed the money into the bag. Perfect. Even at the gate she would seem to be carrying the clothes she said she had come for.

4

XIU LING'S MOTHER HAD *shang chuang*—literally, climbed the bed—more than a hundred times with the benefactor Chang Wing Hing, but now she must defer as a servant, both to the benefactor and to her daughter. She hung her head in a low bow as she admitted Chang to the penthouse. Then, having closed the door, she bowed deeply and stared at the floor as she murmured welcome.

The girl and her mother had been warned by a call from the garage that Chang was on his way up, and Xiu Ling—Little Bell—emerged from the bedroom ready to receive her benefactor. The petite sixteen-year-old girl wore a thin wrapper of flowered silk, open to disclose a black bra, black bikini panties, and a black garter belt attached to thigh-high dark sheer stockings. She came forward to be embraced and kissed.

The mother stood humbly waiting for her daughter's orders.

"Tea," said Xiu Ling.

"Whisky," said Chang.

5

"*DEW NEH LOH MOH,*" Dai Gul Dai grunted to a beggar who approached him as he made his way down the stone steps to the harbor quay. It meant "fuck your mother."

The beggar did not retreat. He snarled in Chinese. "You shit-eating, pox-dripping son of a——"

The rest of his words remained in his throat. A heavy knife, deftly flipped, plunged into his body, just below his sternum. The point penetrated his lung and his heart. His last sensation was of the knife being pulled out and plunged in again. He stumbled off the steps and splashed into the surging waters of the harbor.

The killing had not been without a witness. "*Dew neh loh moh,*" said Anne calmly and quietly—and totally sarcastically—as Dai Gul Dai turned and saw her. "I thank you. In another minute I would have had to use this." She showed him a .32-caliber Colt automatic. "It would have dropped him in the harbor as effectively as your blade—regrettably not as silently."

Dai Gul Dai stepped toward her. As always he wished that circumstances allowed him to *dew* her, and he wondered if his luck would change and the chance would come after all. She wore a raincoat against the drizzle, but it was open, and he could see her black tights and black tank top. She disparaged him as a servant, but someday she would see what gave him his nickname.

"It is not convenient to be here at this hour," he said.

"Do you think it is easy for me? We have much at stake. Tonight. Have you received your orders?"

"Orders?"

"To hand over Chang Po Ka at three this morning."

"Yes. Curse the fly that bit me the moment I heard that order!"

"Do you intend to obey?"

"Suggest an option."

The option he was thinking of was that she might offer herself to him, a reward that would tempt him to violate his obligation to

Chung Yui Hui. But she offered no such thing. Instead, she handed him a red nylon bag and gestured that he should open it.

Dai Gul Dai unzipped the red bag. He saw money! The bottom was covered with yellow thousand-dollar notes. And—he picked up a piece of paper that lay on top of the money. It was a cashier's check on the Hong Kong Bank, made out to "Bearer." The amount was eight million dollars!

"You may count it," she said coldly. "I give you my word there is two million in cash, plus the check—ten million Hong Kong dollars, more than one and a quarter million American dollars."

"And what do you expect of me, Lady, in return for ten million dollars?"

"Chang Po Ka."

Dai Gul Dai drew a deep breath, as deep a breath as a man could draw. "They will kill me."

"No one kills a man who has ten million dollars," she said. "Ten million? That plus the other money I've given you. You can go anywhere in the world and live well. Do you think I am so simple as to suppose you don't have your escape planned? Every man knows where he will go if he must."

"Every *woman*?" Dai Gul Dai asked bluntly.

She understood the implication in his question. She nodded. "Every woman."

"Djakarta," he said. "Singapore. Bangkok."

"Wherever the writ of Chung Yui Hui does not run."

"It is perilous. Extremely perilous," said Dai Gul Dai. "Let me hand him over, then, when everyone is satisfied—"

"They will hide him and his *kwai-pau* in the Chang mansion, inside security that you will be unable to penetrate. Think! You have him in your hands now!"

"Ten million dollars and . . . and *you*, Lady."

She lifted her chin. "Ten million dollars and me," she agreed. "But think! You must be patient a bit. When all is achieved, I will control the resources of the Chang family. Wu Kim Ming will be my ally. Do what you must do about Chang Po Ka. Then flee. Then hide. I will call you back when the time is right."

He grabbed the red nylon bag and trotted up the stone steps from the quay to the street. Out of her sight, he emptied the money from the Adidas bag into a large paper bag that he pulled out from under his shirt. He threw the Adidas bag into the water and walked away.

6

EMILY HAD COME ACROSS the hall and sat in Beth's apartment. With cushions under her, she was able to sit up and not suffer.

"*Qi gong*," she said. "I always supposed it was quackery." She shook her head. "Believe me, it is not."

Beth glanced at Mark Huang. Her thought was that she would not suggest to Emily that it was quackery. If a *qi gong* master had relieved her pain, let it stand at that. Beth could not believe that Emily's pain was psychosomatic, but maybe all pain was psychosomatic to some degree. *Qi gong*, psychiatry, chiropractic, or phrenology . . . faith healing, vitamin-gobbling, holism, or prayers to Jude, the saint of hopeless causes—whatever. Whatever worked. She was not going to discourage Emily in accepting whatever relieved her pain.

"I am adding more security to this building tonight," said Huang. "I had supposed the Chang security was complete, but Bo's thugs had no difficulty snatching Beth out of here last night."

"There may be a simple reason for that," said Beth. "I doubt it *was* General Bo's thugs. He was there . . . but with the Changs' connivance. I have to wonder if Qiao Qichen wasn't there, watching me take my little beating. I wonder who else. John . . ."

"But if what you are suggesting could be true," said Emily, "then Anne—"

"Which is why I am sending a police team into this building. In fact, they are here now," said Huang.

"What's at issue tonight?" Beth asked. "Michael . . . or me?"

7

MICHAEL COULD NOT SLEEP. He had to believe that his transfer to Sha Tau Kok was immensely significant. Besides that, his squalid new prison was not air-conditioned. He didn't have even as much privacy as he'd had before. Apart from the fact that the whole upstairs flat was just one room, plus a bathroom, he was watched by twice the number of guards—including the muttering, threatening Big Mouth. They watched television constantly, whatever was on, and of course they preferred cartoons and silly sitcoms to anything else.

He was handcuffed and shackled. Already, after less than a full day here, his clothes stank of sweat. Gone, too, were the fine meals he had been served. Here he ate what the guards ate: rice and noodles, vegetables and fish, tea.

Wearing handcuffs, he had difficulty cleaning his backside after a bowel movement. It was worse than awkward. Big Mouth made a point of watching and laughing.

He wondered where Beth was. Not for a moment had his vivid memories of her faded. Within an hour or so, it would be exactly one week since she had slipped over the side of the boat in Victoria Harbour. He knew she was alive. He had seen her on television. Qiao Qichen had assured him she was alive. But Dai Gul Dai said she had been severely beaten and was in hospital.

That was a heinous thing to say. He would see Big Prick dead for saying that, if for nothing else.

And Tom—Qiao Qichen—had said it would be impossible for him to marry her. Well . . . the *consigliere* would find out what was and was not impossible. So would his honored father, if it came to that. They were ignorant— The words in his mind stopped. He could not call his honored father ignorant.

Marry "a Chinese girl of respectable family" and keep Beth as a concubine! No! Never! He—

The door opened and Dai Gul Dai stalked in. He was in an angry mood and ordered all his guards to move outside and keep watch from there.

"So, Mikego Chang. I trust you are uncomfortable."

"Uncomfortable, yes. And apprehensive."

"Apprehensive?"

Dai Gul Dai emptied his shirt-bundle of cash, and suddenly Michael's apprehension increased enormously.

8

BETH DRESSED IN THE blue jeans and white T-shirt she had worn the night before, the clothes that had been pulled off her when they beat her. She would have liked for Michael to see her in the catsuit from Guangzhou, or at least the linen jacket and leggings she had bought with General Bo's thousand-dollar note, but Mark Huang had suggested she wear something serviceable and inconspicuous. What they were going to do tonight might prove to be more complicated than had been promised.

A member of his police team came to the door after midnight. He brought Huang something Beth had never seen him carry before: a 9-millimeter Beretta automatic and a soft leather holster. She watched him fasten the holster by its straps and hang the pistol under his left armpit. Little pockets on the harness held two extra clips of ammunition.

To her astonishment he asked her to pull up the right leg of her jeans, and he strapped a thin canvas holster on her calf and shoved down into it a tiny black pistol.

Beth shook her head. "I've never fired a gun in my life. I wouldn't know how."

"Let me show you," he said. "This is the safety. You see, it's in the 'on' position. Push it to the 'off' position, and the pistol will fire when you pull the trigger."

"I couldn't hit anything."

"No one could with this. It's for close range only. You shove it up to within an inch or two of someone's belly or chest or back, and pull the trigger, maybe twice."

She shook her head again. "I don't think I could."

"You can if you have to," he said. "You'll find out. You'll have an immense advantage, in that no one will suspect you have it. Just wear it there on your leg, and let's pray no occasion comes for you to use it. It's called a Baby Browning. It doesn't make much noise, and there's no recoil. It was designed to make it possible for a woman to defend herself if she has to."

9

CHIEF SUPERINTENDENT LIONEL BANNISTER had stood aside from this one. He was letting Senior Inspector Huang Han Gai have his way, confident that Huang would make a fool of himself— or at the very least stir up a destructive mess of political trouble. Huang Han Gai meant "foundation of China." Next year Huang and his like would take over the Hong Kong police. He, Bannister, was going home, as were most of his fellows. All right. Let the wogs, the foundations of China, see what they could do with it. The British establishment in Hong Kong, ranging from the senior bureaucrats who had dominated the higher strata of the civil service like Bannister to the erstwhile taipans that had ruled Jardines and Swires, had watched with dismay and then resignation how quickly the Hong Kong Chinese were displacing them in their political and economic roles even before July 1, 1997. For all practical purposes, the new Chinese billionaires and executives with Harvard MBAs had repossessed Hong Kong in all but name long before the fateful date of the Handover. All the British colonial administration did was stand by with a stiff upper lip. The sun would set on the empire, that's for sure, but the likes of Bannister would have a last fling at authority, with just one year to go. Hence many local and London Brits cheered when Governor Chris Patten took a quixotic stand and challenged China. It did not matter that Patten's action might actually harm Hong Kong in the long run. Suffice that it showed the Brits would not go quietly, not without a fight.

One thing of which Bannister would never have approved was the presence fifty yards or so away of a van filled with electronic monitoring equipment. The technicians in the van were listening to cellular-telephone conversations. During the hours since Senior Inspector Huang called for them, the technicians had identified frequencies being used in the subject apartment building. Almost everything they heard and recorded was innocuous. After midnight the traffic diminished almost to nothing.

Then:

—*"Ni hao?"* Hello?

—"Qiao."

—"When are you leaving?"

—"Now."

—"Be warned that the streets are teeming with Hong Kong police, some in uniform and undoubtedly many who are not. Why do you call?"

—"Chang Po Ji phoned. He doesn't know what is happening tonight, and I didn't tell him. Unfortunately, he has been drinking rather too much, and he said something indiscreet."

—"He often does. What now?"

—"He mentioned Miss Beth Connor. He referred to her as the 'whore with the witch-mark on her tit.' I didn't like that and asked him what he meant. He said she has a mole on her breast. I asked him how he knew, and he laughed and hung up."

—"May all the gods save him if that young woman *has* a mole on her breast!"

Five minutes later a typed transcript of the conversation was delivered to Mark Huang.

"Beth," he said gravely after he read it. "I have to ask you a very personal question. I beg you not to demand of me why I ask it. The 'why' will come out soon enough."

She shrugged, a little impatient with this approach to an inquiry. "What?" she asked.

"Do you have a mole on one of your breasts?"

"Is it important?"

"It may be."

She pulled up her sweatshirt and pulled down her bra just far enough to let him see the small dark mole. "You beg me not to demand—?"

"It identifies one of the men who saw you last night. Not Qiao Qichen. Not Michael's father."

"Then who?"

"Let me find out for sure before we make an error."

10

SHORTLY AFTER ONE O'CLOCK when the streets were dark and quiet, the Hong Kong police made themselves invisible on Arbuthnot Street and Caine Road—so as not to be seen by Qiao Qichen and his guards when they arrived to pick up Beth and Huang. It was a charade. The Chang security men on guard around the apartment building knew full well they were there, just as the police knew *they* were there.

About the same time Huang rang the doorbell at Emily's apartment across the hall. Anne answered.

"Anne," he said, bowing slightly. "I would like to introduce Sergeant Shelley Bai. We have reason to fear some sort of unusual activity tonight, so I would like for her to sit in your apartment overnight."

"What is 'unusual activity'?" asked Anne.

"There seems to be an unusual amount of activity on the streets in this vicinity. Unidentified cars. We have put a police guard around the building and at appropriate points inside. Sergeant Bai will remain awake, and she has her radio."

Anne cast a skeptical and unfriendly eye on the woman, who wore the olive-drab uniform of the Hong Kong police, with her radio fastened at her shoulder, her sidearm hanging in a holster. Anne shrugged. "I'll be glad to have protection," she said dryly.

At one-thirty, promptly, the house phone rang, and the building security guard told Beth there was a car waiting for her outside. She and Huang went down one floor by stairs, so that Anne would not hear the elevator and know they had left. They had no great suspicions of Anne but had decided that what she didn't know wouldn't hurt her—or anybody else. They called the elevator to the floor below and shortly were on the street.

Qiao Qichen was waiting. The car was a black Lexus. Qiao Qichen drove. A guard sat beside him. Beth and Huang sat in the back seat. The car was preceded by one black Honda and followed by another.

Beth recognized the tunnel they entered to cross under the harbor from Hong Kong Island to Kowloon. After they passed through Kowloon they proceeded on highways that led out into the New Territories. The New Territories was by far the largest part of the crown colony in area, though not in population. Traffic was heavy. Huang explained to Beth that the hundreds of big trucks they saw were running to and from Shenzhen, carrying a flourishing trade in the thick of night.

They passed huge apartment developments in clusters of high-rise buildings. Hundreds of thousands of people lived in these developments, which were complete with schools, hospitals, stores, theaters, and clubs. The Hong Kong government made a conscious decision years ago to solve the acute housing crises in Hong Kong

Island and Kowloon by turning farmland in the New Territories just south of the Chinese border into huge satellite cities. But after a time Qiao Qichen followed the lead Honda and turned off the highway and onto a two-lane road. It was the road to Sha Tau Kok, and soon they were the only cars on the road.

They drove slowly and began to pass police vehicles parked by the sides of the road. Eventually they came to a roadblock.

The three cars stopped. The drivers got out and walked forward, into the glare of floodlights. They approached armed men wearing camouflage suits and black berets.

"Field Patrol Detachment, Hong Kong police," Huang murmured to Beth.

"Maybe you should get out and talk to them," she suggested.

He shook his head. "Everything has been arranged. Otherwise we wouldn't be here."

Four policemen had come forward. One, the only Westerner in the group, was a blond, beefy man, substantially taller than the rest. Qiao Qichen talked to him. Only one man looked Chinese. Two others were Asians but didn't seem to Beth to be Chinese.

"Gurkhas," said Huang as though he had read her thought. "Rumor has it they'll be going home shortly."

"Home being?"

"Nepal. The Himalayas. They've served in British armed forces for a very long time. Actually, I don't suppose these fellows will go home directly. They're young. They'll probably wind up somewhere else where Her Majesty needs tough little soldiers. Some of them lived most of their lives here, and their children were born here. After the handover, if they don't go home they must find work, probably as bodyguards to Hong Kong's billionaires."

They looked like tough little soldiers. Small, wiry men carrying automatic weapons cradled under their arms.

Much nodding followed, but no smiling or shaking of hands. Two of the Gurkhas pushed back the barrier, and the three cars passed through.

11

THE TOWN OF SHA Tau Kok was inside a tall fence topped with coils of razor wire. The three cars entered the town through an elaborately guarded gate. The streets were dingy and at this time of night all but deserted.

"Chung Ying Street," Huang said to Beth. "*Chung* means 'Chinese.' *Ying* means 'British.' And this is the border. On this street you can stand with one foot in Hong Kong and one in China."

"It will be best if you two remain in the car," said Qiao Qichen. He himself got out and walked first one way, then the other way, on Chung Ying Street.

They waited. It was now three o'clock. Another black car entered Chung Ying Street. It stopped. Two men got out and walked toward Qiao. They spoke for a moment, then one of them walked away from Qiao and came toward the car.

"Wu Kim Ming . . ." Huang muttered. "I might have known."

Wu walked up to the car and looked in. Huang opened the door. "Senior Inspector. Miss Connor," Wu said cordially. Then he spoke directly to Beth—"I am glad to have been able to be of service to you," he said. "It has been somewhat complex to arrange, but all is in order."

"I am grateful, Mr. Wu," she said.

Wu glanced at his watch. "Any time now," he said.

But three-fifteen came, and three-thirty, with no sign of Michael. Beth was at first tense, then almost tearful. Wu and Qiao made urgent calls on their cell phones and paced. Huang kept silent and watched.

Beth got out of the car and walked up to Wu and Qiao. "*What's wrong?*" she whispered hoarsely. "Where is Michael? Who's holding him now?"

"Dai Gul Dai . . ." Wu said darkly.

"He works for you," she said bluntly.

"He has betrayed me," said Wu. His face was twisted in fury. "He is acting on his own motives. *And he will die!*"

"I don't give a damn!" Beth snapped. "What about Michael?"

Qiao Qichen nodded. "What about Michael indeed. . . ."

THIRTEEN

They could kill Michael before we could reach him.

1

BETH SAT IN THE back of the Lexus, weeping as silently as she could. Huang was out of the car now and stood with Qiao Qichen and Wu Kim Ming, quietly talking while Chang and triad guards stood warily around, scanning the street and all the buildings on both sides.

Wu's face was a carapace of dark fury. "Chang Po Ka," he said, "is within fifty meters of here. I know where. My men and yours could rush the house. But Dai Gul Dai would kill the young man before we could reach him."

"What does *he* expect to gain?" Qiao asked. "What good would it do him to—"

"The gods know," said Wu. "But certainly he expects to gain something. He is no fool, in the larger sense, and he would not have incurred the wrath that is likely to kill him unless he expected to gain something significant."

"Then there is another enterpriser at work here," said Qiao Qichen balefully.

"Bo?" Huang asked.

Wu shook his head. "Why? What motive? He is getting what he wanted. The young man is nothing to him."

"Well, then Chang Po Ji—John," Huang suggested. "*He* has something to gain."

Now Qiao's face darkened. "Yes. I suppose that could be," he said quietly.

Beth wiped her eyes and stiffened her face. She left the Lexus and walked up to the group of men. "So what now?" she asked. "What happens next?"

Neither Wu nor Qiao was accustomed to having a woman interrupt a solemn discussion, and their first reaction was to resent her. Wu glanced at her, though, and then stared for a moment. "We have a serious situation," he said. "I am convinced your fiancé is being held within fifty meters of here. He may indeed be watching us from some window. I know, probably, what window that is. We have men here, with weapons. We could storm the building. But—" He shook his head. "They could kill Michael before we could reach him."

"And they . . ." she said coldly. "They, whoever they are, should know they will certainly die, too. And I assume, Mr. Wu, Mr. Qiao . . . that they will die very painfully. Let me have a red-hot knife to use on Dai Gul Dai! He won't be Dai Gul Dai when I am finished."

"The painful death of Dai Gul Dai means nothing to us if we cause Michael to die," said Huang.

"Alright. Then arrange with them to let me see him," Beth said. "When I'm inside— When I'm facing Dai Gul Dai . . . I have the little gun that's strapped to my leg."

Huang shook his head firmly. "You would surprise him with that, I'm sure. If there were only one of them— No, Beth. You would be killed for sure. Probably Michael, too."

She snapped her head from side to side, looking at the buildings and windows in turn. "Then what do we do, gentlemen?" she asked. "Am I supposed to believe that the powerful Chung Yui Hui and the fabulously wealthy Chang family have been defeated by a sadist thug who goes by the name Big Prick?"

"Someone more clever than that thug," said Qiao Qichen. "Someone who—"

"We are not defeated," Wu interrupted. "We are at a standoff.

We cannot move in and rescue Michael. On the other hand, Dai Gul Dai and whatever allies he has cannot escape Sha Tau Kok. The Field Patrol Detachment has doubled its strength between here and Hong Kong. On the other side, the Bin Fong—that is, the Perimeter Defense Force, the border police—have closed the crossings. Going from here to Hong Kong has always been difficult. Going the other way, into China, has not. Now it will be extremely difficult in both directions."

"This assumes he was ever in Sha Tau Kok," said Beth. "Do we in fact know he was ever here?"

"He was here," said Wu grimly. "He *is* here. On the Chinese side of the line."

"We came in good faith," said Qiao. "We didn't come to use force; we came to effect a negotiated exchange."

"I have only a few men here," said Wu. "In an hour or so I will have many more. But you must understand . . . We are not favored here. The Beijing regime knows us as Taiwanese. I can achieve some things by bribery, others by other means, but—"

Beth turned to Huang. "Can the Hong Kong police arrange to work with the Chinese to mount a joint operation to move in on the house Mr. Wu will identify?"

Huang drew in a deep breath. "I will have to go through my superiors—meaning first through Chief Superintendent Bannister. The bureaucratic process will take time."

Beth stepped away from the men and once again studied the houses. She wondered if Michael could be looking down from one of those dark windows above the street. She sighed loudly. "Alright. I know where I can find help," she said decisively. "Mr. Wu—you say you can achieve things by bribery. Arrange for me to enter China. I want to go to Guangzhou."

Wu shook his head. "In China illegally, you—"

"I have been there illegally before."

"I see what you have in mind," Qiao murmured, shaking his head. "It's a risk, a terrible risk."

"*I* am willing to take it."

"You don't even speak Chinese," said Wu. "I think I know where you mean to go— How can you go there without speaking a word of Chinese?"

"I thought one of you gentlemen might go with me," she said, lifting her chin. "Or one of you might send someone you trust. Mr. Wu? Mr. Qiao? Mark?"

Mark Huang nodded. "I will go with her," he said. "I am, at least, a Senior Inspector of the Hong Kong police."

2

MICHAEL SAW BETH. HE had stood at the window and stared down onto the street—hands cuffed behind his back, a gag stuffed in his mouth so firmly he was all but choking on it. A rope around his neck made certain he would not try a sudden leap through the window.

All that was happening was wholly mysterious to him. He had been brought to Sha Tau Kok for the exchange, obviously, and he saw Tom—Qiao Qichen—and the man he guessed was Wu Kim Ming on the street, with Beth. Yet, no exchange was taking place! Something had gone horribly wrong!

The principals stood around for a long time, then dispersed. All that he had gained from it was a glimpse of Beth. He could see, for sure, that she was alive. What was more, she didn't move like a woman who had been flogged bloody. She was decisive in her movements, emphatic, angry. She was alive . . . *and she was the Beth he knew and loved!* They hadn't hurt her!

Dai Gul Dai stood behind him, watching intently. "So . . ." he whispered hoarsely. "Wu Kim Ming himself! *Ayeeyah!* It is too bad, Mikego Chang, that you could not have a word with your little fat whore, the American—Dai Baw Dai—she of the big tits. Obviously your father has not delivered to Wu Kim Ming everything he asked. The *kwai-pau* was probably one of his demands. Wu Kim Ming has a taste for ones like her. An interesting situation. If the question was, were you to be turned over to your father or was the *kwai-pau* to be turned over to us, you seem to be of less value than the whore."

Michael could not respond. He could not speak. Anyway, he was not thinking of this cretin's insults. He was thinking of the larger questions. He despaired.

3

THE OFFICERS OF BIN Fong, the Chinese border patrol, examined Beth's temporary passport and Huang's Hong Kong identity card. They were humorless and solemnly meticulous, but they overlooked the fact that she did not have the visa she needed to enter China. They casually waved her through. Apparently money had smoothed the way.

Wu had handed to Beth an envelope containing a thick wad of Chinese money—reminbi. As soon as she was out of his sight, she divided the money between herself and Mark Huang. She did not try to count it, but she could see that they had perhaps as much as twenty thousand reminbi. She didn't know the exchange rate exactly but had heard it was not far different from the rate for Hong Kong dollars, so they had more than two thousand dollars in terms of U.S. money. It was more than enough. They did not plan on being in China long.

As the sun rose, two red-and-white taxis waited just outside the village. Huang approached the first of them and told the driver he wanted to be taken to Guangzhou. After twenty minutes of hard bargaining in Cantonese, a thousand reminbi changed hands and Beth and Mark slid into the back seat and set off for Guangzhou.

"It's hard to believe," Beth said.

"What's hard to believe?"

"That it's only a week since I made this trip before. I don't know which way is what, but I have a sense I'm going to be traveling along the same highway as last Monday. I'll tell you, this is a hell of a lot more comfortable."

Huang nodded.

She looked at his face and smiled. "No handcuffs," she said.

4

DRAGON HAD BROUGHT HIS yellow robes with him this time, in his leather case. He rang the bell and was dismayed that it was answered by a uniformed Hong Kong policewoman.

"Uh . . . Anne, please," he said. "I am here to see Anne."

Anne came out of a bedroom and stepped around Sergeant Bai, the policewoman.

"Honored Lady," said Dragon, bowing. "I have come to comfort Miss Parker."

"She will be ready soon. In the meantime, let us step out on the balcony."

The sunshine was oppressively brilliant that morning. It glinted off the angles of the Bank of China and off the multicolored glass of a score of other buildings. The day would be hot. Anne looked down at the working people hurrying along the pavements far below and wondered how they endured the heat.

"It has become impossible to contact Dai Gul Dai," Dragon said ominously. "I stopped by the shop to see if there were messages from him, before I came here. They say the telephone line is dead. It has been dead for some hours."

"The cellular?"

"Dead. They have cut him off."

"*Who* has cut him off?"

Dragon shook his head. "Who could?"

Anne sighed. "The police. The Changs. The triads. Any of them. All of them. Any of them could."

"I only report . . ." said Dragon timidly, as if he were afraid she would blame him."

" 'Big Tits,' " mused Anne. "She is not in the apartment across the hall. Neither is her pet policeman. Sometime in the night they made themselves absent."

"As did Qiao Qichen, from the mansion," said Dragon. "For the meeting at Sha Tau Kok at three this morning. Qiao returned at eight."

"How do you know?"

"I snoop," he said.

"Assiduously," she said dryly.

Dragon showed a pallid smile. "For years my survival depended on my watching and observing—in fact, on my meddling in other people's affairs. They say 'Knowledge is power.' And it is, Gracious Lady, especially when other people don't guess you have the knowledge. Better still, when they think they have concealed it from you."

"*Anyway*, they did not return in triumph with Chang Po Ka. And Big Tits has not returned to the flat across the hall. Something happened! Dai Gul Dai—our friend has done his work!"

"Perhaps only Chang Po Ji stands between you and—"

"Do not think it! Not now." Anne turned away from the view of the streets below. "We must be patient," she said. "Often patience is the very best course. Impatience causes mistakes. We wait. We watch."

Dragon bowed. "As you wish, Lady."

"For now," she said, "you must do all you can for the *kwai-pau* in the bedroom. She may yet prove useful."

Dragon donned his saffron silk robe and went into the bedroom where Emily still lay on her stomach. "Uncomfortable, beautiful Lady Yin?" he gently asked.

Emily turned her head and eyes toward him. " 'Lady Yin'?" she asked. Only Wu Kim Ming had ever used that term for her. "Why do you call me that, *qi gong* Master?"

"Because you merit it," he said. "Let us relieve your pain."

Emily sat up and followed Dragon in the breathing exercise. He asked her to turn her back toward him, and when she did he began to massage her shoulders and her neck. He threw off her sheet and massaged her back. He slipped his hands around in front and massaged her breasts. Finally he moved his right hand down between her legs. Emily moaned quietly.

5

BO YU TANG, NO longer general but an enterpriser with his hand in many sorts of traffic, kept offices here and there. In Hong Kong his office was a luxurious suite of rooms in a first-class hotel, where he lived and worked. To this office he had summoned John Chang, whom he received like a servant.

"I have considered your request," he said with a malicious smile. "But I want to know what you mean to do with the pictures."

"I intend to have them duplicated and then to distribute copies to certain friends."

Bo pondered for a moment. "I am not sure this doesn't violate my agreement with Wu Kim Ming. The witnesses to her punishment were carefully selected."

"Suppose I were to promise you that I will distribute copies only to men who were there."

"Do you so promise?"

John nodded solemnly. "Yes."

"Then—" Bo opened a drawer in his desk and handed John the six Polaroids he had taken of Beth exposed, then beaten, on the yacht. "With my blessing," he chuckled.

"I am grateful, sir," John said as he stuffed the prints into his jacket pocket.

Bo Yu Tang shrugged. "I *saw* her humiliation. I have no need for photographs of your brother's big-titted, big-assed whore. It amused me to take them, but it does not amuse me to look at them."

"It will amuse some people," said John.

6

THIS WAS IN FACT the same highway she had traveled last Monday. It was hard for Beth to believe that only a week had passed since she sat disconsolate in handcuffs on this road, a miserable, frightened prisoner on her way to a Chinese jail.

Time—it was confused for her. Never had a week of time passed so slowly or with so many events crowded one on the other. She wondered if she would remember every detail of it.

Along this highway a brutal reality occurred to her: that she had not telephoned her mother and father in Boston. Of course, they knew she was alive. The propaganda event in Guangzhou had been televised in every country in the world. They had seen her elegantly dressed and shaking hands with Chinese officials and with Xiang Li.

Time—that had been less than a week ago. Maybe they were not concerned that their idiosyncratic daughter had not yet called. Well. What could she have told them? That her fiancé had been kidnapped, she herself almost murdered? That she had worked as a waitress in a Hong Kong . . . whorehouse? That she was a guest of the Chang family in a fine apartment, from which she had been kidnapped and exposed and beaten?

Time—tomorrow she would call, no matter what.

"Guangzhou . . ." said Mark Huang, interrupting her thoughts. "The city ahead is Guangzhou."

She knew. They had indeed traveled on the same superhighway she had seen a week ago. If she recognized nothing else for certain, she recognized the thick multicolored pall of air pollution that hung over the city. Guangzhou, she had learned during the past week, was one of the most prosperous cities in China, with a population of eight million. And Guangdong Province, with seventy million residents, was by far the most prosperous province in China, with its history of Western contacts and proximity to Hong Kong. Dr. Sun Yat-sen, widely hailed as the George Washington of China's revolution that overturned the Qing Dynasty in 1911, hailed from Guangdong. People from Guangdong had emigrated en masse for the past several hundred years and now dominated the landscape of Southeast Asia, dominating the economies of the countries they settled. After China opened up its economy in 1976, Guangdong proved to be a magnet for workers from all over the country; but it was also the focus of every malignancy that uncontrolled urbanization could bring.

Huang noticed her staring at the pollution and explained. "They say Europe and America polluted the world's air and water to generate the industrial economies that give their people so high a standard of living, so why should China restrain itself and deny the same prosperity to its people?"

The highway reached the city on its north side, and the driver turned onto local streets to reach the center. Beth recognized the Guangzhou railroad station, marked by its big clock. She recognized the tall television tower that rose from a hillside above the street.

They turned into a broad street whose name she recalled— Dongfeng Zhonglu—and there she recognized the Sun Yat-sen memorial. Then the driver turned through the gates of the Guangdong Provincial Government Building.

7

"THIS IS AN UNEXPECTED pleasure," said Shek Tin, deputy governor of Guangdong Province. "I did have a bit of advance notice that you were coming. That notice was a surprise, a surprise indeed."

"Who told you we were coming, if I may ask?"

"Qiao Qichen, the counselor of your prospective father-in-law. He telephoned to say you were coming, and he gave me a bit of explanation as to why."

"I came to ask for your help," Beth said quietly.

"Yes. I understand the situation. But I am not sure what help I can give you," said Shek Tin.

Huang said something in Chinese, and Shek responded very briefly in Chinese, glancing apologetically at Beth. As before, he was dressed in a white shirt with a red-and-gold necktie. His jacket hung over a chair. As before, he carried two pens in his shirt pocket, and this time she noticed that one of them was not a ballpoint but rather a Mont Blanc fountain pen that wrote with real ink. She guessed it was better for writing Chinese characters.

"I wish to help you. But what can I do?"

Huang answered. "Send in a brigade of Bin Fong," he said. "The house where Michael Chang is being held is on your side of the border in Sha Tau Kok."

"Sha Tau Kok is a very sensitive situation," said Shek. "Our Bin Fong and your Hong Kong police have been careful not to set off an international incident."

"The Field Patrol Detachment knows exactly what is going on," said Huang. "It can be advised in more detail what you intend to do. It will not interfere."

"Ah, but will it *cooperate*? Suppose these kidnappers rush from the house and flee to the Hong Kong side of the boundary. Will you seize them?"

"We will."

"How is the commander of my brigade to know which house to take?"

"It belongs to Chung Yui Hui. Wu Kim Ming and the triad will cooperate fully."

"Wu Kim Ming . . ." Shek mused. He shook his head. "Wasn't

it Chung Yui Hui that kidnapped Michael Chang and Miss Connor? If so, why would they cooperate with us now?"

"Because they got what they wanted," said Beth. "They got their ransom. Michael is being held by a traitor to Chung Yui Hui, for his own reasons."

Shek swung around in his chair and looked out the window. "You invite me to place myself in a very, very awkward position," he said. "You ask a brigade of Bin Fong to openly assist a triad in solving one of its problems. Not only that, you ask that help for a *Taiwanese* triad."

"Let me suggest two reasons that might persuade you to do it," said Beth. "In the first place, the ransom for which Michael was held involves a multi-billion-dollar investment in a land reclamation project in Hong Kong. Important Chinese on the mainland and elsewhere have a great deal of money tied up in the project. So will Chung Yui Hui. The agreement to release Michael was not just between Michael's father and Wu Kim Ming. It also involved Bo Yu Tang. Suppose Michael is *not* freed, is not returned to his family." She shrugged and turned up the palms of her hands. "I'm not sure the agreement then holds."

"Is this possible?" Shek asked.

"It is. But let me suggest another reason why you should help us." Beth paused and smiled at the provincial governor. "We *do* like good publicity, don't we, Mr. Shek? You could have television cameras in Sha Tau Kok, showing how the People's Republic of China helped liberate the victim of a kidnapping. A gesture of goodwill. This would play well to the American public."

Shek returned her smile. "You are a clever young woman, as I saw last week. But this is a much more sensitive and difficult issue than the one you presented last week. Beijing might not want such an event televised."

"Tape it," she said. "Send them the videotape and let them decide if they want to broadcast it."

"I believe I *will* telephone Beijing," said Shek. "Will you excuse me for a few minutes?"

As they waited in the anteroom outside Shek's office, Huang said very quietly to Beth, "I didn't know you understood so much about Western Reclamation."

"I *don't* know very much. I know part of the story. I guessed the rest."

8

WHATEVER SOMEONE IN BEIJING said, it satisfied Shek Tin. "Very well," he said when they returned to his office. "I will order the operation in Sha Tau Kok. It *must be* a coordinated operation, with the Hong Kong police playing their proper role. Senior Inspector Huang?"

"I will have to call my superior," said Huang.

"Surely you don't propose to call that ass Bannister!" Beth interjected heatedly.

Huang shrugged. "I must. I don't have authority to demand anything from Field Patrol Detachment."

Beth turned to Shek. "Sir," she asked, "do you know the meaning of the American expression 'a horse's ass'?"

Shek nodded.

"And that is what Superintendent Bannister is."

"Then I will speak directly to Bannister's boss, the Commissioner of the Hong Kong police," Shek volunteered.

"Could you allow me to speak for a minute or two with Qiao Qichen first?" Beth asked.

Shek nodded.

She called Qiao and explained the situation him in a few words. His response was, "You are a very clever young woman, Miss Connor. I will telephone the Police Commissioner and reinforce whatever Governor Shek wants to tell him."

"I have a personal request, Mr. Qiao," she said grimly. "See to it that John doesn't know what's coming down. And if he already knows, don't let him go to Sha Tau Kok."

"I understand what you are saying. Please depend on me to be circumspect."

On the telephone, Shek made the arrangements. The Bin Fong Brigade would be dispatched from Shenzhen. Beth and Huang would accompany Shek in the helicopter that would also carry the brigade commander from Guangzhou.

FOURTEEN

"Our son must be avenged . . . at whatever cost!"

1

DRAGON, RETURNING TO THE mansion after his meeting with Anne in the morning, visited Frederick.

His relationship with the dying man was very much the same as his relationship with Anne, in that Frederick desperately wanted to believe the mystic could help him but was too intelligent and practical a man to accept *qi gong*. The breathing and meditating he did with Dragon had sometimes relieved his pain a little, but his disease was not psychosomatic, and his life was not going to be saved or even prolonged by hocus-pocus, not this kind or any other.

"May I be of assistance to you this morning, honored Chang Po Kuok?" Dragon bowed to Frederick.

"Sit down. Let us breathe and meditate together. It may bring me a little comfort."

In fact, it did. The measured breathing brought relaxation, and the meditation focused Frederick's mind on things outside his failing body. It amused him not to tell Dragon what he meditated on. He meditated on his once-superb manliness and the exquisite pleasures it had brought him. He meditated on the erotic girls and women he had known. Sometimes he wondered which one—or if it had been several—had transmitted the disease.

"An effort was made last night to secure the release of your brother," Dragon said when he was about to leave.

"I know," Frederick said wanly, emerging from the half-peaceful state *qi gong* had induced. "It failed."

"How so?"

"All was arranged. Tom went to Sha Tau Kok. The agreement was not honored. My father is in shock. He now believes that my brother is dead. His mother, So Liming, believes he is dead and has gone into mourning."

"John?"

"John is drunk," said Frederick scornfully. "In the middle of the day, he is drunk. That is how my happy little brother pays his respect to his family."

2

JOHN WAS NOT AS drunk as his elder brother supposed. He was drinking Napoleon brandy, but he sat in the living room of his suite, quietly sobbing. The death of Michael meant that he was now the heir. He was drinking to build the courage to seek out his father and mother and join them in their sorrow.

He had in his lap the Polaroid pictures he had wangled from Bo Yu Tang. He had never intended to distribute them as he had said. He had wanted them because they could severely damage the family's name and honor. And that was important. He had begun to suspect several days ago that Michael would never be returned. Everything Four Finger and his triad accomplices wanted had been arranged. They could have returned Michael Friday, Saturday, or Sunday—if he was alive.

With Michael dead and Frederick about to die, he—John—was the heir. The responsibility fell on him as though the weight of the roof had come down on his shoulders.

He stared at the photographs of Beth Connor. *She* would be one of his responsibilities. The family would have to settle money on her and buy her silence. It had been a gross mistake to strip and beat her—no matter with what restraint the beating had been given. Her resentment would make her far more difficult to appease.

Of course, he couldn't have prevented it. No one asked his consent. Still, the problems the beating had created now fell to him. As did a thousand other problems. He had been able until now to live carefree: the cheerfully irresponsible youngest son, of whom little would ever be demanded. If Michael were really dead, salad days were over.

Beth Connor . . . He hadn't felt much sympathy for her Saturday night. He did now. The Polaroid pictures were of an abused and terrified girl. He remembered how she screamed in terror, then howled in agony, and suddenly *all* his sympathy poured out for her.

He wondered if—if *he* could keep her for *his* consort. What tits! What an ass!

John rose from his chair, carrying the pictures with him. He dropped them into a brass bowl and carried them out to his balcony. He returned to his room for a little can of lighter fluid, which he squirted over the pictures, and then set them on fire. As they burned, he sobbed and rubbed his eyes.

3

CHANG WING HING AND So Liming sat on the shady stone-pillared veranda. They were in shock and had begun to mourn their second son. The father had cast aside his jacket and sat in his white shirt with the collar and necktie loose. The mother wore a multicolored silk blouse and a close-fitting knee-length black skirt. She dabbed at her eyes with a white handkerchief.

Qiao Qichen was with them and tried to speak comforting words—

"It doesn't mean that Chang Po Ka is dead. It means only that something went wrong with the exchange. It could be, for example, that Wu's men could not get into Sha Tau Kok, that the officials on the other side have closed the border for some reason. They've been known to do it."

Chang Wing Hing shook his head disconsolately. His eyes and cheeks glistened with tears. For some minutes he had barely spoken and now could not force words out of his constricted throat.

So Liming wept, too, but her face was rigid with fury, and she had words to say. Her grief manifested itself as wrath for injury done her. "Our son must be avenged!" she declared in a hard, clear voice. "At whatever cost! Our family has the power to destroy the triads. Let it be done!"

Qiao Qichen was astonished. Never before had he heard this pretty little woman assert herself at all, much less assert herself so vehemently. He guessed Chang Wing Hing was surprised, too, though who could know what of a woman's character might be seen by a man when he climbed the bed.

"We dare not make war on Chung Yui Hui," Qiao said.

"No?" she asked. "I say we can. My honored husband, in his infinite wisdom, has gradually transferred our loyalty toward those who are coming to govern us next year. They know and they are grateful. Let Chung Yui Hui stand up against *that*."

"They will retreat to Taiwan," said Qiao.

"Ha! Good! Let them be confined to that miserable island," she snapped.

"We don't *know* that your son is—"

"He is," said the father weakly. "All was arranged, all so meticulously arranged. If they didn't hand him over, it was because they couldn't. You said Wu was angry. He was angry because one of his henchmen had killed my son!"

Qiao spoke to So Liming. "Let us rely on Deputy Governor Shek, as you suggest," he said. "The American young woman has gone to Guangzhou to plead for help from that very source. Let us reach no conclusions until she returns."

"*If* she returns," said the mother bitterly.

4

BETH HAD NEVER FLOWN in a helicopter before and had not realized how noisy and shaky the flight would be. Shek Tin and the brigade commander spoke Chinese to each other, but even if they had spoken English Beth would have had difficulty understanding them over the noise of the engine and the repeated *slap-slap* sound of the big rotor.

The commander was a middle-aged officer who wore a crisp, natty uniform and seemed to strive to be charismatic. He smiled, nodded, and chatted enthusiastically with Shek, as if the deputy governor were the most interesting man in the world and this mission were the most challenging and important it had ever been his privilege to command.

The helicopter did not follow the highway. It flew south, down the Pearl River to the sea, then out over the bright wider water of the river mouth. Beth saw the heavy water traffic that moved on the river and the sea beyond. When they were over the open water she took special notice of the fishing boats, wondered which ones were shrimpers, and wondered if she might by chance be looking down at the boat that had picked her up in Victoria Harbour. She stared at the shore and saw fishing villages. Certainly one of them was the one where she had been taken ashore. She wondered what the people there remembered of her. She wondered what they thought she had been.

The helicopter turned east and flew toward Shenzhen, its tall gleaming towers distinctly visible from a great distance. They passed north of the city and came down on a field a little to the east of it. There the helicopter landed.

About a hundred men, wearing camouflage uniforms with red berets, had been sitting on the ground near four trucks. As the chopper settled onto its wheels, they rose and briskly formed themselves into ranks. They were heavily armed with submachine guns, and each one had four canisters strapped to his chest.

"They are an elite brigade," Huang explained to Beth. "They move quickly into a spot where there is trouble. The canisters are tear gas or concussion grenades."

A young officer marched up to the Bin Fong commander, saluted briskly, spun around and saluted Shek. After that he shook hands with both Huang and Beth.

He pointed to a black-and-white van that stood nearby and led the party over to it. He pulled down the rear door. There, spread out over the flat surface, lay a display of large color photographs, taken from the air. They were of the town of Sha Tau Kok, and they were remarkable photographs, so clear that one could have recognized the faces of people walking on the street.

Though Beth had been there only at night, she had no difficulty identifying the spot where the Lexus had been parked and the place where she had stood and talked with Wu Kim Ming and Qiao Qichen. Wu had said that Michael might have been looking down from one of the windows. She could identify the buildings he had meant.

The commander first talked to the junior officer for a moment, then spoke to Shek.

"The difficulty," Shek said to Beth in English, "will be in knowing which building to assault."

"For that," she said, "I think we have to rely on Wu Kim Ming. He knows which building the triad has used before."

Shek frowned deeply. "We have to rely on the word of an archcriminal." He turned to the commander and spoke to him in Chinese. Then Shek spoke again to Beth. "He wants to know if you can reduce the possible number to a few."

Beth nodded. She pointed to four buildings with second-floor windows overlooking the street.

The junior officer pulled a big flat album from beneath the backseat of the vehicle. He spread it open. It contained photographs of buildings in Sha Tau Kok, buildings on both sides of Chung Ying Street—from above, from the front, from the back, and some from the sides. Obviously Bin Fong had done reconnaissance in depth in Sha Tau Kok. Beth wondered if the Field Patrol Detachment of the Hong Kong police had done as much.

A second junior officer trotted toward the utility vehicle. He was carrying a field telephone. He spoke to the commander, who pointed to Huang. Huang took the telephone and listened, then spoke. He nodded and spoke, nodded and spoke, then handed back the field telephone and spoke to Shek. After that he turned to Beth—

"The Field Patrol Detachment has the Hong Kong side closed tight. They have cut off telephone communication between Sha Tau Kok and Hong Kong, though they are monitoring efforts to put calls through. There have been several attempts from Hong Kong to get calls through to one of the buildings on Chung Ying Street."

"Calls from who?" she asked.

"The caller never stays on the line long enough for the trace to be made."

"Does anybody try to call out?"

"Someone picks up the telephone, and when they don't get a dial tone they hang up immediately."

"Who is there? Qiao Qichen?"

Huang shook his head. "And no Chang family security men. But Wu Kim Ming is there. He has as many as twenty men, maybe twenty-five. The Field Detachment had orders to let them into Sha Tau Kok, and the Chief Inspector on the street suspects others have come in from the Chinese side."

"Why has the family sent no one?" she asked.

Huang shook his head. "I don't know, Beth."

"So what happens now?"

"The elite brigade here—the Bin Fong—is going to be moving into Sha Tau Kok from the north. The Field Detachment is already in position—that is to say, it is positioned in force on its own side of the boundary. It will not cross over. The building where we think Michael may be held is on the Chinese side, so it depends on Bin Fong to go in after him."

"So, then, what are you and I supposed to do?" she asked apprehensively.

Mark Huang smiled faintly and wryly. "We are going with them. They count on you to help identify the building."

Beth nodded, holding back tears. "And to identify the body if Michael is dead."

5

MICHAEL LAY FACEDOWN on a tattered, stinking old couch in the room above Chung Ying Street. His hands were cuffed behind his back, his legs were shackled, and he was blindfolded and gagged. Except for being taken to the bathroom, he had lain here since the predawn hour when he had seen Beth on the street. He had not been fed. He'd had nothing to drink. His muscles were cramped. His stomach threatened to spew. He retained little hope.

Dai Gul Dai paced the room, staring down from the window, occasionally picking up a telephone and slamming it back down. Big Mouth, his brother, was the only man in the room who was not afraid to talk to him; even he spoke only occasionally.

There were only five of them: the two brothers and two other men, plus a little girl the men took turns using. A body lay in a corner of the room. That man had complained that they had made a gross error and were trapped, and Dai Gul Dai had flipped a knife into his stomach and then cut his throat. *"Dew neh loh moh!"* he had yelled at the man as the blood gurgled in his mouth and gushed from between his lips.

The girl, hardly more than a child, sat naked on the floor and stared at her feet.

Apart, where Michael couldn't hear him, the brothers talked. "Liu Soong Qin," Dai Gul Dai muttered. *"Dew neh chou hai!"* It meant "fuck your stinking cunt!" He meant Anne.

"Maybe they've got her," his younger brother suggested.

"Or something worse," said Dai Gul Dai. "Where's her fucking miracle man? He's a clever one. He knows how to get in and out of this town."

"With all deference, Honored Brother, I suggest *we* get out. I believe you have a sum of money. . . ."

"You know too much."

"I observe quietly. I do not meddle."

"A problem," said the elder brother. "We will have to kill the two fuckers over there, plus the girl, plus Mikego Chang."

"I ask the privilege of killing that one."

"Granted. We will have to surprise the two fuckers."

"It's a shame, the girl."

Dai Gul Dai glanced at her. Her cheeks were wet with tears, and when she saw he was looking at her, she whimpered. "I'll have her once more," he said. "And maybe you should, too."

"When we go, where do we go?" asked Big Mouth. "To Hong Kong or—"

"No. To Shenzhen. On to Guangzhou. But back to Hong Kong soon. We are going to satisfy your big desire when you put the knife in the belly of Mikego Chang. Today I have developed a new desire. I'm going to *dew* Liu Soong Qin. I am going to *dew* that *chou hai*. I'll *dew* the arrogance out of her."

"Then we'll both be happy men."

"Yes. When we're ready, I want you to go down and check the car, be certain it will start. When we know some fucker hasn't stolen it and that it will start, then we'll finish our work here and leave."

6

THE BIN FONG BRIGADE moved forward in trucks. Beth, Huang, Shek, and the commander rode in the utility vehicle.

"We have reduced the number of possible buildings to three or four," said Shek Tin, "but we will rely on Wu Kim Ming to identify the one building where we may expect to find the young man."

"What are they going do, shoot the place full of tear gas?" Beth asked.

"That is up to the commander. He is an expert at this sort of thing. His men have been thoroughly trained, and they have experience. Last month they moved in on a house in Jiangmen where a gang of heroin smugglers were holding hostages. One of the hostages was slightly injured. Two of the smugglers died during the assault. The others were tried, found guilty, and executed."

"How do you execute people in China?" she asked.

"With a bullet in the back of the head," Shek said almost casually. "The subject is taken out in a field, he kneels, and an officer fires one shot at close range. The matter is not attended by any lengthy procedures or any ceremony: no formal last meal, no prayers, none of the sadistic cruelty of an American execution."

The commander spoke in Chinese to Shek, and Shek translated. "Exit from Sha Tau Kok will shortly be blocked—that is, on our side. The Hong Kong police have blocked the other side. It is essential, we suppose, that our target people not know that. At first, our brigade and the Hong Kong police will keep themselves concealed, so far as possible. That of course means that you, Miss Connor, must not go where you could be spotted, even with powerful lenses. Our targets must not guess what a strong force is being mounted against them."

Beth nodded. "I beg you, Mr. Shek, to make the commander understand that we are here to *save* a life, more than to bring criminals to justice."

"He has been so ordered."

They abandoned the command vehicle and, led by Mark Huang, Beth crossed the boundary line into the territory of the crown colony. They were encountered first by a Gurkha, then by a husky, blond, and thoroughly British soldier-policeman: Chief Inspector Burke Trevelyan of the Field Patrol Detachment.

"Chief Inspector. I am Huang Han Gai, Senior Inspector of the Hong Kong police, stationed in Central. Can you put a telephone call through for me?"

7

THE CALL WAS TO Qiao Qichen.

"The family is in mourning," said Qiao lugubriously.

"Prematurely," said Huang.

"There is a chance?"

"An elite brigade of Bin Fong is here—a heavily reinforced detachment of Field Patrol. The town is surrounded, cut off from the rest of the world. Dai Gul Dai—and I am sure you know the name—will face a Beijing-style execution if he defies the Bin Fong. Can you contact Wu Kim Ming?"

"I can place calls."

"Tell him to cooperate. If he is here, he may face what Dai Gul Dai faces. But he can win his escape if he cooperates with us."

Communication between Chung Yui Hui and Wu Kim Ming, wherever he was, would have been the envy of any national intelligence organization.

"Honored Leader!"

"Speak quickly!"

"The town is surrounded by reinforced Hong King forces and an elite brigade of Bin Fong. They call on you for cooperation."

"I know that. I am in Sha Tau Kok. If you are in further communication with any of these forces, tell them they shall have my full cooperation. I am in contact with their chief inspector here, and you can reinforce the assurances I have already given."

* * *

Anne was distraught. The policewoman who sat on guard in the apartment assigned to Emily had been replaced by another, and Anne wondered if the women were really there to protect her against some real or imaginary hazard, or were there to hold her prisoner.

The telephone rang. She had almost no doubt that everything said on her cellular telephone was monitored, probably recorded, but she answered.

"Lady Yin. Do you recognize the voice?" She did. It was Wu Kim Ming.

"I know you, Lord Yang."

"Your servant has betrayed us both. Do you have any way of reaching him?"

"None, My Lord."

"I regret to hear it. Be patient, My Lady. When you employed your servant, that violated our alliance."

"When I employed him we had no alliance. If I had dreamed we could—"

"If he reaches you, tell him no. Tell him not to do the thing he contemplates. He can be forgiven."

"I only hope I hear from him, Lord Yang."

8

CHIEF INSPECTOR TREVELYAN TROTTED toward Huang. He held before him a small tape recorder/player. "Listen to that, please," he said. "Recognize the voices?"

Huang put the player to his hear and listened. The quality was not good, but he heard—

—"Lady Yin. Do you recognize the voice?"

—"I know you, Lord Yang."

"Thank you very much, Chief Inspector," Huang said. "That is useful."

* * *

Wu Kim Ming sat in a black Honda on a side street off Chung Ying Street. Beth was with him. He had asked for her. She had asked for him. He closed the doors of the car, and they sat alone, cooled by the car's efficient air-conditioning.

Here, in the heat and dust of Sha Tau Kok, Wu wore a dark-blue suit, a dark-blue tie with tiny white dots, a white shirt, polished black loafers, and the points of a carefully folded white handkerchief stood out of his breast pocket.

"Precious Lady Yin," he murmured to Beth.

"I know what that means, Mr. Wu," she said.

"That circumstances could have been otherwise," he said. "But they are not what we might wish. Michael Chang is alive in the building I pointed out to the chief inspector. *He* cannot enter. He is on the wrong side of the border. Over there . . . over there is an elite brigade of the Bin Fong, as you have told me. They are ready to shoot that building full of tear gas and storm it. If they do, your fiancé will, in all likelihood, die. I know Dai Gul Dai. He will kill your lover during the assault. He will do that before he does anything else."

"I know him, too, and I believe it," Beth said.

"I—I and my men alone have a chance to penetrate that building and save Michael. It is a building we have used for years, and I know my way in and out. Dai Gul Dai does not know it as well."

"So—"

"Talk to the people who trust you," said Wu. "Tell them to give me a chance. I have as much interest as any man in the world in destroying the traitor Dai Gul Dai. Tell Shek Tin and his commander to let me have first chance."

Beth frowned and stared for a long moment, then answered him. "On a condition, Mr. Wu," she said. "You will go into the building. You and one or two others? *And me! I* go, Mr. Wu." She pulled up one leg of her jeans and showed him the little automatic Huang had given her. "*I go!*"

Wu shook his head firmly. *"Insane!"*

"Look at it this way," she said equally firmly. "Frankly, Mr. Wu, you don't care if Michael lives or dies. I don't know what your motives are, and I don't care. Shek Tin and his men don't care if Michael lives or dies. They have their own motives. So does my friend Mark Huang. So does the Field Patrol Detachment. I'm the only one here whose sole motive is to save Michael's life."

"You are wrong. It is my motive also," Wu said calmly.

"The rest of my life is involved in this moment," said Beth. "And I won't help you keep the Bin Fong back unless you take me in with you. That's the way it is, Mr. Wu."

"I wonder if you trust me, Miss Connor."

"No. I don't trust you. I *can't* trust you. Deny that you were there Saturday night when they exposed and beat me. I couldn't testify that you were, but I sensed that you were. Senses are reliable sometimes. Deny that my pain and humiliation were part of the deal among your triad, the Chang family, and the PLA. *Deny it!*"

Wu shook his head. "I can't deny it. It *was* a part of the deal, and Michael is alive because of it," he said calmly. "I couldn't prevent it. All I could do was moderate it. Your exposure and humiliation were in lieu of a more severe beating. You were beaten by *my* man. If one of General Bo's men had done it—"

"All right," she interrupted curtly. "I took my flogging, and I don't complain. But the fact that I don't complain might give you some idea of how much I am determined to save Michael. *Lord Yang!* Give me a heavier-caliber pistol. I'm going in with you. I've got more at stake than you do!"

FIFTEEN

*In five minutes we will assume that Wu Kim Ming
and the unhappy American girl are dead.*

1

THE THREE MEN—SHEK TIN, the Bin Fong commander, and Mark
Huang—shook their heads emphatically.

"Do you plan to restrain me?" Beth asked angrily. She thrust
out her hands, fists clenched. "Here! Put handcuffs on me! Tie me
up! Because, if you don't, I'm *going!*"

"You'll get yourself killed," said Huang.

"That's *my* business, isn't it? I have a right to take the risks I
want to take. If you assault the building, they will kill Michael for
sure. Wu Kim Ming says that's the first thing Dai Gul Dai will do,
if he does *nothing* else."

"And what will be different if the assault is by Wu Kim Ming
and some of his triad assassins?" asked Huang.

"He says he knows how to get into the building."

"Then let him tell us how to get in," said Shek.

"I don't think he'll do that," said Beth. "With him it's a matter
of the honor of the triad. He intends to *execute* Dai Gul Dai. He has
a powerful sense of dignity and honor."

"And then escape," said Shek. "Escape from Sha Tau Kok. Escape from *us*. Escape from the Hong Kong police."

Beth nodded. "I don't think he'd have come here if he didn't
have an escape route well planned."

Huang sighed loudly. "What makes you think that *your* being there is going to make any difference?"

"Wu and his men are going in to kill Dai Gul Dai. I'm going in to save Michael. At the very least, I'll be a distraction. But I think I'll be more than that."

The conversation stopped while Shek Tin translated what they had been saying for the commander. He replied briefly.

"He asks if his men are to stand aside and allow the chief of Chung Yui Hui to take their revenge on a disobedient member," Shek translated.

"If someone is to be killed assaulting that place, why is he so anxious that it be him and his men, instead of triad men?"

Shek translated, then translated the commander's response. "He says that is rational thinking. But he also says that for you to go is not rational, is not good thinking."

Beth glanced back and forth over the faces of the frowning men. "Restrain me, or I'm going," she said.

2

BIG MOUTH CHECKED THE ammunition in his pistol. It was an American Colt .45 automatic, the kind that American officers had carried for decades. It was not accurate, but it fired a big, heavy bullet that would knock a man down wherever it hit him.

"I go to check the car," he said to his brother Dai Gul Dai.

The elder brother held the little girl's head between his hands and was pushing her toward his groin. "Be sure it starts," he said. "Be sure the battery is alive."

Big Mouth descended a flight of stairs into the fish shop on the ground level of the building. The sight of the fish reminded him that he had not eaten since early morning, and he decided to stop by the dim sum shop across the street before he checked the car.

As he walked across—into Hong Kong—he noticed something strange: that the street was not as busy and crowded as usual. People were not strolling around, shopping, but seemed edgy and wary.

Inside the dim sum shop he walked up to the proprietor, who knew him because he had often eaten here. "What's upsetting people?" he asked. "Is a typhoon coming?"

"Fucking cops," said the proprietor.

"Whose cops?"

"Fucking Brits. They're all over. Must be afraid some poor Han will cross their fucking border. There must be a thousand of them just outside of town. And plenty in town, too. Don't you see them?"

Big Mouth shrugged. "They're here all the time. It's nothing unusual."

"Well, they make people nervous. The useless, arrogant fuckers are bad for business."

Big Mouth stood in the doorway and looked out. The man was right; there were more fucking Hong Kong cops on the street than usual. Well . . . they'd stay on their own fucking side of the fucking street. Everything he was concerned about was on the Chinese side. He sat down and ordered food.

3

"I'M SURPRISED THEY LET you come," said Wu.

"They were considering handcuffing me to the command van," Beth said dryly. "They don't like it, but I told them they'd have to restrain me to prevent my coming. Do you have a bigger gun for me?"

"No. I don't have a pistol to spare. Anyway, the little Browning you have is well concealed and may make it possible for you to surprise someone."

"I have a little surprise of my own in mind."

Wu stood outside his car. He had left his jacket inside but still wore his white shirt and his necktie. With his jacket off, he revealed a shoulder holster in which rested an ugly black automatic. He unstrapped the holster now and shoved the gun into the waistband of his trousers, immediately in front, where the broad end of his tie covered the grip, making it all but invisible except to someone who stared hard at him.

"Surprise," he said, "is the key, if we are to save your fiancé." He glanced around. "Precious Lady Yin," he said quietly, "may all the gods be with you this afternoon. A man who has your love has the most and the best the world can offer."

"I said I don't trust you," she answered with a short lift of her chin. "Let me change that. I do trust you. You have lied to me, but you lied to help me. I am grateful."

"We are friends?" he asked.

"We are friends," she affirmed.

Wu smiled. "In future," he said, "our friendship may become the origin of great mutual benefit."

"Amen."

He beckoned, and she followed him out of the street where the car was parked. They emerged on Chung Ying Street a full block from the building that contained the fish and poultry shops and the second-floor flat. Wu worked his way along the street, keeping close to the walls of shops, under their awnings.

He nodded toward the other side of the street. "Too many police," he said. "I urged the senior inspector not to be conspicuous."

The men who accompanied them were not conspicuous. Beth searched faces but could not identify a man who might be a member of the triad on his way to enforce the honor of Chung Yui Hui on Dai Gul Dai.

They reached the door of a poultry shop. Live chickens in pens waited to be slaughtered for the wives of Sha Tau Kok, who would stew them for dinner. Adjacent was a fish shop, where fish swam placidly in aquaria, less aware than the chickens that they would be eaten very soon. Plastic tubs with running water were crowded with shrimp. Other tubs teemed with shellfish.

"From the fish shop a stairway leads up to the squalid rooms above where the loathsome Dai Gul Dai holds your fiancé. We cannot go up that way. What the traitors do not know is that we can climb into their flat from *this* shop."

The keepers of the poultry shop were elaborately deferential to Wu Kim Ming. He led Beth to the back of the shop and into a stinking latrine and washroom. There, two men had already stood on a stepladder and pulled down a ceiling panel. In the space above, a variety of pipes was clearly visible. This room shared plumbing with the bathroom in the flat above.

"It is important to know things like this," Wu said quietly to Beth. "Wishing to exit from above, we could easily drop down into the poultry shop and from there out and away."

It surprised Beth that a man she knew as wealthy and powerful would know how to escape from a shabby flat in a slummy building. She remembered how her father used to say that the rich were rich mostly because they knew how to lie, cheat, and steal.

4

A HELICOPTER HOVERED ABOVE Sha Tau Kok, so high that it was hardly noticed. But in the command van the images from its telescopic cameras were sharp and clear.

"They're in," said Shek Tin.

"How much time do we give them?" Huang asked.

"Five minutes," said the commander. "In five minutes they will have done what they went in for, or they are dead. I am moving my brigade forward. In five minutes we will assume that Wu Kim Ming and the unhappy American girl are dead."

5

QIAO QICHEN WALKED FORWARD and offered his hand to Chief Inspector Trevelyan.

"It's all on *their* side of the line," said the chief inspector. "I can't do a thing. Wu Kim Ming is inside the building. So, Mr. Qiao, is the American girl. I don't know what motivates that one—either the most foolish addiction to romantic love I've ever heard of, or the best courage I've ever seen."

6

WU KIM MING'S TWO men were nondescript, so far as Beth was concerned. They were wiry Chinese, dressed in slacks and polo shirts. Though each one carried a pistol and a knife, they did not impress her as very threatening men. She did notice that their pistols were fitted with silencers, which for her defined them as men who used their guns and did not just carry them.

The one at the top of the ladder pressed upward on the wood that had to be part of the floor above. It yielded, and he put his face up and stared out through a narrow crack into the bathroom of the flat. After a moment he eased the trapdoor down again.

"The bastards up there assume the trapdoor is only an entry panel to give plumbers access to the pipes," Wu whispered to Beth. "They don't know that another trapdoor below leads down to this room." He smiled. "I never saw fit to tell anyone."

He then whispered in Chinese to the man on the ladder. The man pushed the trapdoor up and out of the way and climbed up into the bathroom. The second man followed. He reached down and offered a hand to Beth and helped her climb into the room. Finally Wu climbed up, with the same assistance, and all four of them were crowded into the tiny room.

Wu put his mouth to Beth's ear and whispered. "My two men will go first, then I, then you."

Beth shook her head and whispered to him.

Wu frowned, then shrugged.

Quickly, Beth pulled her shirt over her head. She unhooked and dropped her bra. The first of Wu's men kicked the door hard, and Beth stepped into the room. Dai Gal Dai still had the girl on her knees in front of him. His two men gaped at the sight of Beth. Her little diversion worked to perfection. In the single second that the two men stared at her and did not reach for their guns, both of them took 9-millimeter slugs in the chest and sprawled on the floor.

Dai Gul Dai threw the little girl aside, just as the barrel of Wu's pistol crashed down on his skull.

Beth jumped over the body of one of the triad men and dropped to her knees beside Michael. She tore off his blindfold, then his gag, and kissed him fervently.

7

THE HANDCUFFS AND SHACKLES were transferred from Michael to Dai Gul Dai. Beth retrieved and put on her shirt and bra. She and Michael sat together on the couch, embracing and kissing, murmuring to each other. The little girl sat on a chair, weak and sick, quietly sobbing. Wu said something reassuring to her.

"She's a local girl," Michael said. "They just snatched her off the street."

Wu's two men began to search the flat. In a moment they found the girl's clothes, and one of them tossed them to her. She began to dress.

A moment later the other man came to Wu with a large brown paper grocery bag. Wu looked inside. He spotted the eight-million-dollar cashier's check drawn on the Hong Kong Bank. He took it out, folded it, and stuffed it down in his shirt pocket. Then he pulled out a handful of thousand-dollar bills. He handed them—maybe thirty or forty thousand dollars, he did not count—to the girl.

"Where did all this money come from?"

"Dew neh loh moh!" Dai Gul Dai snarled.

Michael translated for Beth, but she had guessed what the words meant—"fuck your mother."

Wu Kim Ming stood and ripped off Dai Gul Dai's shirt. He took a knife from one of his men and drew it across Dai Gul Dai's chest, slicing open a deep, bloody wound. *"Where did the money come from?"* he demanded.

"Dew neh loh moh!"

Wu cut him again, this time from ear to ear across his face. "I know it comes from your other master," he said almost calmly. "What I want to know is, who is your other master?"

Dai Gul Dai spat at him.

Wu put the tip of the knife to Dai Gul Dai's crotch and shoved it forward, through his pants. Dai Gul Dai moaned gutturally.

One of Wu's men hissed a warning. *"Ahyeeyah! Bin Fong!"*

"So . . ." said Wu. "Dai Gul Dai, you are a traitor to Chung Yui Hui. You swore an oath inviting what is now going to happen to you if you betrayed your brothers. I meet your request."

So saying, Wu pushed the point of the knife into Dai Gul Dai's throat. He twisted it and wobbled it back and forth.

One of Wu's men seized the girl and shoved her into the bathroom. He lowered her through the trapdoor by her arms and dropped her into the latrine below. Michael staggered into the bathroom. He had been shackled so long that he could hardly walk. The man dropped him through next. Then he lowered Beth through the same way. Then Wu Kim Ming lowered himself and let himself fall.

"The Bin Fong are our friends," Beth told Michael. "All we have to do is walk out and let them recognize me."

8

BIG MOUTH WATCHED CHUNG Ying Street. He saw the Bin Fong men move in at a trot. Civilians scattered. Obviously the Bin Fong knew where they were going, and quickly faced the fish and poultry shops, forming a menacing line with their submachine guns. Without a doubt, another such line faced the shops from the rear.

Fuck the pig-shit whores! My brother is trapped! Worse than that, the money he brought from Hong King Saturday night is in the flat. Also the fucking Chang!

And the car! They would never manage now to reach the car. And even if they did, the fucking Bin Fong had closed the border!

Big Mouth wondered how he was going to escape. How far could he trust the proprietor of the dim sum shop? Surely there was a room above. Could he pose as a kitchen worker?

"This is bad for business!" the proprietor complained. "They won't buy, and everyone else is afraid of the street while they are out there like that."

"The cops are no man's friend," said Big Mouth.

A black-and-white command vehicle pulled up behind the ranks of Bin Fong. A uniformed officer stepped out. He put a microphone to his mouth and began to speak. His amplified words bounced off all the buildings on Chung Ying Street:

"DAI GUL DAI! SURRENDER! YOU HAVE NO CHANCE! RELEASE YOUR PRISONERS! SURRENDER! YOU HAVE NO CHANCE TO ESCAPE!"

"Fuckers . . ." Big Mouth muttered. They even knew his brother's name! How . . . ?

Suddenly it was all clear. A hunched man lurched out of the poultry shop. He limped. He wore a vest undershirt and dark pants. Under his left arm he carried the bleeding carcass of a chicken, loosely wrapped in newspaper. His right hand clutched to his chest a brown paper bag. The gray hair at his temples proved he was not Dai Gul Dai, and the Bin Fong paid him almost no attention. But

Big Mouth knew him, for certain. He was Wu Kim Ming, slipping away under the noses of the cops, shortly to be out of everyone's reach.

If Wu Kim Ming is coming out of there, alive, then my brother is dead! What's more, that paper bag he is carrying is the bag in which my brother kept the money!

If other evidence was needed, it followed. Mikego Chang! And his big-titted, big-assed American whore! They walked out of the poultry shop and began to nod and smile at the Bin Fong. A civilian from the command car moved forward, smiling and nodding.

Big Mouth was possessed by fury. He pulled from his pants his big American pistol and trotted out of the dim sum shop. They were all staring at the Chang boy and his blond bitch. This would be easy! He would die, but better to die avenging a bitter wrong than poor and friendless—which was what the two brothers' betrayal of Chung Yui Hui left them.

9

WU KIM MING PAUSED for a moment to watch Michael Chang and Beth Connor be received by Shek Tin and the Bin Fong commander. He saw Qiao Qichen hurrying forward. He saw the commander beckon Chief Inspector Trevelyan to come across the line and join the happy reunion. He saw a television camera recording the scene from the back of a truck.

For a brief moment Beth's eyes turned to his and stopped there. She smiled.

And then! Wu saw the wild-eyed Big Mouth trotting unnoticed toward her and Michael, his huge American pistol leveled on them.

Wu dropped the paper bag, then dropped his chicken. It had concealed his own pistol, his supremely engineered and phenomenally accurate 9-millimeter Luger. He took careful aim on Big Mouth. It was not difficult for him to shoot a man. He had done it before. He squeezed the trigger. Big Mouth screamed, stumbled backward, and fired one loud shot in the air before he tumbled on his back.

The Bin Fong swarmed forward and seized Wu Kim Ming.

10

QIAO QICHEN RUSHED UP to embrace Michael, seized him in a bear hug, then broke away from him and hugged Beth. Shek Tin embraced Beth. The commander shook her hand and Michael's. Chief Inspector Trevelyan did the same. Beth trembled. The ugly little man with the big ugly gun had almost— She threw herself into Michael's arms. They wept together.

Half a dozen Bin Fong gathered around Big Mouth. One knelt to examine him. He was dead.

Another half dozen gathered around Wu Kim Ming. He had surrendered his pistol and stood waiting to see what they would do to him. Shek Tin and the commander strode across the street and up to that group.

"You are Wu Kim Ming?" Shek asked.

"I am."

"Then we arrest you for crimes against the People's Republic of China."

"What crimes?" Wu asked.

"Murder. Extortion. Traffic in heroin," said Shek. "Traffic in young girls for prostitution. We have a fat file on you."

Wu glanced around. "Tell your men to move back a few paces," he said. "Tell them to shoot me if I try to run."

The commander gestured to the Bin Fong men to move back, out of earshot.

"Think of this," said Wu. "You wouldn't have caught me if I hadn't stopped to shoot the bastard who would have killed the young Mr. Chang and Miss Connor."

"I expect the People's court will take that into consideration," said Shek.

Wu nodded at the paper bag that lay on the pavement. "In that bag you will find almost two million Hong Kong dollars, plus a cashier's check made out to the bearer in the amount of eight million dollars. Allow me to leave here, and nearly ten million dollars is yours."

"No," said Shek. "It is evidence and must be confiscated as such."

Wu had the courage, maybe just the gall, to smile. "That kind of evidence has a way of disappearing."

"It will not disappear, I assure you."

"Well . . . Let me say just this much. That money is not mine. If it disappears—" He shrugged. "Of course I will be obliged to tell the prosecutor and the People's court that I had ten million dollars in my possession when I was arrested. It is something else I forfeited to save the lives of the young couple."

Shek turned to the commander, who shrugged. Shek picked up the bag and handed it to the colonel. "See to it that this evidence is carefully preserved," he said.

The commander nodded. "Very carefully," he said.

Shek beckoned to Chief Inspector Trevelyan. The chief inspector came over, looking quizzical.

Shek pointed to Wu and spoke in English. "Congratulations, Chief Inspector. You're very smart in having a policeman hidden on the ground on our side of the line. He seems to have saved the whole operation. The chicken was a clever stroke. I wish you'd told us about the man, though. We might have shot him by mistake."

Trevelyan glanced back and forth among Shek, the commander, and Wu, confused at first but keeping his composure. "Sorry about that," he said. "Should have told you, of course. Complicated operation, this, what? Overlooked a detail, sorry to say."

"Well—will you take your man back to your side now?"

The chief inspector nodded at Wu, as if giving him an order.

Wu picked up his chicken and shuffled off down the street.

SIXTEEN

*There will be determined opposition to
our being married.*

1

CARS CARRYING MICHAEL AND Beth, Qiao Qichen and Huang,
and six Chang family bodyguards followed a motorcycle escort of
Hong Kong police up Peak Road.

In the back seat of the second car, Beth and Michael sat alone,
in each other's arms, kissing and quietly reaffirming their passionate love for each other.

"I don't know everything that happened," he said to her. "I
know you risked your life for me."

"You would have done as much for me," she whispered.

"Dai Gul Dai told me you had been beaten."

Beth drew a sharp breath. "Michael . . . tonight I will show you
some welts on my rear—nothing very serious. I was given a caning,
only three strokes, no more than a naughty schoolboy gets, I am
told. We must try to forget it."

"Forget it? I won't forget it!"

"Michael, it is a small matter compared to everything else.
Everything is very complicated. You know it was Wu Kim Ming
who forced his way into the flat and saved your life. Why do you
suppose he did it? It was he who shot Dai Gul Dai's brother, almost
at the cost of his own escape. Why do you suppose he did it? The
deputy provincial governor of Guangdong Province was there. He
led a force of Bin Fong. Why do you suppose he did it? He let Wu

Kim Ming go. Why do you suppose he did *that?* I can answer some of those questions. Not all. But it can't be done in a few words."

He pressed their faces together and kissed her again.

"Michael . . . There will be determined opposition to our being married."

"I don't care. We *will* be married."

"I'm not sure you realize the depth of your family's determined opposition."

"Beth, I am my father's heir now. One day I will be head of the family. My father will gradually step aside. *I* will make the decisions. And I am making this one now."

"Qiao Qichen told me our marrying is simply impossible. He said the family will set me up in a fine apartment, with a generous allowance of money, and that you can see me as you wish. He—"

"In other words, they think I will keep you as a concubine," Michael sneered.

"Your father himself made essentially the same offer. He said I would be a member of what he called your 'extended family' and that your family would respect and even love me."

"But I must marry a Chinese girl of good family. Yes. I can almost recite what they said to you. Also, my wife would know all about you. Their point is that my children must be Chinese. That's what troubles them: the children."

"I have already disgraced your family, Michael. To make some money, so I could stay here, I took a job at the Pearl Club. Only as a waitress, you understand—strictly as a waitress. But I *was* on display in a black leotard and pantyhose. I had to fend off Bo Yu Tang and punched him in the face, giving him a bloody nose. I spent a night in Wu Kim Ming's suite in the Mandarin Oriental Hotel—in a separate room, absolutely, and Mr. Wu never touched me. Then— the flogging. It was very public, Michael. I guess there were twenty men there. They exposed me first, then beat me. God knows who saw me. And someone took pictures of me."

Michael shook his head sadly. "You must hate this city and everyone in it. In just a week, all of this—"

"It *has* been just a week, Michael. At this hour one week ago, you and I were together in that hot-sheet hotel, waiting to be taken to the boat." She sighed. "You say you saw me on television, with Xiang Li. Well, I had spent the twenty-four hours before that in *a jail cell*, in Guangzhou. But—the worst of it was not knowing if you were alive or dead, or if I could do anything to help you. It has been a week I wouldn't want to live again."

"No, and neither would I. I was never so much worried about myself as I was worried about you."

"Michael . . . Could your father disown you?"

"No. He can't. If he is concerned about the family name, he won't even think of doing that. Anyway, that would leave John as his heir, and that is unthinkable. John is at best irresponsible."

"And a liar," Beth added dryly.

"Do you know what disease is killing Frederick?"

She nodded. "Huang told me."

"My father is unfortunate in his sons. One prowled the stews until he brought on himself a fatal illness. One drinks too much and can't be trusted. And—"

"And one," she interrupted, "proposes to marry a notorious American adventuress."

"One proposes to marry the girl he loves," said Michael.

2

WORD THAT MICHAEL WAS coming home had of course preceded him. When the cars pulled up to the gate, it was open, and the Chang family stood smiling and laughing on the lawn just inside.

His father stood just ahead of the group, beaming with joy, his arms open to receive his son. He was almost formally dressed, in a dark-blue pinstriped business suit with white shirt and dark-blue tie. Half a pace behind Chang Wing Hing stood Michael's mother, So Liming, her cheeks wet with happy tears. To the parents' left and another pace back, stood Frederick, leaning on the arm of Anne. To the right, John waited and grinned. Beside him stood Chang Mei Ling—Cheryl—Michael's sister. She had rushed from the tennis court and was wearing tennis whites.

A few more paces back the household servants and guards were assembled. A little apart from them stood Dragon with Emily on his arm.

Michael hurried forward to embrace his father—bringing Beth with him by the hand. Chang Wing Hing sobbed as he clutched his son to his breast. When they separated, he opened his arms to Beth and hugged her. So Liming embraced and kissed Michael first, then Beth.

Qiao Qichen came to Chang Wing Hing, and the two men shook hands gravely. So Liming clasped Qiao's hands in hers and smiled and nodded.

Michael led Beth on toward Frederick. He embraced his elder brother and for a long moment said nothing. Then he introduced Beth to Frederick.

Anne spoke to Beth. "I was frantic with worry when I found you were not in the apartment," she said: "I couldn't find out where you'd gone, and I couldn't imagine. I hope you don't mind, but I took the liberty of bringing some of your clothes here. I thought you'd want . . . uh . . . The honored father commands keys to all the apartments in the building and arranged for me to enter."

"I would like to change," said Beth. "It was thoughtful of you."

Anne herself was dressed for the festive hour in a tight black miniskirt and a black blouse ornamented with silver embroidery. "We will celebrate over dinner," she said. "Your Versace catsuit would be *most* appropriate."

Michael proceeded to shake hands with John.

"I was supposed to meet you at the airport last Sunday," said John.

"So you were," said Michael. "I had forgotten that."

Beth was cool to John. She hurried to Emily.

Emily took Beth aside. "Mr. Wu?" she asked.

Beth smiled and turned up her palms. "Survived," she said. "They let him go."

" 'E promised to myke me 'is number one woman. 'Precious Lady Yin' is what 'e called me."

Beth could only nod.

"I wonder if I'll ever see 'im agyne," said Emily.

3

MICHAEL TOOK BETH BY the arm. "My father wants to have a private conversation with me," he said quietly. "For an hour or more, I'm afraid."

"I can guess the subject," said Beth with a touch of sarcasm.

"No. I don't think so. I think I'm about to be given an intimate look at Wing Lung Properties. I'm about to be initiated into mysteries that Frederick was once initiated into and John will never be."

"Couldn't it wait?"

Michael shook his head. "A nightmare for my father—a nightmare for any Chinese family—is that the father should die leaving no heir prepared to take responsibility for the family fortune. When I went to the States, it was clearly understood that Frederick, as the eldest brother, was the heir. They knew I would be coming home this summer, for a visit only, as I supposed; my father decided to delay giving me the word about Frederick until he could do it personally. Now he wants me to know everything, as quickly as possible."

"Qiao Qichen—"

"No. And please do learn to call him Tom. Tom knows a great deal about the family business, but my father withholds much information even from his trusted *consigliere*. It's a basic technique of control, Beth: to keep certain vital information strictly in pectore. You can trust Tom as much as my father trusts him—about ninety-eight percent. The other two percent . . . in the heart."

"You are about to be trusted with that two percent."

Michael nodded. "While I am with my father, Tom will show you the suite of rooms assigned to us. To *us*, notice. Tonight we will sleep together in this house for the first time. You will be the mistress of this house, Beth. Don't doubt it."

4

MICHAEL WENT INTO THE house with his father. Qiao Qichen came up to Beth and offered to show her the suite. She accepted his suggestion and started to accompany him into the house when John approached and asked if he could join them. Both agreed, and John went with them.

The suite of rooms was more luxurious than the suite Wu Kim Ming had occupied in the Mandarin Oriental Hotel. It consisted of a large sitting room, a very large bedroom equipped with a king-size bed, two huge walk-in closets, a small kitchen with microwave oven and refrigerator, and an astonishing bathroom.

The bathroom initially impressed Beth most. In the center was a green marble whirlpool bath set into the floor and large enough—recalling to her mind a bon mot she had once heard—to float a canoe. Steps led down into it. A person could actually swim a few strokes in it. To one side of the room stood a green marble shower stall. The shower head, the size of a dinner plate, was out of reach above. Nickel-plated pipes surrounded three sides of the stall. They were perforated. They were a needle shower—stinging jets of hot water would massage the body as one stood and turned in the shower. A bidet swung out from one wall.

Two green marble toilets and two green marble basins finished the furnishing of the room. The floor was black marble. The walls were mirrors.

The heavy nickel-plated fixtures suggested that the bathroom had been built seventy years ago, but everything had been maintained as though it were new.

Almost nothing in any of the rooms suggested China. Rather, the decor and furnishings suggested Edwardian England—an Edwardian country house, actually, with a cozy comfort, rather than grandeur. Only a collection of a dozen dark-green jade sculptures on a carved ebony table suggested China.

"Our great-grandfather, Chang Zi Hing, had this bed made," said John, pointing at the immense carved-ebony bed that dominated the bedroom. "It is said that he slept in it with never fewer than three little girls." He grinned.

"Of course, nothing remains of it but the carpentry," said Qiao. "You won't be sleeping on his mattress."

"I am glad you explained that, Tom," said Beth, using that name for him for the first time. "I am sure there are many other things you can explain to me."

Examining closely, she saw that today the original ebony carpentry was just a shell for the contemporary bed frame that fit inside it.

"My mother didn't like it and asked that it be moved to this suite," said John.

"This suite is only temporary for you and Michael," said Qiao.

"You expect that I will be moved somewhere else," Beth suggested. "Like back to the apartment on Arbuthnot Street."

"Much remains to be seen," said Qiao.

They moved to the sitting room and took places on the overstuffed chintz sofa and chairs.

John sighed. "I have brought you something," John said to Beth.

He handed her a small manila envelope. She opened it and saw a muddle of black ashes.

"The Polaroid pictures General Bo took Saturday night," John said. "All of them. I burned them."

Beth handed the envelope to Qiao. "Be so good as to flush these ashes down the toilet, will you, Tom?" she said calmly. When Qiao went to the bathroom, she stared at John and asked, "How did you know Bo took pictures Saturday night?" she asked. "You must have been there."

John closed his eyes and nodded. "I was there."

She glanced toward the bathroom. "Tom?"

"He was not there."

"Did he know?"

Qiao came back. "I heard the question," he said. "Yes, Miss Connor, I knew."

"And Michael's father?" she asked.

"I swear to you that the honored Chang Wing Hing did not know," said Qiao.

"You swear he didn't," she said with quiet skepticism.

"I swear he didn't," said Qiao. "This requires explanation."

"I should think so," said Beth.

"Michael was not kidnapped for money ransom, as you know. A Taiwanese business group with which the Chang family had done much business in the past demanded to be allowed to participate in a multi-billion-dollar land-reclamation project here in Hong Kong. When Chang Wing Hing refused to agree to this participation, the Taiwanese group had Michael kidnapped to force his father to consent."

"The Taiwanese business group is a triad," she said censoriously.

"Not exactly," said Qiao. "Triads are significant investors in many Taiwanese businesses and exert heavy influence. In any event, Chang Wing Hing could not consent to Taiwanese investment in Western Reclamation, because certain important people in China are major investors, and they would not allow themselves to be associated in any way with the Taiwanese."

"To get Michael released," said John, "Tom and my father had to work out a complex deal, getting all the parties together."

"Unfortunately," said Qiao, "one of the major investors was represented by Bo Yu Tang. More unfortunately yet, *you* broke Bo's nose."

"He had it coming," said John, "but it screwed up the negotiations. He wouldn't consent to anything unless you got what he thought you deserved."

"The agreement about you was subtle," said Qiao. "It was negotiated between Bo Yu Tang and Wu Kim Ming. Wu insisted that you be caned only symbolically. To gain that concession from Bo, Wu had to consent to your being humiliated. Bo's reasoning was that you had humiliated him, so *you* must be humiliated. Lest the whole deal—and I mean the Taiwanese investment deal—fall apart, Wu had to consent to your humiliation. All seemed to be in order. Then, at the last moment, Bo demanded that the Chang family *consent* to your ordeal. Not only that, a member of the family had to be present, so that the men who witnessed what happened to you would see a Chang there and know it was done with family consent."

"Which is why I was there," said John. "At first Bo demanded that my father be there, but—"

"*But what?*" Beth demanded angrily.

"Michael's life was at stake," John muttered.

"That is precisely the point, Miss Connor," said Qiao. "You had expressed yourself firmly as willing to accept any sacrifice to save Michael. I took you at your word."

She stared at him, her eyes hard and glittering. "Couldn't you have warned me? Couldn't you somehow have prepared me? I *would have agreed!*"

"But then could you have played the role?" Qiao asked.

Beth didn't temper her angry glare. "Michael suggests I should trust you," she said dubiously.

"We have trusted you with something," said Qiao. "Michael's father did not consent to your ordeal and doesn't know that I consented on the family's behalf. I've trusted you with word of that. I expect you will tell Michael, and I expect he will not tell his father. If either of you do, my position in this family will—".

"Come to an end," she finished his sentence.

Qiao nodded.

"I am going to be mistress of this house, Tom . . . John. I am an

American woman, and I am going to be Michael's partner, not just
an ornament and plaything."

"Michael consents to this?"

"He consents."

"Then I will be working for you?"

Beth nodded and smiled faintly. "I wouldn't be surprised."

5

MICHAEL SAT FACING HIS father's big desk. His father sat behind
it. They had embraced and wept together, then shared some fine
old Napoleon brandy. After that, Chang Wing Hing had explained
in detail just how the deal to secure Michael's release had been
negotiated—except for the element that had involved Beth's flogging, which he didn't know about.

"I regret that it took so long and that you were compelled to suffer so much. But now—Western Reclamation will go forward, and
we will earn a very handsome profit. You should drive out and see
the site, then read all the contracts."

"Frederick?"

Chang Wing Hing shook his head. "He hasn't read them."

This was how Michael had expected his new status in the family to be declared—not by some formal statement, simply by his
slipping into the role. No one had to say anything. The deference
paid him by the household staff, by his elder sister, even by Frederick and Anne, had signified that he was now the recognized heir
and would gradually assume power and control.

"You must learn the names and places of all our accounts," his
father said. "We have money deposited in many places, and some of
those accounts are manifested by no documents. You must be able
to enter a bank and establish your right to the funds on deposit by
reciting code names and numbers. To do that, you must memorize
these matters. This may become more important than ever . . . next

year. In the last war, the Japanese demanded access to all our family accounts. They got some but could not reach others, because no one but your grandfather knew where they were."

6

THE FAMILY GATHERED IN the great formal dining room for dinner. Six tables were set. After only a moment, Beth realized that she was the only person there who was not Chinese and was not, strictly, a member of the Chang family. Qiao Qichen was not there.

She knew where Huang was. He had taken Emily to dinner in the small Austrian restaurant near the apartment on Arbuthnot Road. Dragon, the *qi gong* master, was with them.

She was also the only person at the dinner who could not speak Chinese. No matter. Michael was by no means the only one present who could speak English. Chang Wing Hing could. Frederick and Anne could. John could. Michael's sister Cheryl could. So could others to whom she was introduced but could not immediately identify.

In her garnet-red catsuit she was, as Anne had suggested she would be, not only appropriately dressed but spectacularly. Michael had suggested she not wear the jacket, so she entered the room on his arm wearing the black lace camisole top that left her arms and shoulders bare and displayed deep cleavage.

Anne wore a beautiful dress: black silk so tight it might have been applied to her with a brush, with even deeper cleavage.

Michael's sister wore the latest style from the finest shop.

Beth wondered if she should take as significant the fact she seemed to be treated as though she were Michael's wife—at least his consort—already. She saw that she was to sit beside him at the table where he would sit beside his father, where the others were only So Liming, Frederick, and Anne. John and Cheryl and her husband, sat at another table.

She knew, all the same, that Chang Wing Hing had not consented to her marrying Michael. That, Michael had told her, would be discussed tomorrow.

"I will be the mistress of this house," she whispered to him when they were seated for dinner. "I am being treated almost as if I were its mistress already."

"I promised you," he said almost curtly. "We will settle it tomorrow."

From time to time during the dinner, Chang Wing Hing spoke past Michael and talked to Beth directly. "The flavor of this dish is bird's nest," he explained as they ate a medallion of fried egg whites with crabmeat. "It is a legend in the West, is it not?"

"It is," she agreed.

When she shot a curious glance at Michael as they ate another dish, he explained to her it was sea whelk.

"Whelk?"

"Snail."

Still another dish was based on the webbing cut from the feet of web-footed birds such as geese.

Only once during the dinner did Michael leave her alone: when his father led him from table to table, where they toasted all the guests and were themselves toasted.

Anne toasted Beth. "You are a brave young woman," she said. "I can understand Michael's fascination with you."

"*I* can understand," said Frederick softly, "why he loves you. He is lucky I didn't meet you first."

7

BETH HAD LET HIM see her welts when they were dressing for dinner. Now he insisted that she lie naked on the bed and let him examine them closely, running his fingers gently over them.

By now they were dark swellings, long and narrow, each one

running across her hinder cheeks. She swore to him that they were only a little tender, that she was not in pain.

"Bo Yu Tang," Michael muttered balefully. "He must *die!*"

"Michael . . . It is only a little thing. You and I are alive. That is what counts."

"It is *not* a little thing," said Michael grimly. "Bo—"

"Michael . . . we agreed a long time ago that we would be partners. Now, as a partner with you in whatever we are going to be, I want you to promise me you will not do something foolish over those three little welts. My father never did any such thing, but many a father puts welts like those on his daughters' backsides. It is well to resent it. A year before the Handover, it would be absurd to announce a vendetta against a man who represents unidentified but highly influential people in China—much less to try to kill him."

"Do you forgive him?"

"I will never forgive him. He's a thug. But I anticipate that you and I will encounter him again, and we must be more rational than he is."

"How could you face a man who did that to you?"

"If we stay in Hong Kong, we are going to face a lot of things we never thought to face. Maybe we should go back to Cambridge, if you can't face things rationally and from a practical point of view."

As she turned over and faced him, Michael shook his head and showed a grudging little smile. "You're more Chinese than I am," he grumbled.

She kissed him. "Let's make a little Chinese boy or girl," she said. "I haven't had a pill since I took one in the lavatory on the airliner last Sunday morning, so I'm probably very, very fertile."

"Make a baby before anything is settled?" he asked.

"This is settled—that you and I are going to be together and love each other, one arrangement or another."

"Something else is settled," he said. "You are going to be my wife, not my mistress or concubine."

"I am going to be your partner," she said. "So put that jade stem in me, *ai rien*, and let's make a partnership dividend."

8

IT WAS ALMOST NOON before Michael was summoned to his father's office. Anticipating the call, he had worn gray slacks and a white shirt all morning, and only had to knot his tie and slip on a blue blazer to be ready for what he expected would be a confrontation.

His father sat in the thronelike chair, behind the big desk. Michael sat down in an armchair. They were alone.

Chang Wing Hing opened the discussion with a simple statement: "The marriage would be unsuitable." He elected to speak English.

"What is 'unsuitable,' Dad?" Michael asked respectfully. "Perhaps you mean 'nontraditional.' "

"Let us say it that way. But let us not forget the fact that tradition means a great deal, to all people and particularly to us. We, the so-called Overseas Chinese, have much in common with the Jews. We have suffered through many travails and have emerged more successful and influential than our numbers might justify. One reason is that we are a tight-knit community with traditions we cherish."

"We face a new time, Father. I deeply hope that old traditions will not be discarded, but we must face the fact that Hong Kong is about to be incorporated into the Chinese state. Our society will have to adjust to that."

"You propose, my son, to discard an important tradition."

"To marry the girl I love."

"There is another tradition," said Chang Wing Hing. "Tradition allows a man to find love and comfort outside marriage. A woman may be honored and cherished outside the institution of marriage. Your family will gladly set her up in a handsome home, not just a flat in Arbuthnot Street, and—"

"Why? Why should it be that way?"

"Because she is not one of us. Because she can never learn to understand and be one of us. Besides, are you aware, Po Ka, that she exposed her legs as a waitress in a Kowloon nightclub? And, worse, are you aware that she was exposed naked to the view of a dozen or more men and caned across her bottom?"

"I am aware of it, Dad. Last night I kissed her welts—after *zuo ai*. She may already be carrying your grandchild."

"She is notorious. Her name is known everywhere. Her . . . adventures are known everywhere. In business you may encounter men who witnessed her caning. How will you like that?"

"None will dare mention it," Michael said coldly.

"But they will know."

"Let them. If they give me any evidence of it, they will wish they hadn't."

Chang Wing Hing nodded solemnly. "Your emotions are very strong," he said. "Are they not overwhelming your reason?"

"Have you never done anything unreasonable, Dad? Has not your life been enriched by some of the unreasonable things you have done? Your marriage to my mother was called unreasonable. She brought you her youth, her beauty, and her love—nothing more. Last night someone told me about your dear little one. Is *that* reasonable?"

The father fluttered his hand. "Very well. I will raise another subject. What do you know about Miss Connor's relationship with Deputy Provincial Governor Shek Tin?"

"I know he led the force of Bin Fong that came to Sha Tau Kok to free me. I know she persuaded him to do it. I am sure they did not sleep together. But even if she did, she did it to save my life. I know for a fact that Shek Tin rescued her from a Guangzhou jail when she was being held for illegal entry into China. She told me that last night."

"It appears," said Chang Wing Hing with a measured smile and a brief nod, "that the name Beth Connor is as well known in China as it is in Hong Kong. What is more, she is something of a favorite there. Four years ago she was despised because of the running incident. But her reconciliation with Xiang Li and her graceful little apology to the Beijing government—"

"Plus the fact that she is an exceptionally beautiful young woman with a charismatic personality," Michael interrupted.

"Plus that," the father conceded. "On the other hand, we must accept the fact that Shek exploited her for propaganda purposes. This morning Chinese television began broadcasting an account of your rescue. It shows you and Beth being congratulated by Shek and the Bin Fong colonel. It does not mention Wu Kim Ming. More exploitation. The two of you are being exploited for politburo propaganda."

"A small price to pay for—"

"This morning I received a strange telephone call from Shek Tin, who wanted to tell me he hoped I would extend my parental blessing to your marrying Beth Connor. He said his government would look favorably on it, as evidence that the Chang family is prepared to accept a new order of things. Shek said more. He said that after you are married he would like to receive you as honored guests in Guangzhou, after which you will also be received in Beijing."

"Before television cameras," said Michael.

"Propaganda," said Chang Wing Hing. "Beijing would like to impress the Americans with what generosity and liberality it welcomes the marriage between a prominent Chinese and an American girl."

Michael smiled. "Propaganda to prepare for the Handover."

"It is something more to consider," said the father. "Your marriage may also become a propaganda show."

"Another reason not to marry her?"

"A factor to be considered."

"Dad," said Michael calmly, "I am going to marry the girl I love. I ask your blessing."

Chang Wing Hing stared rigidly at his son for half a minute, his face unmoving.

"I remind you that she risked her life and endured humiliation and agony to save my life."

The father nodded. "I am deeply grateful to her," he said. "I told her I would treat her as a member of the family."

"She will be a member of the family. And you will be proud of her."

"You ask my blessing, not my consent."

"I should like to have both," said Michael. "And I want you to be at our wedding."

Chang Wing Hing stood and stepped around the desk. He offered his hand to Michael. "My son, you have my consent and my blessing. I will welcome . . . Beth into the family. We will speak no more of my reservations."

9

BETH PHONED HER PARENTS in Boston. Her call wakened them, of course. She told them she had experienced some odd things since she had been in Hong Kong, which had prevented her from calling sooner. She would explain everything when she saw them, which would be soon, when they would be in Hong Kong for the wedding.

"We saw you on the eleven o'clock news," her mother said. "With soldiers and the governor of . . . of whatever. The story was that Michael had been kidnapped but had now been returned to his family, thanks to the efforts of the Chinese police. It was all very mysterious. Even the announcer called it mysterious. What has been happening, Mary Elizabeth?"

Her mother called her Mary Elizabeth only when she was annoyed, and Beth was half amused, half concerned. "We'll have plenty of time to discuss it," she said. "I wouldn't even try, right now. Michael sends you his love. I'll call again, probably tomorrow.

Everything is fine now. Tomorrow or the next day we will set the date for the wedding."

"Well . . ." her mother said skeptically. "You seem to be having strange adventures. I wondered if you wouldn't, when you went out there so far and to such a strange place."

10

ANNE STOOD AT THE window from which she could see down onto the stone-pillared veranda. She watched Chang Wing Hing embrace Beth. She watched Beth kiss him on both cheeks and return his embrace.

She turned away from the window, toward Dragon, who was standing behind her.

"It is not finished," she said to the *qi gong* master. "This play is not played out. I will have my way of it yet."

SEVENTEEN

The wedding is next week.
If somebody doesn't get to one of them first.

1

THE WEDDING DATE WAS fixed for September 9—the ninth day of the ninth month, an especially propitious day in Chinese numerology since nine rhymes with the word for "longevity."

Beth's parents and sister would fly to Hong Kong a week before the wedding. Beth sent them airline tickets without explaining who was paying for them. In fact, she already had half a million Hong Kong dollars on deposit to her account in the Hong Kong Bank, put there for her by Chang Hing Wing to spare her the embarrassment of having to ask anyone for money.

Her university roommates were flying to Hong Kong at their own expense.

When the wedding date was agreed on, it seemed a long time off. She found in fact that she didn't have enough days. First, she had to be grounded in Chinese wedding customs. Instruction was given her by Michael's sister Cheryl. She learned that the varied events of the wedding day would begin in the morning and last twenty hours or longer. Besides the ceremony itself, there would be a breakfast, a luncheon, a dinner, receptions, and parties. Every event would have its special significance, and different lists of guests would be invited to each. She had to learn not only the purpose and significance of each event, but also its customs and courtesies. As the day approached she would be briefed thoroughly on who was who and why each person was invited to one event and not to others.

What was more, she had to take a personal part in the planning of everything.

She would be expected to appear in different clothes for each event. A French couturiere appeared at the mansion and explained to Beth that she had been engaged to design and make the wedding dress and all the other dresses for the wedding day. Though she would offer advice, Beth would make all the choices: of style, fabric, color, and so on. The couturiere would bring her samples, sketches, and photographs, they would study them together, and only when Beth was satisfied would the work of making the dresses begin. The wedding dress was of course the most important. The woman's instructions were to make it magnificent.

Beth was also to have a trousseau: clothes appropriate for the wife of Michael Chang. Since she had lost everything she had brought with her from home, she welcomed this. She was astonished, though, by what the couturiere and her several assistants thought it necessary for her to have: clothing from the skin out. It seemed that only her panties, stockings, and maybe items like sweaters could be purchased from stock; her bras and slips were to be made for her, as were her skirts, slacks, and blouses. She would have three sets of clothes: formal wear, day wear, and sports clothes. She had to be measured for each item, then stand still for fittings—which consumed endless hours.

A hairdresser appeared, clucked disapprovingly over her hair as the woman in the Friendship Store in Guangzhou had done, and set to work to treat and style her hair. Then came a cosmetician to experiment with cosmetics and design complex sets of skin cleanser, moisturizer, toner, eyeshadow, lipstick, and so on—each set to be used for its own occasion. The woman spent hours teaching Beth how to use all these products.

Michael was busy much of each day with the family business. The only time she could be sure of seeing him was when they finally went to bed at night.

They had been moved from their first suite into a vastly larger master suite, second only to that occupied by Chang Wing Hing himself. It would be their home for the next few years, and Michael invited Beth to redesign and refurnish the space. A designer appeared to help her. Together they modified the suite. Although it was elegant and richly appointed, Beth found it heavy and gloomy. With the assistance of the designer she changed it, not glaringly but subtly, replacing dark, heavy pieces of Chinese-carved ebony and mahogany with pieces still emphatically Chinese but lighter and more airy. She banished heavy drapes and substituted filmy curtains that admitted light while still preserving privacy. Lighting, she thought, was the key to room design. She encouraged the designer to use his imagination and equip the room with hidden fixtures that would supplement the open fixtures and fill the rooms with cheerful light.

She could have used two more months.

2

ANNE HAD JUST FINISHED playing tennis with Cheryl, and the two women entered the compound through the gate—driven by one of the family drivers and guarded by an armed man who sat in the left front seat.

Wearing her tennis whites, Anne walked into the guest house by the pool, where Emily was living in one of the cabana suites. Dragon opened the door and admitted her into the living room, where the little English girl lay nude on her belly on the couch. Dragon knelt beside her and resumed what he had been doing when the bell sounded: rubbing Emily's bottom with oil. Anne suspected she really did not need these ministrations but that Dragon enjoyed seeing and touching her naked body. She suspected Emily liked it, too. In fact, she was all but certain that Dragon was administering another kind of therapy, nights.

"Oh, Anne!" Emily piped with a wide grin. "The strangest thing 'as 'appened. I got a bit of mail this morning. Sent in care of Beth but for me. From the Bank of China. They sent me a bankbook and a card I can use to withdraw money. It seems I've got one 'undred thousand dollars in an account somebody set up for me."

"How very lucky," said Anne. She sat down and crossed her legs. Dragon turned and stared as her tennis skirt rode up and showed her shiny white nylon panties. She had fluffy little pompons on her shoes. Her black hair was tied back.

"Who could have done it?" Emily asked. "Beth said it wasn't 'er or Michael."

"No," said Anne. "The Changs keep their money in the Hong Kong Bank."

"Then . . . ?"

"My guess would be Wu Kim Ming," said Anne. "He was an admirer of yours."

" 'E's disappeared, 'asn't 'e? Beth told me 'e 'ad much to do with rescuing Michael."

"I doubt that he's disappeared," said Anne. "My guess is that he's just keeping a low profile for a while. I wouldn't be surprised if he reemerges. So, Dragon, I need to talk with you when you're finished there. I'll be in the pool."

When he came out ten minutes later, she *was* in the pool, wearing a colorful, flower-patterned bikini and swimming back and forth with strong, smooth strokes. He sat down in an aluminum-and-webbing chair at the edge of the water, and she lifted herself up and sat on the lip. She had loosened her hair, and it hung around her shoulders, streaming water.

"What word?" she asked.

"It can be done," said Dragon. "For money."

"Of course, money. Anything can be done for money. But I am

not *made* of money. I lost ten million dollars by my bet on Dai Gul Dai—which was a fool's bet; I should never have placed so much trust in that brute."

"He died painfully, I have heard."

"But only once! I wish he were alive again so I could kill him a second time myself." She sighed heavily. "I need to talk to Wu Kim Ming."

"That may be much more difficult. I have inquired. It is suspected he is in Taipei."

"Taiwan . . . The coward has fled?"

"Wu Kim Ming is a shrewd man."

"I need his help. I need money!"

"I have to wonder if he is on your side in this matter, Lady," said Dragon quietly. "Not only did he kill Dai Gul Dai and free Chang Po Ka, he shot the brother who would have killed the young man and the big-titted American. Or so is the story. Who knows what *really* happened at Sha Tau Kok?"

"You have spoken with witnesses," she said dully, unhappily.

"I spoke with the pig of a dim sum seller where Dai Gul Dai's brother was eating just before he went out to be killed. I think his version the most reliable."

"Can the iron hit man supply the substance?"

"He can. He wants two hundred thousand dollars for it."

"Alright. He will have one hundred thousand when he delivers the substance, then a second hundred thousand when Chang Po Ka and Big Tits are dead."

"I will tell him. I am not sure he will accept."

"I intend to use it on the day of the wedding. That means you have just one week to teach me the sleight-of-hand skill I will need to administer the dose effectively and get away with it."

3

BETH AND MICHAEL MET the Connors at Kai Tak Airport. To the amazement of the family from Boston, men in dark suits seized their luggage while they were hugging and shaking hands. To their greater amazement, four black cars waited outside, parked in a no-parking zone. Beth and her parents were guided into one car, Michael and Kathleen into another; the four cars set off in procession.

"Who are the men in the other cars?" Peggy Connor asked Beth. She did not ask who the man driving the car was or who the man sitting beside him was.

"They work for the family," Beth said.

"Kidnapping . . ." her father said. "They're bodyguards!"

"Armed to the teeth," said Beth dryly.

"Do they understand English?" he asked.

"Probably."

Her mother put her hand on Beth's hand. "Is this the life you want, my darling? I mean, do you really want to live under the protection of bodyguards?"

"No. But I want to live in marriage with the man I love. I . . . I risked my life for him—which is nothing more than he would have done for me. I find myself in a situation very different from what I expected. Michael is taking command of a multi-billion-dollar business empire. He didn't know that when we left Boston. He didn't know his elder brother is dying. And I didn't know that the Chang family is one of the wealthiest families in the *world*. I had no idea what responsibilities *I'd* be taking on. But Michael is taking on his responsibilities, gradually, and so am I."

"It's not too late to get out," her mother said gravely.

"It is," said Beth. "Apart from every other reason, I am pregnant."

4

TWO SUITES IN THE mansion were assigned to the Connors. Another would be given to Beth's college roommates, who would arrive in a few days. They, with Kathleen Connor and Emily Parker, would be Beth's maids of honor.

After the Connors slept most of the day, they had cocktails on the veranda, then dinner. They were received by Chang Wing Hing and So Liming, by Frederick and Anne, by John, and by Cheryl and her husband. Beth had briefed her family on all of these people, so they knew who they were meeting.

In a toast to the bride's family, Chang Wing Hing said, "On behalf of my family I would like to repeat our sentiments of deep gratitude for the courage demonstrated so outstandingly by our very dear Beth. Without her, I am afraid my son would not be here this evening. Our family is honored to welcome her among us, and we are honored to meet and to welcome her father, her mother, and her sister. This is the first of many happy occasions when we will share food and drink and fellowship. May all of those occasions be as happy as this one."

Anne rose. "Ordinarily this would be the time for my husband to offer his welcome. He is feeling ill, however, and has asked me to speak for him. Beth . . . We could not be happier. To your family— be assured that this family will cherish your daughter as our new sister."

Beth wore her Versace catsuit that night. Most of her trousseau was ready, but she would not wear anything from it until after the wedding. She might have worn her beautiful *cheong-sam*, Michael's Christmas gift; her mother had brought it; but she judged it better to wear the catsuit in which she had been seen on television all over the world.

Though she would not wear anything from her trousseau until after her wedding, she was wearing the makeup her cosmetologist recommended, and her hair was newly styled. Her mother and sister had noticed that she took longer now to do her face and brush her hair. She had always been casual about these things. She was not anymore.

She stood and said a few words. At the end, she turned to Chang Wing Hing and said, "*Xie xie, Lao Yea.*" It meant "Thank you, Most Reverend Elder," and was a traditional way to address the head of the family.

"*Bu yao ke chi,* Beth," he answered, and she had learned enough Chinese to know he meant "do not stand on ceremony." Also, he had begun to call her Beth, no longer Miss Connor. He had invited her to call him Dad, as Michael did when he was speaking English, and that was how she addressed him on less formal occasions.

At the dinner table, knives and forks, as well as chopsticks, were provided for everyone.

When the first course was put before him, Curran Connor leaned over to Beth and whispered, "Is anybody going to explain to me what I'm eating?"

Beth grinned. "Don't ask," she said.

5

DRAGON FOUND THE ONE they called Iron Hit in his guest house in Chungking Mansions in Tsim Sha Tsui, Kowloon. He was called an iron hit man, or more often just Iron Hit, after the branch of herbal medicine that specified herbs to be applied to heal wounds and injuries. He sold such herbs, also aphrodisiacs and poisons. Iron Hit was also a bordello-keeper. Though scores of so-called guest houses in the huge, squalid high-rise complex operated as bottom-end accommodations for backpackers, the rooms in this one were given over to prostitution.

He might have been called One Tooth—for one was all he had, in front. The story was that all his front teeth had been methodically knocked out by enforcers from a triad he had offended by withholding money that was theirs. He might also have been called No Hair. He was wizened and bent, and he sat in his parlor in a vest undershirt and a pair of shabby blue jeans. Dragon knew very well that Iron Hit was neither weak nor poor. He was a trader in many things, and the tale was that the man had two million dollars somewhere, if anyone could find it. Dragon also knew something about Iron Hit that few people did know—that he had two million *American* dollars, that it was on deposit in Lloyds Bank, that a chartered accountant kept his books and prepared his tax return, and that he paid his 15 percent income tax fully and promptly every year. If he was to have trouble with the law, it would not be over taxes.

Dragon pulled a flimsy wooden chair close to Iron Hit's recliner, so he could speak quietly to him and not be overheard by the prostitutes waiting in the room.

The three girls sat on a couch, watching the flickering image on a black-and-white television set. They wore white panties and bras. Two were Chinese; one was perhaps Polynesian or Indonesian. None was older than twenty. They smoked cigarettes.

"The substance?" Dragon asked.

"I have it. But you impose an unacceptable condition—half my money on delivery, half when the chemical has done its work. What assurance have I that you will administer it correctly? With this condition, I must have one hundred fifty thousand now and one hundred thousand when the deal is done."

Dragon's lids half covered his eyes, and he nodded pensively. "Tell me, what is the substance?"

"Extract of oleander," said Iron Hit.

Dragon shook his head. *"Ineffective!"* he hissed. "Chancy! Men have eaten—"

"Do not show your ignorance," Iron Hit interrupted. "All depends on the plants, on their being the right variety and in healthy condition when harvested, and on skillful work in extracting the alkaloid, the achieving of an effective concentration. When all is done competently, the extract from *one leaf* is a fatal quantity."

"I have heard otherwise," said Dragon.

"Am I to sit here and debate with a *qi gong* charlatan?"

"I—"

They were interrupted by a knock on the door, followed immediately by the entry of two Japanese. The two men bowed politely and pointed to the three girls.

"Five hundred Hong Kong dollars, gentlemen," Iron Hit said to them in Japanese. "Your choice. Pay in advance. Your satisfaction is guaranteed."

The Japanese grinned as they handed over the money. One chose the Polynesian, the other one of the Chinese girls, and the girls led them off to their rooms.

"I know this poison," Dragon persisted. "It is not—"

"It *is*," said Iron Hit. "They will fall to the floor, writhing in agony within half a minute of ingesting it. If a doctor were there and knew just what it was and had the necessary antidote at hand, he could stop the process and give them some chance of living. In fact, no one will guess what the poison is until it is too late to do anything about it."

"Very well, then. But this better work or else . . ." said Dragon.

"I should have asked for twice as much money," said Iron Hit. "I have sold my goods too cheaply."

6

MARK HUANG SAT AT the bar in the Pearl Club. Ilse sat beside him. The statuesque Mama-San wore a liquid black silk dress. She'd had her blond hair cut short, and it stood on her head in a spiky central stripe with no more than bristle covering the rest of her head.

"Where is he?" asked Mark.

Ilse shrugged. "Do you think he would trust me with that information? I don't know where he is."

"The word is around that he's gone to Taiwan."

She shrugged again. "He's not *here*. I promise you that."

"But he's in communication."

"He's alive. Chung Yui Hui is alive. In any case, he sent you a message. Don't press me as to how. Even if I understood how, the information would do you no good."

"So what is the message?"

"When Dai Gul Dai died at Sha Tau Kok, he had in his possession ten million Hong Kong dollars: two million in cash, eight million in the form of a cashier's check drawn on the Hong Kong Bank. Whoever gave him that money meant it as payment for the murder of Michael Chang, maybe also Beth Connor. Whoever paid it is still around somewhere. The person who wanted Michael Chang dead is probably still governed by that motive."

"The wedding is next week."

"If somebody doesn't get to one of them first."

EIGHTEEN

The champagne that Anne complained about . . .
It was poisoned.

1

THE DAY OF THE wedding was fine: sunny with high clouds sailing across the sky, the wind bringing the smell of salt water up to The Peak.

The afternoon before, Michael had moved from the mansion to the Regent's Hotel in Kowloon, from where he and his party would drive to The Peak in mid-morning. He was banned from the compound until then, lest he should by some accident see the bride in her bridal gown before the events of the wedding began.

The first event was an early breakfast for the bride and her party, held in the second-floor family dining room. Beth sat down at a table with her mother; her sister Kathleen; Joan and Diana, her two roommates from Boston; Emily Parker; and Michael's sister Cheryl, who would be close to Beth all day as her adviser. Cheryl's small daughters would follow Beth and carry her train. Even the little girls took tiny sips of the champagne when the toast to the bride was offered.

Her father was Chang Wing Hing's guest in the first-floor dining room, at a breakfast for the men of the family and a few close friends.

Beth was radiant. That was a cliché, but it was what she was: beaming with happiness. Only her mother and Michael knew she was pregnant, and her mother guessed from experience that the child growing within her gave Beth part of her vibrant color. Michael guessed that it was an important element of her happiness.

After the breakfast the bride and her party retired to the master suite that belonged to her and Michael, where the couturiere and her staff, the cosmetologist, and the coiffeuse waited. Beth was the center of their attention, but the others also received appropriate attention. All had been fitted with matching azure gowns, featuring sleek bows on the back. All had been astonished to learn that for the wedding they were to wear new clothes from the skin out: their underwear as well as their silk dresses. No one would wear anything that had ever been worn before.

The mother of the bride was not dressed in anything matronly, but in a slightly more elaborate version of the dresses made for Kathleen, Joan, Diana, Emily, and Cheryl—more elaborate in that the bodice was encrusted with seed pearls and that the Empire waist showed a vigorous décolletage that years and childbearing had not subdued.

In the suite where the bride and her party were dressing, excitement grew. Chinese custom was that the groom and his party would come and offer a price to take the bride away. Bride-price negotiations were an age-old tradition, based on the ancient usage that the family of the man bought the bride from her family. Michael would soon arrive and offer a price for Beth.

2

BETH'S WEDDING GOWN WAS of gleaming white *peau de soie* overlaid with white silk tulle. The bodice was encrusted with seed pearls and iridescent sequins, as were the hemlines of the skirt and train. The bodice was styled with a heart-shaped neckline and an Empire waist that pushed her breasts up and formed a deep, shadowy cleavage. A flower pattern of pearls and sequins decorated the sheer sleeves. The train was a voluminous cloud of tulle, fastened to a seed-pearl tiara. Her white silk slippers were a design by Manolo Blahnik.

A dewdrop pendant of pearls and diamonds hung from the tiara and lay on her forehead. About her throat was a gift from Michael: a strand of lustrous Akoya pearls. Her earrings, also his gift, matched the pendant of her tiara.

At ten the groom and his party arrived in two Rolls-Royces decorated with ribbons and flowers. They were admitted quickly through the gate, while men efficiently denied entry to reporters and cameramen. Spilling out of the Rolls, Michael's friends hurried to the main door of the mansion and knocked loudly.

Joan spoke through the door and pretended that no one inside knew who was there. Cheryl joined in the fun and told the men to go away.

Cheryl's little girls looked out through the leaded-glass windows on both sides of the door and jumped up and down with excitement.

Michael's best man, a friend from his school days, knocked more firmly on the door and said that Michael Chang had come for his bride. Diana said the Connor family had no bride to sell.

But— "If you are willing to pay a penalty, we might be willing to talk to you. See the hoops leaning on the wall beside the door?"

Two of the men held the hoops while the rest of the party jumped through, then turned and jumped back. The hoops were passed to others so that the men who had held them first could jump through.

The women watched through the glass and laughed at the distorted images of the men, clad in black tuxedos, capering around on the lawn, forming lines and jumping back and forth through the hoops.

Finally the hoops were held up for Michael. He was wearing a white double-breasted tuxedo, white shoes, and a black tie with wing-collared shirt. He took off his jacket and ran forward and jumped through the hoops, while all laughed heartily. He turned and ran for the jumps back.

"A song! A love song!" Joan called through the door as Michael picked up his jacket and pulled it on again.

He was prepared for that. Joan had been prompted to ask for it. A string quartet came across the lawn—two violins, a viola, and a cello. Michael had rehearsed with them and was ready to do his best with the love song. The musicians played. The music was from *Phantom of the Opera*. At the appropriate moment, Michael sang part of "All I Ask of You," substituting Beth's name for Christine's.

It was a song they had played often, on a CD player in his Cambridge apartment. Inside the door, Beth's tears ran down her cheeks, causing her mother to dart forward with a tissue and dab before tears streaked her makeup.

Now followed a significant event of the wedding day. Michael's best man knelt at the door and slipped under it a large red envelope embossed with gold characters. This was the bride-price, called the lucky money. The women opened the envelope and showed Beth a check drawn on the Hong Kong Bank for HK $999,999.99. Nine was a lucky number, rhyming in Cantonese with "longevity" and symbolizing longevity for their marriage. The amount was almost one hundred thirty thousand American dollars.

The women opened the doors and admitted Michael and his party to the house. He saw Beth in her wedding dress for the first time and was joyful and tearful. He presented her with her bridal bouquet of white orchids. So as not to smear her makeup, he kissed her gently on the cheek, and she kissed him.

Few concessions were made to the fact that Beth was not Chinese and that the mansion was not her home. A shrine to her ancestors had been set up beside the shrine to the Chang ancestors, to one side of the foyer. Her father and mother had assisted as well as they could in defining the family lines that should be represented, and a calligrapher had inscribed the names in gold characters on red, doing the names as well as he could from descriptions given by the Connors. Thin sticks of incense burned on both shrines, and the couple entered the room and for a moment knelt before the shrines and added more incense.

In a formal parlor furnished and embellished eclectically with Chinese, English, French, and Italian designs, both sets of parents sat and waited. Beth and Michael entered that room, knelt on cushions before their fathers and mothers. Cheryl had explained to Beth that in strictly traditional ceremonies, the bride and groom saluted their parents by touching the floor three times with their foreheads. Beth said she was willing, but Michael said no to that tradition.

An old woman presented the young couple a tray bearing a tea service. Remaining on their knees, they served their parents tea.

To Chang Wing Hing, Beth said, *"Lao yea, hu cha,"* meaning "Dear father-in-law, drink tea. To So Liming she said, *"Lai lai, hu cha."*

When they stood, they proceeded to serve tea to a man and woman identified to Beth as Michael's uncle and aunt, then to Frederick, then to Cheryl, Michael's elder siblings. They served with respectful bows, deep for the uncle and aunt, not so deep for the brother and sister. Finally they served tea to John and to Anne.

Frederick, representing the Chang family, presented gifts to the bride and groom. He gave Michael a packet of lucky money. To Beth he gave a massive piece of jade set in gold and attached to a gold chain, to be worn as a necklace. Though it did not exactly match her gown or the rest of her jewelry, Beth took it from its silk-cushioned package and allowed Michael to help her in fastening the clasp behind her neck.

3

ROLLS-ROYCES AND MERCEDES were lined up to carry the wedding party to the church. Beth and Michael sat in the rear of an open Rolls festooned with broad white and azure ribbons and carrying a huge garland on its hood. The other cars were similarly decorated. The lead cars were first—Hong King police cars, then plain black Toyotas carrying Chang bodyguards. By prearrangement a small flatbed truck was allowed to slip into the procession just ahead of the car carrying the bride and groom. On a wooden platform on its bed, cameramen with telephoto lenses captured every gesture and expression exchanged between the couple. Other cameramen ran along the street as long as they could keep up, then fell aside and waited for their cars to pick them up.

Mark Huang stepped into the road and signaled a white car to the side. It was a police car, and three men in it were in plain clothes and armed to the teeth. Huang wore a black tuxedo. He had not been inside the compound this morning, but he had been invited to the wedding and intended to be present, if not conspicuously present, throughout the rest of the day.

The procession wound slowly down Peak Road and into the streets. It passed Government House where the British colonial governor lived, turned into Garden Road, and came to a stop before Saint Joseph Church. The marriage ceremony would be performed by Father Francis Farren, a Jesuit priest and formerly headmaster of Michael's prep school.

Father Farren was a liberal-minded priest and had agreed to officiate at the wedding even though Beth was not a Catholic. They had talked. She told him she was a Christian. He asked if she would be willing to become Catholic and to rear her children as Catholics. She said she would be willing. He did not ask for a promise.

The limousines lined up and discharged their passengers. They entered a church filled to capacity and were led by ushers to the places reserved for them. Police and Chang bodyguards kept a clear zone. Dozens of cameras flashed and whirred.

Before Beth entered the church a veil was attached to her tiara and lowered over her face.

Michael led her into the church, where they separated, he to go forward with his attendants to the altar, she to join her father who would lead her down the aisle.

Glaring television lights filled the church with unnaturally brilliant light. The best places were given to the cameramen who were doing the family's videotape of the wedding, but many other cameramen were present.

Father Farren, in red-and-white vestments, took his place. The organ swelled with the first notes of "The Wedding March" from *Lohengrin*. Flower girls hurried down the aisle scattering rose petals. Beth's attendants—her sister Kathleen, her roommates Joan and Diana, and her friend Emily followed. Then, on her father's arm, Beth stepped into the sanctuary.

Many people in the church had seen pictures of Beth Connor but had never seen her in person. They stood on tiptoes and swayed back and forth to get a better view of her. Certainly many were astonished. Chang Po Ka was marrying an amazon! She was as tall as he was, and blond, and buxom. That she was a striking bride, dressed in an elegant gown, was beyond denial, but she was nothing like any bride most of them had ever seen before. She walked down the aisle with her head erect, her blue eyes focusing on the people to both sides of her, nodding to the very few she recognized.

There were few to sit on the bride's side of the church, so all but the first two pews on that side were occupied by friends of the Chang family. The front pew was shared with Peggy Connor by friends of the bride—Shek Tin, deputy governor of Guangdong Province; Xiang Li, the Olympic runner; and the Bin Fong commander. The United States consul was there. Beth didn't recognize him but nodded at his assistant, William Hodding.

In the second pew sat Mark Huang and Ilse, the Mama-San from the Pearl Club who had never been invited to a wedding like this in all the years she had spent in Hong Kong. The Australian girl, Barbara, and two other hostesses sat there, too, very modestly dressed and demure in their demeanor.

Beth smiled and nodded at all of them.

She had been told to look for a number of dignitaries on the groom's side, one of whom would be Christopher Patten, the last British colonial governor of Hong Kong. She smiled at a man she took to be Patten. She had no idea who some of the others were, except that she had been told to expect Chan Wah, head of the New China News Agency XinHua (the unofficial Chinese representative under British rule), and C. H. Tung, a shipping magnate widely expected to become the first chief executive of Hong Kong on July 1, 1997, the mayor of Guangzhou, and the mayor of Shanghai.

Father Farren conducted the service in three languages: Chinese, English, and Latin. It was a double-ring ceremony, with the rings tied to ribbons on a white-satin cushion. Beth and Michael held cards on which their responses were printed. At the few points where Beth spoke Chinese, she read the words from a phonetically printed text.

Because she was not Catholic, the service did not include Communion.

At the end, the couple and the priest withdrew into the sacristy to sign the certificate of marriage.

To the notes of Mendelssohn's "Wedding March" from *A Midsummer Night's Dream*, the bride and groom strode up the aisle and out of the church.

4

THE PROCESSION OF CARS moved through the streets to the Mandarin Oriental Hotel, where a ballroom had been reserved for a reception and luncheon. Beth and Michael went immediately to a suite, where they could refresh and relax for a few minutes before going down to greet their guests. Michael changed out of his double-breasted white tuxedo and into a single-breasted black tuxedo. Beth would wear her wedding gown for another two or three hours.

Frederick did not come to the Mandarin Oriental. He was too weak. Qiao Qichen took him home. Frederick insisted, though, that Anne should go to the hotel and enjoy the party—he, after all, would sleep all afternoon and hoped to be able to come to the banquet in the evening.

Though Anne was not one of the bride's attendants, she wore a flowing silk dress of the same azure that they wore. Her shoulders were bare, and her dress was cut in deep Vs in back and front. She was an impressive figure, as she always had been, and she attracted much attention from the photographers. In the ballroom, guests clustered around her.

The afternoon reception and luncheon was for the young friends of the bride and groom, also for foreigners: Americans, British, Taiwanese, Japanese, Filipinos, and Australians who were business associates of the Chang family.

Ilse came to the ballroom on the arm of Mark Huang. She knew, and the Chang security men knew, that among the guests at this affair were half a dozen armed Hong Kong police detectives. Chief Inspector Burke Trevelyan was there—in civilian clothes but carrying a pistol inside his jacket. Huang himself was carrying his 9-millimeter Beretta, strapped in his left armpit.

A few short speeches were offered. Christopher Patten spoke briefly, saying that the marriage of Michael Chang to Mary Elizabeth Connor was a most auspicious event for Hong Kong and that he hoped it would set a precedent for other marriages between prominent Chinese families and prominent families from other nations. He could not help but add a healthy dose of politics to his concluding remarks, saying that Hong Kong might yet show China what freedom meant, just as the new bride had shown the Changs what courage meant through her ordeal. The last remark caused the many pro-Chinese guests to wince.

The diplomatic representatives present had appointed the United States consul to speak for them, and he spoke, too, saying he had only once met Michael but that he was honored to have known the rest of the family well.

The managing director of Swire—the taipan of the once-famous British Hong that imported opium to China and ruled Hong

Kong until it was overshadowed in recent years by Chinese tycoons like the Changs—spoke for the foreign business community.

Beth and Michael circulated among the guests, greeting each of them. Beth used a few words of Chinese, saying, "Welcome to you" to some guests and, "It is an honor to have your presence" to the governor and the diplomats. She smiled warmly at Chief Inspector Trevelyan and told him she was glad to see him. Some of Michael's friends made small jokes. A good deal of the conversation at this function was in English. That made it possible for Beth to understand, though in this mixed crowd most of the talk would have been in English anyway.

Michael's father acted as a sort of master of ceremonies, and he called the bridal couple to come to the table where the three-tiered wedding cake waited.

As everyone gathered and smiled in anticipation, Beth and Michael came through their assembled guests to the table. A waiter brought a tray filled with champagne flutes, and the maître d'hôtel brought forth a bottle of Heidsick Dry Monopole champagne. The stems of two of the champagne flutes were tied with white and azure ribbons.

The maître d' raised one ribboned glass high and poured. Anne had slipped in between him and the bridal couple, took the glass from him, and handed it to Michael. She handed the second glass to Beth.

Beth turned and courteously, with a small bow, handed her glass to So Liming, her new mother-in-law. All watching were surprised. It was an unprecedented breach of Chinese wedding etiquette. But it was graceful, and So Liming accepted the glass with a faint smile and a bow of her own. Michael turned and handed his glass to Beth's mother.

Anne interceded. "Stop," she said firmly. "This wine is not to be drunk. I speak quietly and do not wish to make a scene, but no one should drink from this bottle. I now notice that the fool there has served the wine without removing the lead foil from the neck of the bottle. That means that each glass poured from it will bear lead poisoning." She reached for the two glasses.

"Anne . . ." Michael murmured. "Isn't it a small matter?"

Anne's eyes flared. "Is it a small matter that the champagne served now should be *poisoned*, however slightly? What could bring worse luck?" She poured the champagne from the two glasses onto the tablecloth. "Another bottle, properly served!" she snapped at the confused maître d'.

Other bottles were ready. The man opened another and stripped off the foil. He poured again, and Anne handed the flutes to Beth and Michael. Once again, Beth handed her flute to So Liming, and Michael handed his to Mrs. Connor. More glasses were filled and passed, until the entire wedding party, including Anne herself, had champagne. Then Beth and Michael intertwined their arms, and each held a glass to the other's lips. The crowd applauded with enthusiasm.

They cut and served the cake then, Michael serving cake to Beth, she serving cake to him.

When all moved away from the table, Mark Huang stopped the abashed maître d'. "Hong Kong police," he said. "I want that bottle the woman said had lead in it."

"She is a fool." The man grunted.

"I wish I could think so," said Huang. He picked up a napkin and began to blot up the wine that had been poured on the tablecloth.

5

IN THE EVENING THE marriage was celebrated with a banquet at the Regent Hotel in Kowloon. This event, thirty-eight tables in all, was for the families and friends of the Chang family—chiefly business friends. It was for the most part a different group than had come to the luncheon and reception.

As guests arrived, each stopped at a table and signed a piece of red cloth, which would be preserved in memory of the day. Almost all signed in Chinese characters. Then they stepped up to the bride and groom and handed them packets containing their wedding presents.

The presents were money: cash and checks. No packet contained less than one thousand American dollars; most contained more. Beth and Michael received the packets with thanks and did not open them, knowing what they contained. They did open one—

Mark Huang handed a packet to Beth. "That is not from me," he said. "Ilse gave it to me this afternoon, to be delivered to you this evening. It is from Wu Kim Ming."

Beth opened the packet. It was a cashier's check on the Bank of China, for one million Hong Kong dollars—a hundred and thirty thousand, U.S.

"I need to talk with you two as soon as possible," said Huang. "Don't eat or drink anything until you talk to me."

The guests moved around the room, looking for their tables, picking up drinks. Some gathered around a large television set where the videotape of the church wedding was being played.

When the last guest had arrived and the last present had been received, Michael and Beth took a break in a suite in the hotel, where Beth would change into another dress. Huang went with them.

They sat down in the parlor of the suite, and Beth kicked off her shoes.

Huang spoke grimly. "The champagne that Anne complained about . . . It *was* poisoned. But not with lead. The poison is a botanical. It is deadly. What is more, the poison was not in the bottle. It was in the wine she poured on the tablecloth but not in the wine left in the bottle."

Beth flushed. "Anne took the glasses from the maître d'. She was the only one who touched them, or came near them, after they were poured."

Michael nodded. "When you handed your glass to my mother and I handed mine to yours, she had to intervene. That's why she complained about the lead foil."

"Where is she now?" Huang asked.

"In the banquet room," said Michael.

"Don't eat or drink anything she touches," said Huang. "I've assigned four men to watch her every movement. Also, I've had two men arrested—Dragon, her *qi gong* master, and a dealer in exotic botanicals called Iron Hit. They're sweating in two cells right now. I wouldn't be surprised if they have something to tell us. But be careful. If she tries again, it may not be with poison."

Beth closed her eyes, and tears were squeezed out. "Why, Michael?" she whispered. "Why?"

"Money," he said. "The family obsession."

6

FOR THE BANQUET BETH wore a *cheong-sam*; red silk embroidered with gold and silver thread. The high collar covered her throat. The skirt was split to six inches above her knees.

Beth and Michael ate only a little of the elaborate banquet. It was their duty now to visit each of the tables, drink toasts, and again welcome and thank all their four hundred guests.

Anne sat at a table near the head table, smiling, laughing, nodding—all animated. She was wearing a sleek, skintight black dress featuring a black lace bodice. Strategically placed black blossoms covered her nipples; otherwise her upper body was plainly visible through the open lace. Her glossy black hair fell to her shoulders.

As the bride and groom moved among the tables, drinking many toasts, it was a game for the guests to encourage them to drink and get them drunk. Michael's attendants seized the glasses from him as soon as he had taken a small sip and drank some of the champagne themselves. John was enthusiastic about this duty and soon was wobbly on his feet. Diana, Joan, and Emily performed the duty for Beth.

Emily proved almost immune to alcohol. "Y' grow up in a East End Pub, y' learn t' hold yer liquor," she explained.

In spite of the help given him, Michael was a little unsteady when he stood on the stage and spoke into a handheld microphone. Even so, he thanked his parents and Beth's parents, then thanked all the guests. Chang Wing Hing took the microphone and talked for a few minutes about the joy of this day. He thanked Shek Tin in particular and saluted the dignitaries from China. Curran Connor spoke just a few words, which Cheryl translated for him. He said his daughter had had unbelievably good fortune in having discovered Michael Chang and having had the good sense to fall in love with him. It was the luck of the Irish, he said. Few knew what that meant, but all applauded.

A judge came to the stage to say a few words. A leader in the Hong Kong legislative body, recently knighted by Queen Elizabeth, spoke. Finally, Chan Wah, head of the New China News Agency XinHua, came up. He offered his congratulations and good wishes.

7

ENTERTAINMENT WOULD FOLLOW. ONCE again, the bridal couple went to their suite for a few minutes. Once again, Mark Huang went up with them.

In the suite, Michael went for glasses of water and offered Beth two evil-looking black pills.

"What's this?"

"Chinese herbal medicine," he said. "Good for ingrown toenails, dandruff, and everything between." He gulped two himself.

Skeptically, Beth swallowed the two pills. "When in China, do as the Chinese do," she murmured.

Michael looked at Mark Huang. "Senior Inspector Huang?"

"It is strange how a little friendly persuasion loosens mouths," said Huang. "The dealer in botanicals spoke first. He sold Dragon, the *qi gong* master, a quantity of concentrate from the leaves of oleander. It is a botanical of the dogbane family and, when properly refined, is as deadly as cyanide, almost. When the *qi gong* quack was confronted with this confession, including the amount paid and other corroborating details, he thought it wise to make a self-protective statement. All he did, he says, was teach Liu Soong Qin, Anne, a bit of stage trickery to enable her to . . . Well, he says to put an aphrodisiac in your wine, as a joke. That's what he was told the oleander was: harmless Spanish fly."

"You understand, of course, what she had in mind," said Michael.

Huang nodded. "I'm prepared to arrest her now."

"No," said Beth. "Let her hang herself."

8

BEFORE RETURNING TO THE banquet hall, Beth changed clothes again. For the final event of the evening she wore a deep-violet gown with a sequined bodice. She wore the jade-and-gold necklace the Chang family had given her in the morning and jade earrings that Michael gave her just before they went down.

The entertainment had begun. Hong Kong's best-known actor, Jackie Chan, was speaking on the stage. He had the audience laughing, and when he saw Beth and Michael return, he summoned them to the stage. Michael could trade jokes with him, a little. She, of course, could not. Jackie spoke fluent English, proficient enough to be very funny in it.

Standing on the stage, enduring what was for her nothing better than an embarrassment, Beth looked around and spotted Anne. She also saw Huang, not far from Anne.

Jackie Chan asked her to sing a song. She smiled politely and firmly declined. She took Jackie's hand, clasped it warmly, and walked off the stage. Michael had no choice but to follow.

Beth walked directly up to Anne. "Sister," she said. "I've drunk a toast with everyone but you."

Anne grinned. "Possibly so," she said.

Michael beckoned to a waiter and pointed to an unopened bottle of champagne. The man brought it, in its ice bucket, and opened it. He poured one glass. Anne reached for it, took it, and handed it to Beth.

"You took care of us so well this morning by seeing to it that we did not taste wine that had the least bit of lead in it," Beth said. "I'd appreciate it if you would taste this for us before we drink it."

"It's good, I assure you," Anne said crisply.

Beth grabbed Anne's left wrist. She was much stronger than Anne, and Anne could not pull loose. Beth used her other hand to pry open Anne's clenched fingers. "It would be good," she growled, "except for what's in this little vial you carry."

Mark Huang now grasped Anne's right arm. One of his men took her left.

"Will you come with us peaceably, or do we have to make a scene?" he asked.

Anne looked at Michael, then at Beth, and then her eyes fell. She walked out of the banquet in custody of the two policemen. Only when they reached the police van did they handcuff her hands behind her back.

9

WHEN THE FAMILY WAS back at the mansion Michael and Beth sat down with Chang Wing Hing, John, and Qiao Qichen and told them what had happened.

"Frederick must not know," said Michael.

"Do you think the police will release her?" Beth asked. "I mean, if he doesn't see her—"

"Senior Inspector Huang will release her in my custody," said Chang Wing Hing. "She will remain here, confined to the mansion, so long as Frederick lives. After that—" He shrugged.

"She will be committed to a mental hospital," said Michael.

"But—"

"It would not be good for the family name to have her prosecuted and imprisoned. We will put out the word that the death of her husband destroyed her reason and that she requires treatment. There is a hospital on Lantau Island that prominent families occasionally use in cases like this."

"And she'll be kept there—?"

"For the rest of her life," said Michael. "If she behaves herself, she will have a comfortable room, television, books . . . whatever she likes."

"For the rest of her life," Beth whispered.

"She tried to kill you. She tried to kill me. She tried to kill our child," said Michael. "Yes. For the rest of her life."

10

IN THEIR SUITE, BETH and Michael did what they had learned to do in Boston and loved to do—took a shower together. Then they went to bed as husband and wife. Tomorrow they would fly to Beijing for the first days of their honeymoon, to be followed by a longer visit to Boston.